STRONGHOLDS

Also by L. M. Boston
Yew Hall

Strongholds

by

L. M. Boston

HARCOURT, BRACE & WORLD, INC.

NEW YORK

To my only Persephone with unchanged love

PART I

Silverstone Tower

1946

It was a sodden Sunday evening in late August, such a downpour as visitors to the fells most dislike. The brown bents and tremble grass were knee-high, the bracken waist-high, and these, with the wide soppy leaves overhead that bent under the rain to the shape of dripping umbrellas, made it wetter than any winter storm, a welter of scented, steaming drench. Persie had fed the pigs and hens on her grandfather's farm and at the first free moment was out and away. She was fifteen, and the absorbing passion that other girls of her age might have for a horse, or dancing, she felt for the countryside in which she lived. It was a challenging joy every minute and gave her a gaiety that nothing else in her circumstances warranted. Rain to her was just one of the more private moods of her world.

She made now for a big yew tree in the centre of a wood on a neighbouring hilltop. With her shabby mackintosh wrapped tightly round her, she flung herself down on the spongy needle-covered earth under the wide boughs. Her shoes were soaked, the leather turned slippery like fish skin. Her hair dripped down her neck and into her eyes. She drank the rain that ran down her face. She saw a red squirrel as wet as herself and laughed to hear how he grumbled. There was a world of sound to listen to, but the yew tree was silent in the rain. Its leaves offered no surface for patter, its easy swinging branches shook the wet off in mist. The only sound under it was made by big drops collecting under the loop of the boughs and falling to the ground like beetles. A neighbouring beech took the rain angrily, hissing in the downpour. Its trunk and branches were as wet as her own legs and neck. The clustering hazel leaves drummed, and the grass sighed. Persie called to mind the sound of rain skidding on the smooth boulders that lay along the shore like whales' backs, pittering on the mud flats of the estuary and stinging the river winding between them. As she travelled in imagination over the country she listened for all of it, as if hers were the only ears that could maintain it whole in con-

3

sciousness. Rain swilled in rivulets down the hills; it gurgled, trilled, seeped, and cascaded. Over the meadows it dived like descending larks; along the hedgerows it leapt, swinging from one dipping branch to another. It laughed, it sighed, it grew eager. Only against the windowpanes of houses it wept. Coming back from this flight of thought to where she lay, she heard the faint silky sound of a blade of grass that had deposited its weight of water and now slid upright again.

The low continuous clouds passed over and through the woods where she lay, but down the hill the fields would detach themselves from the grey ceiling, and under it the farm horses, turned out for a day's rest, would be moving with steaming sides and rumps and shaking waterfalls from their necks. Down there, out of sight from where she lay, the fields were dominated by the ruined Tower, among whose outlying debris and hummocky turfs the horses were wandering.

The Tower—which gave its name to old Stalker's farm, humbly built of its fallen masonry only just clear of its shadow—was a massive roofless stone keep, rising from the grass in such isolation that it was hard to imagine what it had ever been meant to protect. Even the schoolteacher knew nothing except that there were similar ruins scattered about the border counties. Three of its walls were standing, nine feet thick and varying in height, their crumbled sky line crowned at the highest point by an elder bush. This was at the top of one of the corkscrew stairs which climbed the inside of each angle. Many steps were missing, and at each level, where once had been a floor, stone arches gave onto precarious foothold from which one could look down into the central pit. The local boys of course had all climbed it at some time, but Persie, who lived under it, did so frequently. The thrift, harebells, pimpernel, scabious, and lady's-slipper that grew in the crevices were planted there by her in co-operation with the wind and the birds. The missing fourth wall had split away from the rest and fallen outward all in one piece, flinging off its loosened corners as it went. It lay like a wrecked ship at an unnatural angle, its base anchored in the stone and rubble that had buried the first floor, over which the springy turf had now spread.

Often when perched on the top of the winding stair and equally often when snug in her bed, Persie had wondered at the fall of that wall. How could such a thing happen? Could it have been riven by lightning, like a tree? Or did some enemy lord, filling the tower with brushwood, set it alight and burst the side out with heat? As she thought of it now, seeing in imagination the driven cloud torn as it

4

passed over the jutting stone, seeing the walls running in unbroken sheets of water, feeling the squelch of the well-known turf round its base, where on such days every footstep caused a miniature spring, imagining the pressure on the earth of that weight of masonry, she suddenly wondered if it had collapsed, undermined and washed asunder by sheer force of rain—such a rain as this. She sprang to her feet and ran as fast as her flapping wetness allowed her through the woods to the nearest point from which she could see the Tower, anxious lest another wall should be gone.

It stood as she had always seen it, its two indomitable right angles as sharply cut as when it was built, everything else softly weathered, ancient, and useless, its reserves all exposed, its secrets forever kept, a happy place that only she appeared to love. Joyful at the sight and remembering also the pleasures of food and dry clothes, she set off homeward at a light pace, a smile on her face down which the rain splashed quite unnoticed.

The four cottages along the lane leading to the Tower were so modest that unless they boasted geraniums on the window sills there was little to distinguish the dwelling from the outbuildings, all in whitewashed stone. One cottage had a tiny garden at the side with a fuchsia hedge and a row of sweetpeas. This was Dick's, the cowman. It was he who woke her in the morning under her window. She helped him to milk the cows while the others were still in bed. Beside Dick's was another which looked as if the windows were never opened to the air nor the door to guests. The garden was abandoned to nettles, old cans, broken wheels, and the inimitable wreckage proper to children. The owner took his pleasure elsewhere and his wife perforce kept herself to herself. Sam Cudthrop was his name, the slaughterer. Persie detested and feared him, having seen him from her earliest childhood outside the door of his scene of action, wearing the dreadful waders and rubber apron of his calling, his arms red with blood to the elbows. Her mother always told her he was a good-natured man, but to Persie one of the nightmarish things about him was the more than life-sized good humour of his comings and goings. He was big, thick, and red. He ate so much meat that looking at him one was conscious that he was made of it. During the war he and old Stalker had been thick in the black market together. Their furtive midnight work, so much more like murder because it was mean and hugger-mugger, brutal and whispered, was the only repercusison of the general slaughter that reached this outlying hamlet. Even the

5

young men like Dick had stayed at their work. But the war was over now. It was a word that had never taken on a personal meaning in Persie's childhood.

Tower Farm, standing several fields back from the lane, was the largest building in the hamlet. It had a porch, but without geraniums. It stood on the open sward surrounded by a path of cobbles from which a branch slippery with muck led to the cowsheds. A salt sour smell came from the back kitchen and dairy, a sweet smell from the shippen, and an unspeakable one from the sties. The farm windows were small and deep-set, so that (Persie hoped) one would not notice the shabby curtains. There was no sign at all of money spent on comfort or pleasure.

Her mother, Bess Stalker, was standing in the porch looking out for her. She was not in Sunday clothes. She had none. In any case she never thought about her clothes at all. There were a great many things she never thought about. You could not say her loose brown hair was untidy, for that presupposes an idea of how hair should be done. The most you could say was that it was pinned out of the way. Bess had the pleasant shapelessness of real country women. Under her loose blouse, washed to the colour of stones in a brook, her plump flesh hung comfortably round her like a cushion that needs shaking up. She was sturdy and easygoing on her feet, a good walker. She had eyes like those of a farm dog not too well treated, and a ready good-natured smile, as unconscious of the absences and vagaries of her teeth as if they were in a gapped rake and not part of her at all. In fact, as a general rule in her relations with other people she was conscious of nothing but good nature. Persie loved her dearly. She had seen with shocked surprise other mothers who nagged, clouted, and snatched their children, hauling them by the arm, hurling spite at their heads, dumping them in chairs, promising that their father should leather them. Her mother had never raised a hand against anyone, or shouted except with laughter in the bar on market day.

"Come on in now. Tea's on the table," was all she said as Persie came along the cobbles. "I've made potato cakes for us today."

Persie took off her sodden shoes and mackintosh and left them in the porch, crossing the kitchen floor in long hops to the foot of the stairs. The kitchen was bare except for essentials, and for that reason, in its way, beautiful. There was a crooked wooden dresser reaching to the ceiling. Among the plates and cups space had been found for

6

personal treasures. There was a pair of brass candlesticks that had belonged to Bess's mother, a round china box with a pictured lid, such as gentlemen keep their studs and cuff links in, and, most admired by Persie, a solid glass dome with brilliant prismatic patterns showing inside. Bess had few possessions of her own. Persie had been taught to hallow them. The table had been scrubbed for so many generations that the grain was raised in a pattern which Persie's infant fingers had explored and approved. One end was covered with a scarlet-and-white cloth, fringed and much split at the edges, on which the tea was set. The chairs were of heavy ash, without cushions except for one with arms in which old Stalker sat to smoke his pipe. The floor was of stone slabs, still fresh from the weekly scrubbing.

Her grandfather, who was sitting at the table, turned round when he saw her and spat on the floor, making a concession to manners by rubbing the sole of his boot over the place.

"Nay, Father," said Bess.

"Neigh's what the old mare said. And don't try to learn me what I'll do in my own house, Bess Stalker. You're no one to be talking. I'll do as I like. You get on and pour out the tea."

Persie, behind her grandfather's chair, put out her tongue at him and waved to her mother.

"Go on with you now," said Bess, "and be quick about it." Persie's bedroom was a tiny square of dank Reckitt's blue plaster, containing a sagging iron bed, a row of wooden pegs for hats and coats, and a meagre self-willed chest of drawers with a loud voice when disturbed. The window looked to the Tower and caught the morning sun. On the window sill was a small cup filled with harebells and fuchsia, on one side of it a shell and on the other a fir cone. She had a few books, school prizes, and a coloured reproduction, out of an old Christmas number, of St. Ursula's bedroom by Carpaccio; but how was she to know that? She did not even know it was supposed to be good. This picture was her model and inspiration, for it was not from Bess that she had learnt neatness. Bess's room, larger and more furnished than her own, had all the more scope for disorder. The bed was hardly distinguishable among the general strew, and it was made only when it failed to provide a good night's rest. It did not occur to Persie to criticise her mother's habits or to feel less than affection for her because she slept in her own litter as warm and comfortable, and with as easy a mind, as the cows who settled their soft flesh in the straw of

7

their stalls, and communed with each other in the night with a breath of their nostrils, or perhaps with a soft lowing on one deep note. It was not a derogatory comparison. It was all in the natural pattern.

Persie changed the wettest of her clothes and, with her damp hair combed flat over her small skull, she went down. The tea was strong and the potato cakes were cold, but her grandfather had gone. Sunday night was the second best of the seven pub nights of the week.

"Mums," said Persie meditatively, bent over her tea with her feet on the crossbar of her chair, "why did you call me Persephone?" She pronounced it Percyfown as her mother did, only in her mind she heard its real music, learnt at school.

"Your dad wanted it. I should never have chosen a foreign name like that, but he asked for it." Bess looked enquiringly at her daughter and then added: "You're old enough to know a thing or two now, I suppose. Might as well tell you. I was never really married, you know."

"Yes, Mums, I know."

"It had to be that way. But you took after his side. I suppose he'd never thought that might happen. At first he was beside himself with affection. Then it began to worry him. It seems there mustn't be bastards looking like *them*. Too much like being one himself. He was only nineteen, poor boy."

She stopped as if for a deep sigh, but it never came, and she continued without it.

"In the end he shot himself."

"Oh poor Mums!" said Persie, having trouble with tears that would not go back into her eyes however hard she forced them. "I suppose you loved him very much."

"Like everyone else who is in love, I daresay. We're all alike when it comes to that. But you stick to your own class, my girl. Don't have anything to do with the gentry."

"You were too good for him, I expect."

"Good! If he hadn't been bothering so much about what was good and what wasn't, he might have been alive now. I knew all along he couldn't marry me. See me as her Ladyship!"

"Was he a lord?"

"No. He was plain Mister. It was one of those families with two surnames. You're Mr. This half your life, and then suddenly you're Lord That."

"Lord what?"

"Let be. There's no point in talking about it. I reckon if he minded enough to shoot himself it's best to let it drop."

It was many years since Bess had talked so freely. She felt embarrassed and empty, as if in saying the words she had killed the fact, as if the things she had said were part of her and had left a cavity. She rubbed her knuckles.

"I'll have another cup of tea if there is anything left in the pot," she said.

Persephone tipped it vertically, holding the lid on with her other hand, and as the cup slowly filled, so in her mind the concept of her mother's lonely life on the farm, formed now for the first time, filled with the dignity of an everlasting love; the sort of love for which she herself one day, unless she was very unlucky, would be the tender container. She let out the sigh that her mother had not found, but it was not bitter. It was sweet, like a starling's descending note.

❖

The next day promised to be fine, but when the cows were turned out after milking in the early morning it was still nearly as wet as the day before, only now all the moisture was going upward. They moved out at an unenthusiastic pace to consider the possibilities of the meadow, thrusting their heads through the chiffon mist and wearing it about their shoulders. Their lowing was subdued but not discontented. The hens, who all the day before had harped on one maddening tremolo note, were excessively busy and kept up an animated if ridiculous family conversation with a great deal of backbiting. Persie, as she drove down the track through the meadow, stood up in the milk float the better to enjoy its rollicking action and the gay dance of the milk cans. She laughed at the mad piglets who easily outpaced her, nimble and humorous. Doomed to be bacon, in their brief life they have more *joie de vivre* than any other youngsters in creation.

As she turned into the sunken road between hedges of bramble, ivy, and stiff ash saplings, changing the lurching of the rutted track for the purr of wheels and click of hoofs on the macadam, it was still only half daylight, but the sky between the ash leaves was golden, turning as she raised her eyes to green and then palest blue, where the moon lingered insubstantial and aloof. At the fork which led off into the woods, where yesterday she had been enjoying the rain, a young man came out carrying an enormous camping bundle on his shoulders and a suitcase in one hand.

"Are you carrying those for fun?" Persie shrilled as she rattled past him, "or would you like to throw them on here?" The pony was tackling a hill in good heart, so she did not want to pull him up in case it should not be necessary, but she turned to catch the stranger's response. He broke into a laboured run and just managed to hurl his suitcase on to the back of the float.

"Wait, wait! For God's sake, you provoking pair of creatures!" he gasped, freeing his arms from the shoulder bands of his pack. "What's the good of offering if you won't stop?"

The pony, feeling the added burden, slackened to a walk, and with Persie's help the bundle was transferred to the top of the milk cans.

"You'll have to walk up the hill," she said, still moving on, balanced on the float slight and straight as a cowslip.

The young man, using his long legs with relief and ease, grinned up at her from alongside.

"All right, all right! What a tartar you are! I can walk."

"It's only for the pony," she said, blushing.

"I suppose you don't count?"

"I get off when it's very steep, especially downhill. Where have you been camping?"

"Back there in the wood. But I was washed out yesterday evening."

"I was there yesterday, but I didn't see you."

"What were you doing there?"

"Nothing," said Persie, going pink again.

"I suppose you don't happen to live down a rabbit hole?"

"No. If you want to know, I live in a nice little donkey's stable."

"Sorry. I deserved that one. But you know, it was very wet for anyone who had a house they could have stayed in. You are very ready to box a chap's ears. My name's Geoff. What's yours?"

"Persephone," she said with a defiant lilt in her voice.

"Did I hear right? Would you be so good as to say that again?"

"Most people pronounce it Percyfown," she conceded, really pink this time at having committed the social sin of being highbrow.

Geoff, looking at her with kind eyes, laughed so that it did one good to be with him.

The crown of the hill being reached, she pulled up the pony and sat down, inviting Geoff to join her. He sat on the near corner, draping his legs over the shaft.

"I suppose it's the station you want to go to? The Central Dairy is quite near there."

"As a matter of fact, I want to go to the Red Rose. I am sick of lying in a swamp and finding wood lice in my coffee. I've got a few days left and I propose to be comfortable. What's the Red Rose like? Ever been in it?"

"Oh yes. I take the milk every day. But I've never been inside. It smells terribly of beer and new linoleum."

"The beer sounds all right."

The sun was now awake, and, like someone who comes last for breakfast and immediately takes charge, was tidying up the mist, putting a brass polish on the leaves and a silver one on the road, and pulling up the blinds that hid the expanses of the estuary and the distant fells. The noises of the day began one by one. The first train rumbled across the viaduct. Somewhere a horse was whinnying as its companion was led away to begin work. Voices of approaching cyclists were heard before they themselves were seen, and the barking of dogs newly released reminded one that it was long since the cockcrow had the echoing sky to itself. It was no longer a personal secret to be up. The boss was there. It was now a pressing obligation on everybody.

The bright reality of the morning brought her happiness into sharper focus. Persie was enjoying the encounter as much as if her vitality had been doubled. She was therefore serious. Joys were not to be crazily frittered away. They deserved attention. She looked, to Geoff's eyes, suddenly aloof and abstracted, while she flicked her lash between the pony's ears so delicately that it was a caress.

At a brisk trot, joggling on their wooden seat, with the cans clattering behind them, it was not so easy to talk. Half a mile passed without a word. Then Geoff's resilience asserted itself again.

"Do you come this way every day?"

"Yes."

"What! At a quarter past six every day! Strewth!"

"That's nothing. I help to milk the cows first."

"Is it your father's farm?"

"It's my grandfather's."

"I don't think I'd like farming. Too much manure before breakfast."

"What do you do?"

"Phys. Chem.," said Geoff casually, thinking only of her young throat, which was longer and more flexible than the normal human pattern, and gave her head a poise that teased his mind, searching for a parallel. It reminded him—of what? When she bends down, it's like a flower with a bumblebee in it. When she looks over her shoulder, it's like a deer. No call to be so sentimental. It's like a ping-pong ball balanced on a jet of water. In other words, it's like a giraffe! Boys, my baby's got a neck like a baby giraffe. That would make a good song!

"Fizz kem!" Persie was repeating. "What's that, please?"

"Sorry. That's what we call it. My old man keeps a little shop where we sell ginger pop and aspirin."

This time they laughed together, but Persie was not laughing at his joke. She was laughing at what she thought was the truth.

"Somehow I never thought you'd be doing that!"

"I'm not really made for it. I tend to give one humbug over the ounce. In a little shop you can't afford to be generous."

"I thought you'd be doing something more exciting."

"Such as?"

"Putting up telegraph posts. I think that's a lovely job, don't you?"

So it came about that when Persie said good-bye at the Red Rose to the most enjoyable companion she had ever met, she had no idea that this young man, who looked at her with the laughing eyes and snowy teeth of a young dog, was that dangerous creature that her mother had warned her against. The name on his suitcase, G. de Fol, she imagined over the window of a little shop where, if she was lucky enough to live near, a girl might go in to buy a pair of shoelaces.

Geoff had insisted on her coming back to breakfast with him after delivering the milk at the Central Dairy. The landlady, in honour of Geoff, addressed her as Miss Stalker, though she had known her all her life as Persie.

The dining room of the Red Rose was, even on the most romantic occasion, repellent. It was furnished with the tawdry cast-offs of respectability. The pompous sideboard carried a platoon of sauces and pickles, a fantastic silvered cruet like a cluster of church spires, and a vase of paper sweetpeas. The overmantel was complicated with little alcoves and shelves, in each of which was at least one object, no matter what. These and the pictures were mere stage props, the minimum of what everyone is expected to expect. The wallpaper aimed at refinement but only succeeded in being squeamish.

Persie did not know what it was that made her feel so out of place. Even the use of cutlery—she was given two forks and three knives—seemed a formidable matter, as difficult as if she were using it for the first time. It all required concentration; but though she was silent and nervous, sitting with both feet pressed to the bearer of her chair, her elbows tight to her sides, she would not have changed places with anybody.

None of the other visitors had yet got out of bed. From the table in the window Persie and Geoff overlooked the river and the fells. The tide was sweeping upstream, bringing an immense renewal to the dead end of mud flats and to the idle little village, which, existing only for summer visitors, had caught a permanently time-wasting outlook. The boatman dangling his legs over the sea wall was rounded with long sitting till he took the curves of a roll of fishing net folded and pushed up onto the parapet. With his pipe he could remain unbored the whole day long. Near him a cluster of rowing boats for hire, newly released from the clamping sand by the tide, were nosing together and fidgeting their sterns like shore donkeys.

Geoff, as if he had ordered all this with his breakfast, was ease itself, leaning back to smoke with his arm along the back of a spare chair and one foot on the seat of another. He was not overawed. He joked and talked, and waited with indulgent patience till her eyes came up from their thoughtful middle distance and met his with a quick innocent stare.

When Persie got home, she ate a second breakfast like any other adolescent—in fact, with a better appetite than she had had for the first. Then she went to relieve Dick, who was driving the cutter over the second crop of clover. Dick always contrived to give her the light jobs in consideration of her fifteen years. It was hard to remember she was even that, she was so small. Old Stalker had no mercy. He used her like a cheap animal that is not expected to be any good. You get what you can out of it. If it cracks up, that proves you were right.

Driving the cutter was a treat for her. With a mind as free from care as the summer air, she perched on the high iron seat and drove the horse-drawn machine round the field like a moving weir that tumbled the clover down to a quiet level. The surface before her flashed sparks of almost kingfisher-blue under the splendid sun, and the clatter of the crossing blades was a pleasant accompaniment to her mood. In the field alongside, stooks of corn were set up like the tents of an army as pictured in a history book. They curved in beautiful lines over the rise of the land, and each time she came round to that side again, the rooks and pigeons flew up. She drove with care, leaving behind her, as she neared the centre of the field, a square pattern like a silk quilt.

Her grandfather had gone to Kendal to market, and when he was away even the animals on the farm seemed more contented. At midday, walking with the reins in the curve of her elbow as if arm in arm with the mare, Persie led her to the trough for a drink. In the yard, Dick was trimming the necks and backs of the other two horses, shearing off thick greasy hair like an old rug and leaving a smooth plush, the colour of sawn wood. As he worked, he whistled with loving concentration the only kind of music he knew. This time it was "Love is where you find it," and the precision that he brought to it robbed it of vulgarity and made it into something as natural and delightful as a robin's song. The tune lodged in Persie's brain, so that all afternoon, as she continued her solitary and satisfying job, "Love is where you find it" burst from her in interjected bars whenever there was a hiatus in her thoughts. The scent of clover and hay mounted round her till by evening it was as pervasive as the setting sun. Persie had a prehistoric sense of smell. She could think in smells as other people did in words.

On her early drive the next morning, as she passed the corner where she had met Geoff with his bundle, the place gave her a special sensation, as distinctive and strong as a scent—an early morning's surrender of its secrets, a heady inhalation. All the way to Silverstone she relived the former drive, moment by moment. She left the milk as usual at the back door of the Red Rose without waste of time, seeing nobody, not even the landlady; for she had no idea of calling on Geoff. G. de Fol—a name most musical to her—she knew did not willingly get up early.

It was a day of unusual heat. Persie rode the haymaker to finish the job. The round bubble of her happiness was not quite perfect. Old Stalker was about, finding fault everywhere and lashing out at the dog. The old man who did odd jobs of repairing about the farm buildings was told he was not worth his wages. He ought to go into a home. The weather was too hot to trust. The wheat must be carted in before night, however long it took them. Everyone would have to turn out. Persie was accused of sitting up there as idle as a slug in a cabbage. He supposed that if the old mare chose to lie down she would sit beside her and fan the flies off. He then delivered a sudden whack on the mare's rump that set her in motion so violently that Persie was nearly thrown backward among the rakes. She kept her seat, however, and went off singing "Love is where you find it" as loud as she could, going through it to the end, which she regarded as the height of sarcasm.

By noon everybody was on the cornfield except old Stalker himself, who had taken a horse with a loose shoe down to the smithy. Bess was there, enjoying what was for her a social occasion. Sam Cudthrop was there, obligingly lending a hand. He worked between Bess and her daughter on one side of the wagon. Persie would have crossed over and gone between Dick and the old man, but Dick's wife was there, enjoying a day out of doors beside her husband, and anyway, country rhythms are settled and compelling. Bess seemed in unusually high spirits. Her pointed jokes provoked the obvious repartee, and that, again, general laughter. These simple but almost ritual exchanges worked in with the lifting of the sheaves and helped to keep the human machine working. Most of Bess's jokes were aimed at Sam, and under cover of them Persie worked with as much remoteness from him as she could. In the course of the afternoon, as she was hoisting up a sheaf as big as herself onto the cart, she caught sight of Geoff coming down the hill past the Tower in the direction of Silverstone. She waved joyfully, hoping to make clear by her vigour that she could not interrupt the work to come to him. He waved back and, after a moment's pause, went on his way.

"Who's your friend?" Dick called out for the others, who were all looking.

"Just someone who's staying at the Red Rose," she said. She was happy that she had seen him, even passing by. He had remembered where she lived.

Halfway through the work, but when Geoff was already far away, Bess produced beer for all. This she would never have dared to do in her father's presence. Pressed by her, Sam drank a double share. His gusto was such that generous people plied him to watch his enjoyment; but the average man watched to see that he did not help himself unasked. After the beer, hotter than ever, they went back to loading the carts. Old Stalker was right: it was freak weather. The heat was overwhelming. The ground was like an oven plate and the stubble bit into Persie's ankles and sandalled insteps. Bess's face and arms were scarlet. She was not used to exposure, spending her time in the dairy and washhouse, and her skin had caught the sun.

Persie was damp all over and out of breath. Her hair ribbon had come off, so that her hair flopped like warm curtains over her face. What could be seen of her was moist and flushed, with swollen eyelids and parted lips. The neck of her blouse was open, but the material clung to her back and ribs and the waist had worked loose from

15

her skirt. She brushed the stifling hair back from her face and met Sam's eye, fixed and jolly like a boar's. She let her hair fall back over her face and worked on without looking up again, keeping a fixed, vague stare. Bess's fund of jokes had died in the heat; but Sam, who throve like a Roman under the weight of the sun, began directing remarks at Persie under his breath, each of which was like a dirty nudge. She was thankful when at last it was milking time and she could escape.

It was restful in the half dark of the shippen, where those cows that had not yet been milked lowed softly and monotonously to each other like women complaining in a queue. Bella, Daisy, Cowslip, Buttercup, Maidy, Curley, Violet, Nancy, Strawberry, and Star—simple creatures untroubled by pedigrees. Persie leaned her head into the sighing flank of Bella, and the music of the milk playing into the pail was repeated in syncopation by Dick milking at the other end of the row. The clank of pails and shifting of milking stools took the place of speech between the two who shared this primal labour every day.

The milking done, she fed the hens, and the silken piglets, whose enthusiasm for their trough of swill was innocence itself and blotted out all thoughts but happy ones.

By this time the sheaves were all gathered. The carts were led in, the patient horses turned out to roll and scratch their fly-bitten backs, and, with a fine flourish of their awkward legs in the air, to keel over and lie flat for a moment's abandon.

Bess and Persie had hurried in to set out high tea for all the exhausted workers, and for old Stalker, who was sourly silent. He had evidently imbibed much beer before returning, and was in the best mood anyone could hope for from him. Though morose, he could be ignored. He took the head of the table and ate, sucking his teeth and wiping his hot neck with a corner of the tablecloth.

Enclosed in the crowded room, which was hot, noisy, foggy with acrid tobacco smoke, and smelling as if it were full of foxes, Persie longed to be alone in the woods. As soon as she could she slipped away, making an excuse that she had lost her hair ribbon on the field.

In the golden evening light the binder stood idle, familiar and beautiful. The rooks flew up off the bleached stubble for the last time as Persie came out, and flapped away all in one direction. The shadows were very long across the hills, for the sun was dropping behind the headland, between which and her home hills the tidal wave was due to be coming up. Perhaps even now, in an as yet uncollected momentum, the wide ripple was making its way across the breadth of the bay, drawing behind it an irresistible invasion of water and the cool winds of the open sea. However unspectacular the leading wave might be, in almost no time the empty river bed would be covered with sea water whose restless edge seemed ravenous to devour the sand. Along the central current the water would undulate in steely switchbacks sweeping on towards the piers of the viaduct, whence the roaring of the hampered onrush could be heard all over the land.

On the rocks beyond the farthest field of the farm she could sit and bathe her tired feet, and hear the lapping of encroaching ripples, the cries of gulls, curlews, and sandpipers all in commotion, and at the same time the last notes of the blackbird calling "Eight o'clock on a quiet evening and all's well." But she was tired, and too ruffled for the evening star.

She turned instead, for company, into the shippen, which in the afternoon had seemed so full of comfort. Some of the cows, who were due to calve, were kept in and given extra hay, and these were lying down with sides rounded like the fells, their hind hoofs crooked under them. They turned their heads as she entered, and all their jaws moved together with a soft grinding. Daisy, Curly, Violet, and Nancy. They were placid and relaxed, their black eyes half closed. Persie stood listening to their breathing. It seemed a little deeper than necessary, as if they enjoyed it every time. It was hypnotic. She let it flow in and out of her mind, disposing her to sleep. Presently she was aware, with stiffened senses, that there was breathing of quite another quality behind her, tense and rough. She whipped round—to see Sam, over life-size and horribly jocose.

"So that's where you've got to, you little monkey! A fine dance you've led me. You told me you were going to the wheat field."

"I didn't say anything to you at all," she replied, turning her back on him.

"Oh yes, you did! I know that look in a girl's eyes when I see it. Look up, look down, and I'm going to look for my hair ribbon. So I came to help you to find your hair ribbon, see?"

Sam was laughing, and it was a nasty sound. Against her will she turned her head to take stock of the danger, and his arms suddenly imprisoned her. She fought with all the force of her wiry body; she remembered how many an animal had struggled in his hands and never one but had been brought to the sacrificial position. Her strength was not equal to that of a calf or a pig or a sheep, but Sam's laughter, half-brutal, half-sentimental, fired her with wild rage. She made a feint of submission, withholding only her face, while shudders of disgust followed the greedy movements of his hands.

"That's Sam's little maid," he said, shifting his hold to enable him to carry her to the reserve of hay in the last stall; but he was too confident, and she slipped between his arms, between his knees, and out of immediate reach. All this time, the cows remained undisturbed, munching with closed eyes.

Persie stood taut and wild with her back to the wall, for Sam was between her and the door; and there on a ledge her blind fingers closed over the handle of a mislaid billhook. She did not at first take in its possible use, but Sam was approaching, in the attitude of some-one rounding up a runaway animal, one hand on the end of the wooden division of the stalls, the other spread out to block the passage. His knees were bent and feet wide apart.

"No! No! No!" she screamed, swinging a blow at his fingers with the billhook. He saw it coming and jerked his hand away. The blade bit into the wooden post and stuck there quivering.

"What a savage little girl it is!" said Sam, delighted. But he could not resist trying the billhook to see how far the blade had gone in, and looking lovingly at his fingers. Persie streaked past him and was gone.

The back door was open, and inside were friends and safety, but it was not possible to face them in her present state of shame and dis-order.

She ran past the door and made without conscious choice for the Tower, sobbing as she ran. She had no memory afterwards of how she climbed the broken stairs; but on her ledge at the top she lay, controlling her shaking as much as she could to listen for any rattle of displaced rubble or grate of boots on a stone. Now and again panic seized her lest in the difficulty of her breathing she had failed to hear. Then she would hold her breath and hear the night air sighing, the horses munching below in the meadow, sounds from the house of doors shutting, of steps on the cobbles, of the dog's chain rattling out and in, her mother's voice. All these, to her ears straining for ghosts of furtive noise, seemed surprisingly loud.

From her viewpoint she covered most, but not all, of the space between the foot of the Tower and the house. She fixed that bit of field, now indistinct in the late twilight, with straining eyes. It was hummocky and shadowy, and any shadow on which she concentrated for long appeared to move.

She heard kind Dick go off home in the opposite direction talking to his wife. Their voices faded away. No sound or sign revealed Sam's whereabouts. She never thought the danger would be of less duration than her fear. It was impossible not to suppose that anything so evil must also be lasting, cunning, and persistent. She had only one thought—if he comes up here I'll push him over—and in the shelter of that decision she lay for a long time. The stone was unremittingly cold, as if the heat of the day had made no impression on it at all. The restless breezes of the night plucked up the edges of her short cotton sleeves and chilled her armpits. They ignored the skimpy skirt wrapped tightly round her thighs, but worked into the whole surface of her skin. They persistently touched her between the shoulder blades.

Though the sun had gone quite away from the world and its last attributes of twilight and mist had gone too, the darkness had never become total. It was silvered in advance by the moon, long before she rose. When the bright, icy disc sailed up over the hilltop, Persie found herself looking out from her Tower over a world of quiet splendour. The arc of the sky was distanced by stars so faint she could not be sure she saw them, immeasurably farther off than the familiar blue into which the skylark mounts. Below her, the massive slabs of the Tower were reared in strong contrasts of bone-silver and black, shadows that were impenetrable enough to simulate roof and buttresses. A wealth of mother-of-pearl boulders lay about the meadows, and among them, copying their shapes on the tender sward, the horses slept, and the cows. Over the middle distance, the loose stone walls separating the fields followed the contours like necklaces over sleeping shoulders, disappearing into hollows and rising again over mounds. The distant fells, cloudless, seemed to lie tilted, opened out on the curve of the earth, and pallid magic flowed down their sides. It was a scene to disarm fear, and it had its effect on Persie. She received the detached serenity in some part of her imagination that was not available to her then, being crowded out of consciousness by the vehemence of her agitation. At the time it only seemed to her that the cold and the fatigue had become intolerable under the added burden of all this brilliance. Later on, however, looking back, she rediscovered the moonrise on the Tower with feelings of beatitude.

In the end, hearing no one and seeing no one, she became weary even of fear and began to clamber down. The stairway would have been dark had it not lacked most of its inner wall, like a spiral shell broken open. The well was zebraed with crisp moonlight and shadow, unfamiliar to sight and imagination, deceptive in colour, size, and substance. It was familiar only to her feet, which took her down step by step as if they had an intelligence separate from hers, and, where there were no steps, fumbled confidently for the familiar foothold. Except for a misjudged jump and a few nasty grazes, caused by her obsession with the black square of the floor below and what might be standing there, she came without accident to the bottom, where, opposite the doorway into the shadowed interior, there was another out into the floodlit earth. She slid through this and ran—more now to get warm than from present fear—towards the farm.

Old Stalker always locked up at half past ten without even enquiring if his granddaughter was in or not, but she had a way to her own bedroom window over the scullery roof, which was known to Bess, who was thus absolved from making scenes with her father on the subject. They would in any case have been useless. The dog's eyes shone in the moonlight from the opening of his kennel, and Persie heard his tail swish in the straw but he did not bark. From a low wall, via the water butt, she reached the sloping roof and crawled up it to her window.

She had thought longingly of her bed and the sleep it would bring, but in that she was deceived. Experiences that were too violent had put her brain into commotion—the image of the sublime moonlit world being the one that made sleep finally impossible, like an open door. She tossed and ached and stared at darkness till the tension hurt. She felt too vulnerable, unable to bear, without counsel and support, a world that had such horror in it. At last, trembling and wretched, she took her candle and crept quietly to her mother's room, thinking to slip into Bess's bed and perhaps sleep till dawn in the lee of her comfortable body. What she would say if questioned she did not know. Perhaps Bess would be too lazy to query when she woke up and found her daughter there. Perhaps she would just say, "Hullo, ducks!"

Persie turned the handle noiselessly and went in. The candle flame that had leant backward and given almost no light as she walked, now stood upright and seemed to give an ample fiery light, in which she saw Bess asleep with her head on a mottled, powerful body above which Sam's hated bristly face lolled sideways on the pillow, his arm hanging over the side of the bed and his ogre hand relaxed in sleep.

❖

Possibly the breath retreating into Persie's body caused some kind of mechanical cry, but she made no conscious sign. It was as if she had been struck senseless. With no will, meaning, or life, she withdrew as quietly as she had come, a walking body from which the soul had been stolen. She returned to her room and sat on the bed, possessed by a clarity that was empty of all thought. Presently she rose and dressed and began putting her few things into a bass basket. There was little enough and nothing to choose from, so it was soon finished as mechanically as it began. At the sound of the first cockcrow she began to hurry. She went down to the kitchen and found a piece of paper and a pen. She wrote a message that she thought could prevent pursuit or enquiry.

I have gone away with a man. I'll be all right.

Her mother would be pleased that she was fixed up. She understood, with the false logic of disgust, that her mother would be glad that she was out of the way.

She picked up her bass basket and with a white face and an expression that was both vague and taut she left the farm. She walked with a slightly swaying step down across the fields and towards the highroad. A few minutes after she had gone, Sam, who had been wakened by the cockcrow, came down and washed his head under the sink tap. Oblivious of what he had brought about, he returned to his home and to his wife, who scolded him as she loved him, which was without measure.

❖

Persie set off into the fields and followed a footpath at random, looking, from a moon's-eye view as she crossed the billowy eiderdown of the world, like a lost feather that moves without volition. In fact, she had no chosen destination. There were simply a number of places to which she could not go—neighbours' homes where explanations would have to be given; and if she could not tell the first half of her story, still less could she tell the second. It was thus that she came eventually before the schoolteacher's house, which seemed to offer some hope of human counsel. It was at least not an outstanding impossibility.

She passed into the garden and sat down on the wooden bench in a grotto made of ivy, facing the windows. White linen blinds were drawn over them like lowered eyelids. Not only Miss Thwaites slept. The house itself seemed to nod and the garden to be shut out from it like a lonely and anxious dog. Persie was even more of an outsider as she sat there, her feet drenched in dew, and fixed her unhappy eyes on the face of the house, which was so austere and withdrawn.

The dawn had begun, but its advent was lost in the pervasive radiance of the moon. The influence of oncoming day could only creep along the surface of the earth, giving a little more weight to the greens of oak and larch, a little more reality to the ground under one's feet. Its touch was cold and burdensome, and it drew up a mist like a yield of sad thoughts. While these planetary revolutions were taking place the tide, which had swung in after the rising moon and poured its great surplus up the valley, had turned again and called up a rain-laden west wind. Persie sat on in Miss Thwaites's arbour, a solitary figure quite out of place.

Her thoughts floated on currents at different levels with no direction. They were just the furniture of her mind grown unfamiliar with the erasure of the joy that had hitherto accompanied her through life. This erasure detached her almost completely from that self which existed in the lie of the land, the shapes of the fells, the direction of the paths, and the scents, sounds, and visual and muscular impact that belonged to each footfall. She received passively the impression of every detail of the garden in its bleak lack of significance.

Of what use could Miss Thwaites be, rooted as she was in the village and responsible to the parents, not to the children? Once there had been a doctor, a friend of Miss Thwaites's, who had been very kind to Persie. She had seemed to know that young things were more than pieces of a family group. She had recently left the district and gone to Kendal.

The repeated scolding of a blackbird reminded her that Dick was now throwing stones at her window to wake her for the milking. She saw herself in a series like a cinema reel of almost identical pictures, milking in the shippen among the soft welcoming creatures she had known for so long, Bella, Daisy, and the rest. Star would have her calf today. Persie sprang up wildly. She must get away. She would go to Kendal.

❖

Every morning at half past six Dr. Masters' housekeeper took her a cup of tea in bed, and then went down to prepare breakfast. After that, she cleaned the surgery for opening time at seven-thirty, because

Kendal, being the centre of a farming community, is a place of early risers and early workers. This morning she was back again, tapping on the bedroom door before Dr. Masters was even out of bed.

"I'm sorry to disturb you, Doctor, but there is a girl downstairs that perhaps you ought to see. I found her at the back door when I opened up, and I said, 'What might you be wanting'—a little thing she is— and she said, 'I want to speak to Dr. Masters,' she said, and I said, 'She isn't up, but I'll take a message for you if it's something urgent,' I said, 'otherwise you can come back at seven-thirty when surgery opens,' I said. 'Are you a patient?' 'Yes,' she said. 'No,' she said, and down she went flop. I'd better go now and see to her till you come. She's lying on the kitchen floor."

"I'll be there in a minute." Dr. Masters was already in her dressing gown and putting a comb through her soft grey hair.

When she entered the kitchen, Persie was propped, lax and unconscious, in a wicker chair to which the housekeeper had dragged her, her head hanging backward so that the dank hair fell away from her high, unexpectedly severe forehead. Her nose jutted out like a corpse's.

"No, no—no more cold water! She's like ice. Get some hot bottles and blankets, as quickly as you can. Never mind my breakfast."

It's the Stalker child, she recognised, as she felt for her pulse and sounded the flower-like chest with a pity that was not bounded by the clock and the pressure of work.

When Persie finally opened her eyes on a shudder, she found herself lying on a sofa wrapped in blankets. Dr. Masters was sitting beside her, stethoscope round her neck and a cup of tea in her hand.

"Don't move," she said, putting aside her breakfast. "Just tell me about it. Is your mother in town?"

"No."

"Your grandfather?"

"No."

"There's been an accident?"

"No."

"Do they know you are here?"

Persie made a great effort to sit up.

"Don't tell them—please don't tell them!" Her face went from white to scarlet and stayed heavily flushed with a visible pulse on her temple as she gave way and lay back again.

Dr. Masters sat watching her. She knew her home and history.

23

She had attended her mother at her birth, and at various miscarriages since.

"How old are you?" she asked, after a pause.

"Sixteen."

The doctor calculated. Hardly, she thought, but let it pass for the moment, turning the general situation over in her mind. "I suppose you have run away?"

Persie nodded.

"Somebody frightened you?"

Another nod.

"Who was it? You'd better tell me."

"Sam," said Persie, bringing out the name between slow sobs, clearly unable to say more.

Dr. Masters knew a great deal about Sam, both personally and by repute. It seemed to her that most of the babies she had delivered in Silverstone were attributed to him, whether their mothers were married or unmarried—and this was not counting the nine who were legitimately his.

"Did he do anything to you?"

Persie shook her head, the root of her desolation still untouched.

"Well, what did happen?"

"I tried to get him with a billhook but I missed."

"Just as well," said Dr. Masters, her soft, clipped speech showing nothing of her alarm. "You're sure he's not hurt?"

"Yes," said Persie, but now so obviously distressed, with her head turning from side to side and the tears pouring down into her chattering teeth, that Dr. Masters decided to ask no further. Besides, into her mind had come the memory of rumours linking Sam and Bess. She quietened Persie with promises to say nothing to her mother, at least for the present; and with that, she called the housekeeper and they took Persie upstairs and put her to bed in the spare room. She was given a hot drink and an injection and left with drawn curtains and orders not to move. Dr. Masters, having had no breakfast, went on into the surgery.

During the day's work she kept her ears open for gossip, and she searched the local newspapers for a paragraph about a missing child.

By evening, when she looked in on Persie for the third time, it was clear she had a touch of pneumonia. Unless they were going to send her to the hospital—which meant filling in all her papers and informing her mother—she would have to stay where she was. It was not at all correct professional behaviour, but Nan was inclined to see if she could put it through without getting into trouble. So long as the child was not seriously ill and nobody asked questions.

After supper, she rang up her friend Miss Thwaites and had a long chat, drawing her out on village news. Miss Thwaites had much to say about juvenile and parental misdeeds, but there was no mention of Persie. Finally Nan asked outright: "How's my little Persephone Stalker?"

"Oh, all right, I think. She's working on the farm. You could still pick her up and put her in your pocket, but she seems tough. Brainy little thing. I hoped she would have gone on, but she's a bit of a mystery. No friends."

Nan went up to visit her where she lay tossing between shocked consciousness and snatches of nightmare, coughing and breathless. To Persie, Nan was a comforting vision. Although she came and went almost like the other figures in her fever, each time it happened she brought confidence and quietness; which, after she had gone, remained awhile as if she had changed the atmosphere of the room. As a doctor, she had no professional manner. The manner that she had was her attitude to life. She was slow in movement because to hurry is to overlook something, sparing of words because they distract from thought, kind without condescension, and at times immovably stern. She had asked Persie no further questions. She would deal with the pneumonia first. She made her comfortable for the night, soothed her by saying she had done right to come to her and was not to worry, propped the spare-room door open and her own, which was at right angles to it, and after completing her noiseless and leisurely preparations, lay down in a dressing gown for night duty.

❖

As soon as time is loosed from the pressure of before and after, if consciousness falls out of the race and lies on one side, enduring but not moving, then a second is, to experience, as long as an age—for both are without limit or comparison. As Persie lay broiling in her fever, as much without a future as without a past (for the revulsion she felt from her mother seemed to have smashed her memories as an image is smashed when a mirror falls), the busy ticking seconds that skidded, skidded on her ears without advancing, piled up into a buffering no man's time between herself and yesterday, which, when the muscles of time should be active again and forcing her along, would be found to have isolated the consciousness of shock from the activities projected by it. Meanwhile she lay, and the indomitable floral wallpaper, the flapping navy blue curtains, and the feel under her fingers of the cups and ridges of the honeycomb bedspread seemed to take on themselves the whole of her personality. She had become surface only.

No enquiries, no police notices, no spiced-up stories in the papers came to trouble Dr. Masters on the subject of her visitor, whose young body had responded admirably to treatment and gave no cause for anxiety. At the end of a week she was sitting up in bed, wrapped in shawls and eating everything the good housekeeper brought her. She was fascinated and amused by the whole tradition of correct trays —the crocheted cloth, Devonshire pottery, cruets, toast rack, napkin, and layout. The housekeeper had evolved the idea, neither prompted nor repudiated by her employer, that Persie was her niece or cousin, and was treating her as one of the family.

Dr. Masters had decided that the time had come to review the position and make plans for the future.

She went upstairs and sat down by the bed. Persie put aside *David Copperfield* and turned to greet her with smiles held in abeyance, as so often, till she was sure they were welcome. To the doctor's enquiry she replied: "Oh, yes, I'm quite all right now. Ready for anything."

"Where were you on your way to when you dropped in here?"

"That's exactly what I did do, isn't it!"

"Was it only because you were ill that you came?"

"I didn't know I was ill till I flopped. I came because I thought you would help me to find a place to work. You see, I haven't any money at all."

"How did you get here?"

"I hitchhiked."

"Alone?"

"Yes," said Persie, surprised that anyone should ask.

Nan paused and tacked.

"What kind of a place do you want? Something livelier, such as shops or factories?"

"Oh, no! I don't want to be in a town. I thought somebody would be sure to want a farm girl or stable girl. I can lift quite big sacks. . . ."

"Well, you should be all right in another fortnight. We will look at the advertisements and I'll give you a reference. I'll get hold of the *Stockbreeder* and the *Agricultural Times* and perhaps *Country Life*, and you can look through them. By the way, Miss Thwaites rang up today and gave me the Silverstone account of your running away."

Persie blushed and lifted tear-pricked eyes to Nan, with the steady look of the most practised liar, which she so oddly wore when most vulnerable and most candid.

"I thought it would stop Mums trying to find me. That was all I minded at the time. But now I hate Dick thinking that of me."

"Dick hates it too. Was it quite untrue?"

"Yes, of course. There wasn't anybody."

"No young man at the Red Rose?"

"How beastly, how *beastly* they are! Who said that? I never did."

She pushed her trembling hands under the bedclothes, but fiery anger blazed in her face as if she would blister her opponents. Then she suddenly laughed.

"Dear G. de Fol!" she added tenderly. "I only met him once. He was nice. We had breakfast at the Red Rose."

"That would be quite enough for the village, you know."

"Is it wrong to have breakfast with someone? I didn't think. I wish Dick knew the message wasn't true. At the time I think I liked it being horrid because I was angry. I have been thinking about Dick a lot, but I don't like to write. Not that he'd give me away, but everyone would see the postman come."

"It would be kind to tell your mother that you are all right."

Persie's gentle and quicksilver face became blank and unapproachable as she gazed at her feet sticking up under the bedclothes. She did not answer.

"I could send Dick a private message by Miss Thwaites."

"Oh yes, please, please do that."

❖

There were not many situations for land-girls offered where Dr. Masters—anxious that, having unlawfully taken parental responsibility, she should not fall short of it—was satisfied that the living conditions were good enough for anyone so young and innocent. Persie, however, found in *Country Life* an advertisement for a girl as trainee undergardener, and showed it with great enthusiasm. That would be much better; she would prefer it to anything else by far.

ST. HILARION, PORT TRISTRAM, CORNWALL.
Nominal wages for first six months.
Board and lodging. Community life.
Reply Bursar.

Dr. Masters sent a letter recommending her protégée, stating that she was under sixteen and had no proper home, and that she wished to send her where she would be personally looked after.

The reply, written on good paper in a fine cultured hand, assured her that such a child would be particularly welcome, and that they would all do their best to make a home for her. It was signed "Bursar," and under that a signature of indecipherable modesty, as if the writer was not interested to be known. It looked like "Clare X," but must be meant for "C. Larex." Dr. Masters consulted the medical directory for the doctors in that part of Cornwall, and found an Irishman whom she had known well in Liverpool actually practising in Port Tristram. To her letter asking if he knew St. Hilarion and if it was a suitable situation for a girl of fifteen, she received an answer by wire: DON'T MAKE ME LAUGH. NOTHING BETTER THIS SIDE OF PARADISE.

❖

Persie, to whom an electric iron was a wonder, carefully pressed her shabby skirt, her two faded cotton blouses, her best pink cardigan, her deplorable knickers, her skimpy flannelette nighties, and her red hair ribbon, regarding her work with satisfaction and folding up what she did with pride. Nan, watching her, had to fight down her longing to fit the child out properly. Maybe by doing so she would undercut Persie's confidence in herself, which was so much more valuable than any confidence based on new clothes. It would also certainly spoil the disarming appeal she must make on arrival just as she was. She therefore confined her generosity to having the worn country shoes and sandals soled and heeled, and buying two pairs of brown dungarees and a mackintosh. The whole wardrobe still fitted easily into the bass bag.

PART II

St. Hilarion

The journey was long. Dr. Masters had put her on the night train at Preston, recommending her to the guard and to the ladies in the compartment. She was not due at her destination till late the following day.

The carefully imparted freshness did not stay long on her old clothes. By morning they had reverted to their true age and condition. Also, the sleeve of her jacket, too narrow at the shoulder and stopping short above her wrist, had split at the armhole when she had helped a lady to lift a suitcase off the rack. She had been excited and interested since daylight, watching the rounded fields rolling past like a green ocean ever widening between herself, penned in the brown, stale-smelling compartment, and all that she had known and loved. Ranges and valleys wheeled past and sank away, until even the important stations where the train stopped had names she had never heard of. When the journey had exceeded all limits and began to seem to have lost the attribute of progression, in spite of the eddying landscape, she tried to fill the vacuum with images of a wealth of velvet pansies and quilted bachelor's-buttons, to be touched and watered by her; of sweetpea seeds dropped one by one into holes made with the first finger; of yellow and orange leaves to be swept up with the wind in one's hair; of beds of polyanthus as bright as the morning from between whose leaves one pulled up young Vs of grass or soft unresisting chickweed. Such things on the smallest possible scale she had sometimes done on a Saturday afternoon to help Miss Thwaites.

Suddenly and at last she had arrived at Port Tristram, as much taken by surprise as if she had never really expected a destination; and now she hopped out with her bass bag, joyful to leave the train and to be able to smell and hear the country that for so many hours had been only a panorama behind dirty glass. The soft, sea-cooled air was delicious to her lungs and temples—almost, it seemed to her, to her lips. The little station had a look of total leisure. The single, jolly-looking porter was the host, delighted to welcome his guests, with an air always of expecting more than actually came. This time there was only one. He greeted with fatherly solicitude the light-footed bit of a thing whose lifted nostrils were sampling the air as if she were a foal.

"Anybody with you, love?"

"No. Can you tell me, please, how to get to St. Hilarion?"

He studied her again with a look of surprise.

"You wouldn't be Miss Stalker, I suppose?"

"Yes, I am!" She remembered that she had been called so once before, long ago, at the Red Rose. She nodded to confirm what she had said.

"Ah, miss, I'm glad to see you. I've been told to look after you and put you on the bus. Where's your luggage?"

"It's here, thank you. I've got it." She waved the bass bag. She was cheerful, hungry, anticipatory.

"There's not a bus for forty minutes," he said. "And when this train pulls out there's not another for two hours. So I was going to make myself a cup of tea. You come along and have one. It'll help to pass the time for both of us."

Persie sat in the porter's room, curling her bare legs round the legs of a high stool, which, he told her, was the one on which he usually sat to write his entries in the station book. They each had a tin mug of good strong tea with plenty of milk and sugar. The porter leant against the grimy wall opposite her.

"What do you do when there are no trains?" asked Persie, gaily inaugurating the conversation.

"I write up my books. And sweep the platform and light the lamps. And I look after the station garden."

"I'm going to be a gardener. That's what I've come for."

"You, miss? You couldn't push a barrow-load of muck."

"I could, I'm very strong. You'd be surprised."

"I am surprised."

Persie looked at him with provocatively protruding eyes over the top of her mug of tea, and then laughed.

For forty minutes they got on like a house on fire. When finally the bus carried her away, waving to him through the glass, the porter pushed his cap back and scratched his head.

❂

The bus stopped for her at a large white gate, and here her feeling of giddy independence left her. The place she was approaching had been hidden from her along its roadside boundary by trees and shrubs, and now she set off along a steep and curving drive, looking round her for indications of what she was to expect. It was sunset, and somewhere a quiet bell was ringing. The drive was long, but soon came out of its bordering shrubs, giving her a view of a small open park in which, at first sight, she thought there were deer grazing. She quickly realised that these beautiful creatures must be Jersey cattle, which she had previously seen only in pictures. They had been recently milked and were unsociable, ignoring all her blandishments. She stopped for some time to look at them and to watch the sun setting beyond the hill that she was climbing. It was all very serene, with a positive quality of beatitude added to the stillness. She loitered, reluctant to have arrived. At last, rounding a dense clump of trees, she saw the house. It was a long cluster of buildings of no particular style, plastered and cream-washed, with square sash windows throughout. Owing to the medley of adjoining blocks and wings of different heights and aspect, the windows came at many levels, making a pleasant, lively impression, with the setting sun reflected in rosy flashes from the polished glass.

The house faced down the valley. Here was the garden of Persie's hopes, its lavender hedge throwing long shadows in the sunset, the September roses taking a deeper flush.

She wondered which of the many doors she should go to, and finally, deciding it was politer for a stranger to go to the front, she stepped into a porch full of geraniums and other flowers, unknown to her, and rang the bell. It was a pull bell, and her first modest effort seemed to her to have had no result. She therefore, after a moment, pulled harder; but the embarrassing ding-dong of her success was such that, the door opening simultaneously, she was not able to speak against the noise, but stood startled and abashed in the smiling presence of the opener.

The figure was an abstraction, like a Druid or a Viking, suddenly leaping the gap between the not easily credible pictures in school history books and present reality. Persie hazarded a guess that she must be a nun. Had she been an angel, she could hardly have been more impressive. She was tall and very thin, wearing her pleated brown robe with gentle grace; all her face except what you might call the soul of it, was enclosed in white face bands and a starched bonnet. From out of these her wood-agate eyes (one of which was tilted towards her temple like a doe's, the other straight) and her dividing smile—dividing Persie's experience into the time before she had seen such a thing and the time after—considered the visitor and instantly received her into her own unbounded good will.

"Is it Persephone?" she asked gaily.

Staring, she could only whisper, "Yes."

"I am Sister Clare. It was I who wrote to you. Come in. You've had a very long journey, I know."

The entrance hall was spacious and white, with an oak staircase, uncarpeted, and a tiled floor. There was little furniture, so that the one picture was conspicuous. It was unintelligible to Persie, showing a figure kneeling with arms outstretched and receiving, apparently, a stroke of lightning through each palm. Under this was the largest vase of flowers she had ever seen, arranged with rose-coloured lilies and traveller's-joy. The lilies also were something she had never seen before. She put out her hand to touch them, with a gasp and a sigh. Sister Clare watched her gesture with assent, and gave her time to finish it.

"I see you will be an enthusiastic gardener. How glad Sister Monica will be. She badly needs help. I will just take you in to see Reverend Mother, and then you will want to wash and tidy before supper. You have come just at the right time. You must be hungry."

Sister Clare pressed a bell as she spoke. A rather breathless little nun came out of the door beyond the stairs.

"Oh, Sister Agnes, could you please find Sister Monica and ask her to come to Reverend Mother's room?"

"Yes, Sister Clare."

"Now, Persephone, will you come with me?"

She led the way, opening a door that proved merely an added layer to the privacy of a second door, a wall's thickness behind it. On this she knocked gently, bending to listen for a reply with a face of love.

In Tower Farm there had been neither deference nor discipline—merely license and a politic yielding to tyranny and bad temper. In school, the teacher had imposed a discipline but had not expected or wished for deference. Comradeship had been her losing game. At the Central Dairy the clerk who knocked at the manager's office showed a mixture of sycophancy and intention to outwit. In the hospital where she had once been, the passage of the specialist was brisk and ludicrously ritual. The moment he had gone, there was laughter all

34

round, beginning with the whispered joke between nurse and nurse. In the hierarchies of Persephone's life there had been no deference of the quality that she now sensed with wonder.

On a reply from within, Sister Clare opened the door.

"It's Sister Clare, Reverend Mother. The girl who is to be the new garden apprentice is here. Will you see her? Yes, my dear, Reverend Mother will see you now. Will you come in? Reverend Mother, this is Persephone Stalker."

The room was large and comfortable, but unencumbered. Opposite the door, through a pair of windows, Persie could see down the valley to the distant sea. The sun was just disappearing, leaving along the surface of the water a blaze of crimson and orange which shot across the lower green of the valley and struck into the room, lighting up on the mantelpiece a painting of a Mother and Child, set like a jewel in a polished brass frame encrusted with shining spokes like the rays of the sun, now burnished by the sun itself to dazzle Persie's eyes. She had to turn away to find the voice that greeted her.

"Good evening, my child."

"Good evening, ma'am." Persie was already conscious of her shabbiness, her littleness, of the train soot on her hands, the mud on her bare ankles, of the whiskery bass bag that she still held in front of her. It seemed suddenly to smell of poultry.

The Mother Superior had presence. Her smooth skin was so fair that it and the starched white funnel enclosing it exchanged reflections, making the white less cold, the flesh more remote. Her voluminous clothing could not obliterate the strength of the human personality beneath it, but left it mysterious. One only saw, held in the snowy linen, a noble face, rather long, with almond-shaped light-blue eyes, wide apart and wide open. It was a piercing glance to meet, almost a glare, which her fastidious narrow mouth did not much help to soften. Her manner was warm and gracious, imposing because one felt at once that she imposed it rigorously upon herself.

In contrast with Sister Clare's limpid simplicity, Reverend Mother had the long practice of worldly graces behind her, to which was added the suavity of authority.

"Come round here, where the sun is not blinding you. That's better. Did you say *Persephone*, Sister Clare? How oddly and delightfully pagan that sounds among us. It puts us among the early Christians."

They laughed lightly together like two intimate friends.

"Well, Persephone, I am glad to see you here. I hope the porter at the station was helpful?"

Persie tried to feel more grown up and to speak as older girls she knew would do.

"He was right friendly, and gave me a cup of tea."

Reverend Mother smiled again. "So, even after the North Country, you got quite a good first impression of us. I hope you won't be homesick."

"No," said Persie. "What lovely cows you have. Would they be Jerseys?"

"Yes; those are Sister Veronica's beloved Jerseys. Are you used to cows, Persephone?"

"Oh yes. I come from a farm, you know. I've always looked after cows."

"Have you really? How very nice and how very useful. Are you quite well again? I believe you have been ill. Pneumonia, wasn't it?"

"Thank you. I am quite well again."

"That's good. Well now, Persephone, I won't keep you any longer tonight. You must be tired and hungry. We will have a talk in the morning about your duties. Sister Monica will look after you now."

"I have sent for her to come here, Reverend Mother," said Sister Clare.

"Oh, thank you. I really want to see you for a few minutes. You may sit down, Persephone. Look at this, Sister Clare, read this letter from Lord Penhellion. What am I to say? Lady Penhellion wants to come again."

"I wouldn't like to advise you what to say, Reverend Mother. The truth would be most embarrassing. She set the whole place at sixes and sevens."

"I know. I should think half the sisters are still confessing the things she made them think."

Persie listened, enjoying their high clear voices and not trying to understand what was being said. She was a born mimic, and this way of speaking, which seemed to use the roof of the mouth as a sounding board, in fact to use the upper part of the face so much and the cheeks and underlip so little, made her by contrast think of the dialect she knew as being framed by drooping cart-horse lips—a thought that made her laugh aloud.

Reverend Mother looked round, startled and severe, but at that moment there was a knock on the door and Sister Monica had arrived.

"This is Sister Monica, who is in charge of the garden. Sister Monica, will you look after Persephone and show her to her room, please. You can let her sleep late tomorrow, because she has been all night in the train. I shall want to see her after breakfast."

"Yes, Reverend Mother."

"You may go with Sister Monica, Persephone."

"Yes, thank you."

"You may call me Reverend Mother."

"Yes, thank you."

"Yes, *Reverend Mother.*"

"Yes, Reverend Mother," said Persephone, her eyes round with fun.

When she had gone out with Sister Monica, leaving the two friends alone, Reverend Mother leant back in her chair and exclaimed: "What an odd discomforting little thing! Sister Bridget would say she was a changeling."

"I thought her very sweet. I would have said one of St. Ursula's eleven thousand virgins."

"Let's hope she's that at least. Now, let us see Lord Penhellion's letter again. I didn't like her laughing out like that about the sisters' confessions. That was like a changeling."

"Reverend Mother, we were laughing ourselves. It was your joke."

"So it was. We shouldn't have been talking like that in front of her, I suppose. But we laugh with a difference. She was just wickedly gay. It was as if a little devil had suddenly burbled with joy out of the armchair."

"Why not a little angel? They must sometimes laugh at the sisters' confessions, silly creatures that we are."

"The most likely supposition is that she really is a total pagan. After all, they are the big majority now. Well, now, where's that letter? I must answer it."

"*Must* we have Lady Penhellion again, Reverend Mother? I think I have never felt so far below my vocation."

❧

Meanwhile Persie was trotting after Sister Monica along the corridors. There was an appetising smell as they passed the kitchen and little Sister Agnes came out with a tray of crockery. They also passed a closed door from behind which came the sound of voices and laughter. Sister Monica said that that was the Common Room. "We all go there in our free time and after supper." Sister Monica was a silent person, withdrawn into hours of solitary work. She had nothing to say except the minimum of information. Persie was puzzled. Nobody had said anything yet to enlighten her as to what kind of a place she had come to.

At the end of the north block they climbed the stairs to the top.

"This is your room."

Persie entered a little white room, spotlessly clean, containing a bed and a chest of drawers and—most wonderful to her—a basin with taps.

"What a nice ornament," she said, picking up a porcelain Madonna and Child off the chest of drawers and looking underneath to see if it was hollow. Then she looked out of the window, over the top of a spinney which clothed the hill. There was an ebony cross on the wall, and beneath it a chair, of which the narrow seat was only eight inches from the ground, the back being the usual height but topped by a shelf.

"What's that for?" asked Persie, curious where everything was unexpected.

Sister Monica, who had already had one shock, looked at her almost with fear.

"It's a *prie-dieu*."

"A what, please? I don't understand."

"A *prie-dieu*. For saying your prayers."

"Oh. Have I got to do that? I don't know any."

"You must know some. Don't you know the Pater Noster?"

"What, please?"

"Our Father Which art in Heaven—"

"Oh, *that*! We used to say that before school."

Sister Monica grew pink inside her bonnet.

"Where is the rest of your luggage?" she asked, to change the subject.

"There isn't any more. Everything's in here. It holds a lot. Dr. Masters gave me some lovely new dungarees, for gardening in. Look!"

She pulled her treasures out onto the bed, and Sister Monica saw the whole contents of the basket.

"I want to learn gardening more than anything. I wonder if I have green fingers?"

Sister Monica smiled suddenly—not a nun's smile, but a personal one.

"You have the right name. Who should have green fingers if not you?"

At this Persie smiled too, and it was as if the spring had come.

"You had better wash now and get ready for supper. Don't be long, because it's nearly time. Make yourself as tidy as you can and come down to the Common Room. Can you find your way? In any case, I'll take you down and introduce you. I think you had better put on your cardigan. You won't be so naked."

"I'm not *naked*!" Persie laughed. "I've got a blouse on."

"Well, you look naked, anyway. Be quick. I'll come back for you in a minute."

Persie put her clothes away in the drawer and folded a nightie on her pillow. She enjoyed a good wash in her hot-and-cold basin. She kept her clean blouse for the interview with Reverend Mother next day, and was glad to hide the crumpled one under her cardigan. She considered the *prie-dieu* again. Prayers at school had been a meaningless routine. Over the Scripture classes taken by the Silverstone Vicar, a droning old man, despairing and impatient, sham lay thick like the dust of centuries, effectively preventing her from regarding them as anything but another of the government's inexplicable impositions. Nevertheless, for curiosity, she tried out the *prie-dieu*. It really felt as if it was meant for something. She felt oddly shy. When Sister Monica came back she was leaning out the window.

✪

The Common Room was full of robed figures with faces enclosed in starched linen, all gracious, all smiling, all untroubled. Persie felt like a small moorland rabbit that had been put into an enclosure of Angoras. Their smooth movements, the mildness of their speech, made her feel by contrast wild, tense, and awkward. The sister who happened to be the nearest to her asked her kindly if it was the first time she had been away from her mother. Persephone knew nothing about social procedure or conversational opening gambits. She had imagined that what nobody knew, nobody would touch upon. She felt suddenly faint. Her tongue refused to answer. Luckily, at that moment the bell rang and silence fell. The sisters trooped out in procession, Persephone bringing up the rear behind Sister Monica, who murmured in her ear that there was a rule of silence at mealtimes.

39

When every sister was standing beside her chair at the table, Reverend Mother entered, moving with immense dignity among her flowing pleats. She stood at the head of the table to say grace, after which she and every sister made the sign of the cross, watched by an electrified stranger, so rigid that when all sat down she was left standing. Sister Monica touched her arm and pointed to her chair.

Two sisters were waiting at table, handing the dishes to each in turn. There was much for Persie to look at before they reached her. The table was polished oak. How odd to have no cloth, only straw mats. There were wooden candlesticks up the centre whose light coloured the eight grave faces on each side and also the shining oval which was the unconscious vehicle of Persie's stare. Opposite her sat an old lady in black whose skin was like rice paper. She was the only other person not wearing a habit.

Whole-meal bread was served in dishes of polished wood. When at last the kedgeree, of which there was still happily an ample portion, was offered her, Persie automatically said "Thank you." The spoken word, though not loud, seemed to her to ring through the silence like an oath, but not a glance was lifted and not a head turned. Had someone but frowned, the incident would have been over. As it was, it was left in mid-air for the duration of the meal, sometimes seeming to Persie's memory to have been whispered, sometimes suddenly looming in imagination as a positive shout, heard by all.

When at last the meal, which Persie spent, as it were, in the stocks, was over, grace after meat spoken, and the nuns preparing to file out, Sister Clare, from the far end of the table, looked down to a tired child with eyes like harebells, keeping an obstinately straight neck, her hands locked behind her. She smiled and signed to her to wait. It has already been noticed that Sister Clare's smile was of an extraordinary sweetness, but sweetness was not its only quality. It was touched with something incalculable that perhaps went with the glance of her tiptilted eye. She was drawn to Persie as she would have been to a lost leveret. She touched Persie's elbow, saying: "I shall see that you go straight to bed. You are tired out. Come with me now to say good night to Reverend Mother. And don't forget—*Reverend Mother!* We all do revere her very much."

Persie followed as if drawn along and protected in the flow of Sister Clare's movement, and in the Common Room, where the Mother Superior was sitting among the sisters, she said her piece. Sister Clare asked permission to go up with her to see that she had what she needed. Reverend Mother gave permission and said good night to Persephone with a gentleness that was like a kiss. Sister Clare led her away.

"We do not go into each other's rooms unless someone is ill, but tonight you are still our guest. Do you like your little room?

"You will be going to bed with the birds. I see you like plenty of fresh air. There's no moon tonight; it will be soft and dark until the stars come out. You must go to sleep quickly. You will want a bath, I expect. Tomorrow you will be given your regular time to have them. I'll show you the bathroom."

Persephone had lost her first nervous uncertainty of bathrooms while staying with Dr. Masters. She had come to regard them as luxurious toys and had a great love of lying in the clouds of steam. She was surprised and delighted to find that such indulgences were to continue. In that she was to be disillusioned, because, although a daily bath was obligatory, the water was never more than lukewarm. Even on the coldest day the lifeless surface hardly gave off a breath of steam. One was tempted to hold a mirror over it. But now she looked into the bathroom with Sister Clare and gave what she thought was a sophisticated nod. Sister Clare laughed inwardly at such contented shining eyes.

"Well, I'll leave you to it now. Don't forget your prayers. I'll tell Sister Monica to wake you in time to dress for Mass."

"For what, please?"

"For Mass. For Communion in the Chapel."

"But tomorrow isn't Sunday. It's only Saturday."

"My dear child! We don't *skimp* it like that. What were you brought up—Catholic, Anglican, or Nonconformist?"

"I don't know the difference. I suppose it was Church of England at school, but I've never been to church. What must I put on? I was going to wear my new dungarees for working in."

"Now I remember; Reverend Mother said you need not get up tomorrow till breakfast. Don't take any notice of the bells. Sister Monica shall call you before she goes to Mass and you can dress then. Your dungarees will be quite all right. Good night now, my little Persephone. I hope you will soon feel one of the family. We shall enjoy having a younger sister to look after."

"Good night, Sister Clare."

Persephone was fascinated by the strangeness of the atmosphere and quite dazzled by Sister Clare's kindness. Willing to please her in

41

every way, she knelt for the second time at her *prie-dieu*, and for the first time in her life considered the words of the Lord's Prayer as she said them. They struck her, separated from the headlong singsong gabble of school, as august words, good to say. She got into bed in a state of total surprise about everything, but as her head touched the pillow she fell asleep.

❖

She was wakened, as she thought, by Dick's pebble on the window, which after a moment she identified as Sister Monica's discreet knock. Almost immediately the Chapel bell began ringing somewhere over the building. When she had called out an answer to the knock, she heard the rustle of the habit as Sister Monica moved away, and before she got out of bed another followed it down the corridor. Muffled in the heavy pleats, the actual footfalls were hardly heard. Persephone hung out of the window, and now she could see the bell swinging under a little roof of its own above the gable end of what looked like a barn. She could see the jerking rope that disappeared through the thatch.

She dressed with deliberation, almost with solemnity, for her initiation into the profession of gardening. She was full of ambition, and knew it was important for apprentices to make a good impression. She wished to look willing and bright. She made sure that her dungarees were tidily put on, the extra length of shoulder strap, which her diminutive height did not require, well tucked in out of sight. And round her head, to keep the hair out of her eyes, she tied a jolly red hair ribbon, a trophy from a chocolate box given her by the proprietress of the Red Rose by way of a Christmas tip. She tidied her room and, before leaving, paused a moment by the *prie-dieu*. Was she supposed to do it again? She decided to wait for definite instruction on that point, and went down through empty passages to the room where supper had been served the night before. Over the door was printed REFECTORY. The door stood open, and there was no one inside. The table was laid; the big windows were open. As she leant out she breathed the tangy smell of chrysanthemums still wet with dew and the honey of dwarf Michaelmas daisies. There was no sign of human life. Persephone knocked diffidently on the kitchen door, meaning to ask if it was all right for her to wait in the Refectory. The kitchen was empty. Steaming pans were on the range, empty porringers waiting. Everything was spotless, organised to the last detail, glittering with aluminium and white enamel, purring with refrigerators.

Only the long wooden table in the centre, scrubbed to the colour of bread, struck her as human, and lovable. The Chapel bell tolled once, startling her. She presumed they would be coming out, as at weddings, but no peal followed. She posted herself outside the Refectory door to wait. The bell rang again in the otherwise total silence. Persephone began to feel nervous, fidgety. She looked forward anxiously to the chance of a word with Sister Clare, and, if not to babble, at least to hear voices and be able to ask for reassurance. She longed suddenly for a gay thoughtless passage of words with G. de Fol. Her heart, till now adventurous and willing, contracted with a stab at the picture of her own country which sprang vivid and whole into her consciousness around the thought of him. The girl who stood rollicking in the milk float, wholly given up to the enjoyment of the rattling vibration up her legs and back, ready without thought to tease and leave behind so precious a stranger, seemed someone in another life, whose only connection with herself was the gossamer thread of memory. The rustling procession took her by surprise, filling the corridor and bearing down on her, led by Sister Clare, who smiled as Persephone made an irrepressible movement towards her, but laid a finger on her lips and went straight on into the Refectory. Persephone stepped back downcast. Another silent meal! She fell in naturally at the end, after the old lady in black, who did not even look at her. When they were all standing in their places Reverend Mother swept in as before.

After breakfast Sister Monica came to tell her to wait in the Common Room till Reverend Mother sent for her. Her manner was distant. You would never think I was here to help her, even if I am only a pupil, Persie thought as she wandered round the empty Common Room. All the sisters had vanished, presumably to their different tasks. Subdued voices were heard about the house. From the kitchen came cheerful homely noises, gay talk over the washing up, and Sister Agnes' laughter jerked out of her by the vigour of her scrubbing.

At last someone came to summon her, a sister whom she had not noticed before, with a plump ordinary face, good-natured and impatient, who passed into the kitchen and was heard giving orders with rather petulant authority.

Persephone knocked at Reverend Mother's door and went in. Reverend Mother was sitting behind her writing table as before, but without yesterday's tide of fire from the setting sun the room looked stern and official, a headquarters rather than a personal study. Reverend Mother was awe-inspiring, statuesque in her folds, noble in her pose. Her hands were small and well kept. Her fingers tapping on the desk thudded so distinctly that it was hard to tell for a minute whether it was indeed finger tips or the end of a pencil. Beside her stood a sister who seemed to droop under the weight of her habit. Persephone had come already to accept the faces of nuns as beautiful, so that the commonness of the cook's face seen a moment ago had surprised her. The face of this sister was unearthly to such a degree that one doubted if it was even made of flesh. She might be a ghost, a dream, and under her habit there was perhaps nothing. It was impossible to suggest any age that she might be, but the bodies of the young are not so easily discarded. She carried an air of infinity about her, a difficult infinity, a fighting beatitude. Persephone received some such impression strongly if vaguely, and felt an instant devotion.

"Good morning, Persephone," said Reverend Mother with warmth and smiling charm. "Come in. Please sit, Sister Veronica."

"Good morning, Reverend Mother."

"I hope you slept well and feel ready for work?"

"Yes, thank you."

"Yes, thank you, Reverend Mother," came the correction smilingly.

"Yes, Reverend Mother."

"I am rather afraid that what I am going to ask you may be a little disappointment to you. You came here, I know, to learn gardening. Did someone decide that for you, or was it your own preference, and have you chosen it as a definite career?"

"Yes, Reverend Mother. I want to learn it."

"Have you always wanted to?"

"No, Reverend Mother. But I do now."

"Well, Persephone, I will explain the difficulty that we are in, and why we want your help. This is Sister Veronica, who is in charge of the cows and chickens."

Sister Veronica smiled out of her infinity, and it lit up her ghost's face without moving the muscles.

"I am sorry I have come to trouble you, Persephone," she said. Her voice was soft and Scottish.

"Sister Veronica had a strong young sister to help her, but she was called away yesterday evening to nurse a dying father. Now you told me yesterday that you were used to farm work, so it seemed to me that the person we needed had been sent to us before we had asked, before we knew we should need her. All the sisters would be glad to help

44

Sister Monica in the garden in their free time, but cows and calves need constant care from someone who understands them. You will realise before you have been with us very long that here nobody does what she personally wants to do, but each one does what is best for the community. I have sent for you to ask if you will help Sister Veronica. Think a moment before you answer. I don't want to hurry you into it."

Persephone listened with a growing sense of loss and disillusionment. She had not known how anxious she was to leave Persie Stalker behind, to shed her like last year's leaves. She did not know why gardening had seemed to her so important—the innocent world of pansies and primroses, the cool silk of roses, the sun worship and rain worship, and the humble tending of the anonymous soil. She felt the sick despair of those who find, after imagined escape, that they are still face to face with themselves.

On the other hand, there was no need for Reverend Mother's pious sentiments about each doing what is needed. On a farm it is always like that. Had Dick or the old shepherd grumbled? But gardening was the first personal wish that Persephone had ever adopted. To give it up was harder than Reverend Mother had any idea of. Besides, from the point of view of a labour exchange, what she was asking was quite unfair, a kind of blackmail, because, as Persephone understood it, there was now no position as garden apprentice being offered her. She was to be a farm girl or go back to impose on dear Dr. Masters, or else where?

She stood looking fixedly at Reverend Mother with all these emotions—despair, acceptance, and even woman-to-woman criticism—present in her face. Then she looked at Sister Veronica, and acceptance was natural.

"Yes, Reverend Mother," she said tonelessly.

"That's all right then. I am very glad you have decided that way."

"Thank you, Persephone. It will be a great help to me," said Sister Veronica.

"You will, of course, get a little more money as a farm girl, because you will not be an apprentice. You will have a day off once a fortnight from milking time to milking time. Sister Veronica will explain everything to you. I shall expect you to attend High Mass on Sundays and Vespers and Compline always. Sister Clare tells me you have had no religious teaching. I will arrange a time when she can explain to you the meaning of what we do here. I mustn't keep you now, because Sister Veronica is behind time and wants your help. We are grateful to you for being so ready to fall in with our arrangements." She paused a moment, and then added, "It is a good start." The smile was an afterthought.

She rose to dismiss them, and came over to Persephone in the most friendly way, putting a hand on her shoulder.

"While you are with us, my dear, although you are not one of the community, I want you to look as neat, as discreet, as you can. Let me arrange your hair ribbon for you. It's just a little—flamboyant. I'll tie your hair back on the nape of your neck—so—neat and practical and really much nicer. You know, I am in the position of everyone's mother here. There. Let me hear good things of you from Sister Veronica."

Persephone went out like a pricked bubble. At the door she met Sister Clare, just coming in. Sister Clare always looked as happy as if she never had a trouble of her own, and as sympathetic as if she had known them all.

"Good morning, my little sister Persephone. I am sorry to hear you have to be torn away from your beloved flowers. You look just as *she* must have looked in the underworld, poor thing. It must have made Pluto quite unhappy. But cheer up. It is a great privilege to work with Sister Veronica, enough to make anyone happy. Look after her well. We all worry about her. She works herself to death. Don't let her carry heavy buckets. And her Jerseys are very beautiful."

"Yes, they are," said Persephone, pulling herself together and smiling. "Thank you, Sister Clare. I'll run after her." She skipped away and Sister Clare went in to the Mother Superior.

"I don't know what to think of that child," said the latter. "I wonder if she's not a liar. Her expression doesn't match her words."

"I should say, Reverend Mother, that her expression is not confined to her words. It overflows them in every direction. She is obviously very intelligent and hypersensitive."

"Do you think so? She gave me at one moment quite a hard-boiled stare."

Meanwhile Persephone had caught up with Sister Veronica, wondering greatly how anyone could clean the cowshed in those clothes. At the back door there was a cloakroom where shoes were changed. Here Sister Veronica put on gum boots, and, turning up the bottom half of her habit, pinned it firmly behind her waist. Her large sleeves she also turned up and fastened at the shoulder.

"Your clothes are certainly more practical," she said, smiling, "but I manage very well like this. First of all we had better feed the hens."

They set off together, Persie carrying two buckets of wet mash in a yoke, and Sister Veronica the bucket of dry corn. A heavy bucket straining on each shoulder is a brake on conversation, but in the walk from the back door to the field where the hens were Persie discarded her first ambition, never to brood over it again, and orientated herself to serving Sister Veronica.

While they took the traditional breather and watched the hens to see who was peaky or off her food, Persie began a professional conversation.

"How many cows have you, Sister Veronica?"

"They are not mine, you know, though dear Sister Clare jokingly calls them mine. They belong to the community. There are twelve, eight in milk and four in calf. Then there are the heifers. When we began there were only three. I bought them for Reverend Mother at a big farm sale."

"You bought them?" Persie tried to imagine Sister Veronica in the cattle market at Kendal.

"Yes. I used to be a veterinary surgeon before I joined the community. I have known Reverend Mother all my life and when she started here she asked me to come and take charge. The first three cows were Zenobia, Dido, and Theodosia. They are getting old now. The others are their calves."

"What funny names!"

"Yes. It's getting difficult to think of enough queens. Some of the great queens were saints, but Reverend Mother does not like that. I can't help thinking of animals as being good. I would prefer Helena to Helen, but Helen it is. She is certainly a beauty."

"I've never seen Jerseys before. Ours were all shorthorns. Do you keep a bull?"

"No. We haven't a man here to look after it. But I get the local vet in to help me with a difficult calving. Have you ever helped at one?"

"I've sometimes been there when it happened by itself, but I've never helped in a difficult one. My grandfather isn't a very good farmer. Once he let a cow die. Dick cried."

"Is Dick your little brother?"

"No! Dick is a cowman. He is awfully nice. He was mad with Grandfather. Grandfather was drunk and obstinate."

"Ah, poor cow! You may find me obstinate but you'll never find me drunk. Come and see the calves. They must be fed now. Eleanor, Isabella, and Christina. It's Christina making all that noise. She's only just been taken away from her mother."

Sister Veronica's transparent face had not a great range of expression. It was always rapt. The smiles or looks of sympathy that modified it were at one remove, reflected on it from the world she had left. Her conversation was like her face. She spoke with intelligence and humour but quite without urgency, as if at any moment her voice might die away and be heard no more. Nevertheless what she said was practical, not dreamy, and Persephone was soon convinced that she knew more about cows than Silverstone Tower Farm had ever dreamed of. Together they dosed Isabella for scald, and treated Hecuba for a wound beside her eye. "That was Zenobia's doing. The old lady is growing rather crotchety and bossy."

❈

By the end of the day Persephone had struck roots in her new home. She was accepting and accepted, gratefully aware of the unassuming welcome that each sister seemed to offer. When, after supper, Persephone joined the gathering in the Common Room, she already knew most of the sisters by name, and was taking for granted things which until that morning had been outside her imagination. In the Common Room hung coloured reproductions of Botticelli, of Memling, of Fra Angelico and Piero della Francesca, which Persephone examined, going from one to the other with cumulative awe. They were revelations of an unknown world, and stimulated her with nervous thrills. For the rest, the room was carpetless, surrounded by deep low cupboards, and furnished with a number of low-seated, straight-backed chairs, which the sisters drew into groups according to what they were doing. Some were making or mending habits or their white bonnets; others were doing fine embroidery on frames. Sister Sophia, the librarian, was bookbinding. She was so tall and thin that when she sat down on a low chair it was like folding up a map. Her exact hands were immensely long. Her brow, of course, was hidden by a white band; but under that the line of her nose, lips, and chin prolonged itself smoothly, without any thought of littleness, so that it was a pleasurable sensation to follow it down. Her eyes, with their tired blue lids, were for reading and meditation only. She would

48

be no more enclosed in her thought with them shut than with them open.

There was in the Common Room a grand piano on which, she was told, Reverend Mother often played to them; but on this second evening of Persephone's life here she was absent from the Common Room, where the time between supper and Compline passed in natural chatter and laughter in which Persephone was easily included. Sister Veronica also was absent, having, because of her frailty, special permission to rest in her own room. Because Persephone was enjoying her first evening as much as if she were at a party, and did not wish to be anywhere else, she accepted the fact that one needed permission to withdraw, without realising its implications. As she looked round the Common Room, where the groups of sisters made a satisfying interrelated whole, equable and tranquil, she was ashamed of her skimpiness, her personal insufficiency.

Not many days passed before she let down her skirt to its utmost length—though it showed a wide band of unfaded material round the bottom. Even so, she felt all legs, and bare legs at that. She exceeded Reverend Mother's wishes in the matter of her hair, and now flattened back her curly fringe, revealing a high Memling forehead that delighted Sister Clare.

In the weeks that followed, modelling herself on the sisters, she consciously modified her North Country accent towards that of the educated South—not out of snobbery, but as though it were a mark of the Order. Their ways of talking, of moving, of smiling were all alike there for her admiration, to be acquired, together with humility and serenity. She learned to observe the Greater and Lesser Silences. She collected with avidity the meanings of such strange words, heard in conversation, as sext and terce, wimple and scapular, feria and octave, thurible and chasuble. She modulated her frank vigorous movements towards a gliding stillness, very difficult to achieve without the habit, so much dignity was carried in its mere fullness and flow. Reverend Mother, when opportunity occurred, would always stop and talk to her, gently, gaily, and personally. Persephone was too ingenuous to know that this was a cultivated and deliberately practised grace. She laid it gratefully to her uprooted heart.

Persephone's progress in the ways of St. Hilarion was meteoric. Nothing in her former life had given her even a glimpse of what she was now offered. The poetry of the religion they taught she accepted without opposition. Genuflection and the making of the sign of the cross on her breast were joys to her, as if her instincts had always prompted just that.

❖

The Chapel which Persephone attended so gladly had been allowed to keep undisguised its barnlike features of rough beams and rafters and uneven stone walls. Reverend Mother had rigorously excluded anything sanctimonious in converting the building to its new function, content that it should recall the scene of the Nativity. It was constructed with cruck and tie beams whose succession down its length gave it a Gothic pattern. The cross that hung above the altar was formed of two rough pieces of wood similar to those used in the roof. It had kept its brick floor, and the windows were mere slits between vertical stones. The ceiling was plastered between the rafters and the walls pointed, but these were the only concessions. A curtain of Sister Clare's weaving hung behind the altar, and upon it were the fine embroidered cloths and laces worked in the Common Room. The sacristan was Sister Anne, and the maintenance of the Chapel and altars was her special duty. Persephone would have expected one who daily handled the holy vessels to be of an august seriousness. But Sister Anne was the merriest of the sisters, her odd irregular features so disguised under the lightness of her expression that no one thought of her as ugly. The Chapel was lit at all times with candles, and at festivals was sweet with fresh flowers. Reverend Mother was very particular that these should never show a shrinking petal or curled leaf. Here Persephone knelt open-eyed through many prayers, watching and listening, soul and senses satisfied.

Equally, when she went alone in the early morning to bring in the cows from the paddock, where they lay like islands of warm amber steaming in the morning mist, as she called to each by name, affectionately slapping the lazy ones who lay munching with their eyes shut pretending not to have heard, she abandoned herself to the sensuous and spiritual impulses that stirred in the autumn world. Prayer to her was a way of understanding these otherwise overwhelming impressions.

❖

It was a slow, glorious autumn. The sky was empty of everything but light, the air so mild that the leaves, which had lost all functional connection with the trees, were not dislodged, but remained lifted as if floating, each stalk adhering to the tree by the kind of magnetism that holds flotsam to the riverbank. When the moment came they would glide off, adventuring capricious and incaculable flights. The blood-red cherry leaves, canoe-shaped, would travel far; the golden elm swerve, tease, and frolic like children playing catch; the brown beech slip off purposefully one after the other, like bees leaving the hive; the pear leaves, rounder and thicker in texture, would flick-flack slowly down in a well of still air. But the heavier leaves of chestnut and sycamore that had made the summer umbrella of shade and swaddled the valley with green to hold the warmth at night, these, however gorgeous against the sky, had no vitality left, but when the air stirred would simply fall to the ground, instantly becoming so much lifeless litter to be shuffled and trodden.

The time for all these weaving rhythms was, however, miraculously delayed. To Persephone, as one quiet day followed another, it was as if all change—and therefore all fear—was in abeyance, and she herself lost in the gap between one second and the next. She would find herself moving as slowly and smoothly as the cows, lest by a careless turn of the head she should precipitate the clatter of time and the leering of the demons that inhabit it. Sister Veronica, who waited for her at the shippen, unconsciously prolonged the mood. She was there only because she had not been wafted away or brushed by the wing of a bird. Change and fear she had long since forgotten.

The fall, when it came, was not the gentle dissolution that the ripening days had seemed to promise. An Atlantic gale burst upon the coast and, increasing in fury all day, lashed up the valley, jerking every loose fibre of it into the air. Leaves, whirled up, down, and around were mixed in turmoil with sticks, straws, labouring birds, and tatters of cloud, as Persephone's hair was mixed with her eyes and mouth. The trees rocked and cracked, and the grasses were flattened as in the wake of an aeroplane. The troubled hens, whose voices were blown out of earshot, had their feathers back to front, looking like dinghies with too much canvas, and were shoved about by the wind as they scratched in the flying debris. The mooing of the cows who were clustered by the gate came to Persephone in tattered bursts like distress signals from distant tossing ships.

In the afternoon, as she fought her way against the gale towards the gate where the cows clamoured for her, while the wind caught in her nostrils and cut her breath and bent her eyelashes into her eyes, she found herself obsessed with thoughts of Silverstone Tower. Perhaps when in the night the rattling of the windows and doors had disturbed her in deep sleep, some forbidden memory had escaped from her dreams, and had remained to remind her that however hard she struggled to put one foot in front of the other, no step would bring her nearer home, not now or ever. If only in a lull between gusts she might hear the roaring of the tide through the piers of the viaduct. If only instead of Sister Veronica's ghostly kindness she could have a wide crooked smile from Dick! She missed her mother so much that it came to her like hatred, most painfully.

Sister Veronica, trying to secure the shippen door so that it should not be flogged off its hinges, was in trouble with her bonnet. As she bent down the wind blew her veil forward over her face, revealing the back of her close-cropped sandy-white head. When she turned, facing the wind, to rearrange herself, a gust caught in the scuttle of starched linen and jerked her head back by the chin strap. Then the whole thing was dragged askew over one ear, and the veil came forward again and was plastered over her mouth. It was the only time Persephone had ever seen her put out. She looked as if it were a martyrdom. Finally, nearly in tears, she went into the shippen and removed the bonnet, leaving only the face bands, over which she tied the veil under her chin. She was hardly recognisable, pink, agitated, and old.

"I feel so ashamed," she said. "I must look like a witch. Imagine the scene if I flew in at the Common Room window!"

"Sister Clare would smile, and the witch would pop out of you."

"It would be a mercy if I met Sister Clare before Reverend Mother had time to excommunicate me. She would act quickly. She believes passionately in the power of evil, such as witches and the Devil."

"Don't you believe in the Devil, Sister Veronica?"

"I do, because we are told to. You can't pick and choose which bit you will believe and which not. But I always think, if there is a Devil, compared with God he is just puny."

"But not compared with us," said Persephone, in whose imagery the Devil was Sam Cudthrop with a tail.

"No, not compared with us. Reverend Mother's business is to look after us."

Sister Veronica's bonnet hung over the end of Dido's stall. Persephone, wrenching her mind away from Sam, thought of trying it on the beautiful primrose cow. Her dreamy, heavy-lidded eyes, long nose somewhat turned up, and wide pale mouth would look very like Sister Sophia.

❖

From the moment of her arrival Persephone had looked forward, as only the young can, to going down to the sea, the open sapphire-blue sea, as she imagined it, with Atlantic rollers and high cliffs. Hitherto she had only known the sheltered reaches of an estuary, the daily crossing of salt water with fresh. Now she could see the sea at the far end of the valley all the time, like the section of a saucer, a grey half-moon with a hard upper edge, or more recently, in the quiet weather, a diaphanous tender azure melting into a primrose sky. Its attraction was almost like a physical pull. Strictly speaking she was free every day from the end of her work until supper, but half of that time was taken by Sister Clare's daily instruction, which Persephone did not grudge. The remaining forty minutes did not give her time to get to the sea and back, though she frequently walked along the ridge to get a wider view. Her first half-day being on the Patronal Festival, she spent it helping in the kitchen so that little Sister Agnes could be free to help the others in the decoration of the Chapel. The second, a fortnight later, was therefore the more keenly anticipated. When it dawned fine and still, Persephone, skipping out to bring in the cows, saw sea and sky wrapped together in their own breath like sleeping sisters, in a world so quiet that the cries of sea gulls gliding far out over the water came to her ears as poetry without a trace of harshness. She was radiant with expectation and went gladly to Reverend Mother's room in answer to a summons, entering with her newly acquired nunnish decorum, through which her natural alacrity showed charmingly.

Reverend Mother was kind and smiling, but perhaps a little absent-minded. It occurred to Persephone that it would not be easy to ask her anything. Her pleasantness was imperturbable, her attention distant.

"Good morning, Persephone. I believe today is your day off?"

"Yes, Reverend Mother."

"Sister Margaret is going into town today by bus to do some shopping, and it occurred to me that, since you have no one to go out with you, it would be a good idea for you to go with her. It will be company for you and a change, and an opportunity to buy some of the things you need. I have told Sister Margaret that I want you to have proper winter underclothes and stockings. These are necessities and will be provided for you by the community. The winter is very cold here."

"Thank you, Reverend Mother," said Persephone, meeting the generous, gracious smile with her pinkest, most unconvincing expression, her hopes quite dashed and an overwhelming dislike of all underclothes seething in her heart. She was paying back what she owed to Dr. Masters week by week and detested this arbitrary charity.

"Thank you, Reverend Mother," she said again, but it was no better than the first time.

The bus had borne her away inland, and all the afternoon she had stood behind Sister Margaret in chandler's, in corn merchant's, in grocer's, in coal merchant's, in ironmonger's, carrying parcels and waiting while Sister Margaret havered and changed her mind, and talked and talked. The underclothes were bought in a little old-fashioned shop where Sister Margaret seemed well known. Brown woven knickers were first produced to match the habit, but Sister Margaret explained that Persephone was not a member of the community, so these would not be suitable. Saxe blue was chosen instead.

"My skirt is brownish," said Persephone. "Couldn't I have brown?"

"No," said Sister Margaret. "It is not suitable that you should have the same as the sisters."

"Are these made specially for St. Hilarion?" asked Persephone.

"Oh no!" said the shopwoman, smiling. "Lots of schoolgirls wear them."

Persephone turned again to Sister Margaret.

"No," said the latter, turning a dull pink. "It wouldn't be suitable. Reverend Mother might not like it."

Every minute of all the day Persephone was feelingly not at the sea, not hearing the gulls, not treading the sand, not drinking the wind, above all not alone. Sister Margaret pointed out to her that it was just like Reverend Mother to think of everyone in every way, and to provide a treat for Persephone, who would otherwise have to go out quite alone. Not very nice for a young girl. Sister Margaret made it sound very nasty.

"I'm used to being alone," said Persephone sadly.

"Well, that's all different now," Sister Margaret replied breezily.

Persephone gave a snort that was more whimsical than rude, and walked up the drive, in spite of all the parcels she was carrying, a little faster than Sister Margaret could manage, till she reached the

54

front of the house. From there she could see the sea, lying like molten metal under a sky the colour of a gas jet.

"Ah, well," she said. "Thank you, Sister Margaret, for my shopping."

❂

That was a fortnight ago. In between, the great gale had occurred, and the troubles that Persephone had hidden from herself had had their covering ripped off and were exposed and sore.

She achieved her day by the sea soon after the gale and before the turbulence had subsided. As she leapt off the bus and the wind snatched all in one action at her nostrils and at her mackintosh, the first thing she became aware of was the shouting of the sea. Over the roar and hiss of its inrush and the grinding landslide that followed it back, there was a sensation of immensity, an accumulation of seething sounds individually unheard in a world of vigorous din. She wondered whether the sough of the wind was formed in the shell of her own ear or whether it was really carved by the cliffs into a note and whistling in the spirals of its upcurrent. The thick ceiling of cloud, which let no gleam of the sun lighten the sea, was hustled along by the wind just high enough to clear the cliff top and streamed endlessly inland, sagging and tattered but still holding back its rain.

The rim of the cove was piled with the wrack of seaweed torn off the rocks, giving off a new and exhilarating smell. The narrow beach shelved steeply to where the waves, enclosed and tossing, jostled like bulls. The flying spume was animal too. This was not the deep-blue sea of songs. It was fish-coloured, a monster made like the sunless caverns of its lair, turning in a wash of churned rock and seaweed blood. Persephone was alone beside it, except for a wildly barking white French poodle which seemed to expect she would throw sticks into the sea for him, though nothing was going to induce him to retrieve them. Actually, when she threw one from a cautious distance, it was whirled from her hand in the opposite direction, up-shore. She examined the crisp beach of pounded shell, so different from her home mud flats. In the fragments that composed it there were tough limpet shells, but otherwise only the tiniest and most fragile pink and golden treasures had remained intact. But it was no day for delicate observation. As she bent over her sifted handful, thus bringing her ear nearer the shrilling of the moving water edge, an unexpectedly thrusting wave swept over her ankles and wrist, and in its retreat snatched her feet from under her, so that she sat down in the spume.

She was wet and startled. She picked herself up and removed the bracelets and anklets of slithering seaweed ribbon that were wrapped round her, and thereafter she was more careful. The sea seemed to be heaped up and likely to pour down on her. She had no sea lore, tending to expect stupendous tidal waves every time the wall of water curled over in an unbroken front. More intimidating still were the long ridges like the roofs of a row of cottages that formed farther out, advancing into the cove at a speed that, though constant, was indeterminable, so much was every drop alive to the next, and the waves, though separate, bound together by a terrifying muscular cohesion. These ridges following one behind the other gave themselves up at the last minute as willing breakers, so that the rocks received at close quarters the impact of projected tons and the whole view was curtained in spray. It was some time before Persephone could stand her ground.

There was no sign of human life. The cliff-top fields, cracked at the edges and leaning outwards, or having lost a section in an avalanche of clay and stones, looked as uninhabited as the ocean, except for the gulls who had forsaken the latter for the land and were resting on every ledge. There was a well-marked footpath along the headland which she decided to follow. A scramble warmed her up, while every step revealed more of the coast line and the assaulting surf. The dog ceased his senseless barking and went with her, causing innumerable gulls to open their wings and swing off with far-carrying cries. From unseen caves sounds like muffled gunfire reached her, and the earth trembled. She could see how every feature of the coast tended to be top-heavy, hollowed out underneath by the persistent leaping of the sea, whose tongue she had already felt on her wrist, rough like a file.

The path was well in from the cliff edge except in places where there had been a recent landfall. The dog evidently knew his way about. Now and again he seemed to run over the edge, but reappeared in a moment, tongue out and eyes unseeing but happy. When Persephone approached the edge the wind rose vertically like a fury to push her back, and then as suddenly seized her in its arms to throw her over. She lay flat to avoid its jostling while she looked down. She found herself above a rectangular inlet, three sides of which were sheer stone, creviced and worn like masonry, with here and there pillars, or slabs accidentally jacked up on a ledge, that suggested sculpture of a prehistoric cult. The fourth wall had succumbed to ceaseless battering and infiltration, and now lay prone in a barrier of broken rock at the entrance. Round this the swirling umber opened and closed, or met in a clap of spray; or the divided crests came together again, each combing through the foam of the other with a frenzied rattle. Once the obstruction had been leapt, enveloped in heaving shoulders, scarified in roaring foam, or bypassed in rapids, the water raved into the narrow compass of the walls, crisscrossed and boiled and climbed, threw up ropes of spume and foam that slithered sideways down the dark granite, and now and again a breaker, reforming with some reserve of strength, would boom on the lower hollows, or smack full against the rock face, so that the foam came up to Persephone's mouth. All the while, the dry grass at the earth's edge twittered hysterically as it flicked one stalk against another.

Persephone thought of Silverstone Tower and of the fear that once had waited at the bottom of it for her. She shuddered with the memory, which had taken on itself the chill of the wind and her wet clothes. For the first time in her life it made her dizzy to look down. She turned away from the cliff, and found the dog lying beside her, tongue dripping and ribs heaving, his face split with a happy smile. She embraced him with rapid talk to pacify herself. He received it with amiability and willingly allowed her to search his collar for the inscription: WILLI. LORD PENHELLION. COBOLD'S WHIN.

They set off together again along the cliff top. The track now led up and down among monoliths around whose bases the grass was smooth like a bed. These rocks were of massive and suggestive shapes, in groups with a distinct family likeness, and posed as if they lived there. Many gave the impression of sitting majestically, looking out to sea, others of crouching to avoid recognition. They were, moreover, covered with dry pale hair that felt to the hand like the bristles of a soft broom. She was accustomed to the flat lichen of the north, with curled edges like blistered paint. These silent unmoving presences, clustered round secret hammocks of turf, first awed and then discomforted her. She was afraid of the rocks themselves, lest they should turn their stony heads after she had gone by, but she was also afraid of what she might see behind them. She found that her teeth were chattering and that she had to force herself to walk on. When presently the path led between vertical slabs like doorposts, she came to a standstill, unable to pass through. She turned and ran back the way she had come till she could run no more. Out of breath and with a stitch in her side she reached a heather-covered slope facing inland, from which she could see, not the ocean, but the road along which her bus had come and the rough fields beyond it.

Down this road a large car was approaching, noticed by Persephone vacantly but by Willi with hypersensitive ears and nose. Even his eyes were focused and keen. Before it had pulled up he had streaked away, and by the time the occupants had got out he was there, giving a frantic welcome, mixed with abasement, to a lady who, after the first scolding acknowledgement, took no more notice of him. With a man who had accompanied her in the car, she began to walk up the slope on which Persephone was sitting. She walked superbly, hatless and breasting the wind as if defying it to smooth her faultless clothes even closer to her figure. It was hard to guess her age, for she had the poise of maturity and the arrogance of youth, but her companion was a man much younger than she, to judge by his gaucherie. He ran first to one side of her and then to the other, taking her elbow and looking as if he would be glad to carry her rather than risk her placing a foot wrong, though in these antics he alone stumbled. As they advanced along the path leading to the camps of boulders that Persephone had so precipitately left, she observed the lady's face. It was withdrawn and treacherous, like the stones themselves. Sister Veronica, she reflected, had said Reverend Mother believed in witches. This was a face for moonset. As the lady drew level she glanced at Persephone in passing, and perhaps because of the foolish subjugation of her escort, who was pressing her to accept an altogether unnecessary walking stick, perhaps because crouching there on the fringe of the heather Persephone looked like a wild creature, a timid relation of the passionate elements, she directed at her a smile so confederating and vital that Persephone was startled into love, thinking her as beautiful as Helen of Troy. She made sense of legends. With a low-pitched laugh she led her young man towards the privacies of the cliff path. Willi also, as he passed Persephone, permitted himself a slight lowering of the tail and a hardly perceptible wag, as to an acquaintance made outside one's class.

❈

"How did you enjoy your day by the sea, Zephy?" asked little Sister Agnes in the Common Room. Abbreviations were little used at St. Hilarion, because saints' names must be treated with respect, but with a pagan name liberties may be taken.

"It was very stormy."

"Weren't you lonely?" asked Sister Margaret, bent over her darning. "I'm sure there was no one else there. It would give me the shudders. I don't like the sea. I always think it sounds so wet."

Reverend Mother laughed fullheartedly, without ridicule.

"Sister Margaret thinks in terms of batter consistency and cake mixture," she said. "She would like the waves to plop like whipped cream. Was anyone else down there, Persephone?"

"No, Reverend Mother. I was alone, except for Willi. I picked him up on the beach and he came along with me."

Every head was raised from its occupation and every pair of eyes looked at Persephone, like a peacefully grazing herd when a strange dog enters the paddock.

"Who is Willi, Persephone?" asked Reverend Mother with distant modulated calm. The eyes went down to their work again.

"Willi is—a dog," said Persephone, maintaining her gaiety in spite of feeling herself for some reason under criticism. "He was lovely company. But he left me when Lady Penhellion came, and pretended not to know me." All the eyes were raised again, the busy hands held in keen stillness.

"She is very beautiful, isn't she?" Persephone continued, seeing that they were all waiting for her to speak. "She was with a gentleman, but he couldn't have been Lord Penhellion, because Willi didn't know him."

A slight rustle throughout the room, underlining the silence that had preceded it, indicated a resumption of activity. A cotton bobbin rolled noisily across the polished floor.

"There are always a great many visitors at Cobold's Whin," said Reverend Mother in her measured voice, which put a full stop to the conversation. "I think we will have some music," she added, moving to the piano, which Persephone jumped up to open for her. "What shall I play, Persephone?"

" 'Sanctify us by thy goodness,' *please*, Reverend Mother."

❖

Sister Clare was the first to notice a change in Persephone, a tenseness, an avidity for doctrine and ritual where hitherto she had shown only astonished delight. She had been entranced by a pupil who laughed with joy at the holy legends, whose heart accepted the Massacre of the Innocents for the sake of their future status as the first martyrs, the darlings of the Blessed Virgin, who, now that her Son was King, would take them up from playing round her feet and set them in her lap for His childhood's sake. Persephone had returned

59

constantly to the Holy Innocents. If there was a Pope Innocent could there not be a Sister Innocent? Why was nobody ever christened Innocence? Sister Clare now noticed that the emphasis had shifted to sin, that Persephone shook when she spoke of it, and that after every evening lesson she herself was left wondering unhappily if she had said the right thing in the right way. When after painful hesitation she spoke of her anxiety to Reverend Mother she was answered with unusual sharpness. Reverend Mother told her to beware of fantastic and sentimental ideas about an emotional girl of unstable inheritance.

Sister Clare flushed a deep angry pink, but after a moment she replied: "I will remember what you say, Reverend Mother. You think perhaps I am making it seem too easy. But I came to ask you whether you will let Persephone have Latin lessons with Sister Sophia. It was her own suggestion. She is not glib. She says she wants to use the language, not just to make the sounds. She is, after all, still a school-girl. Learning is no trouble to her."

"Sister Sophia has her novices' class. She cannot be asked to give up her time to one girl's fancy. Let Persephone wait. She doesn't understand the meaning of the English yet. But I see I have disappointed you. I am sorry. Why do you feel so much about this?"

"I have the impression that she is fighting for security, that in casting her anchor she wants to be sure the prongs are barbed. She is leaving nothing undone that might help."

"You are always impressionable, Sister Clare. It is not Latin that Persephone needs."

Sister Clare stood looking at the ikon on Reverend Mother's mantelshelf. Then she added: "In any case, Reverend Mother, as soon as All Saints is over I must hand Persephone on to you, because she wishes to be confirmed."

❖

The responsibility of preparing any inmate of St. Hilarion for confirmation, though in the usual order of things it happened rarely, because infidels were infrequent there, naturally rested with the Mother Superior. From the moment that she took over Persephone's instruction, religion ceased to be pure joy. It became not the natural attitude of the soul, but the most difficult attitude possible. Reverend Mother was also of the opinion that for Persephone it must be even harder than for others. The challenge was accepted.

Reverend Mother had to admit to herself that her pupil was serious and diligent, but Sister Clare, now a distant onlooker, and cut off from even receiving confidences from Persephone because that would be like going behind Reverend Mother's back, would have given much to be able to ask Reverend Mother how things were going between them. But even this was a disloyalty that she had to confess with bitter shame to the Warden. It was not in the category of sins that one merely acknowledged as requiring repentance. It was a close distress almost impossible to utter.

Father Cuthbert, the Warden, who celebrated Mass in the Chapel and confessed the sisters, lived nearby with his mother, the old lady in black whom Persephone had seen on her first night, who came in at intervals to make her retreat.

On Sundays and special feast days the Warden, or whatever visiting priest was taking his place, lunched with the community, and afterwards in the Common Room talked with the sisters. Persephone, unused to the mannerisms of the clergy, was unpleasantly surprised by the joviality, not to say levity, of these encounters. She was startled by the excitement and coyness of the sisters' reactions. Many of them, though ageless, were still to her eyes not young enough for this sort of behaviour. The priests seemed to her to enjoy playing on the margin of what, by agreement, should not have been uneasy. Reverend Mother, watching how these gentlemen gravitated breezily towards Persephone, who, with regular meals and hours, was rapidly acquiring the most charming curves, noticed with displeasure how her eyes were raised slowly, as if unwillingly, how a smile, almost a jeer, twitched her mouth. She judged it provocative. Father Cuthbert found it virginal and most disturbing. He took hold of her elbow.

"Well, my dear child, so we want to be confirmed, do we? That's good. That's very good."

❧

Sister Veronica was the one who saw most of Persephone at this time, but though she was humorous and gentle, and quick to see anything wrong with her animals, she was not observant of Persephone. She allowed her presence with the detached affection of someone about to move on, whose trunks are already in the train while she talks to a pleasant stranger on the platform. This relationship Persephone accepted with gratitude. It gave her, in the enclosure of the convent, a refuge from examination. Her character had been moulded in freedom, blissful and beneficent to her, but regarded here as an aberration.

It would no doubt have been better for Persephone if she had been gardening, if everything she did had not reminded her, if only by contrast, of what she did at home. In the mild weather, when the cows had only come in for milking, she had swilled and cleaned out the shippens daily with pleasure, and sprayed them with dairy DDT, thinking how much better this was than the mucky stalls at home, which in the summer, when there was no straw bedding, were not considered worth cleaning out at all. Sister Veronica had told her how in the summer it would be her job to wash the cows over with antifly lotion, so that they fed and lay in peace. Then she remembered how Dick had shared her distress when the poor beasts' faces were a crawling mass of flies which they had given up even trying to dislodge. These refinements seemed to her in keeping with the disciplined cleanliness of St. Hilarion, where Reverend Mother was as impatient of anything in less than spotless order as she was of wasteful old-fashioned toil. The kitchens and dairy were fitted with every practical modern device. When, however, the cold weather set in, Persephone noticed that Reverend Mother was less conscious of Adam's curse than of Eve's. The chicken houses were tolerable, but the cowsheds were mediaeval. Sister Veronica said smilingly, when Persephone dared to express surprise, that every time she asked Reverend Mother if the shippens could not be modernised it coincided with an access of grief that there was so little money for the missions. Reverend Mother just had a blind spot for cows. Sister Veronica seemed not at all disturbed, though it was impossible to maintain her rigorous standard of clean milk except by suffering tortures oneself. It was to Persephone an affront that the floor of the shippen had no runnel, so that not only was the straw continually sodden, but also each cow, as she got to her feet for milking, was found to be coated with muck. There was only cold water, from a pump, so Persephone staggered down each morning and evening under a yoke with two buckets of hot water, and with this, which was all too soon cold, the rumps and udders had to be washed. On the first such morning as, with clean warm water, she meticulously washed the first cow, increasingly conscious of the silky warmth, the soft maternal weight of its flesh, her hands caressing the divisions that reminded her of the quartering of a big creamy rose, she suddenly found that scalding tears were running down her face into the animal's flank, and that Sister Veronica was saying: "Move along, Persephone. It's only muck you are washing off, not mortal sin. Nothing to weep about."

Persephone, as if stung by a gadfly, clattered with her pail into the next stall, thinking now consciously of her mother, with a corrosive anger in which Reverend Mother was bracketed for tolerating this unnecessary filth. Ever after, in spite of her love for the animals, she felt an obsessional dread and resentment for this part of her work, the more so as her hands, in the freezing weather to follow, became so sore with cracks and chilblains that she could hardly dress and undress herself. Sister Veronica's prayer-stilled hands were in equally bad condition, but she seemed not to notice. She dressed the worst sores and she treated Persephone's too, but only as she would have treated the cows' feet or ears. It was her duty to see to it. No other aspect concerned her.

Another sister who saw much of Persephone was Sister Sophia. The library, her domain, was not grandiose. It was a large room filled with books on carpenter's shelves, but it received atmosphere and dignity from the presence of Sister Sophia, who used it for her study. She sat at her writing table bending her distant, questing face over a pile of reference books, often in Latin or Greek. She told Persephone that she was doing research into the history of the Armenian Christians during the Crusades. Sister Margaret had once remarked, with resentful laughter, that Sister Sophia's Christianity was all Greek to her. Certainly it was of a different quality. Persephone found in its aura a relief from the pressure of the convent. Sister Sophia's discipline was internal, not imposed from without; and Persephone soon sensed, if only from a tone of voice in discussing a picture, that she had simply no sense of heresy.

As the wet dark afternoons set in, she nearly always came to the library in her free time between Vespers and supper, less often to read than to look at books of reproductions which Sister Sophia chose for her. Like the illiterates of the Middle Ages, she absorbed an attitude of mind from what was shown her. In these pictures she lost herself completely, but refound, to her surprise, Sister Veronica's face, Sister Sophia's immensely long hands and feet and the very folding of the pleats over her gaunt limbs. Reverend Mother she found heading processions, receiving saints.

In reply to Reverend Mother's question as to whether she found Persephone restless or unstable, Sister Sophia answered with a vague smile that she always seemed perfectly happy.

✤

Christmas at Silverstone Tower had never meant more than a joint of pork and a very heavy Christmas pudding. Sometimes Bess contrived a little present secretly out of the money given her for house-keeping. Last year, Dick had given Persephone a hyacinth bulb, fat and glazed with purple, a great treasure. The sisters at St. Hilarion were literally penniless, obliged to ask the Mother Superior for permission to write to their families, and provided by her with blank cards on which they could inscribe suitable religious greetings or paint angels and cribs. Zephy was better off, having her small wages to dispose of. She had been commanded by Reverend Mother, as part of her confirmation exercises, to write to Bess, and this she felt she would die if she tried to do. She wanted to send a present to Dr. Masters and another to her kind housekeeper, for which reason she welcomed, this time, an outing with Sister Margaret. She had a plan to avoid writing to her mother. She would buy a card of the kind Bess liked, a puddingy one with robins. She had a horror of anything that would look like spiritual "side."

The occupations in the Common Room had changed. Now, in the evening, all were making toys for sick children. Sister Clare made cloth donkeys and woolly lambs. Persephone, who had had few toys, was entranced. Her hands being too sore and rough for fine sewing, she stuffed the animals for Sister Clare. Most of the sisters dressed baby dolls, with touching pleasure. It was the nearest they ever got to maternity. The older ones seemed to have dwindled back to a sterile childhood, treating the dolls as puppet babies; but Sister Agnes, the youngest, had tears in her eyes, thinking of the child who would play with the doll she had made—a little girl sitting up in a cot.

When the toys were finished, inspected by Reverend Mother, counted and sent off, the remaining evenings were devoted to the cards. Zephy did one for Dick. She might have known that Reverend Mother would ask if the letter to Bess was written. She had not thought it would have to be shown. When Reverend Mother saw the card, she threw it straight into the fire with an exclamation of disgust. No such card should go out from St. Hilarion. If her mother did not know that Christmas meant more than pudding, then Persephone could tell her. She was sent away to write a proper letter. Confronted with the absolutely impossible she did what she could, paying for it with headache and sickness.

Dear Mums,

 I have been a long time in writing to you. I am sorry if you were worried. The note I left you was all lies. I should not have said it. I am quite well. I am working in a convent. They are all very

kind to me. I think I should like to be a nun. There are beautiful
Jersey cows here.

> *Wishing you a happy Christmas,*
> *From*
> *Persie*

This letter was allowed to go. Perhaps Reverend Mother was too busy to insist on a better one. Perhaps she had the delicacy to leave it unread.

The celebration of Christmas was pure delight. Persephone, not being one of the community, was excluded from the arrangement of the Crib and the decoration of the altars, but that only made her like the solitary child for whom a Christmas tree is lighted. She enjoyed the carols, singing with boyish clarity, which Reverend Mother, who rehearsed the singing, could not but appreciate as one asset at least if Persephone should eventually stay with them. After the Christmas joy came the Christmas pleasure—a turkey feast where all could chatter, Father Cuthbert carving; and if there were no paper hats, there were painted cardboard angels all down the centre of the table among the Christmas roses.

❧

Persephone was baptised, made her first confession, and was confirmed on the Eve of Epiphany, when the Bishop stayed overnight at the convent. Confession was what she had looked forward to with most hope of consolation. Her insufferable resentment towards her mother she knew was a sin, because it corroded and distressed her, although she felt compelled to give it full rein. Her incipient and suppressed hatred of Reverend Mother she knew would be considered a far worse sin, and she did her best to stamp it out although it had an element of pleasure. To confess the first and ask for help would be a luxury; to confess the latter, horrific. Little did she guess that the Bishop heard it in confession more than any other sin. The sisters, determined to love their sufferings, too often found that the natural dislike had been driven out only to settle on the one who allotted to each her special hardship. Hearing that his little penitent "sometimes didn't feel obedient," he passed it over with almost indulgent exhortation. She was hardly more explicit, stammering in her outpouring, about poor Bess. She was bidden to repent of her anger, to remember that God loved sinners however hardened, and to pray that her mother might repent of her bad life. It might be your prayers, she was told, that would change your mother's heart.

She left the confessional stupefied by the anticlimax. It was not the sinfulness of her mother's conduct that poisoned her, but disgust. Of Bess's two sins, one had given her life and the other had made it not worth having. Yet by the book, one was as bad as the other. But Bess was not bad. She was gentle, she was long-suffering, she vaunted not herself. Since she had been in the convent, Persephone knew better how little Bess vaunted herself. She repudiated all idea of changing Bess's heart, that loving easygoing heart that had been everything she needed. She just wanted something not to have happened that had happened, and it was because she realised that she was up against the impossible that her limbs trembled and sometimes she hardly heard what was said to her.

Then there were the hints, never pressed home, because the impurity of the idea was such that once deeply implanted it might prove stronger than any prayer, that she was in need of special grace in order not to grow like her mother. Once confirmed, she would be in the courtyard of that fortress from which she might, perhaps, defeat her special relentless devil. In fact, innocent as she was, she was considered tainted. Whom should she hate most for that, Mother or Reverend Mother? Why would they not simply let her worship? Because you can't do it if you are angry or disgusted. But they were more disgusted still than she was, with turned-up spiritual noses. And yet, shocked as they were, there was so much that had never been told. All that Reverend Mother or anyone else at St. Hilarion knew was that Bess was unmarried, and that Zephy had run away from what Dr. Masters had described as an unsuitable home. All that her confessor heard from her own lips (though he was primed privately by Reverend Mother) was that she hated her mother because of something she had done. Of Sam, in relation to either her mother or herself, it was inconceivable ever to speak.

Her brain sifted and tussled, resisted and contrasted and went back on its tracks till she was exhausted. But it is not to be supposed that the results of all this thinking were at all clear to her consciousness. That was just an unhappy mess. There was only one way open to her—to confess again to the Warden with the utmost sincerity that she had not felt obedient to the Bishop. It was a formula that, as time went on, was to be used despairingly to express her nameless trouble.

Nevertheless, when with a white face and stammering voice she had followed the Bishop through her confirmation, the kiss she received from Reverend Mother was very comforting to her.

66

"God bless you, my dear little Josephine." Josephine was the name chosen for her instead of her pagan one. Reverend Mother pronounced it as if she had just buried someone. But it was Sister Clare, unable any longer to see such an unhappy face without asking what was wrong, who received on her shoulder the weariness of tears, and was appealed to for a ruling as to whether she was lost in advance because of her mother's sin.

"What nonsense, Zephy darling," she said, unconsciously digging up the child that Reverend Mother had buried. "Why, if it comes to that, even Reverend Mother is a daughter of Eve."

"Ah! Tell that to her!" said Zephy, breaking away. Which was just one more thing to be confessed: this time—though Zephy never guessed it—by both of them.

❖

A few days later Bess's dreaded reply arrived. It was worse than Zephy could have imagined. Beginning "My own darling little baby girl, I have always been so proud of you, and now I can't forgive myself. I never believed what you had written O what must you have thought," and so on through pages of cringing tear-stained abasement that Zephy found only repulsive. Bess's lack of dignity was worse than her lack of scruple. It was more than she could bear.

Confirmation, Confession, and Communion had all been added to her armoury, but Zephy found no peace. She decided that this must be because she was not throwing herself into it far enough. Perhaps for her there would be no peace except in total abnegation. She must cease to have a self. She therefore decided to ask Reverend Mother if she might be received as a postulant.

Outside, a heavy sea mist covered all the inland fields. It lay dead and immovable in the valley bottom, only rolling uneasily in an upper drift of air marking the valley's course. The cold was gnawing and hostile. Zephy had felt it like a personal persecutor all day. She had changed her clothes in her north-facing bedroom, where the window was always open by order. It seemed to have added the chill of its own plaster to the cold of the mist, and in contrast with its wooden floor the earth that was giving off so much clammy vapour was, in imagination, heated by subterranean fire. The Mother Superior's room was warm. She sat in an armchair by the fire and laid by, as Persephone came in, the book she had been reading. Above the architectural layers of her habit that with powerful anonymity represented the Church, she carried a proud head. Her blue eyes, concentrated by the enclosing wimple and levelled as if to conform to the line laid down by the linen that bound her brow, beat upon the outsider who stood there trembling with a plea to be received. "Suffer the little children to come unto Me" was not the text that came into Reverend Mother's mind. Her experience when in the world had been bitter, and had given her cause to believe that the beauty of the body was the cause of more sin, more injustice, and more lamentable failure to attain to God than even riches. It was not for her to imagine Persephone's beauty in terms of Iris, who wore the rainbow scarf that was herself. As she looked at the young neck that rose from a faultless spinal column and lost itself in ferny curls, at the throat sleeking upward to an under-chin like an eider feather and downward to a hollow that would hold dew, where now her heart seemed to be pulsing; as she appraised against her will and almost with revulsion the soft and vital body whose curves were enhanced by a waist too small to be functional—it could hardly contain the organs one is known to have—Reverend Mother's face hardened against her will and she touched the cross on her breast with firm white fingers as she hesitated. Then she addressed Persephone with the warmth and interest that she could produce at will.

"You know it is a very hard undertaking, my little Josephine, and not everybody can hold the course to the end."

Zephy's frozen fingers were burning as if her hands were held in the fire. She nodded.

"Yes, Reverend Mother."

"We do not encourage anybody to try unless we are satisfied that she sincerely intends to go through with it. You are young, and your background is not one to give you stability. But it cannot have been by accident that you came here. You were certainly sent to us. We all love you, and we will pray that God, who has touched your heart, will grant you a true vocation. I will ask you to pray about it for another week, and I will do the same. Then if you still hold to your purpose come back to me, and I will tell you whether I have decided to admit you."

Persephone had never yet left Reverend Mother's room without feeling a little unhappier than when she entered it. But at least she had not been refused.

When she had gone, Reverend Mother rang for Sister Clare. She had questions of organisation to discuss with her and the general life of the convent. These topics she lingered over with less than her usual decision, so that Sister Clare sensed that there was something more to come.

"I think that is all," said Reverend Mother, and let Sister Clare get as far as the door before she added: "I am troubled, Sister Clare. Our elfin Josephine has asked if she may be received as a postulant. All my instincts tell me that she has no vocation. But that is not in my hands. I know without asking that you would be in favour of receiving her."

Sister Clare stood silent for a moment before saying: "She will make a sweet little nun. I am sure of it."

"A sweet little nun!" repeated Reverend Mother slowly, as if letting the words drop into astonished ears. "Sister Clare, I did not know you had it in you to be so vulgar."

Sister Clare crimsoned and stood for a moment almost like a fury. "O clement, O loving, O sweet," she quoted almost under her breath.

It was against the rule for any sister accused by authority to defend or excuse herself. She had made herself guilty both of that and of attempting to correct the Mother Superior. They faced each other with rising heat for a moment, but the words that had been used were potent. They hung in the air and distilled in Reverend Mother's consciousness. She stopped drumming on the book with her fingers, and then looked up and smiled at her friend.

"I apologise to you, Sister Clare," she said.

A week later it was announced, after the Rule for the Day had been read, that the recently confirmed Josephine had been received as a postulant. The assembled sisters were bidden to pray for her to the Mother of Mercy and to St. Joseph, guardian of virgins. A Salve Regina and the Litany of St. Joseph were said in special intention for her. Persephone was present at the reading of the rule for the first time, sick with wonder that she had been received and also with fright such as one feels before an operation that is to put one right. *As sick to a Physician,* she repeated over and over to herself. As they came out of the Chapel the Mother Superior and each sister kissed her on both cheeks.

❖

Now that she had accepted the way of life shown to her, the way of love, that is to say, and had been put on her probation, she found that with the very act of acceptance the way of life had changed. The love seemed to have dropped out of it. Reverend Mother was no longer smooth and gracious with her. She had become critical, adamant, distant. Persephone was disorientated by the change and at a loss what to think. There were no other postulants at the time, so she had no opportunity of judging how much of the severity was on the curriculum and how much was directed at her personally. The fear of reproof made her nervous, and nervousness made her commit mistakes and forget what she should have remembered. Mistakes of this kind —running to do what she was told when she should have glided silently, dropping plates when she was in mortal agitation, the blacking out of the answers to questions that she knew perfectly—were treated as a lack of attention to God's will. She had also to learn, which was even harder, to accept reproof for what she had not done without defending herself. This seemed to her to happen unfairly often, as if Reverend Mother chose to presume that every time a dirty pair of gum boots was left in the cloakroom, or gate left open, or chair scraped during grace, or book dropped during Mass, it must have been done by her.

She was given a veil and a plain brown dress, in which she lost her individuality without gaining a feeling of unity with the sisters. She felt less one of the family than she had done before. Then she had been in a permanent, known position. Now she was on trial. In this altered atmosphere she came to notice the predicament of Sister Faith, who seemed unhappier than herself. She was from a slightly lower social class than the other sisters. But that was not the trouble. She just lacked something. It was too easy to pass her over. She herself never felt she was one of them. She did the laundry and was vastly useful. She was of mediocre intelligence, of no self-confidence, and she squirmed at the sight of the Mother Superior. As a result she almost automatically evoked a piece of wounding irony. She had been used to the loose uncritical affection of a large family of brothers and sisters. They were her only topic of conversation, already ten years out of date, which was why the sisters lost interest. They were kind and civil to her. Perhaps they thought she had found some comfortable corner in the body of the Church Universal, but she had not the brain to hold abstractions like that. She looked forward to Heaven, and in her loneliness had more dignity than anyone gave her credit for. Even Sister Clare felt an embarrassment with her, chiefly due to her clear perception of Reverend Mother's brutality—for so she sometimes judged it—but also to the irritation caused by a person who cannot be helped, who has suffered a disillusion and is wrongly placed. She always smiled at Sister Faith, but had slipped into the habit of making only cheerful remarks that needed no answer. In this way silence closed gradually and solidly round poor Sister Faith, who had believed in love on earth. She had a moon face of real gentleness that was lost in disappointment.

In contrast, much envied by Sister Faith, whom she carelessly befriended, Sister Bridget took everything as it came. She was scatter-brained, and could act when scolded with the most nunnish humility. No face more easily assumed the proper expressions or more quickly took them off again with an Irish joke. She appeared, if not very fitted for a religious life, particularly fitted for that of a community of women. She had found a good billet.

As for Persephone, in the old days when she was running wild over her own country she had had a serviceable enough skin against taunts or criticism and could hold her own in a high-spirited fashion. Now she was the shorn lamb, and Reverend Mother did not consider it one of her prerogatives to temper the wind. Rather the reverse.

❖

That February was the coldest for many years. The drifting Cornish mist was the best of the weather's vagaries. On such mornings, when Zephy went out at five-thirty to begin milking, she felt like a phantom in limbo as, with her two buckets that precluded the use of a lantern, she picked her way step by step through the curling earth-hugging cloud. Somewhere in it sometimes she heard a thrush try his first brief cadence. It seemed to express an anguish of desire. Driving sleet on a howling north wind was worse, but the mere battling against it was a distraction; its roughness could make one laugh and be glad to arrive at a door. Coldest of all were the iron days without mist when a sullen chill glided in from the sea and penetrated to the bone beneath numb and suffering flesh. The hours before daylight did not deserve the name of dawn. They lay in the dark like sleepers who have been cold all night and cling to the last minute of inertia.

Persephone went downhill carefully, straining her eyes in the neutral off-dark in an effort to choose her foothold between ice, rut, and stone, all equally treacherous. She did in fact slip, and spilled half of her precious hot water. In the shippen she lit the lantern, and remembering that Sister Veronica had been at Lauds and Mattins in the Chapel at midnight, it being the beginning of Lent, she left the bucket with hot water for her and began work with cold. It drew a gasp from her when she first plunged her hands into it. Sister Veronica came in a moment later. They did not speak, because morning milking took place within the Greater Silence, which lasted from

Compline until after Mass. Persephone looked up and saw Sister Veronica's face grey with cold, her lips moving in silent intercession. She would have supposed she wanted help but that her eyes were not raised. They settled down to work, and there was no sound but the shifting of animals in the straw, the rattle of halter loops, the splash of buckets, or the coughed protest of a cow as Persephone's icy water was applied to its flesh. She herself was nearly weeping with cold and pain in her hands, but determined no sound should escape her. The windows had changed from indigo slits to pewter; the lantern no longer heaped up mammoth shadows behind the cows, but merely coloured the colourless. Persephone was finishing milking her fourth cow when she noticed that Sister Veronica was only moving towards her second. She laboured with her pail, setting it down with a clang, and she whose movements were normally so weightless fell, rather than sat, on the milking stool. The cow turned her head, reaching an inquisitive muzzle towards her, and at the familiar touch of the hand on her teats lowed softly and was still. No music of milk in the pail followed, but instead a sound uttered by Sister Veronica that brought Persephone, big-eyed, to the stall. Sister Veronica was sitting slumped over her knees, her arms, with hands as white as candles, hanging inert before her. An inhuman noise came with her breathing, and before Persephone could catch her she had toppled over and lay in the straw. Persephone tried to sit her up, but the cow, startled by the fall, had backed and set her forefoot on the veil, close beside the face which was no longer the one Persephone knew. She had first to coax the incalculable beast away, to prevent her pushing with her stupid instinctive head the unwanted bundle that lay in her stall. Then she had to drag Sister Veronica away, twisting in the cramped space and impeded by the overturned pail and stool. When at last she had succeeded in propping her against a bundle of straw in a safe corner, she saw with wild distress that the face had become again the one she loved, but beyond all recall, and round its nobility the veil hung torn and awry. The habit too was fouled and stuck with clots of straw. Oh, poor Sister Veronica! Nobody must ever see her like that! Automatically she began cleaning the habit, devotedly, with the rough means at her disposal, arranging the folds, hiding the tear in the veil, till suddenly, with the bonneted head in her hands, she was seized with panic. Sister Veronica was dead. Everything she was doing was wrong. Reverend Mother would be as angry as God. She should have gone for help. Perhaps Sister Veronica need not have died. They would all have gone into Chapel, and she was too late to get help now.

She ran towards the house. The stony uphill path seemed endless, like Hell; every moment she expected to hear the Chapel bell that would make her message impossible to deliver. She could no longer remember or calculate at all how long she had been, or even if she had heard the Angelus.

She did not wait to change her boots or to tidy and compose herself. Startled sisters saw her plunge unannounced, with hardly a knock, into Reverend Mother's room, but the Greater Silence was still in force and nobody questioned her. Reverend Mother was kneeling at her private devotions. She ignored the gasping interruption and calmly pursued her Collect to the end. Then she rose to her feet and considered the figure backed against her door with palms outspread and flattened to it, whose breath was drawn so sharply it was almost like laughter.

"Josephine!" said Reverend Mother, who alone consistently used this name. "Control yourself. I do not know what has happened, but that is no way to break in. You look more like a gipsy than a postulant. Come away from the door. Stand here in front of me. Now tell me what is the matter. Has Sister Veronica sent you to me?"

Persephone stood with her knees knocking together and her jaws working, but no words came.

"If you cannot speak, it is no use standing there. You had better go, and come back after Mass when you are in control of yourself."

But Persephone could not go either. She brought out in a chattering whisper: "Sister Veronica is dead."

Reverend Mother straightened herself and became very still.

"Speak up, Josephine. Say what you have to say properly."

"Sister Veronica is dead, Reverend Mother," came out this time too loud, almost a shout, and everything else after it pell-mell. "She was milking. She made a noise and fell over. Theodosia nearly trod on her face. Her veil is all torn. The milk pail was knocked over. The milking isn't finished. I—I—I left the gate open, I thought—I ran—" The recital ended in sobbing.

Reverend Mother moved to the table and rang the bell. To the sister who answered it she said: "Sister Pauline, send for Sister Mildred and tell her to take three others and go at once to the shippen, where Sister Veronica has been taken ill. It may already be too late. Then telephone to the doctor. Tell Sister Clare to read Prime for me

73

if necessary, and ask Father Cuthbert to come straight in to me. In that order, please."

"Yes, Reverend Mother," said Sister Pauline, and withdrew as quietly as she had come.

Reverend Mother put her hand on Persephone's shoulder. "Are you sure she is dead, and has not merely fainted?"

Persephone nodded. She had seen pigs, calves, lambs, horses that were dead. Dead is different. At the thought of Sister Veronica's face she wept again.

"Come, my child. Have we taught you nothing? That is not the way to behave when a sister dies. Have you forgotten the Resurrection and the Life, and the Company of Saints?"

"I didn't know what to do."

"Did you think of saying a prayer for her?"

"No." Persephone remembered now that her ears had heard the Angelus while she was washing the dung from Sister Veronica's habit, and that she had not even stopped to say "Holy Mary, Mother of God, pray for us sinners now, and at the hour of our death. Amen."

"Then we will pray for her now, together. Come here with me."

They knelt side by side in front of the crucifix, and Reverend Mother began the Pater Noster, of which the familiarity, the everyday quality, was at first impossible and then consoling. Then followed the Ave Maria, of which Persephone managed to say her part steadily. Reverend Mother, as if she had, on this day, no other thing to see to, commanded Persephone to say every sentence clearly after her and to think of its meaning.

"I recommend thee, dear Sister, to the almighty God, and commit thee to his care whose creature thou art; that when thou shalt have paid the debt of all mankind by death thou mayest return to thy Maker who formed thee of the slime of the earth. When thy soul therefore shall depart from thy body let the resplendent multitude of angels meet thee; let the court of apostles come unto thee; let the triumphant army of martyrs conduct thee. . . . May Christ who was vouchsafed to die for thee deliver thee from death. May Christ the Son of God place thee in the ever-pleasant garden of his Paradise, and may He, the true Shepherd, number thee amongst his sheep. Mayest thou see thy Redeemer face to face, and standing always in his presence behold with happy eyes the most clear truth. Mayest thou be placed amongst the company of the blessed and enjoy the sweetness of the contemplation of thy God for ever. Amen."

74

While they were going through this long prayer, the passing bell began to toll. Reverend Mother continued to the end.

"Now go and make yourself ready for Mass," she said, in dismissal. "And remember in future that what we teach you has real meaning for things when they really happen."

❧

Some people's faces when in distress seem to be all mouth. It is the mouth that is enlarged, distorted, out of control, and whimpering, or perhaps pressed shut in a grim rictus across the face. Persephone seemed to be all eyes and forehead, wet with tears and dewed with sweat. Her eyes seemed larger, rounding out the lids lowered over them in a kind of lonely reserve, her forehead more prominent because the damp curls had gone back from it like seaweed on an ebb tide. Sister Clare, during the silent Lenten breakfast, looked down the table at this mask for a Pietà, remembering the evening of her arrival barely six months earlier. How much she had grown in suffering since then, and how well she bore it! It was professional for sisters to sit with lowered eyelids during a silent meal. Except in the case of the finest spirits it was apt, alas, to give them an appearance of complacently concentrating on their food. This morning all must be presumed to be sorrowing, but Sister Clare had come to see Persephone's face with fear. She was anxious for an opportunity to show her sympathy and love. This did not come until the end of the day, after the evening Angelus, for Sister Veronica's death had naturally given her a great deal to see to, and Persephone also was working overtime, though helped by Sister Monica. By evening she was without any emotion but fatigue. When questioned, she told Sister Clare all that had happened, monotonously and gently, remembering that Sister Veronica was Sister Clare's old and dear friend; but because of her own great need she told her too what most haunted her.

"My poor little Zephy! Poor darling, try never to think of that again. It's only natural that the body should feel a dreadful spasm when the spirit leaves it. But it was *only* the body that felt it, and Sister Veronica never thought of the body at all—certainly not then. Say your private alleluias in Compline for her and afterwards sleep well. I shall be watching tonight. I shall join you to all my prayers."

Persephone was comforted. Sister Veronica's body lay before the altar, the sisters taking it in turns to pray beside it day and night, while the many services took place around it as if Sister Veronica were still one of the community. Persephone was not, of course, allotted an official turn to keep watch, and her day was now very full. Her classes with Reverend Mother entailed "study," which she was beginning to find, for the first time in her life, elusive to memorise. There seemed no way of fixing the answers so that they were available when Reverend Mother asked for them. On the night before Sister Veronica was buried, she rose at midnight for the Vigil of the Dead at Lauds, in order to pay her last respects. It was the only time she could find.

The door creaked as Persephone entered. The Chapel was dark, lit only by the four tall candles round the open coffin, a candle at the entrance, and another at each of the two desks. Two sisters, anonymous in their veils and posture, were kneeling near the coffin. The light fell on their shoulders and on Reverend Mother's face. A multitude of shadows like moving presences consorted with the timbers supporting the roof, bulky and simple by the wall, intricate and winged on the ceiling. An eerie luminosity slowly penetrated the gloom enclosed by the stone walls. It was some minutes before she could distinguish the outline of the big crucifix above the altar, where there were neither candles nor ornaments.

Sister Agnes' voice was taking the responses. Other sisters were dimly there, their wimples showing through the dark like the blaze on horses in a field at night. Persephone had not known so many left their beds at midnight. Along the brick floor the draught flowed over her ankles like cold water. The old timbers creaked and almost seemed to lurch in the wind, giving out loud cracks. The shadows swirled, and sometimes the candle flames were flattened down as if they must go out. After each such eclipse they leapt up again valiant as ever.

The murmuring voices of Reverend Mother and Sister Agnes came and went like the candlelight. Only occasionally, when the words were very familiar, could she pick them out, or when Reverend Mother turned her head in turning a page.

"As long as I live I will praise thee in this manner and lift up my hands in thy name . . ." and again, much later, "O Lord, I am oppressed. Undertake for me."

Persephone knew—had she not held it in her hands?—the face that lay in the coffin, around which this vigil was kept. The obscure congregation of nuns made neither sound nor movement, but their prayer could be felt. The reading of Psalms went on like thoughts in a sleepless night that keep time with one's heartbeats. There would still be many hours of dark before the Angelus. In the Chapel was an induced, a cherished endlessness, in which Reverend Mother, raising her voice to the least that all could hear began: "O praise God in his holiness. Praise him in the firmament of his power."

"Praise him in his noble acts. Praise him according to his excellent greatness" came in a long breath from all the sisters. From this time on the ritual was as familiar as rapturous, leading to the inspired, because inevitable, *"Requiem aeternam dona eis Domine."*

Lauds being over, the sisters by the coffin gave up their places to others, and the rest, except for Reverend Mother, who remained in her stall, slipped quietly away. Persephone returned, freezing, to her cold bed, where she lay awake, as she thought, and in spirit still in the Chapel, till the alarum clock shattered the illusion. She had barely had time to get warm again.

❖

A farm girl from the neighbouring village was hired to give temporary help to Persephone until a proper bailiff could be found to take Sister Veronica's place. Her name was Moira, a hearty girl with a flat nose and so sanguine a complexion that the high colour could not be contained in her cheeks but spread permanently over her temples. She had great physical strength and elemental ease of mind, if mind it could be called. She was buxom, with buttocks like a horse and a wide toothy grin. She was a force. She attacked Persephone's attitude of mind as amiably as a cow might munch a hedge. She found the shippens beneath consideration and did not hesitate to say so, grumbling continually in a way that had more of contempt in that it had nothing of querulousness. While she was doing with no apparent personal discomfort the work that was so hard for Persephone and Sister Veronica, swinging the pails or wielding the hay truss on the fork without an alteration in breathing or facial expression, she aired her opinions. Because Zephy—"Saintly," she called her—was supposed to keep silence, Moira had it all her own way and kept the conversation moving singlehanded.

"What a place!" she said. "I wonder you stay here, I really do. I wouldn't. I've promised for a month just to help them out, and I'll stick to it. But don't you be such a fool as to promise for longer. Do you hear, Saintly? They'd never get anybody round here to take it on. Why, there's no convenience at all. It's just making work. People who put up with dirty linhays should put up with dirty milk. Ah, there's a lump dropped in. Just what I was saying. I don't wonder your old girl

77

died, I don't really. I see in the paper she was seventy. Your Reverend Mother, as you call her, must be nuts. So must the old girl have been, come to that. She was a trained vet once. Did you know that, Saintly? Dad says she was a shrewd one too. Must say there's nothing wrong with her cows, except their outlandish names. And some of them are getting too old. I'd kill off old Say-no-beer, she'll never do no good again. Hey! Saintly! What's the matter with you? Can't you answer? Talking keeps the circulation going."

"I'm not really supposed to talk until after Mass, unless it's necessary."

"Aw, you're nuts too. You're all nuts, if you ask me. It is necessary to keep the circulation going. Look at your hands! I suppose you'd let your fingers drop off and never say Oh. I don't suppose you have got anything proper inside you either, have you? Hey, Saintly! I said, what have you had for breakfast?"

"We don't have anything until after Mass," said Zephy, breaking the rule again, but after all, St. Francis had said: "God is also courtesy."

"Good life! It makes no sense. Bloody silly, I call it. I'll bring you a tot of rum tomorrow to drink with some milk."

"Oh no! Please don't!" Zephy was pleading like a threatened child.

"All right, all right! Good life!" said Moira again, with large unruffled amiability. "I wish everybody had a bit of sense. Too much to hope, I suppose. Come on, now we've got to carry the milk in. A tractor would be nice, now, wouldn't it? Let alone the boy driving it. What do you think, Saintly? But no. You've got to yoke yourself like a donkey and carry the stuff there."

"St. Joseph's little donkey," said Zephy suddenly, laughing happily.

"What's that? Don't know what you're talking about. But laughter's free for all."

At first, coming in immediate contrast with the memory of Sister Veronica, Zephy found every syllable that Moira said shocking and offensive. Particularly she resented with passion any belittling reference to Sister Veronica, whose frail head she still held in her hands unless she consciously put the image from her. Nevertheless Moira's vulgarity was so warm and large, her vitality so contagious, that no one but a prig could have resisted her preposterous good nature for long. Laughter, as she said, was free for all. There was no malice in hers, and very soon Zephy discovered that she could laugh at Moira as

78

one can laugh at the antics of a young dog, without disturbing their relationship.

Moira's conversation was as inexhaustible as her vitality. If Zephy thought they had finished with the tragic incident of Sister Veronica's death, she was proved wrong. Next morning Moira was still exploiting it.

"I can't get over thinking of that poor old girl flopping down here like that, just where I'm milking. And it had to be Saintly that found her! A poor little lost kitten sure to be more cut up than anyone else. Now if it had been me, it would have been different. I'm fond of my old grannie, see, and she comes over like that often, so I know what to do."

"What would you have done?" (The Greater Silence must lapse. You can't do it unless the other person does too.)

"Well, to start with, I bet you propped her up."

"Yes, I did."

"Well, you shouldn't have done. You should have laid her down. And then you should have taken her teeth out so she couldn't swallow them. Poor old thing. She should have had someone looking after her, a nice cup of strong tea, warm in bed, and then get up later and poddle round giving an eye to things if she felt like it. Now take our grannie; it's all you can do to stop her working—old folk get like that—but Mum's real good to her. She'd never let her do a job like this. Your Reverend Nuts must have a heart of iron."

Persephone had been deeply impressed by Reverend Mother's bearing at the time of Sister Veronica's death. It had seemed to her noble in its impassivity, its imperturbable carrying on with the next ordered step, its leisure in rigid routine, so that even in such an emergency she had time to spare for teaching the humblest postulant. Persephone had never so truly admired her. Nevertheless alongside her awed and grateful thoughts a completely different incorrigible feeling seethed in her, in which Reverend Mother was hated as a person who let her oldest friend die and thought if she said prayers for her it was all right. This was monstrous, and Persephone repudiated it, but it was always there, and Moira voiced it, giving to it the dynamism of her own personality.

❖

During Lent people from outside came in to make their retreat. Twelve were expected on the Friday following Sister Veronica's death. They slept in a separate wing, had a separate table in the refectory—at which Zephy was appointed to wait—and had their own director, who happened on this occasion to be a striking-looking man in his early forties called Father Anselm. He confessed the retreatants, guided their meditations, and had a room set apart where he could talk with any of them who felt they had special difficulties. With this exception, the retreatants were supposed to keep absolute silence for four days. They were, however, received in the Common Room on the night of their arrival, and after that they sat in the library or in their own rooms. Their arrival caused a considerable stir in the convent. To begin with, the domestic work was doubled. For once the sisters' steps betrayed an agitation and their voices, in handing on instructions of work to be done, sometimes lapsed into a worldly sharpness. A certain amount of curiosity also was unavoidable in a place where a new face was an event. By suppertime Zephy noticed even a hint of resentment. When she went into the kitchen to ask how she was to set the table she heard Sister Margaret say, replying to something Sister Monica had said from the back door, "Again! It's disgusting."

Each sister when passing another in the corridor had something to say under her breath. Sister Mildred had a positively impish grin as she said to Sister Clare, "Now for it!"

Zephy was too nervous under the responsibility of waiting to think of anything else, or to connect these various phenomena with anything but household pressure.

Towards the table where she was to wait twelve strange women were filing in. There was nothing about them that marked them out from the rest of the world. The only thing they had in common was the black veil of chiffon or voile that they now wore loosely over their heads, and they had adopted a churchgoing gait, very different from the swiftly moving grace of the sisters. As Zephy, with lowered eyes, stood waiting for them to take their places, sensing rather than seeing the different types that went past, her eye was suddenly caught by a pair of wonderful shoes, shoes unlike any she had ever seen, only proper to the feet that wore them and the legs above them. Startled by such smooth beauties, whose slimness of ankle was more suggestive of dimple than of bone, whose gait was anything but churchgoing, a carriage that allowed every happy muscle contributing to it to be sensed, her eyes escaped her control and reverted to stare. A dress that made black seem more voluptuous than colour, a veil of real black lace that showed off to perfection the pearls and the sullen crimson mouth—she had no difficulty in recognising that face.

Perhaps responding unconsciously to her stare, Lady Penhellion's wandering eyes came suddenly to rest on hers, and just as Reverend Mother was sweeping in to her place, Persephone received from her Ladyship an outrageous wink. She blushed slowly and thoroughly, and a rapid flick of Reverend Mother's eyelid as she passed them left no doubt that she had seen the flush if not the cause.

The waiting went off without any serious blunder on her part. The salt, however, had been forgotten, and it required a long pantomime from Lady Penhellion's pliant red-tipped hands to show Zephy what was missing. She nearly ran to get it, but remembered in time and glided instead. Thereafter Lady Penhellion watched her with open but not unkind amusement. She found her exquisitely funny, the only creature worth looking at in the convent.

Persephone did not see the reception in the Common Room, because she was washing up in Sister Agnes' place while the latter went to talk to her sister, who was a retreatant. She heard all about it from Sister Agnes before Compline. Reverend Mother had laughed and talked with Lady Penhellion, and according to Sister Agnes had made a great fuss of her. Then Sister Sophia, who in private life had a title that took precedence of Lady Penhellion's, had taken over, and the two of them had sat exchanging news of each other's relations while Reverend Mother went round and spoke to the others. Sister Agnes said they were all listening to Sister Sophia and Lady Penhellion calling each other Catherine and Cassidy, and could hardly keep their attention on Reverend Mother at all. Father Anselm was there too, but only marking time. His real business would come later. But when he went to pay his civilities to Lady Penhellion there was no more conversation in the room at all, so that Reverend Mother had to go and join them to save her face. She had been talking to old Mrs. Bridge, but she just wasn't listening, so Reverend Mother swept away with a superb "Please excuse me." "It was like that last time—everything absolutely topsy-turvy. It makes you ashamed. And all because she's wicked."

"She's beautiful," said Zephy.

"The Devil gave it her at her christening, then, and the holy water just didn't take, like some inoculations."

"I suppose he gave her her lovely scent too."

Reverend Mother had not failed to notice the exchange between Josephine, as she never failed to call her, and Lady Penhellion. It caused her concern out of all proportion to the incident. She was able, without putting her thoughts into words or allowing them conscious recognition, to react strongly to various horrible possibilities. Watchful that there should be no further communication between them, she replaced "Josephine" by a sister to wait on the visitors. Persephone suffered, thinking she must have been more awkward, more noisy, and more silly-looking even than she feared. She remembered how Lady Penhellion's laughing eyes had followed her round. She was oppressed with the unmanageableness of life. The more she tried, the harder it became. Every little thing that used to be easy was now a burden. Every personal distress that used to be nobody's business but her own was now also a sin. She was hungry with fasting. One job followed so mercilessly on the other that it seemed the day would never end.

In such conditions the preposterous Moira was like a lift to a tired hiker. Her confidence had an overplus that carried Zephy along, and her good humour was such that she did for Zephy all that the latter had done for Sister Veronica without taking account of it. She, no less than Reverend Mother and Lady Penhellion, considered Zephy an oddity, but she had taken a liking to her, not only maternal, since it went so far as to honour her early-morning silence, or at least to address to her only remarks requiring no answer. On the second day of the retreat she was silent almost to moroseness, but Zephy was sick with hunger and did not notice.

Zephy saw Lady Penhellion at Mass, kneeling among the other retreatants at the back of the Chapel, conspicuous for her elegance, her black lace veil, and her wandering eyes. At breakfast Zephy was waiting on Reverend Mother and Father Anselm, which was even more agitating, and she forgot the other's presence.

She had changed into her working clothes and was just coming down when Reverend Mother, meeting her in the hall, asked her to take a note to Sister Sophia in the library. To reach the library, where the retreatants would be gathered, she had to pass along the corridor where their rooms were situated. At the door of one of these Sister Bridget, whose business it was to do their rooms, was waving at Sister Pauline what Zephy at first thought was Lady Penhellion's veil, but she was mistaken.

"All to match, right down to the panties," said Sister Bridget, spreading them out. "The scent in this room is like a conservatory."

Having done her commission and feeling considerably better after breakfast, Zephy set out to join Moira, who went home for her meals on a motor bicycle. It was in looking after the calves and hens that she had time to enjoy the outside world, to exchange heedless jokes and to forget herself. The garden as she went through it was full of snowdrops and crocuses. The bitter weather had eased. Underfoot in the lane there was slippery deep mud, but the dead grass was showing spikes of green. The sun caught the hedge tops above stone walls, where brown fronds curled behind hoops of bare bramble. There was even a solitary violet among the ivy. At home—it was months since that word had come into her mind, and it gave her a shock—the tiny violets that grew in the lee of boulders on the commons would not appear until May. There were newcomers among the birds, and the trees etched in purple against the sky swayed like brooms as if to sweep winter away. Zephy hurried with her pails of calf food, glad to feel the moist life of February around her. This was the day's escape, to Moira and her admirable rudeness.

For try as she would, the Chapel where such imposed penitence went on had begun to feel a little arid. A thrush's song ringing in the sunless but budding wood meant more to her than the intoning of Lenten psalms. She felt more certainty that the bird's song reached the ears of its Creator than that her responses did. She made a round mouth like a boy chanting. "Ho-ho, Moira! It's going to be a lovely day."

Moira turned a glum look. "I'm not friends with you," she said. "You've made a fool of me."

"Why, Moira, what have I done?"

"I thought it was supposed to be a holy house up there, and everybody good, even if they are all crackers. Something sort of different."

"Well, it is different."

"Then what's that woman doing there? Tell me that, Saintly. Why's she there? I keep telling my dad about you, and today he laughed and said, 'Your Saintly keeps fine company.' I thought he meant a boy, and I said, 'She does no such thing, Dad, and I don't care who says it. She does no such thing.' 'Well,' he said, 'Lady Penhellion is up at your precious convent now, and she'll learn them a thing or two.' "

"She's in retreat, for Lent."

"Worn out and wants a rest, I should say. If I behaved like she does my dad would flay me."

"If she's so bad, she must have more to repent of than other people."

"Repent, my bum! I bet your Reverend Nuts, with her staring cat's eyes, isn't taken in by that. It's his Lordship's money she's after. A nice fat sub for helping to keep up appearances. You hop it just once and do what Pin-hell-on-you does all the time and see if Reverend Nuts is as sweet on you when you come back. You try!"

"The Church ought to be for everybody," said Zephy, quite sure of what she was saying but quite unsure of herself saying it. "The worse she is, the more she should be there."

"Good old Saintly! You couldn't look down your nose if you tried. Do you know what she did at the Agricultural Show? Well— After all, I don't think I'll tell you."

❧

Saturday evening was the time for Confession. There were two confessionals in the Chapel, one of which was devoted for the time being to the retreatants. Zephy, who had been washing up after supper, went to the Chapel shortly before Compline. A long row of retreatants was waiting at a discreet distance from their box, some reading or kneeling, some showing signs of exhausted patience as the murmur went on and the curtain never parted. Zephy took her place among the sisters on the opposite side, and when she had made her confession the line of retreatants had not changed except in length. When Sister Anne, the sacristan, rang the bell for Compline, the final act of the day, Father Anselm came out of the box in haste, looking grim and ruffled. The bell had finished ringing before Lady Penhellion followed, slowly, but freshly made up and trailing a faint heady scent. As she took her place, the retreatants all moved along and made more room for her.

By Sunday breakfast time something like consternation was noticeable at St. Hilarion. Although the meal was silent out of courtesy to the retreatants, a suppressed buzz could be felt, vibration without sound. The eyes of those whose position faced the visitors' table were continually met by those whose backs were turned to it. There was throughout the room an unconscious surface of shoulder movements, twitching fingers, and sighs. Some retreatants were frowning in attitudes of determined resignation. Even Reverend Mother's smooth face was recognised as an act of discipline. Sister Clare looked angelic but miserable. And yet the tilted eyebrow on the side of her face that was doe-eyed sometimes went a little higher. Everybody knew that of the twelve retreatants, only four, including Lady Penhellion, had been able to make their confession. The rest had had to make do with a private act of contrition.

When breakfast was over and the sisters had filed out, with Zephy bringing up the rear, she had opportunity to observe how the retreatants fell back to let Lady Penhellion go first, as if in society; how they smirked at her, if with too much determination; and how solidly they closed up their ranks when she had passed.

Lady Penhellion, making for the garden, caught up with Persephone.

"What a lot of putrid snobs," she said. "They're all as angry as hell with me, and they can't even show it. Their smiles are screwed on. I like you better. You go scarlet every time I look at you, but you hold your ground. Who are you?"

"Nobody," said Zephy, and added childishly, absurdly, to blush about it for the rest of her life, "but I love you."

"Good God!" said Lady Penhellion, looking at her with hatred. She turned on her heel and walked off into the garden.

✾

Father Anselm was like a Zurburán saint, in that there was no doubt about it. He was young enough to be extremely handsome and old enough for the strength of his face to be underlined, the fine bones showing. He had a gift of quiet eloquence; consequently each of the retreatants thought of him as sharing the intimacy of her deepest aspirations. The fact that he was celibate added a heady aetherealism to their relationship.

Lady Penhellion sat opposite him. Her eyes were no longer wandering; they were fixed day-long on him, wide and almost vacant, whether she listened to his addresses, or knelt, or stood holding the prayer book, or sat at meals separated from him by the width of the room.

When the day's devotions were over Father Anselm sat in his study, where anyone might visit him between supper and Compline. The majority of the retreatants had resolved their doubts long ago. Some had doubts that they had decided they must live with as best they could and keep to themselves. His usual visitors were either ladies who must talk or die, who went apologetic but determined, or

85

else those who emphasised their piety by hair-splitting questions of correct ruling. Lady Penhellion had been brought up as a Catholic and had made her retreat often before, never unmoved. She was noticeably absent from the library where the others sat reading the lives of the saints. The only comfortable armchair was reserved for her by her book on the seat. Sister Sophia sat in a hard-backed chair, her eyelids with the blue veins in them lowered as she bent over the Greek text. Her serenity was always distant and mysterious; it was something both inside and outside the Order. Now, as she sat un-ruffled and apart, her long and sensitive lips laid lightly one upon the other, it was impossible to tell how much or how little she saw of what went on around her.

The fidgety old Mrs. Bridge, who was on the right of Lady Penhel-lion's empty chair, had been counting how many pages of the life of St. Bernard she had still to read. She presently leant over and picked up the discarded book on the next seat. It was *La Joie* by Bernanos, in the original French, a language which she could not read and which meant to her, in book form, simply indecency. She held it up for her neighbour to see, nodding her head and shooting out her lips. This incident, too much for Sister Sophia, was afterwards told in confi-dence to Sister Winifred, who had been brought up in France, and it went to swell the pool of gossip. Mrs. Bridge, who really couldn't help it, was then impelled to go and consult Father Anselm about the mar-ried life of her daughter. She found, as she had hoped, that he was engaged. This too on her return was conveyed in dumb show to the room, in case any others had thought of going. The minutes ticked by, and faced by that provocative chair the lives of the saints failed altogether to hold attention. After half an hour, another retreatant was assailed with a query about the book she was reading and went tiptoeing out. She waited obstinately in the passage, where presently she was joined by Sister Clare, who urgently needed to speak to Fa-ther about the arrangements for the next day, which was the last day of the retreat. When at last the bell rang for Compline, Lady Penhel-lion came out, ravaged with weeping and hysteria. She made no at-tempt to hide her tears, but walked with desperate eyes slowly through the assembling sisters, shaken at long intervals by a dry and rattling sob, and climbed the stairs to her room. Zephy, small and inconspicuous in a doorway, saw and heard, and identified herself with the sorrow.

❖

86

The Chapel, being originally one of the farm outhouses, was not far from the back door, where Zephy filled her pails. Sister Anne, the happy sacristan, whose face was so ready to smile at persons or things outside herself that one hardly thought of her as having a face of her own, was standing outside the Chapel door. Tears of exasperation were running down her cheeks. Could this be the face she had always had? It was more than plain—a mere lopsided lump with a nose like a swinging door. She was talking to Sister Mildred, whose quick wit and interest in life were such that she never could refuse to hear anything. Afterwards she would pigeonhole it where it belonged, frown at it if it should never have been said or listened to, and if it had an element of humour, being human and needing laughter, she would repeat it in confidence; but only to the person least likely to be interested. She was now listening with keen-eyed sympathy. Sister Anne was unable to clean the Chapel, which it was her business to do between breakfast and Sext.

"You know how dusty it gets in there. I don't know where it all comes from, but of course it was an old barn. But you know, I sweep up *clouds*, I must, and she's been lying there since Lauds, except during Mass. Surely that's long enough for anybody? I don't like to keep walking backwards and forwards round and over her, but I've got to brush down the altar curtains. And I can't do anything at all about the carpet. She's right on it, crouching in front of the altar. It's as if Lilith, or *an animal*, were there. It's horrible. I find myself wanting to kick her; in front of my altar that I spend my whole life reverencing and keeping beautiful. I feel I simply can't stay in there with her. I daren't."

"I'll come in with you," said Sister Mildred. "Perhaps two of us can do it more quietly than one. I'll help to move the chairs." She took Sister Anne by the hand and they went in together. They knelt side by side at the back of the Chapel for a moment, facing the side altar, so that the figure of Lady Penhellion did not come directly between them and their prayers. They then worked quietly together, repeatedly passing those inescapable haunches, which were at once ampler, finer, richer in facets, sleeker in line, firmer and suppler than one would have thought the human frame could achieve, a miracle of fleshliness. Her waist nicked in sharply above the hip bones, and from there her back, arms, and neck seemed to cascade to the ground, ending in a pool of black lace covering her abandoned head and crumpled at one side in a clenched fist. The two nuns worked on, till all was done but the carpet before the altar on which she lay. Sister Anne paused there, miserably considering it. Then she hurried across to Sister Mildred.

"I believe she's asleep!" she said. "Probably been asleep all the time."

"Then that makes things a lot easier." Sister Mildred picked up a pile of hymnbooks, walked near the sleeper, and deliberately dropped them on the floor. Lady Penhellion stirred, groaned, raised her body, and absently rubbed her knees and her eyes. Sister Mildred was beside her at once, helping her to her feet and turning her towards the door.

"Can you stand? You had better go to bed now and have a good sleep, if you have been watching all night. I'll come with you to see you don't faint." She turned to show Sister Anne her laughing eyes above a properly pursed mouth as she guided her patient away. Lady Penhellion seemed dazed and without resistance. Sister Mildred literally put her to bed, taking off and folding up the crumpled frillies, putting aside the long nylons and the exquisite shoes, of which the toes were ruined by the night's vigil; she offered her from the chest of drawers a choice of fresh nightgowns, committing their luxury to memory as she did so. Finally, using her authority as Dispensing Sister, she took her up a tray of coffee and rolls. Lady Penhellion never spoke except to say thank you. Her eyes were blank and motionless. She munched without thinking. Sister Mildred tucked her in bed, and remarking, "You should not be so excessive in everything," trotted silently off to make up the time she had lost.

❖

The retreatants assembled again in Reverend Mother's room for tea, to say good-bye to each other and to her. Lady Penhellion had slept the day out, arriving for tea in what Sister Agnes, peering through the door, called her going-away clothes—a costume of daffodil yellow tweed. Sister Clare afterwards said it was both hand-woven and hand-spun. She wore it with primrose calf shoes and heavy gold bangles. Her hair shone like a hunter's neck. Lord Penhellion had come to fetch her, and as she took his arm and led him to Sister Sophia, her welcome and her scent filled the room. Compared with her, the other retreatants, good unselfish women, wearing for the most part lisle stockings, stretched jumpers, and baggy tweed skirts, looked as if the world they belonged to had little to offer them. The brown habits of the sisters, on the contrary, gained rather than lost in comparison with Lady Penhellion's worldly perfection. They were royal, she a mere court figure. Sister Clare looked as if, given her choice of all the shops and fashions in the world, she had found the dress of her desire, so perfect that in wearing it she need never think of what she wore. It could perhaps be said of Reverend Mother that she gave her habit a build-up, that she carried it magnificently. Sister Sophia, gaunt and stylised like a figure in a mosaic, looked royal in her own right, bending from her great height and pressing her long and lovely fingers together. Sister Pauline, it must be conceded, looked dressed for mortification. She was slim, straight, and brisk, and after five years in the convent still looked as if she would feel better if only she could pin her scapular to her bodice with a *diamanté* brooch.

These four only were entertaining the departing visitors in the Mother Superior's room. Zephy and Sister Agnes had merely wheeled in the trolley with tea. From the refectory window they later saw Reverend Mother and Sister Sophia saying good-bye to Lord and Lady Penhellion at the front door. Willi was in the car, sitting beside the chauffeur. When they had gone, Father Anselm left his study and joined the others.

❖

Lenten piety settled in on St. Hilarion a little heavily after so much excitement. Reverend Mother was disposed to extra strictness. Fasting and watching were harder than before. Zephy's hunger was cumulative and she often had headaches. The feeling that her activity, her position on the convent map, was pinpointed for every moment of every day and night became oppressive. During the endless repetition of the psalms, rich as they are with imagery of the mountainous earth, homesickness like hunger overwhelmed her. The woods of her own country afflicted her. That was the heaven from which she was separated. In them, she had known innocent bliss.

At meals she ate ravenously, though the hunger was of the heart, and she often felt sick. Today she could not eat, because she had forgotten the gate yet again, being late for Mass, and the heifers had escaped. The yard had two gates, a five-bar gate giving on to the paddock and lane, and, round the corner by the pump, a hand gate for short cuts to the house. This was the one Zephy had left unlatched, and presumably Moira, before going home, had let the heifers out into the yard. They had gone up the hill towards the neighbouring farmer's pasture. During breakfast their distant uneasy calling had been heard by all. Zephy had gone crimson and then white as Reverend Mother's eyes found her and pinned her sin on her.

As soon as breakfast was over she ran out, leaving the boundaries of St. Hilarion for the first time in months. She passed through the copse whose treetops began under her bedroom window. They were still bare but the sun was twinkling on top of them as it does on the surface of a brook, and long rays stole down and round the boles. Zephy laid her hands and brow on a smooth ash trunk, and it seemed to her that she could feel its being alive. From the wood she passed out onto a stretch of common with labyrinths of furze tempting her with alcoves private and windless. The grass was nibbled close by rabbits, which sprang away in every direction. She climbed towards the sound of the heifers, who were now making the hullabaloo of the lost and foolish. As she went, she looked round as if she herself were the runaway, happy beyond words to be alone. From the top of the hill she could see the heifers wandering up and down outside a grass padded wall, on the other side of which a strange herd ignored their clamour. Zephy too ignored it, turning her back and looking out to the sea whose surface laughed in the distance. The sky was a dim gentle blue, the moon just glazed enough to be seen, the sun just warm enough to be felt. It lay on Zephy's brow like a benediction, it covered her body as with an extra layer of wool. The turf held it; the cushions of thrift and whorls of primrose leaves relaxed their frost-pinched rigidity as if filling their veins with it.

Before her was the sea, rounding the horizon and half the globe beyond that, a kingdom in which man was as rare and unimportant as newts on land. Inland from the cliff edge, the smooth and consequent downland flowed over hill and combe almost shadowless, winter grass and grey furze distancing to blue. Small birds chased each other in and out of the bushes, diving into openings as well known to them as tracks are to the rabbits. Travelling across the sky were occasional small white clouds. As they lay over the sea, their firm snow was reflected in its mirror, broken and ruffled, as though a light shone up from below. When they passed over the land they trailed instead lengths of shadow, under which the opening leaves were checked and held back their sap like breath, and the pale twirl of the primrose bud remained prim for more imperious coaxing. Zephy, lying on a flat rock, chose a puff of cloud far out to sea and watched it move towards her. She felt the chill as it cut off the sun and waited, enjoying the cold in anticipation of the returning warmth. As the sun shone out, a lark flew up in song from beside her, shaking a shower of joy out of the sky.

Convent discipline softly vapoured away. The world was here, lying in the hand of its Creator, not yet finished, being shaped every minute, as she was also. This easing bliss, so necessary to her that she submitted to it without a backward thought, might have ended in a long re-creating sleep, as inexplicable by convent standards as it would be inexcusable when she confessed it there. She was saved this disgrace by the heifers running aimlessly towards her before the snapping, high spirits of a stray dog. When she had driven the dog away, the heifers were willing enough to be guided home, whence, as they approached, came tolerant moos in answer to their high trumpet calls.

Moira meanwhile had done without grudging the work of two. When Zephy brought the heifers into the yard she was there, her feet planted well apart, tossing forkfuls of litter with a swing of her massive hips, apparently with as much ease and enjoyment as a pig tossing with its nose or a cock with the back stroke of his legs. She turned her scarlet face, opened in a wide smile.

"I bet you left that gate open on purpose. Don't blame you. Bet you feel like screaming sometimes in there. Nice day for a walk. Turn them into the paddock, there's a dear. I've cleaned out the shed."

❖

It was amazing how much Reverend Mother always knew about anything that approximated to private life among her sisters. Sister Monica, pulling up leeks at the farthest corner of the vegetable garden, had seen the direction taken by Zephy as she set out, and much later had spoken with the farmer's son, who had brought his cart and horse to shift last year's stable manure from the yard to the garden for her. It was on his land that the heifers were trespassing. In answer to her query as to whether the animals had done any damage, he told her he had seen "the little 'un" lying out on a boulder sea-gazing. "First day of spring," he said. "Even you ladies must notice that." Sister Monica had no intention of giving Zephy away when she said to Sister Margaret, as she handed in the baskets of vegetables for lunch, "That child is too young for a convent."

When Zephy went to Reverend Mother's room for religious instruction that evening, she was asked to account for her morning, beginning with the leaving open of the gate.

"I am sorry, Reverend Mother. I suppose I must have been thinking of something else."

"Can you think back now, and tell me what it was that prevented you from being reliable? I have to scold you for leaving the gate open at least once every week. It hardly seems possible you could forget every time, you, a farmer's daughter—or, I should have said, brought up on a farm."

"That was the reason," said Zephy dwindling under the wide-eyed stare. "I was homesick."

Reverend Mother continued to look steadily at her. Then she said: "It seems a sad waste of emotion to be moping for something that shocked you so much that you ran away from it. You ran away. I didn't take you prisoner. You became a postulant at your own repeated asking. Cross out your past life, which seems to me to have had little good in it. Don't let it come, in what form I cannot imagine, between you and your duty. Somebody else had to do your work while you were chasing after the heifers. Why then were you idling away the time lying admiring the view?"

"Reverend Mother," said Zephy, clasping a wet ball of a handkerchief between her sweating palms, "why is it so much easier to love God outside? Up there on the headland it was so beautiful"—here she lost her *élan* and could only repeat questioningly "it was so beautiful."

"The most beautiful thing God ever did, and the only truly beautiful thing for us to think of, is the Passion, by which we were given life. To be lost in love of the material creation, when we could be contemplating God's mercy, is as much a waste of time as for you to be hankering after a bad home when you have chosen to be a postulant."

"Why then was the world made so beautiful, Reverend Mother, if we are not to love it?"

"I sometimes think God made it like that for the animals, to make up to them for their short life and necessary death."

"Do you mean, Reverend Mother, that He made *all that* just for the animals? The rabbits and the birds? That *would* be grace abounding!" Zephy was aghast and delighted with this measurement of "more than we can ask or need."

"What were you more than a rabbit or a bird when you lay there enjoying the sun on your skin, the scent in your nose, the sounds in your ears? Couldn't they do as much?"

Passionately Zephy admitted to herself that she believed they did all that, even as she. Passionately she denied that that was the whole of her experience. But she sat downcast and said nothing. Reverend

Mother talked on, but Zephy's mind was occupied with the questions that had been raised. That the animals loved their home coverts and hills as she loved hers—yes. That was easily imaginable. That the birds loved the air and the light and the wind and the flutter of leaves through which they had their known paths, there was nothing impossible in that. Would that mean that they really felt as she did? If so, where was she different? The gulls, she thought, equally at home on the sea or on the wind, knowing no bounds at all, had perhaps—turning their steely necks this way and that, plunging or gliding—a better idea of the whole, as a whole, than any other creature, if wholeness was the criterion.

"Are you paying attention, Josephine?"

"Yes, Reverend Mother." That was it. The gulls had never been separated from the whole. They are just part of it, made of the elements. The larks too, and all the rest. They weave in and out of something that is still God. They see nothing from the outside. To see from the outside is sorrow and joy in one breathful, is real desire.

Reverend Mother's words running concurrently with Zephy's thoughts cut in and made part of them.

"It is no use hankering after the Garden of Eden. We have lost it forever. But we are offered the chance of something better. Don't lose the future in foolish homesickness for the past. There are other glories compared with which spring and summer are material, temporary, and, to us, worthless. Go into the Chapel before Compline and make an act of contrition for this morning's heedlessness, and try to think of these things."

Zephy went to the Chapel as she was bidden and knelt willingly in its dusk, which to her always seemed laden with the golden motes that hover in barns, and lit as with St. Joseph's lantern. She had never yet repeated a prayer mechanically or in hypocrisy. An act of contrition for having lain in God's hand she did not find possible. Why should it be supposed that God was only to be found in thinking of sin and death? Defiantly she opened her book, whose pages glimmered in the light of the candle nearest her and rustled between her fingers like mice in sheaves. She turned to the Benedicite and repeated it with a bounding heart, aware that she was on the edge of heresy.

"O all ye works of the Lord, bless ye the Lord. Praise him and magnify him for ever."

As she read, she re-created each word with all her senses. The

93

powers heaped up the mountains and the tides, and from a mysterious seed called out a human being great and weak with worship. The angels were omnipresent, unseen for dazzle, the heavens opened and the stars receded for ever. She felt the showers on her neck, the dew on her feet, the wind in her ears, while all the trees chanted. The earth turned hugely for winter and summer, requiring time and meditation for so profound a ritual. It spun for night and day, helter-skelter with happiness. Once she had known that. The mountains and hills were her own, they sang with the becks of the North Country, she felt them under her feet, she drank deeply of the wells.

She sat on in happy repose, watching Sister Anne, who was now lighting candle after candle for Compline. She thought with love of the warm and beautiful cows in their stalls; of the calves curled up together in deep straw like a huddle of angular puppies, their large eyes lidded in smoky velvet; of dear Moira, strong and easy and simple like an oak tree or a good farm horse. Among the sisters who gathered for Compline, none performed that poetical office with such fresh delight as Zephy, nor did the Confession seem to her other than admirable words for an attitude essential to humans, to which she subscribed and which bound her to the rest of mankind.

❈

The next morning was full spring. The cows were turned out after milking. They hesitated in the doorway as if unable to believe in their release. They mooed into unanswering space, and called to each other in the yard like countrywomen gathering for a treat. They ran hither and thither, and finally, led by Zenobia, they headed for the park. Zephy, who was still keeping the Greater Silence, and Moira, who now treated it as a game, imitated the cows to each other and waved their arms. Moira tried to head Zephy away into freedom after the last rump had lurched through the gate. Zenobia was heavy with calf, the skin strained over her hips with the weight it carried. She was followed by younger matrons with sides high, round, and promising like barrels. They walked staidly, but once in the park the others overtook them, bursting into clumsy gallop on unsteady winter legs. They were disappointed in the grass, but found some novelty in munching the tips of hedges. Their voices exploring and commenting made Zephy smile as she came back through the yard where the litter was smoking in the sun. She waved in passing to the little old man who came up from the village and spent the night with a fire and a

94

camp bed in the disused saddle room to keep an eye on the cows who might calve in the night.

"The old one won't go beyond tonight," he said. "But it won't be as fine a calf as last week's two. Beauties, they are. It's a treat to feel them suck your fingers."

After breakfast Zephy received a message to go to Reverend Mother's room. "There's a new bailiff," whispered Sister Agnes, before gliding away into the kitchen.

Zephy remembered with a pang that Moira's month had only another week to run. But worse was to follow.

Reverend Mother was alone. She was distant. She might have been talking on the telephone to someone invisible. Although Zephy often wished she could remain unseen, the unspoken command to do so she felt unnerving. She felt her hands and feet too big, her elbows too angular. It was difficult not to jut anywhere into space not allotted to one. She felt out of place, wildly peculiar. She received Reverend Mother's orders in a numbness that momentarily robbed them of their sting. She was to be transferred to indoor work. Sister Winifred had damaged her knee and could no longer do the stairs and corridors. Reverend Mother was well satisfied with this new arrangement; it would give Josephine more time both for study and for attending the Chapel. It would, in fact, give her the opportunity of keeping Holy Week as it should be kept. She was to begin her new work at once under Sister Mildred's orders.

Zephy's mouth came open with the intention of asking who was to do her work, but questions of that kind were considered improper. She closed her lips therefore, but Reverend Mother received a characteristic direct, meditative gaze, also improper, before the docile "Yes, Reverend Mother" with which Zephy withdrew.

❖

Aseptic corridors were now her world, whose only decoration was the pattern of the window sashes that the sun cast on the inner wall. Progressing backwards on her knees below the level of the window sills, she had only linoleum to look at. It was the event of the day to polish instead the oak wood of the stairs. She examined the grain, followed its rhythms in polishing, could have kissed it for belonging to her own world. As she sat back on her heels surveying her shine and letting her thoughts wander as she rested her arms, Sister Mildred looked over the bannisters.

"There's no time to waste," she said. "The new retreatants come this evening, so you have the library block to do as well. You can do that this afternoon."

Zephy looked up electrified. "Is—" she ventured.

"No. No sensationalism this time. You have time to scrub the hall before lunch. Remember not to clank the handle of the bucket. Reverend Mother insists on absolute silence."

It is difficult to move a heavy bucket about on tiles in an echoing hall without making any noise. Zephy seemed to herself, however hard she tried, to make a noise like a blacksmith. She grew sticky with anxiety, and the blood, rising to her face, turned it to a moist faint lilac. Every minute she expected the appearance of Reverend Mother, whose rebuke would classify her clumsiness as sin. By lunchtime she was feeling very sick, but the hall was done, and the only criticism was from Sister Mildred—whose gaiety was equalled by her strictness—who told her she had left it much too wet; it looked as if there had been a cloudburst. The retreatants had not been told to bring galoshes. She must learn to wring the cloth out properly.

That night she was kept awake in spite of her weariness by sad roars from the cowshed, where old Zenobia was in labour. Through the open window she heard hobnailed boots crossing and recrossing the yard and the cracked voice of the old man in consultation with strangers. When at last she fell asleep, she dreamt that the new bailiff was Sam Cudthrop, and it was not Zenobia but Bess who was in labour.

For the first time, morning brought no cold outside air, no fading stars, no bird song, no movement of warm, soft-eyed animals with wide, unthinking brows; only the floor and chair legs of the refectory and the library, and the dirty gates. The retreatants were as retreatants should be, so many unknown souls; to Zephy, so many more feet going up and down her passages. After breakfast, when she was clearing the table, she learnt from Sister Margaret that Zenobia had died in the night, through lack of the experience and devotion of Sister Veronica. It was a bull calf, not much good, but it would come in for Whitsun. Mr. Curry said he would have got rid of Zenobia anyway. He didn't believe in keeping old cows. Sister Veronica, after all, was an old lady herself and getting a bit sentimental.

"Who is Mr. Curry?"

"He's the new bailiff. His wife is doing your work."

"Has Moira gone?"

"I don't know, I'm sure."

Outside the kitchen door, the cobbles shone rose and blue in the March sun. A merry din of cockerels filled the near distance, and beyond that the cries of calves and the uninhibited clank and clatter of farm activity. Zephy listened for any echo of Moira's full voice or monstrous laugh, but heard none.

There were two four-day retreats in quick succession, doubling the housework for all the indoor sisters. Zephy had no idea of complaining—she was taking her vocation seriously—but, cut off from the open air and faced only with her linoleum, she became the victim of her own thoughts. It was as though a cloud of these, like evil mosquitoes that she had been waving away, that had been following her at close range waiting for an unguarded moment, had found it as she crouched on all fours, gazing at nothing and monotonously working her arms. The first day that their horror came into the open, it was just a continuation of her bad dream—one of those things like a headache or a bilious attack that has to be borne; but after a day or two, she found that the mere getting down to her humble position and taking the scrubbing brush or polisher in her hand was the signal for the attack to begin, and that each time it was more corroding, more exhausting.

There was no possible distraction. The life of the convent went over her at a higher stratum—feet passed her fingers, skirts brushed against her bucket, her eyes were level with blind knees moving behind woollen folds. She had not even the social contacts of a hotel scrubbing woman, who, rounding a gilded pillar on all fours, setting her paraphernalia before her, may come face to face with another of her kind and exchange a morsel of juicy gossip or a boiled sweet before each is drawn away, retreating backwards before the arabesques of her scrubbing brush. Zephy fought her thoughts in solitary battles lasting for hours. She embraced her work, welcomed her aching wrists and shoulders, trying to make a power out of it that should defend her from the obsessing turntable of her mind, which, presenting first innocently the features of her own countryside, would trip her suddenly into a melodrama where she held the billhook in her hand and wished she might have her chance again to murder Sam, and so never have to see what she had seen.

For the first week, she tried to ward off these attacks of nightmare by the meticulous polishing of floors as if they were holy vessels. She spent so long on awkward corners, or the bend in the stairs where the

97

bannisters were double, that Sister Mildred was continually telling her not to spend more time than there was.

"I must. It's not clean," said Zephy dully, looking at her in distant distress.

Sister Mildred was never in so much of a hurry that she did not take in what she saw. She did not like the look of Zephy. Losing weight, she noticed professionally. Bad colour. Wasn't like that two months ago.

On Saturday, when the second batch of retreatants had gone and the final polish for Sunday was under way, Zephy, quite tired out, not having been out of doors all week, was trying to close her mind against its swarming torments by timing the strokes of her polisher to the rhythm of desperate prayer. With the weight of her body on her arms, she forced her Ave Maria this way and that, and when Sister Mildred spoke to her she looked up but her lips continued to move.

Sister Mildred was entirely devout and had been a nun ever since she ceased to be a hospital sister. Her medical training had drawn a circle in red ink round religious practice and experience—thus far shalt thou go and no further. She endeavoured at all times to keep religion sane. Mysticism was a harder "case" than doubt because it had gone over the edge and there was no reasonable way of countering it. She dreaded above all things a muttering nun. She turned her attention to Zephy, and devised what she might put in motion to relieve her. Her influence, because it was selfless and always reasonable, and because she had learnt never to let her dynamism come into recognition, was very strong with Reverend Mother, who gave way to her without noticing that she had done so. Whereas even the Bishop found Reverend Mother hard to move.

So it came about that, in the evening, Zephy was told that a certain Father Martin, cousin of Sister Clare, was to celebrate Mass on the Patronal Festival of a tiny church beside the sea; and, it being mid-Lent and Refreshment Sunday, Reverend Mother had given permission for him to take with him in his car Sister Clare and Sister Sophia—both indoor sisters needing a rest and a breath of sea air—and Josephine. If the day was fine, they were to spend the afternoon by the sea and return in time for Vespers. Sister Mildred's hand did not appear in this. The news broke on Zephy with the dazzle of a miracle. It was Sister Margaret who told her, with undisguised envy —for was not she the hardest worked of all the sisters? "I often almost wish I were not blessed with perfect health and strength. If I get tired, nobody thinks it matters."

Forewarned, Zephy received her summons to Reverend Mother's room before Compline, trembling, but for once not with fear.

❧

A quiet blue dawn ushered in one of those days when people begin to wonder whether the daffodils will not be over before Easter. Zephy, from the earliest light, had been studying the prospects from every window that she passed, so important was it that the weather should be mild enough for them to stay out.

Father Martin bore a family likeness to Sister Clare, being tall and spare, with something of her sweetness in his expression; but in him it was tired and at a distance, in her it was eternally fresh. With Sister Sophia's gaunt six foot one they made a trio in cassock and habits like a group of church statues, compared with which Zephy, in her postulant's little brown dress and veil, looked like a sort of holy toy.

The tiny church, dedicated to a saint of whom nothing was known but his garbled name—whose saint's day was therefore a matter of arrangement—was pressed into the side of a combe overlooking a small bay. It was built of mortared cobbles and had a tough octagonal tower trimmed to the wind, reminiscent of harbour lights. It was august in direct ratio to its smallness, which suggested the great gesture of a pioneer community establishing in stone what had been initiated in the open air and acknowledged in a log chapel. There was assembled a congregation of three persons, one of whom rang the space-exploring old-toned bell. The contingent from St. Hilarion had the satisfaction of doubling the congregation and of reasserting the honour of the ancient place in the present day.

As they walked down to the beach after Mass, the three seniors discussed the little church and its history while Zephy, as befitted her position, kept silence and enjoyed the Atlantic horizon and her thoughts.

The tide was out when they arrived. Zephy saw for the first time what the sea can do to the land. Her life on the estuary had prepared her for it, and yet she was overwhelmed. The cove was deserted as if from all time. After their luncheon, eaten on dry flat rocks in the lee of the wind, Father Martin withdrew to read. Sister Sophia closed her eyes and rested her head against the sunny cliff. Her long lids and what could be seen of her venerable temples were, though wrinkled, as

99

delicate in skin and vein as a baby's—to be blessed, thought Zephy, with kisses. Sister Clare sat with her hands clasped over one bent knee, an unregarded attitude that she would never have assumed in the convent. She blinked up at the gulls, she smiled at the breeze. Zephy risked asking if she might take her stockings and shoes off to go on the shore. Sister Clare nodded, her finger on her lips as she looked towards Sister Sophia's preparation for a doze.

Zephy stood for a while on the edge of the shingle, ashamed to trespass where all was so divinely washed, smoothed, luminous, and glistening. She took in the significant and stupendous shapes of the rocks, the softening and streamlining of all their curves and crevices for the receiving of water. She understood, awe-struck, that the cove was the sea in reverse—its negative, its vessel, hollowed and polished by the sea to receive itself. The brown seaweed hung in orderly fringes round the lower rocks, beneath a buttercup-yellow frieze of lichen. Each sloping sandbank was perfect—the very shape of a gentle withdrawal, the arm of a sleeping child that its mother lifts and lays on its breast. The trickles of fresh water finding their way down the beach moved in sleek opening fans between sands ridged as by a wood carver.

Zephy set foot on the kissing sand and ran towards the sea. It took her some time to get there, for she was diverted by the richness of detail at every step, the tabernacle splendour of the rock pools, so much too richly curtained and bejewelled for the foolish shrimps who lived in them or the small furtive crabs. Precious pebbles lay on the twilight bottom, each too individual and too perfect to be left behind without a pang.

As she neared the sea, the prospect became more breath-taking, and closed round between her and the land, cutting her off in the unfamiliar. Those rocks and inlets from which the sea had recently withdrawn had kept something of its mystery about them. Huge boulders, still wet, showed themselves veined and coloured, blood-red, purple, or green. The underside of overhanging cliffs was iridescent with flickers of ripple light.

The waves of the ebb tide broke with sleepy regularity on the sand at the entrance to the cove, their sound almost lost in the emptiness of the sky. Zephy now and again forgot to hear them in the silence, and then, at a turn of her head, caught their plashing again. She blamed herself, as if in listening to music she had dreamed off and missed a

100

bar or two. She was wakened from one such oblivion by a sharp wave with a special shiver of excitement in it. Something was happening, something was different. Gulls were materialising in the sky, calling urgent signals one to another. A little fitful wind blew in off the sea, and a long arc of foam, like a priest's skirt of lace, was spread widely over the sand beyond the line hitherto reached by the waves. The creator of the cove was returning to it.

Zephy's impulse was to retreat in haste, but she soon discovered that this was no sudden business. It was only the deep breath of a sleeper about to awake, one whose work was too great to be hurried, requiring all time. She was impatient, fearing the summons for the return journey before she should have seen what she must see.

The warmth of the afternoon held, however, and perhaps she was not the only one reluctant to be re-enclosed, for no move was made, and the waves, gathering momentum, took back group after group of rocks—first encircling the base, then lifting up the seaweed like hair, running it through, tossing it this way and that and finally passing deeply over it, leaving it upright and swaying beneath unbroken water, its fronds spaciously deployed, its nodules plump like berries.

The sound of the surge increased greatly once it was enclosed by the sides of the cove. It was no longer possible to ignore it for a second. Zephy, whose thoughts naturally ran in the imagery with which she was daily supplied, found herself repeating St. Francis' hymn:

> "Thou flowing water, pure and clear,
> Make music for thy Lord to hear.
> Alleluia."

Alleluia seemed to her to be the sound the waves actually made as they surged, broke, and spread—repeated for ever, rich, flowing, weighted syllables. Why, she wondered, were waves always described as battering, fighting with the rocks? It was love that she was watching, the creator returning to its work, the lover to the loved. Every boulder was embraced, encircled, revived, contained, sung over; every form delineated again and again. The descending spray lingered over the rock face like fingers tracing the brow, the eyelids, and the nose of a dear face; but all the time it was forming and changing what it touched, transmuting stone into sea. She watched the process at work, the white jets of foam running up and down the cracks that would eventually separate blocks standing cliff-high; or the plunging

101

surf that changed from a syphon of roaring bubbles to a dome of blue glaze dividing over a boulder, smoothing, sleeking, establishing a perfect oneness with a sigh.

Driven from one rock islet to another, Zephy returned to Sister Clare with a handful of lustrous pebbles. Her feet were puce with the cold sea water, and she gratefully accepted a drink of tea from the thermos flask, and went across to Father Martin to ask if he would have some.

"Is this a precious stone?" she asked him. "Porphyry or some lovely name like that?"

"I should say, a piece of bottle thrown overboard by a drunken sailor," he said, smiling at her face.

Zephy examined the semiopaque disc lying in her palm. It was pale greeny-blue, like summer dawn when the moon is in the sky. It had also the colour and almost the texture of the neck of a wave against the light. The surface was so hatched and pitted, and after that again filed so smooth, it held its colour so deeply you could not tell whether it came from within or without. This was surely a gem in its own right—whatever you called it, however it began.

"How long would it take to turn into this?"

"The oldest glass in the world looks something like that in texture when it is dug up out of the earth—though, of course, its edges are sharp. But I don't think we can be so romantic about this piece. You almost never find sharp broken glass on the beaches, so I suppose it is ground down pretty quickly."

Zephy returned and sat down beside the sisters, caressing the egg-shell-surfaced glass pebble with her fingers, and studied the scene. On one side of the cove every surface was sea-old, pushing out open fingers into the sea, offering wave-run and polished spray-courses, rounded basins, faceless corbels, wind-smoothed overhang. On the other side, a recent landfall had heaped the shore with jagged slabs of basalt, tilted like wrecked ships, splintered and pointed. On the cliff face from which they had fallen their outline could clearly be seen, bare of all lichen or weathering. These uncompromising hulks, newly foundered, must also be worked upon, brought into harmony. How long? There was all time for it. There was no hurry.

Suddenly there came clear-cut into her mind an image of grace—grace that inhabited all time, that created its vessel only by withdrawing from it, and returned again to fill it; that perpetually moulded and altered, flowing under and over, that, knowing no limit, knew no resistance. Everything must and would be made in its image. Why then these terrified heartbeats and cries of "While there is yet time"? She did not believe God was short of time. Everything must succumb, if not now, then later. Sin was just silly—a drunken man throwing bottles that turned into gems. For the first time, she called Sam and her mother to mind deliberately, like someone trying a sprain to see if it still hurts. She easily pictured Sam as the faceless corbel on the cliff. It made her laugh. Her mother she saw as a smooth, salt-washed rock with flowing hair. God was embracing and compelling everything, everywhere. *God was not shocked*. In bliss, she slid against Sister Clare's shoulder, and presently heard her say: "Wake up, Zephy, it's time we went home."

Her ears were filled with organ-loud noise, and the waves were racing almost to her feet.

"Sister Sophia was feeling cold. She and Father Martin have gone on ahead to the car. We must catch them up."

Once on the headland turf, Sister Clare picked up the skirts of her habit and ran, showing long boyish legs. Zephy danced, skipped, and sidled, and shot away downhill like a rabbit.

Sister Clare later went in to Reverend Mother to thank her for their day's indulgence. Reverend Mother knew the little church well and was interested in every detail. The sisters of St. Hilarion had themselves embroidered and presented the altar cloths, and funds were sent from the sale of their produce.

"I love to hear that old bell," she said, when Sister Clare had finished her account. "Dear old Abel can hardly have the strength to swing it now."

"His grandson was with him. He is thirteen and bigger than the old man already. Father Martin asked Abel to let the boy try his hand."

"How did Josephine behave towards Father Martin? Sometimes she is still painfully coltish."

"She behaved perfectly. I was so happy, Reverend Mother, that you had the idea of letting her come. I wish you could have seen her eyes when she was by the sea."

"What should I have seen if I had seen her eyes?"

"They were Byzantine. They seemed to take in everything and to give everything out again. They were so large they filled her whole face, and nothing else was necessary to know her by."

"You are very lyrical, Sister Clare."

"Reverend Mother, you *know* I think her very remarkable. Father Martin thought so too."

"They all do," said Reverend Mother.

❖

Vesper and Compline passed for Zephy in a murmur of spiritual repose. It was not until Mass the next morning that she grasped the meaning for her of her experience. Inside the shell of the Chapel she heard the sea in her ears. Resting her eyes on its homely limits she let her imagination sail into the security of the limitless. Nothing was required of her but love and a lack of self-importance. She worshipped in exaltation, momentarily invulnerable. At a lower level of consciousness there passed thoughts of Sam. In this light he was no worse than her grandfather's grinning old boar. It had never occurred to her specially to detest that. It would take more than an old boar to outwit the power she was concerned with. The question of Bess she consciously laid aside. It was incomparably harder and bitterer, but she knew which way to approach it. It would need practice. The Gloria, the Sanctus, and the Benedictus were wings to her exaltation, and where the words of the Mass were less relevant to the particular orientation of her vision, her adoration carried her along. Love was offered her. Nothing but love was required of her.

Afterwards, as she was collecting her cleaning paraphernalia from the cupboard, Sister Clare passed her. They exchanged, without speaking, those rare smiles that are mysterious, not, like Mona Lisa's, for what they conceal, but because they flower unconsciously in a candour beyond normal experience. Zephy now swished her semicircles of soapy water in succession like the least of waves, and looked at her gleaming tiles with eyes that still saw the sea-blessed sands. She did not hear Reverend Mother coming till she was there, her path obstructed by the bucket and Zephy's heels. She rose to make way, absently flattening herself against the wall, not raising her eyes.

Reverend Mother stopped, and putting a finger under Zephy's chin raised her face.

"Lift your head, Josephine, while I look at you. I do not like to see that face held so conspicuously high during Mass, when everyone else is bowed in humility. What were you doing? Worshipping some little god of your own?" She tapped Zephy's cheek, as if to show that the rebuke was meant gently, and passed on.

Zephy stood still, paralysed by a blaze of anger such as she had never felt or imagined. Blasphemy such as this should be struck dead.

But Reverend Mother had passed immune down the corridor, and it was she, Zephy, whom the thunderbolt had struck, she it was who was incandescent. Reverend Mother had come like the Devil, now, at this first moment of firmly grasped release, to stamp it out, to push her back, with deliberate obliteration that the offensive tap on her cheek only exposed. She felt violently sick, but was too angry to give way to it. Hurriedly, unconscientiously, anyhow, she finished the hall, to get away before Reverend Mother should make her return—lest she, Zephy, should damn her own immortal soul by the words she would say.

Sister Mildred, who, observing Zephy at breakfast, had preened herself on the success beyond expectation of her manoeuvre, was startled to find herself so soon afterwards in charge of an automaton badly out of order. If, before, Zephy had worked too well, she now worked too badly. She was capable of walking away with her kneeling mat and leaving the pail of dirty water in the hall all the morning. Her broom and tins of wax were abandoned all over the place. Polish was put on door handles and never wiped off. She was reminded and chidden from morning till night without showing either repentance, resentment, or improvement. The climax came later in the week. Sister Margaret reported water dripping through the larder ceiling, while Sister Clare in the linen room heard a sound like the fountains of Rome in the bathroom. Zephy, who had been sent in to clean the bath, had absent-mindedly walked out again, leaving the tap on. Sister Clare, by making no fuss about the number of towels used for mopping up—for it was she who had charge of the linen—succeeded in preventing serious damage. She managed also to belittle the affair to the indignant Sister Margaret—"Just some spilt water"—and to come to a tacit agreement with Sister Mildred that nothing need be said. Sister Mildred, in any case, preferred to keep what she could in her own hands rather than call in higher authority. She was a born husher-up.

❖

Sunday ushered in Passion Week, during which the officiating priest was to be Father Durham, an Oxford scholar and an old friend of Sister Sophia, whom he had known since her Somerville days. He stayed as Reverend Mother's guest and was loved by all the convent.

Zephy had been feeling, in utter wretchedness, that St. Hilarion—at least as interpreted by Reverend Mother—had, after all, nothing to offer her. She was in the desolation of disillusion. She had not lost faith, but she had lost confidence in the vehicle. She despaired of ever bowing among the others anonymously in the unity of faith. What else could she worship but her own God? She thought of Sister Veronica, whose personal opinions, though she still had them, had become as indifferent to her as her nose. She looked longingly towards Sister Clare and Sister Sophia, to either of whom she would have entrusted herself. Sister Clare, she knew, would only refer her back to the Mother Superior. Sister Sophia she did not dare to approach. She also hazarded a guess that Sister Sophia was able to agree with Reverend Mother only by keeping silence. Zephy's solitude in these circumstances was like a madness. Where should she go if she could not honestly stay at St. Hilarion? What other home had she? What would become of her? The short night allotted to her she spent awake for fear of dreams—in vain, as she invariably dropped off before morning and the nightmares were punctual to meet her at the gates of sleep. More than once she overslept and Sister Mildred had to wake her. The first time, she shook her by the shoulder—but the result was a scream.

Father Durham appeared at this juncture like an angel. She knew almost at once that to him she could say anything, and that the answer would be for her.

At first sight one laughed. He so much resembled an elephant—if an elephant can be imagined without heaviness, refined to a delicate ghost. He had a high, domed forehead, big ears, drooping nose, and receding chin. Everything about him drooped—his long silver hair, his wrinkled eyelids, his cheeks, his aged shoulders, his baggy pockets, his shoelaces. He walked as slowly and uncertainly and with as little weight as someone walking in deep water. The skin that covered the bones of his face was creased into countless whirlpools wherever the contour offered a protuberance that could be encircled. Wrinkles travelled round the oval of his face, crossing into a complex network round his eyes, round his cheekbones, round his mouth, round his chin. All were capable of movement, combined or discriminated, and yet the general effect was still. His expression was ambivalent. It was very merry. It was also profoundly sad. Between these extremes there was no opposition; they were somehow sublimely the same thing.

Zephy, waiting on him at table, offered him food with as much emotion as if she laid sacrifices before the Archangel Gabriel. And yet she could not but laugh, as he did then in return at her, the pleasure seeming both immediate and emanating from a base very far away.

After supper she was privileged to take the coffee in to Reverend Mother's room, where, to her joyful surprise, Reverend Mother presented her to Father Durham and told him she would be the one who would do his room and wait on him in any way he required.

"Above all, Josephine, see that there is a good fire both in Father Durham's room and in the library. Try not to disturb him and don't move his things about. That's right, isn't it, Father?"

"She need not be afraid of disturbing me, Mother Cecilia. It is rather the other way round, I am afraid, my dear," he said, turning to Zephy with a smile slowly growing like a ripple round a sinking stone. "I am afraid I have grown very absent-minded. You must not be offended if I sometimes do not even notice you have come in, or do not hear the first time you speak. Forgive me at these times. When I do see you it will always be with pleasure. As for my things, as Mother Cecilia so kindly warned you, if you find a heap of books on the floor with my slippers on top and my medicine bottle in one of the slippers, that is how I want them. And don't gather all my loose sheets and letters into a tidy heap. Let one lie here and another there, just as they were. Try to imagine that my brain is bestowed here and there about the room and I don't like the coils disturbed."

Zephy let out a little cadence of laughter, and Father Durham, turning back to Reverend Mother with the smile still in his eyes but working outward to mingle with the solitary grandeurs of his temples, caught her unawares, staring at Zephy with wide unyielding eyes.

"You may go now, Josephine," she said.

Sister Mildred's dismay when she heard who was appointed to look after Father Durham was unjustified. The week of his visit was a reprieve for Zephy. She was devoted to her new ministry and carried out her duties with a passion of precision that affected her other work as well. She loved the old priest with her whole heart, and was best satisfied with herself when she succeeded in waiting on him unnoticed. The progress of Passion Week was a positive rest for her. Following in Father Durham's wake her doubts were merely unanswered questions. Her God could not be less than included in his God. It was only a question of understanding. Her mind was little, his was vast and wise. His idea of God would contain hers but not reject it.

It was on the Friday that Zephy, after knocking like a bird, slid into Father Durham's room and silently brought to him a tea tray on which the cup played a long tremolo in the saucer. When this was stilled on the table beside him, he looked up from his writing and smiled at her as if they had not met for a long time.

"My dear child," he said, "I am afraid I was deep in thought. Did you say something?"

Zephy looked into the mysterious wrinkled oval that contained his expression. A long strand of hair fell over it like the lock characteristic of young men, but this was limp and silver.

"Father, may I ask you a question?" She slid into his smile, she was herself the stone that set the ripples moving. "I suppose there isn't really any such thing as righteous anger?"

"That's not a question. That's your answer to it. But of course there is! It's the besetting sin of the righteous. When people try all the time with all their power to be good, it's only natural to think sometimes that they have done it, if only for a minute. That's the Devil's chance to slip in in disguise. I use the Devil as a figure of speech. He is nearly always disguised, generally as good, even as God. He stops at nothing. In any case, anger—plain unrighteous anger—is the besetting sin of religious houses because it is the obverse of love. We are wretched elastic creatures—if we go a long way in one direction we tire and flip back in the other. We resent people interfering with our being good. It's very silly. And then, of course, anger can be a great pleasure—an orgy."

"No! It nearly kills me."

Father Durham looked at the pencil trembling on his table from Zephy's proximity. He got up and went to his armchair by the fire.

"Sit down, Zephy, and tell me about it."

How did he, so dreamy and distant, know her pet name?

"I mustn't. Reverend Mother will be—Reverend Mother said I was not to disturb you. And it is my reading time now."

"Never mind that. There is a time for reading and a time for talking. Sit down. I will answer for it to Reverend Mother. Why do you suppose she chose you to wait on me?"

Zephy sat down precipitately on the hearthrug.

"That will do, then. Sit there with your arms round the dear, humble coal scuttle as if it were a dog."

Zephy saw that she was indeed caressing the coal scuttle, but she did not move. It surprised her to be gently teased from such a distance. It seemed to her that though his body must be vaguely aware of being laid in that particular armchair in the room, his consciousness was so expanded with learning and experience that it touched far margins of space and time, and it was from this remove of receptivity that he had noticed a foolish little girl.

"I suppose you are never angry any more," she said, speculative and tender.

"Not often, now. I say it as a drunkard might say 'not for months.' "

"Perhaps that is why you look so sad."

"Sad? God forbid that I should look sad. But you have said something surprisingly wise and penetrating. How old are you?"

"Sixteen and a bit."

"Well, tell me how you came to know so soon that it is, humanly speaking, sad to be without indignation."

❧

On the Saturday of his departure, Father Durham took coffee with the Mother Superior and Sister Clare. Zephy carried his cup from Reverend Mother's hand across to him, then stood, solicitously watching him take it, her hands behind her and midriff thrust forward like a child.

"Thank you, Josephine. You can go now. Sister Clare and I will serve each other."

"Yes, Reverend Mother. May I say good-bye to Father Durham?"

"Good-bye, Zephy," said Father Durham, getting to his feet and going to open the door for her. "Thank you for looking after me so kindly."

"Good-bye, Father. I hope you have a good journey."

Sister Clare saw that this prim speech was said with brimming eyes, but Reverend Mother only saw the old man holding her hand in both of his.

When Zephy had gone, she asked him how he had found their little postulant. "Has she really looked after you well? She is, regrettably, still somewhat incalculable."

"She looked after me perfectly. I am only sorry I can't take her with me."

"Ah, you may joke, Father, but I could almost wish the same thing. I am not at all happy about her. Father, you have an unrivalled experience of young people. I would greatly value your advice. Do you think that child can have a vocation? One cannot quite override all one's instincts; they form one's judgment whether one will or no. Did I do right to receive her as a postulant?"

Father Durham polished his glasses and temporised. Then he said:

"You certainly did not do wrong. Forbid them not, you know. She is signed and sealed, but it may be a long time yet before she is delivered. Some people who are all-loving have got to love all things at all levels. I think she may be one of those."

"You too think she has no vocation."

"I did not say so. But I should enjoy christening her babies."

"I fear they might be illegitimate ones. She comes from the worst of homes."

"Not the worst, Mother Cecilia. Her mother is gentle, and affectionate and unprotected."

"Unprotected is the thing I dread. Like mother, like daughter. That is why I received her as a postulant against my better judgment. That is why I fear so terribly what will happen if her vocation does not hold. Here she would be safe—if, perhaps, troublesome later on."

"One can be too anxious about safety, I think. After all, the Magdalene would not have been the kind of saint she was if she had not been the woman she was. It takes all sorts to make a calendar. Now, Mother Cecilia, if you will forgive me, before I get ready for the train I want to slip up to Catherine—I should say Sister Sophia, my memory slips back—to speak to her about the translation she is doing for me. There is one point I forgot to make clear."

When the door had closed behind his ambling timelessness Reverend Mother turned on Sister Clare a face distorted by exasperation. Her eyes were bright like daggers.

"It seems to me that *all* men are utterly irresponsible, even Father Durham. To hear him speak, you would think it's all one to him if she goes on the streets."

Sister Clare did not answer. She was sitting with her head between her hands.

"Sister Clare!" said Reverend Mother sharply.

"Forgive me, Reverend Mother. I am afraid I am ill. May I go and see Sister Mildred? I didn't want to give in just now. I hoped it would pass off."

Reverend Mother rang the bell and crossed to Sister Clare.

"My dear, what is the matter? Tell me. You know I can't bear to see you ill. Ah, Sister Agnes! Please ask Sister Mildred to come down at once. Oh my dear! Your hands are like ice and your cheeks are burning. How blind of me not to see. What have I been thinking of?"

❖

There were always casualties during the rigours of Lent. Influenza
crept in from the outside world, and the fastings and vigils exposed
the weaker sisters to illness. Though the weather was less bitter than
at the beginning, the hours in the unheated Chapel were longer. The
feet of the kneelers, once they had turned to blocks of ice on the brick
floor, had no time to thaw before they were back there again. Sister
Margaret, who got well warmed up in the kitchen, was the one who
complained most about the Chapel. In its draughts her nose turned to
a rosy button on her pink face, above which her blue eyes stared out
into the cold like windowpanes reflecting the weather. Sister Sophia,
because of her age, had a special indulgence for Shetland underwear;
but she gave the impression of withstanding the cold chiefly by having no impetuosity to cool. Nor did she seem to require food, though
she ate Sister Margaret's whole-meal scones with gaiety. Sister Clare
was always delicate. She was like a filament, all brightness and no
reserves. She began Holy Week in bed with a severe quinsy, nursed
by Sister Mildred, who became twice herself when she had a real
patient.

❖

The bright and windy March weather flattened and pummelled the
growing world like an obstreperous schoolboy who cannot leave his
friends alone. Windows rattled, flues moaned, trees lurched sideways
and righted themselves, birds stiffened their wings to soar on the up-
currents and dived again for fun. The daffodils turned their backs to
the wind, holding their hats. Because the sun was never very high,
everything reflected it at an easy eye level. The earth hid her rising
tenderness, her warm spring blood, under a diamond glitter. Zephy
saw all this through the windows, adding to it in imagination the encircling sea with spray like needles, but she scarcely went out,
even in her brief free time. For the moment, she knew that Reverend
Mother was right. The Garden of Eden was lost. She was an exile,
full of fears. The only refuge open to her was the convent.

When she tried to imagine her future there, her instincts set up a
clamour like birds when an owl is among them. She could not reason
because the balance of love and aversion was too close. Every thought
of staying, after a moment of sweet relief, came face to face with the
Gorgon's head of self-perjury. She trembled like a rabbit round whom
the standing corn is being cut. It crouches in the hope of being over-

looked, but ultimately it must be exposed. She stayed indoors, doing what she had to do with indifference, as people do in a house where they are waiting for someone to die. Even the calves she had only visited once. The new bailiff had been there, a big man neither young nor old, standing lean-hipped with his thumbs in his waistcoat armholes. On meeting his amiable, amused eyes, she had taken fright and hurried away, puzzled to find herself so shy.

Unknown to herself, she had now reached a state of very high tension, but this did not remain unnoticed by other people. She was out of breath when she spoke, and did not easily take in what was said to her. Sister Agnes, wondering during the Gospel why her chair tickled her, noticed that it was touching Zephy's chair and that she was quivering like a motor. The ordered rituals of Holy Week, in contrast with her unhappy emotional tangle, she entered into as it were with the personal guarantee of Father Durham, and with a degree of sensibility and imagination that exceeded her previous capacity. Sometimes she could watch her mind selecting out of a store of vivid and tumultuous symbols the associations that were most evocative; reflecting this on to that, combining a whole range of feelings in one sheaf, nameless but known for future reference; or startled by the intrusion of metaphors that came in from outside like meteorites.

The same curious stimulation and contact with a mind she did not recognise as her own pursued her in dreams, most of which were now staged in the Chapel. She dreamt, for instance, that she was praying ardently in the Chapel about something of tremendous but unspecified importance, when Reverend Mother came quietly in with a rustle of robes and an unusual, soft, dragging sound. This was caused by a fowling net which she carried, and which she now began to spread over all the chairs to catch a little brown bird which she would drive into it. But she, Zephy, had taken refuge in the curtained alcove near the west door where the brushes and pails were kept. From there, she saw Reverend Mother moving down the Chapel, which had become a shippen. Now and again, she stood quite still, like a cat listening. Beside the last unexamined corner she spread her skirt out wide and approached, bending as Sam had once done before, with a trapper's grotesque action. This was so dreadful to see that Zephy flew out. Reverend Mother then seized the rope and tolled the bell, while the sisters, dressed—she knew it—for an execution, filed in. Zephy beat her wings against the east end, but could not hold a flight that did not advance. She gradually fluttered downwards. Reverend Mother now came forward holding a large book, as boys at school had held them for killing flies. Sister Mildred followed her with a dustpan and brush. The bell was like a tocsin.

She woke, still terrified, and realised it was ringing for the midnight offices. Sitting up, grasping the bedclothes which had been, she supposed, both her wings and the fowler's net, she was ashamed of her dream. It was hateful, wicked, and vulgar. Father Durham had said that the Devil loved disguises. That would be easiest of all in dreams. She tried to compose her mind. She got out of bed and knelt at her *prie-dieu,* opening the book at the psalm they would now be saying in Chapel.

"Open me the gates of righteousness that I may go into them . . ." was the verse she chose as the proper antidote to her dream. She took the crucifix down off the wall and laid it beside her pillow as she prepared to sleep again.

Almost at once she was back in the Chapel. She examined it dubiously lest it should be the same dream repeated, but everything seemed this time to be all right. . . . It was Christmas. The Crib was there and a real cow lay munching beside it. Sister Veronica must have arranged that. This was not the shippen but really the Chapel. It was as full of birds as any wood and their singing was an ecstasy. They fluttered up and down like angels. All the sisters were smiling. Everything was all right—just. She must be very careful. She was coming to be clothed. Lady Penhellion was there, ultrareal, spotlighted, and looking at her with amusement. She then saw with shame that, instead of a spotless shift, she was wearing Bess's grubby pink-flannel nightdress. The nuns gave no sign of noticing, but Lady Penhellion laughed woundingly and pointed to the bundle which all this time Zephy had been carrying, presuming it to be the habit she was to be clothed in. "It's *Samson,*" she said in her carrying contralto, and laughed again. The bundle weighed like a baby, and now was heaved by movement from within. Zephy turned back a fold, and uncovered a snake's head pushing out, questing and evil. She dropped it, screaming as if she could never stop.

Sister Mildred was holding her hands.

"Hush, hush! Zephy! You are making the most dreadful noise. You will disturb Sister Clare. She has just fallen into the most lovely sleep. There. Are you properly awake? I don't like these dreams of yours. What do you think causes them? Is it your liver? Perhaps you miss the outdoor exercise? No one who has attended Compline ought to have bad dreams."

As she spoke, she saw the crucifix beside the pillow.

"I see," she said, with one of her uncanny flashes of insight, "the dreams are as bad as that. Have you talked to Reverend Mother about them? Are you sure there isn't something you haven't confessed?"

Zephy shook her head wearily.

"I've confessed and confessed, but it won't come right. Who thinks of such awful dreams? I'm sure it's not me. Oh dear, I'm so tired. Is it time to get up?"

"Not yet. You have another hour. I'll bring you some hot milk. I got it for Sister Clare, but she's asleep and doesn't need it. Then you can settle off again. I'll come and go between you and Sister Clare, and I'll wake you up in plenty of time. Don't worry. It's only dreams, not real things."

"I wish I could be sure," said Zephy.

Sister Mildred went away thoughtful. Reverend Mother had the defects of her great qualities. She had too much personality. If she didn't take to someone, she frightened them off without meaning to. It was not the first time Sister Mildred had seen it happen.

❖

Cards were sent out for Easter as for Christmas. This was a custom Zephy had never heard of. This time she had no money, for though Sister Clare had made her keep her employment card, since she was not yet one of the community, she did not take her wages, but paid them back into the convent account. She had therefore now to ask Reverend Mother for the allotted two cards and two stamps. She sent one to Dr. Masters, towards whom she was ever grateful and loving. After long hesitation, she sent one also to her mother, who would see no point in it, but Zephy had never answered her letter and thought, with double guilt, that an Easter card would answer it while underlining that they had no common meeting ground. For this, afterwards, she felt not merely guilt but remorse. She had become like Reverend Mother, or at least tarred with the same brush.

❖

Sister Faith was always very anxious when she had to wash such special "articles," as she called them, as the fair linen for Easter.

"I sweat till they are safely done," she told Zephy, between whom and herself she felt no barrier. Zephy had not been in the laundry before. She had just been sent down by Sister Mildred with a towel that had been overlooked. She stood a moment watching Sister Faith ironing lace with fearful care. She sighed as the last fold-over was successfully done.

"Isn't it lovely?" said Zephy. "You do it beautifully. I wish I could learn." But she dared not stay. "Good-bye, Sister Faith. I'd love to stay and watch, but I must go. Don't worry. They will look wonderful."

Sister Monica and her fortunate helpers had brought in, on the preceding night, baths full of daffodils, jonquils, and hyacinths, ready to decorate the Altar of Repose, which they did before Prime on Maundy Thursday. The end of Holy Week, as so often happens, brought an early heat wave, too sudden, exhausting to bodies unprepared for it, and trying to tempers. But in the early morning it was fresh. Too much heat was difficult to imagine. When Sister Monica had finished coming and going and the mess was roughly cleared up, Zephy was standing with her pail ready to scrub the covered passage leading to the Chapel. Just before she began, Sister Pauline, hurrying past to deliver to Sister Anne the clean altar clothes over which Sister Faith had sweated with anxiety, now loosely wrapped in tissue paper, slipped on a stray daffodil leaf and caught the surface of her package on a door latch. There was a sound of tearing.

"Heavens!" she said. "I nearly broke my neck."

She put her hand over her mouth as if to push the words back into it, for she had broken the silence. Zephy pointed to the disturbed wrappings, but Sister Pauline's shrug indicated, "Only the paper. It's my ankle that matters," and she went hobbling off into the Chapel.

❈

Zephy had never been to a theatre or seen a pageant or a procession. In this respect, as in so many others, she came to Maundy Thursday with a mediaeval outlook, the ritual affecting her as profoundly as the originators intended. The commemoration of, and actual participation in, the Last Supper; the procession to the glorious Altar of Repose, where for the first time she prostrated herself; the stripping of the High Altar; and lastly, at Tenebrae, the putting out of all the lights until only one was left, to symbolise the One Light of the World, and that too extinguished—these were not obscure rituals that had to be explained, but her own emotions, wonderfully embodied. The sisters, and Zephy also, had in turns kept two-hour vigils before the Altar of Repose during the day, kneeling upright in the hot afternoon with the added heat of the banks of candles and the headachy scent of flowers. All kept vigil there during the Holy Hour, and remained in the Chapel thereafter until it was time for Sister Anne to prepare it for the Good Friday services.

Still fasting, throughout a still more blazing day, the community continued to celebrate its rituals, each more emotionally exacting than the last: the Veneration of the Cross; the procession from the Altar of Repose to the High Altar, stripped like a scaffold; the stark Mass, and the Devotion of Three Hours to the culmination at three in the afternoon. Faintness was in itself an emotion, marking this off from any other day. By the end all other emotions were exhausted except that of a participated ordeal. Only Sister Clare had been absent, alone on her sickbed.

Hot-cross buns were distributed to the fasting when they came out of Chapel. Zephy could hardly keep her schoolgirl teeth out of hers long enough for decency. She and Sister Bridget moved off across the garden looking for coolness and shade after the stuffiness of the Chapel. They sat down on a garden seat under the wall of the house, and, wordless after all they had gone through, began to eat, too tired to move again unless driven.

The seat happened to be underneath the window of Sister Clare's room, which like every other was wide open. Inside they heard Reverend Mother's voice.

"How are you, my dear? Has Sister Mildred not been up yet with your gruel? I told her to see to you first of all."

"Thank you, Reverend Mother. She will be bringing it. But what about you? Have you had anything yourself?"

"Not yet. I wanted to see you first. We missed you."

"It has been dreadful to be alone here away from you all. I could see it all in my mind, but it is not the same. Anyway, Reverend Mother, I am really quite all right again, so I won't have to miss Easter."

"There is no question of your getting up for Easter. The doctor and Sister Mildred are agreed about that."

"But Reverend Mother, I *must*. I can't miss Easter Sunday. I am quite all right again now, really I am."

"I am sorry, my dear. I must forbid it. I am still blaming myself for Sister Veronica's death, although I know it was not anybody's fault. She was hopelessly obstinate—but one loved her for being it. She died for her obstinacy, and one loved her for that too. This was the first Good Friday without her. And without you too, my two first. I thought of you both. I cannot take any risks with you, my dear. Once for all, *no*."

"But it's quite different. I haven't a weak heart—only a sore throat, and that's cured. I must, *please*, go on Sunday. I must be at Zephy's first Easter." Sister Clare's voice had the brittle-tempered unreasonableness of convalescence.

Reverend Mother's reply was on a sharper note still.

"First it's Easter Communion and then it's Zephy, as you all persist in calling her; perhaps with more prescience than I had." It was as if a wind suddenly rose in the room, Pentecost in reverse. "What can that little country baggage add to your Easter Communion?"

"How dare you speak like that, Reverend Mother? She is one of us."

"One of us! Hah, she has a long way to go before she becomes that."

"If she doesn't, it will be your doing. You try to break her. You are a spiritual tyrant. You always were."

"Sister Clare, hold your tongue."

"I won't hold my tongue. I've known you a long time. I know you better than anyone. You think you're St. Peter holding the keys, and you like shutting people out. *You like it*—especially when you are jealous."

For a moment there were two voices in indistinguishable passion, and then the window sash was slammed down.

Zephy was as white as those muslin anemones that open among the scarlets and purples.

"Holy Mother of God, pray for us!" said Sister Bridget. "When those two quarrel they really show you how to do it! We all know Reverend Mother's got a temper like the Devil, sit on it how she will. But you'd never think Sister Clare would let fly like that. Mercy! What a tongue! Little they guess we heard it all. It's a fine stern face Reverend Mother will be wearing at supper."

But Zephy had left her.

❖

There were several absentees at supper. Sister Sophia was at the head of the table. Rumour ran that Reverend Mother had fainted in her room and was resting. Sister Clare had had a relapse, and Sister Mildred was with her. This was at the head of the hierarchy. At the bottom, Zephy lay on her bed prone and sick. But they were all judged quite normal Good Friday casualties. The meal was silent.

The time of Compline had been advanced and the Office of Tenebrae added to it by anticipation, so that all could have an unbroken night. Reverend Mother was present in the Chapel, but the office was taken for her by Sister Sophia.

Holy Saturday was another brilliantly fine day. The atmosphere of the convent was relaxed and happy. Sister Monica and Sister Pauline were cutting flowers again; Sister Anne and Sister Winifred had the Chapel to prepare for the First Mass of Easter, at midnight. Zephy was back on her knees in the hall.

There was an early hitch in the proceedings. Sister Anne came to Reverend Mother's room in consternation, with the fair linen hanging over her arm. There was a seven-inch rip in the lace edging. She showed it to Zephy as she waited for an answer to her knock. It was impossible to mend it in time. The Altar for Easter, the apex of her year's care of it, would have to have a tear *hidden*. Sister Anne was shocked to the verge of fear.

She was not long with Reverend Mother, but was followed after a moment by Sister Faith, weeping openly.

"Tell her you didn't do it," said Zephy, catching at her hand.

The second interview was even shorter. Sister Faith was not weeping when she came out. The tears had dried and her face looked sizzled.

"I wasn't allowed to say anything. She said no one had handled it but me, and it was just stupid cowardice not to have shown it at once. I hate it here. I hate it," she repeated, as if surprised to hear her own voice saying it. "I wish I was at home with my own people."

"Why don't you go?"

"I can't. They would think it shameful. A runaway nun! It would be as much a disgrace to them as an escaped convict. They wouldn't understand. I should be as lonely there now as I am here. I don't care. I'll be dead someday. A mumbling old woman saying her prayers."

❁

Easter, for all its pomp and rejoicing, and in spite of Zephy's sincere preparation for it, meant when it came nothing at all to her. It went on over her head as unnoticed as the play of aeroplanes over someone who is burying her love. She tried hard during Mass to drag a prayer out of her stupor, but all her thoughts were engaged in the ordeal that was before her. Easter Monday was to be her zero hour.

However, on Easter Monday Reverend Mother was away attending a conference called by the Bishop. It was a long day. As far as possible it had been arranged as a rest for the sisters, who sat in the garden talking gaily together or closing their eyes against the brightness of the sky. Zephy sat amongst these latter, silent as they, her thoughts unguessed. Nor did any of them, relaxed as all living bodies should be when resting in the sun, notice that one among them was unmoving and solitary.

Persephone had to perform the impossible, the unthinkable. She presented herself on Tuesday morning at Reverend Mother's room.

Reverend Mother sat at her desk, in poise and panoply, composed as always; but ironically, on this occasion when Persephone longed for distance, she was more approachable than ever before. She smiled a welcome.

"Come in, my little postulant. What is it you want to see me about?"

Persephone went into action. "Reverend Mother, I cannot be clothed."

Reverend Mother's face went to pieces and reassembled itself into something harder.

"That is not a decision for you to take like that from one day to the next without discussion or advice. If you have difficulties you should tell me."

Zephy stood silent.

"Have you talked to Father Cuthbert, at least? When you made your Easter confession?"

She shook her head.

"Come now, Josephine. This is a very serious matter and you are not a child to stand there dumb. Tell me why you cannot be clothed."

Zephy searched for something that was sayable. The face of Sister Faith presented itself to her mind, and being, in the oppressive silence that waited to be broken, unable to choose her words, she spoke crudely.

"I don't approve of things that are done here."

Reverend Mother turned a dull crimson which her white face bands incorruptibly emphasised.

"Who are you," she blazed, from the height of her august position, "to disapprove of what we do here—you, a worse than homeless vagabond whom we took in and sheltered? You were uncouth and we taught you manners. You were ignorant and we gave you all you know of culture. You were a pagan and we taught you true religion.

And now you do not approve! We have done everything for you. When you came you had not even any underclothes." Zephy's eyes came up and fixed her steadily for a moment with a look of enforced revaluation, then sank, not to be raised again in any contact with Reverend Mother.

"Do you know that it is a rule here that if any postulant decides she has no vocation she must leave *at once*? Have you thought of that? Where will you go? To the home you ran away from? It will be incomparably worse if you go back to that life after knowing this than if you had never been here. What will you do?"

"I will go back to Dr. Masters, and I will earn my living like any other girl."

"You may earn your living like some other girls if you cut yourself off from the means of grace. Josephine, I—implore you—" Reverend Mother made a supreme professional effort, but after many minutes they were where they had started, except that the sweat had broken out on Zephy's forehead. Reverend Mother even, as her last appeal, brought out—"I don't know how I am to tell Sister Clare. She is very fond of you." She did not guess that Zephy knew the measure of her self-abasement. But her penitence came too late.

"Promise me at least that you will not go home."

Zephy was silent. There had come unbidden to her memory the lighthearted tune that had accompanied her last day at home, that she had sung defiantly against her grandfather's scolding. What were the words? *Love is where you find it!*

"You are going away from God," said Reverend Mother finally, and Zephy answered, taking the words that came of themselves:

"God is where you find Him."

❖

When she had closed the door behind her and gone dizzily away to find and send down Sister Mildred, she brought out of her pocket a letter which had come that morning. It was from Dr. Masters, and she had kept it in reserve for a tonic when the worst was over.

Dear Persie,

I have got some news that you may find very unexpected. I am getting married on Easter Monday to a Canadian, Doctor Simpson, who has been over here six months. We are leaving immediately after for Canada. I am so glad you are staying on at St. Hilarion, especially since I shall not be here to look after you. I hope you

*will be very happy. I will write there later and give you my new
address.*

> *Your affectionate*
> *Nan Masters*

Sister Mildred came upstairs again looking grieved and horrified.
She told her that a ticket to Kendal would be provided for her tomorrow, with two pounds for emergencies, both of which she must
consider as debts to be repaid when she could. She was on no account to speak to any of the sisters about her decision to leave.

"But will they know I went of my own accord? They won't think I
was turned out?"

"They will know nothing at all."

"Could I possibly say good-bye to Sister Clare?"

"I am afraid not. But if you wish, after you have gone, I will tell
her you sent your love."

"Thank you, Sister Mildred."

As always, somehow the news was whispered round. Coming out of
supper, Sister Sophia fell out of line and came back to Zephy at the
end. She shook hands with her and said, "Good-bye, Persephone, I
wish you good luck," adding with her faint smile, "in the name of the
Lord." In the Common Room, Zephy felt herself shunned, if only out
of embarrassment, by all but a few. Sister Bridget was amused,
brightly watching from face to face, when she was sure of not being
watched herself. Sister Mildred was kind, like a wardress before an
execution. Sister Pauline, lacemaker, was repairing the fair linen that
she herself had torn. Zephy was already as good as gone, as far as she
was concerned. Zephy risked going up to Reverend Mother's chair
and asking if she might be excused this evening, at which every head
was bent down to its work. She remembered the evening when she
had talked about the dog Willi. Now she was bracketed with Lady
Penhellion in the sisters' minds. She was to sin for them, to be the
reason for their existence.

Reverend Mother said: "Yes, you may go. Good night, Josephine,"
with almost no change in her voice, and yet it was noticed.

"Good night, Sisters," said Zephy weakly.

She had not yet closed the door behind her when Reverend
Mother at the piano struck into the flowing notes of "Sanctify us by
thy goodness." It was quite deliberate, and as the music followed her
along the passage, for the first time in her ordeal Zephy wept.

She was to leave before Mass, so there were no more good-byes. Only Sister Faith contrived to emerge from the washhouse to give her a wet kiss. Sister Mildred saw her to the door and gave her her ticket; money, employment card, and sandwiches.

"If you get into difficulties, go to the Moral Welfare Officer. She'll perhaps be of more practical help than the priest. Try to be good. I'm glad you have got Dr. Masters."

With her bass bag in her hand Zephy walked alone through the park, past the newly milked Jerseys, who knew her as someone to take no notice of. As she reached the gate on the main road the Chapel bell began to ring.

PART III

Symington's Hospital

The convent had discarded Zephy. It was laid down in the rule, and when the momentary awkwardness was over, the life of security was resumed within. The pain of the closed door was enough to keep Zephy moving as far as the train. From the moment she sat down in her compartment the impetus was spent. For an hour or two she wrestled with a diminishing sense of necessity. There was no point in going to Kendal. There was no reason why she should get out at any one station more than another. At first the train stopped frequently, but she was resting after so great an effort. Then it ceased stopping at all and whirled across meaningless space. When it drew into a large station the guard came down the platform shouting instructions. He looked into her compartment and asked to see her ticket.

"You change here, miss," he said. "The next train on this side." She picked up her bass bag and put it on the seat beside her, but the guard had moved on and she still sat there. The station looked infinitely discouraging. Her train drew out again. For hours it rocked her in its degrading smell. She had a consciousness of acute tension and terror, outside her body, which seemed so passive and disconnected as to be almost part of the grimy plush upholstery on which it lay.

She was ultimately turned out by a ticket collector. This was not the train for Kendal. She should have changed. He put her out at Swindon, telling her all the changes she would now have to make. He assumed that the intention to get to Kendal would be strong enough to push her through feats of endurance. He helpfully gave her into the hands of a porter who set her off unresisting on the next stage of the imaginary journey, but after that she was lost.

She found herself sitting in a large station waiting room on a bench upholstered in American cloth. People came in and out all the time. The door never stopped swinging. It was very exhausting.

"Are you waiting for someone, ducks?" said the attendant. Zephy shook her head.

An hour later she came again. "Are you all right, ducks? Don't you want some tea?" Zephy had not moved. She tried to answer, but the stammer was too difficult. Her predicament was something words could not convey. She gave it up and wept for weariness. The woman was due to go off duty at six, and as she handed over to her successor she pointed Zephy out to her.

"Been there four hours. Something wrong." She tapped her forehead.

"Is there?" said the much brisker newcomer. "Then I'll get the policewoman. I'm not being left here with a loony."

The policewoman came in with her own version of a constable's portentous roll. She asked for Zephy's ticket and put it in her pocketbook. She asked for Zephy's handbag. She had none. That put her at the very bottom of the human scale. She ransacked the bass bag, sorting out its contents. To her it represented nothing but destitution. No incense, no whispers of prayer shook out of the faded clothes. She found the National Insurance card.

"Percyfown Stalker. Is that you?"

The stammering began again.

"Okay. Stay where you are." She vanished, to return shortly with a police doctor. Zephy was whisked away like a corpse, a drunk, or a foundling.

The attendant automatically dusted the bench where she had sat, and went back to her inner sanctum, where pennies need not always be put in the slot. Some could drop into her pocket.

❖

If there was any one thing that frightened Persephone more than another it was the thought of the specialist into whose judgment she was to be committed. He had at his command unknown powers and procedures which she feared as much as whipping, red-hot pokers, or gouging out. He might say there was nothing the matter. SHAMMING! He might condemn her as lost, to be shut up for ever. When she had, by coaxing and superior force, been inserted into the specialist's room and stood there like Joan of Arc, it was all so easy as to be a complete anticlimax. He asked her questions far from any relevance to her troubles, so that even her stammer was found not to be there. Her name? Her age? Type of farm work? Did she like it? Why had she left?

"It was a convent," was all Zephy could muster, but it seemed sufficient. Did she leave of her own choice? Good. After that he asked her to draw a straight line, to look at his pencil, to raise her arms to shoulder height, to twiddle her toes. "Any pains? Your chest? I'd better examine that. Nothing wrong there. Thank you. That is all I want of you for the present. We'll start by giving you a long rest in bed. Does that seem to you a good idea? Then I'll see you again."

What unimaginable mercy was this bed that was to be hers! And yet she felt as anxious as a dog on the table in the vet's surgery. Everything she had was taken from her, even her nail file and hairpins. She sat up in bed weeping, but the sister soon came with some capsules, and confused oblivion received her.

❖

While Persephone was sleeping out her drugged eternity enquiries were made. She was traced to St. Hilarion and to her home. The Mother Superior and Sister Mildred sent in their account of her, Sister Mildred stressing that in spite of her depressed condition she had not lost faith, and then, her medical training coming uppermost, mentioning the muttering of Ave Marias as she scrubbed. Reverend Mother had added that she had found Persephone histrionic and resentful of discipline. She stressed the instability of her background. Bess had written humbly asking if her daughter was going to be shut up and if she could write to her.

❖

It was in real time a fortnight before Persephone, with the lessening of the opiates, surfaced enough to take in a general idea of her surroundings. It was a gradual process. Some things that she had thought were dreams persisted into reality. On the bed next to hers a heavy middle-aged woman was lying, fully dressed, in an attitude of sultry, sensual brooding that, though not offering anything a nurse could forbid or correct, was yet unfit to be seen. Opposite was an old granny sitting with idle hands and scalded eyes weeping silently. Another patient sat in front of a sheet of paper, pencil in hand. But nothing was ever written day after day. The inmates did not mix with each other. Each was sunk in isolated misery.

The nurses were breezy and efficient. Though they moved as quickly and quietly as nuns, it was with an odd wag of their haunches as they walked, as if the stiff apron, with its belt and pockets and fountain pen and scissors, was a façade behind which moved somebody quite different and much more rakish. Their patience, their kindness and optimism seemed also put on with the uniform—not less hypnotic for that, but who was there when the uniform was taken off? One never wonders that about nuns. Their habit is an expression of their ultimate selves.

Persephone was a neutral creature when she lay in bed and was not disturbed. The difficulty began when anything was asked of her. The first and often the only result of any effort was a wet trickle down her face. She could not be told to dress and left to it. There was neither energy nor desire sufficient to get her arms into a dressing gown or her feet into shoes. If she got as far as sitting on the edge of the bed, that bankrupted her and she stayed there. The pain in her chest and an obscure and fearful helplessness were the only symptoms she was aware of. She did not see the bland and trivial Bishop again. No, not the Bishop. That was somewhere else. The specialist. After her fortnight's sleep she saw a different man, Dr. Richards.

The doctors in Symington's Hospital fell roughly into two categories. There were those who looked as if they were, or had been, or might at any moment become, patients; and on the other hand those who had achieved an ironclad normality established beyond any possibility of lapsing, arid and superior. The former were naturally enough preferred by the patients. At the worst they were equals, at the best understanding. The second group inspired deep mistrust. They knew and dealt with personalities as impersonally as if they were pruning shrubs, setting watches, or neutralising acids.

Dr. Richards was outstandingly of the first category. He was slightly deformed, with fine dark eyes and the overlarge, overfull lips that often go with imagination. When Persephone was shown into his bleak consulting room she walked into a haven of sympathy. And yet haven is the wrong word, for it was a tragic world that he inhabited. Like Father Durham he had come through to the far side of human indignation, but had lost all joy on the way. His was the melancholy of a poet debunking poetry. To this sad citadel she was invited.

On the first visit there was little beyond kind conversational enquiries and some very simple mental arithmetic, which however she could not do. On the second they got down to work. His voice was sleepy but trustworthy, helping to allay her great fear. All his movements had the softness, the studied lack of suddenness, that Zephy associated with vets and the owner of the pet shop in Kendal—the hand that was insinuated to catch a goldfish, or closed over the wings of a bird. He gave her a tray with a heap of small coloured blocks and invited her, gently but without a smile, to make a pattern. She was very slow, agitated by a conviction that vital significance lay in this est, such as is attached to ordinary things in dreams. On this pattern performed under his sombre eyes everything hung. She forced her fingers to pick up the sterile but threatening cubes. She made a long cross from side to side.

"That's all right," he said. "Now we'll do something easier. I am going to show you some photographs, and all you have to do is to say which people you like and which you don't like. Just as if you were sitting in a train looking at the people opposite."

At the words "people you like" Zephy had a clear vision of Sister Clare's smile and happy tilted eyes. She held out her hand for the first photograph as if, being significant, it must be of her. She longed to see it, knowing she was childish and that her logic was slipping. When she saw the face she was given she put her hand over her mouth with a cry.

"Why do you cry out?" asked Dr. Richards casually, making marks in a sort of diagram on his desk.

"I didn't expect anything so horrid."

"Here's a different one then."

Now she was cautious, forcing herself to take them one by one, and each was an abomination, nightmare faces, cumulatively threatening.

"What's the matter? They are just people. Suppose one of them had to take you home after a party, which would you choose?"

"None. They are all awful. I would rather be alone. They scare me."

"Suppose you were lost and had to ask the way?"

"I wouldn't ask any of those."

"Not even this woman?" He pushed a card to her without even looking up.

Zephy looked again at the classically handsome secretary or house-keeper, the bend of whose head was fixed so that the eyes looked out sideways, as if from a great distance inside, leaving the rest of her face as a mask, not used for expression, hardly even for speech, and immo-bile in the sense of something infinitely treacherous and steadily aimed.

"No. No."

"Is she the worst then?"

"They are all hateful. Why do you show me such frightening things?"

"Don't think about them any more. That's all for today."

However, two days later she was given another set of faces, with the same result. To take the taste away, ink-blot patterns were shown her, such as school children make by folding paper along the line of a wet signature. These were less alarming, almost fun. What were they like? Dr. Richards even smiled at her. "Why, butterflies, bats—" But it was not all so easy. "Two servers genuflecting at Mass, but they are very queer. A kind of palace, not really like a church; I don't like the door."

"Go on."

"A bullock's skull. A sheepskin rug."

"Why do you frown at those? Don't you like sheepskin rugs?"

"Yes, I suppose so. Mums had one by her bed. I thought it was rather a horrid present. I don't like things being killed."

"And why is this not like a church?"

"I don't like the door."

❖

The peculiar tests to which she was submitted appeared to Zephy quite pointless. At first she was relieved that effort and decision were allowed to slide in a stream of apparent nonsense. Later, when she was able to take frightened stock of what went on round her, she made one more of a crowd in limbo, all asking why they took such odd tests, what the results had been, what was supposed to be wrong with them, how long they would be there, and, hidden in their innermost fear, the question whether they would ever be let out. Less hidden, more constantly pressing, was the fear of treatment, that unknown torture house of ingenuities to the application of which they had signed themselves away in advance. Resistance to treatment was liable to downgrade them and cause a transfer to Block B. Beyond that was Block C, a symbol too terrifying to have any meaning more explicit than the sweat that broke out at the thought of it. Nothing was ever explained. Crude rumours and horrific guesses were passed by the patients to each other as elementary knowledge and the formidable labels of the different treatments were on everybody's lips.

In the corridors that Zephy traversed to the different doctors' consulting rooms, she saw men in doubtfully clean white overalls like children's rompers, fat men who joked with each other, who looked completely irresponsible, who were neither doctors nor patients nor male nurses; who looked like nothing so much as back-room executioners. What exactly did these clowns do? In Renaissance pictures of martyrdoms there were always men like these among the executioners. From the ward patients were daily wheeled out under an anaesthetic and brought back in a far worse condition.

Dr. Richards had now moved Persephone to a ward where all the inmates were sufficiently alike in the degree of their illness to be companionable.

Sympathy was the first of her faculties to return. She suffered for all the others, the more so as she herself was let off lightly. None of the alarming physical treatments were applied to her, and whereas she was grateful for somewhere merely to be, the others were all torn out of a normal life, separated from husband or small children or from a career that was going to ruin in their absence. These all talked as women will, pouring out their life history and difficulties to each other and explaining away why they were there. Zephy would have talked if she could, both to show friendliness by repaying confidence with confidence, and also, if she could, to feel less peculiar. It was known from her stammering answers that she had no father and an unkind grandfather—anyone could understand that—and also that she had left a convent. Nobody had the verbal currency to exchange on that subject. A convent! Fancy that.

Characteristic ways of walking distinguished the patients—a dejected shuffle was the norm. There was also the implacably obstinate stride; the uncertain balance, one hand feeling for the rail of the bed; or the action of an anxious hen, each foot in turn lifted too high and held a moment in air while the hands were tightly clasped and the head poked forward rhythmically with each advance. Among these Zephy's gliding ways and her habit of standing to attention when spoken to like a child about to recite seemed to the others truly peculiar. And it was an odd fact that having left the convent she felt compelled to be even more conventual in her behaviour than when she was in it.

Confusion reigned in her head, as if her mind were a honeycomb in which the cell divisions had been damaged and the honey was seeping uncontrolled. The faculty of surprise had left her. She found she was to be subjected to a new form of confession, and that the confessor appointed to her was Dr. Evelyn Fisher. She was introduced into a small white room containing a couch on which the patient was installed, and a large desk, where the doctor sat facing her with her back to the window. This was net-curtained to hide the soulless view into a light well.

Dr. Evelyn Fisher was a woman with a fine-drawn, severely boned

131

face and a mouth of delicate passion. She should have been beautiful but had never humanly achieved it. She was marred by an aggressive integrity that had run amok on personal idiosyncrasies too small for such a charge. Her intellectual eyes were ill set and had no direct outward glance. They had, when she was a child, been tender and confiding, but now had a resentful glitter. Looking at her one was uncertain whether the creases on her forehead were caused by the weight of her abundant screwed-up hair dragging her scalp backward, against which the muscles of her eyebrows battled through the day, or whether her eyebrows had shot up, accordion-pleating her forehead, in the first surprise of finding how bitter life was, and were fixed there. She wore these signs of stress with arrogance. She knew that her contacts with the outer world were unrewarding. She had found no other outlet for emotion but belief. She believed that she and her school of thought were right, and that all variants and other systems were wrong. Into this channel flowed the turbulence of her disappointed life. She was the daughter of an eminent scientist and as a child had absorbed from him the doctrine that materialism was a truth demanding all one's powers, for the saving of course of mankind; that atheism was the only adult belief possible and required courage to the uttermost. The need of courage was perhaps true in some aspects when her father was young, but now she was riding the flood tide of accepted materialism and her passion was left useless on her hands. Her courage now was only required to face the hateful world of her choice. That, and an unhappiness equal to their own, was what she had to offer her patients.

❖

"Now, Persephone," she began mechanically like a recitation (and while she spoke, as if to make sure the pace did not degenerate into a gabble, her fingers, which would have been lovely if they were not rigid, pushed the brooch that fastened her collar to left and right to the extent of its pin, like a metronome), "I want you to try to relax. You are simply to talk to me for as long as you can. Don't try to pick out what you think is important. If you have ever tried to make a speech in public you will know that it is very hard to make the important things spin out for even five minutes. We have forty minutes allowed us, and I want you to go on as long as you can. The important thing is to make no effort of it. Don't pick and choose. Say what comes into your head. I shan't find that you are either sillier or more shocking than other people. I see from your papers here that you have run away twice. That's as good a starting point as any. Begin then with your home, how many people were in the house, how they got on with each other and all about it. Begin." She looked at her watch.

When in later years Persephone tried to recall these sessions, she found that in memory they were much telescoped. Although they were in fact many and wearisome, filling long months, she could recover the impression of only two or three. What she herself had said was vague and irrecoverable. The few comments of the doctor were expanded almost to a continuous lecture, amplified by her own reactions to them, which she came to think of as things the doctor had said concentrated to sledge-hammer force. It is as she remembered them that they are reported, though in her memory there were also periods of apparently infinite duration when she could think of nothing that would make words. Often she was reduced to remarks like "These walls are dead" or personal remarks about Dr. Fisher, always there before her eyes. "Your fingers are like lizard's feet when you press them back." "Your hair is screwed up till it hurts me." "Somehow your face just couldn't be in a convent, but Dr. Richards is like a renegade priest."

"Come now," said Dr. Fisher on this first visit, "make a start. Where did you live?"

The word "Westmorland" proved enough. Persie's thoughts wandered on familiar paths, always away from the farm. But while she tried to describe the woods and riverside of the North it often happened that she switched to the headlands and tossing salt breakers of Cornwall, and the word *"vivificantem"* would slip in out of the liturgies of St. Hilarion. The soliloquy was halting and muddled, without beginning or end, and charged with distress.

Dr. Fisher listened, fountain pen in hand. She rubbed the permanent puckers over her eyebrow with the end of the pen. Finally when Zephy was stuck for the name of a wild flower that grew in a certain field, and was getting into a state of anxiety because she could not remember it, Dr. Fisher interrupted, not unkindly.

"I'm sure you always got the nature prize at school. Or was all this wandering done in school time? Were you playing truant?" The fountain pen was lifted hopefully again.

"No, I went in the holidays and on Sundays, or in the early morning, or in the middle of the night."

"Do you mean you were sleepwalking? No. Well, was it at all like sleepwalking? Did you know where you were?"

"Oh yes. To the inch almost."

Still the fountain pen hovered.

"Well then, you were not escaping from school. What were you escaping from?"

How could Zephy, poor flustered underdog, explain that it had not been escaping from but running to? Though now in retrospect she was escaping from things that couldn't be said and therefore was caught on the wrong foot.

"It's just that I am like that," she said. "It's quite natural. I'm that kind of person."

"You must see that all this roving about was pure escapism. You were a child, I know, but what you chose to do was solitary and entirely useless, simply an alternative to doing anything or meeting anybody. It was neither learning nor playing, nor earning, nor making anything. It was no good to you or to anyone else. It was also eccentric. Now what were you escaping from? I am not talking about the convent. I gather you ran away from that too. It seems quite an established technique with you. But considering the unnatural life there it hardly needs explaining."

"It was a lovely place. I was terribly happy there."

"But you ran away from it all the same."

Zephy remembered certain conversations with Reverend Mother that had been very similar to this.

"Yes, Reverend Mother."

Dr. Fisher made a quick annotation in one of the columns of her ledger.

"You are not in the convent now. Tell me about your home. Your grandfather, now. Little girls are often their grandfather's darling. Did he spoil you badly?"

The unreality of the conversation made the effort to speak almost too great. Zephy pressed her hands to her forehead. She began about her grandfather. He was dirty and bad-tempered. He was often drunk. He was miserly and allowed her mother hardly any money. His animals were neglected, he worked lame horses, mated the bitch with a good dog and then destroyed her and kept the puppies. He used cruel traps and forgot to visit them. Sometimes a rabbit cried so terribly in the night that she got out through her window and went to let it out. It was hard to find them in the dark with only the screaming to guide you, and afterwards she lay shaking in bed. He was always horrid to her mother. He spat on the floor.

"I see. You feared your grandfather and resented him."

"No. I wasn't afraid of him. He didn't count. I was sorry for the animals, but he didn't seem to have anything to do with me. He was hardly human."

"But he was your grandfather all the same."

"It seemed too far away to matter. There was Mums and her mother in between. And perhaps he wasn't even Mums' father."

"I see." At last the fountain pen was writing. "Your papers give your mother as unmarried. Have you any reason to suppose your grandmother's life was irregular?"

"No, but anything would be better than Grandfather." As she said it Zephy thought of Sam, and the sweat poured off her.

"Have you ever thought there was any mystery about your birth?"

"Yes, there was, in a way."

Dr. Fisher was too busy writing in her clear positive hand to look up.

"Mums never told me his name, but he was a lord."

"Did you ever wonder if he was somebody really important—the King, for instance?"

Zephy under other circumstances would have laughed, but now she was furious. She felt she was being sneered at, and things she had never thought were being written down about her. She was tired to death, and this was all bullying and nonsense.

"What makes you think your mother was telling the truth?"

How could she acknowledge that it was her own nature, so different in every way, that sufficiently proved it? She truly was of other stock and could not fail to know it. But proof!

"Mums had some of his things."

"Go on. Describe them to me."

"She had a china box with a picture on the lid of shells and sea-weed, which he kept his studs in."

Dr. Fisher did not laugh, but, scornful in spite of herself, with only an undertone of pity, she commented: "An empty shaving-soap container, I expect. That doesn't prove much. Are you sure your mother was not making it up? She wouldn't be the first girl to get into trouble and try to make it sound more romantic than it was. It's only natural."

"She wasn't making it up. And she told me to have nothing to do with gentlemen, because my father shot himself."

Dr. Fisher, when she took up her pen to write, did so as if something satisfactory to her had just been proved. She was making a case.

"During the time that you lived at home, did your mother seem to have men friends?"

Zephy was sick, and the interview was ended. Dr. Fisher rang for the nurse, and sat on at her desk, carefully ruling parallel lines under the end of her paragraph.

❖

The Ward Sister had to be sent for to march Zephy in to her next interview two days later. Up to the very door she protested that she could not go in, she was going to be sick.

"Dr. Fisher will know what to do if you are. She is used to it. In you go!"

"I am sorry to have upset you last time, Persephone, but these are questions that have to be asked. I take it that you have answered in the affirmative. Your mother had men friends. Now try to tell me about your mother. What is the earliest thing you can remember?"

"Being comforted when I thought Sam was going to kill his baby. Sam was the s-slaughterer."

"Go on about Sam. Did you see much of him?"

"As little as I could, but he lived quite near. He was always about."

"Did you see much of him when you were a child? Tell me what you can remember."

"I always knew when he was there because of his great loud laugh, so I kept away. He had a red face and rough black bristles and a smell that I thought came from always killing things. And he was so grinning and jolly when he had no right to be, and always made himself at home in other people's houses."

"Do you mean specially yours?"

"Yes. I hated him. Grandfather didn't seem to mind him at all. I suppose they had killing things in common. But I never could understand why Mums—" Zephy stopped, a lurid spotlight playing back on her childhood's memories.

"I see." Dr. Fisher saw with finality. "Go on. What is it you can't say? Was he your mother's lover?"

Zephy's nod was no more than the movement of the head when one swallows.

"Come, there's nothing to be so upset about in that. It's perfectly natural. She had no husband. I suppose the convent stuffed you up with ideas of chastity."

Zephy seemed to herself to have spent a lifetime in never being able to put across the simple truth. She had needed no one to give her ideas of chastity. They had come of themselves.

"It is a fundamental law of nature and the most natural thing in the world for male and female to come together. It must happen and it does happen, and it has a very bad effect on people indeed if it doesn't happen. Every adult person knows that. Young girls, of course, such as you were at the time, have an equally natural squeamishness—we presume it to be a biological phase necessary to preserve them from too early mating. You should be adult now. What is so disgusting about your mother being simply normal? Are you jealous, like tiny children? Did it take her affection away from you?"

"He is a disgusting person. He is too disgusting. My father was a gentleman. How *could* she?"

"It doesn't concern you how she could. Perhaps it was just because your father was a gentleman. I think you said he shot himself. That must have been very humiliating for her. Perhaps when she came, miserable, home to the farm Sam was the only person who was kind to her. Perhaps she was comfortable with him because they understood each other and he didn't ask more of her than she could be."

Zephy remembered her mother's confidence on that last Sunday at home, and acknowledged that there was possible meaning in this. She remembered also her own reaction of love and honour towards Bess at the time.

"She should have been faithful to my father."

"Stuff and nonsense. Romantic rubbish. It may often be sensible and sometimes heroic to be constant to the living, but to be constant to the dead is unreal and without any purpose at all. Besides which there is, you know, nothing to prove that Sam was not your father. Your mother may have been very constant."

Zephy was like a chattering monkey with rage.

"That seems to make you very angry. But nobody can choose her own father, you know. Calm down now. Begin again at the beginning. You were saying he was always about the place. Just see how much you can remember. Any *particular* incident when you were a child."

"He can't have been my father because he made—because he tried —with me."

"My dear child! You are very ignorant. He was that kind of man. Lots of my patients are women whose fathers molested them, and lots of Dr. Richards' are the fathers who can't help doing it. It's quite ordinary, but in that case you were right to go away."

If Zephy in the convent had found confession and the constant assumption of guilt to be burdensome, this new form of confession where all values were systematically undone and the soul as it were unharnessed from its armour and left bare was infinitely more painful. The headaches and trembling and the bolting of her heart after these sessions were the most panic-bearing experience she had ever known. What subhuman thing would she be if they went on like this? It even happened during some of the later sessions that, unable to go over her childhood's experiences any longer because she felt with repugnance the gradual building up of Dr. Fisher's ideas in her, she broke into passionate repetitions of "Suffer me not to be separated from Thee" and wept bitterly.

Dr. Fisher, writing with her long fingers and finicky pen, speaking coldly without looking up, interrupted her. "I want your own thoughts, Persephone, and not a litany expressly designed to stop you thinking them."

Jerked out of her prayers and confronted with that intense aquiline face that could never possibly be imagined in a convent, but which in its arrogance and denial and unhappy contracted forehead would make a convincing sculpture portrait of the Devil, Zephy felt at the same time revulsion and a fascinated dependence. She was trapped; the process of undoing had begun, had indeed gone too far to be revoked. They were taking out her vitals. She had no more volition of her own.

As she was going back from Dr. Fisher to her own part of the building, slowly climbing the stairs with a sharp renewal of the old pain in her chest, two sisters in their going-out clothes hurried tip-tapping down in high-heeled shoes. They seemed to her to present the sinister alteration of the possessed, as if their ward personality had been left empty across the bed with the print dress and apron, and their bodies, ravenous and ruthless for pleasure, were jaunting off. No patient could appeal to them now. They forgot her as soon as they had passed her but their resumed conversation followed her up.

"—nothing but one obscenity after another. I've never heard better. Where she learnt it or thought it up! And the poor old parson praying beside her till the sweat poured off him. It would be funny if it wasn't pathetic. I believe she was his organist."

❖

Persephone was no longer confined to her own ward, but had liberty to mix with patients from other wards both male and female. There was a large measure of freedom for the hours when they had no treatment, but occupation and social life were also organized. She never went into the dining room without a pang for the remembered refectory. The tables had plastic tops on which saucerless cups stood each in a ring of its own liquid. The food was unpalatable, every meal tasting the same as the last, as though in the huge pressure cookers the remains of the day before were thrown in to make weight. Each patient fetched his or her allotted portion from the serving table where a sister presided. There was a perpetual scraping of chairs and social disorder. The noise of voices had none of the stimulation that comes when people are talking to others who listen. There were here as everywhere individuals who talked unceasingly, but where so many were exhausted the convention of listening had been allowed to lapse. The talkers were lucky if the person nearest to them was too tired to move away. In any case they seemed content merely to pour it out. Some sat talking to themselves. Laughter was rare and too often confined to the maker of the supposed witticism. To be shared, a joke had to be aimed at the authorities. Discussion of treatment, though forbidden, was popular, and often sensational. Among those who still looked forward to a possible, not too distant, release, the pressure of fear and sorrow was physically felt. It was something they all suffered and that grew with sharing. Among many intolerable burdens, the bitterest was the degradation of being considered less than human, creatures who had no valid judgment of their own, to whom anything could be done, even to the removal by surgery of part of their brain, in order to make them conform to a pattern to which, at the moment, they did not subscribe. If there were for each of them topics on which judgment was obscured by the physical disturbances of sweat, tremor, and agitation which accompanied any approach to them, there were other things about which they were abnormally clear, such as the human value of their fellow inmates. The solidarity of the deranged had a profound wisdom. They knew something about the nature of man that is hidden from the world outside.

Persephone had become shy of men, and ventured into this difficult world in the lee of a motherly person called Biddy, whose face was stamped with grief but whose conversation was simple and uncomplaining. She was fat in the way that seems made for the cuddling of infants. Her features were a series of pleasant bumps, with little to choose between nose, cheekbones, and chin. Her eyes were brown and soft and had no power to detain. She had the sweet faculty of being negligible without resentment, and when she took Zephy under her wing it was protection with nothing taken in exchange. When Zephy asked her what treatment she was having, she replied, "None. I am under observation. I suppose they'll let me go sometime. I have been here two months. I want to go back to my children, poor loves."

"Who's looking after them?"

"My husband and his mother."

It was some time before Biddy's reserve would allow her to tell the rest of her story. Her husband's form of pleasure was to threaten her with knives and boiling kettles, or to say he would turn the bedroom gas on if she went to sleep. She bore it as long as she could, but finally, fearing for the children as well as for herself, she went to the doctor. He interviewed her husband, who denied it all and said she was always making up things like that. His mother said the same.

"They had manners that imposed on people," said Biddy. "The gift of putting it across." The doctor found them harder to disbelieve than Biddy. He tricked her into going to a "convalescent home" for a rest, which she certainly needed, and there she was.

"It seems to me that as long as I say the truth they'll keep me here. I don't mind for myself. It's safer than being at home, but I want the children."

A great many patients thought they were there by malice or mistake, but Biddy was believed absolutely by her ward mates.

❖

Zephy had left St. Hilarion in March and it was already May when she was given the liberty of the extensive hospital grounds. Biddy told her that beyond the garden there were fields and woods, with bluebells, and towards these they set off together.

The broken white clouds tumbling about the sky revealed, when their rolling manoeuvres left an empty circle, a gay, high blue far beyond, streaming with warm light. The wind that played boisterously among the heaped-up cumuli was too high up to trouble the trees. Only an occasional gust, cannoned off a cushion of cloud, disturbed them, and after it had gone they shook out their new leaves to smooth away the creases. Over all the natural earth wild growth was pushing up, jostling for space, clinging, creeping through, burrowing under, every inch claimed many times over. What happy idle hours would be needed to enjoy all that was there! Ground ivy, trefoil, and moss, enriched with ladybirds and beetles, and drifting delicate para-chutes of seeds, held their place in the grass which crowded and pro-tected them. Its emerald and blue blades, or the exploding star of a rolling dewdrop, flashed back to the sky. All this within reach of the forearm if a watcher lay propped on his elbows, and in the hedge-row nearby as much again. Wild chervil for blessed indolence, lords-and-ladies for sorcery, hawthorn and dog rose for nests and the fixed eye of the sitting bird.

When in their romping the winds had herded the clouds to some other part of the sky, and the sun's warmth poured steadily down, colour vibrations filled the mysterious and versatile air, which trans-mitted a world of scent to be drunk by the lungful, quivered with the hum of bees, and rang with the pealing of birds from their tree belfries. And if, because of their challenging sound, one has compared the birds with bell ringers, what comparison could suggest the deafen-ing din, from several fields away, of the sheep? Well fed and untrou-bled, they made a pleasure out of anxiety, each ewe of the flock call-ing on a different note to her lamb; and, receiving no answer from the careless fatling, blared again her maternal foghorn, together maintain-ing daylong a raucous, contented bedlam, sometimes muffled by the wind or softened by a burst of sun. To enjoy the dynamism of May requires a robust nervous system.

Zephy, leaving the hospital for the first time since she had been admitted, set out with Biddy. Her head and feet felt both too heavy and too light, and the short walk was an effort. Biddy said at intervals, "It's nice, isn't it, love?" The pasture land lacked the magnificent stony backbone she was used to in Westmorland and Cornwall. Per-haps that accounted for her disappointment, but it was rich land and spread up and down rounded hills that had once been invisible under a cover of forest.

"Are you tired? Sit down here. We needn't go as far as the woods today."

Zephy lay down on the grass. She would begin to like it after she had rested a little. With her eyes closed against the violence of the new green, she received the full blast of the sheep's orchestra, and also the swaying crescendo and diminuendo of the rooks. A thrush was stabbing the blind world with notes intended to be heard in Val-halla. She opened her eyes to ease the concentration on her ears, and looked at the tress of stalks into which she had thrust her open fin-gers. She knew all their names, and once had had a live reaction to

141

each, but now they meant nothing. She picked a little bunch, con-
founded to find that she could not give them what they lacked. Something in me must be dead, she thought with terror. She threw the
bunch away, and as it lay scattered on the grass it filled her with
disgust. The ground was wet and cold under her where the sun could
not strike it.

"Are you enjoying it? I'm used to the town, you know. I don't
understand the country. There's nothing to look at, is there? But I
suppose it's peaceful."

Stubborn and limp, Zephy sat on for five minutes that felt like
hours, but then the restless, ear- and eye-splitting activity of the fields
bombarding the cavity that was herself became unbearable.

"It's cold," she said, with chattering teeth, "and I don't know why,
but I'm tired. Let's go back."

They dragged themselves back in single file along the footpath to
the hospital and sat down to rest on one of the seats by the asphalt
drive. It was better to be where there was nothing. Asphalt. My head
is like a knob of soft tar.

"Are you rested? What are you thinking about, love? We've been
here for ages."

❖

Zephy, who found talking in a void such a burden, was willing
enough, after repeating thoughts like a gramophone record till she
could not bear to say them even once again, to tell Dr. Fisher something different. She was frightened by her recent outing.

"It's like looking for myself and finding I've disappeared. I can't tell
you what it's like. I used to feel when I looked at that sort of thing as
if it were an end in itself, a natural end like dying and going to
heaven." Dr. Fisher swung her foot. "But now it's as if I were dead.
It's the other things that are alive, and I have no part in them. The
Holy Spirit has been taken away from me. There's nothing there. I'm
empty, like a poppy pod when the seed has run out." Her restless
fingers unconsciously crushed and powdered up the dry husk she was
thinking of.

Dr. Fisher, seeing her patient so cast away and undone, may have
felt personal sympathy, and did certainly feel professional, humanitar-
ian sympathy. She enquired carefully whether Zephy believed she
really was dead; whether she thought her head really was a knob of
tar; whether she thought her brains really had run out like seeds.
Satisfied at last that these were figures of speech ("Though some-

thing in me *must* be dead," said Zephy), she gave her a little lecture on the dangers of dramatising herself, and assured her that her condition was highly satisfactory and showed that the treatment was having an excellent effect.

"You can't go back to your childhood if you wanted to, so it's a good thing you don't want to. It doesn't mean a thing to you any more. So now you must find something else to interest you, and take a step forward."

Zephy glowered, all eyes. This was Reverend Mother over again. They were both certain that the soul has no instinct for its own fulfillment, but can be chopped and beaten and pressed into something else.

❖

At intervals dances were arranged for the patients. Had Zephy not been afflicted with heartache and headache and dragging feet, had she in fact not been in a hospital, she would have been among the keenest dancers. And dancing classes were included in the occupational therapy.

Biddy took Persephone along, hoping it would raise her spirits. She was inwardly worried about "the child's" lack of clothes, wondering if any young man would ask a timid goosegirl to take the floor with him.

As they went along the corridor towards the dance room they heard an odd sound behind them and turned to see what was happening. A very tall, one-legged man was approaching in vigorous hops, each hop lifting and flopping his long dark hair, so that his progress reminded Zephy of an incoming wave. He overtook them, his face sharpened with exertion, but as they made way for him to pass he thanked them with a smile both charming and defiant. His empty trouser leg was looped up through his belt and the end hung down like a sporran.

"Well!" said Biddy when he had gone.

"What a lovely face," sighed Zephy. It was indeed the first lovely thing she had seen since she left St. Hilarion.

Huddled beside Biddy in the dance room Zephy looked round her. There was little of the glamour of an ordinary dance about it, which Zephy had never known but instinctively expected. Everybody knew it was just more therapy, but a few patients had visitors who brought a spark of atmosphere with them and so doubled the nostalgia of those who had none. For the rest, as at all dances, only more so here, aging women with hungry eyes presented themselves perseveringly, and young men sulked, not to be cajoled onto the floor by anyone at all. She soon saw the one-legged man standing with his hands on the back of a chesterfield, talking rapidly to a group of young men. He was well knit and very thin. He gained added height from his hair, which though uncut was vital and stood up an inch or so on either side of his parting before falling round his face. His eyes had a wide leonine set, but it was a gentle face. Though his lips were marked with the long endurance of pain, his smile was like firelight, which other people see playing over a face but of which the person watched is unconscious. Zephy was astonished that she had never noticed him before. "I must have been going about like a nun, looking at the ground."

A ward sister bustled up to him with the usual mixture of authority sweetened with archness, but with less than the usual assurance.

"Shaft," she addressed him, wagging her finger, "at your tricks again! Why don't you wear your leg? You make such a disturbance hopping round the place like that. Besides, we want as many young men as possible dancing. I want to dance with you myself. I brought your leg down and gave it to someone to put in the men's cloakroom. So do go and put it on, there's a dear."

Shaft, as he was called, replied at once, amiable but unmoved.

"Did you really carry that contraption of aluminium and leather downstairs lovingly in your bosom? It would be touching if it were not macabre, even for here. You seem to think that the artificial leg is what walks. I am what walks. I am what I am and I walk because it is my nature. If you cut off the other leg I shall walk on my hands. But I WON'T be finally bracketed with, and limited by, a piece of metal. One can choose."

"Why not choose to dance? Here's—" the sister looked round—"little Zephy, for instance. She's not been here long and doesn't know anyone yet. I'm sure she's light as a feather."

He looked down quizzically from his six foot three at Zephy's stargazing eyes.

"Little Zephy! So that's your name. We met in the corridor just now." His eyes were bright and compelling beyond any look that Zephy had ever borne. "If you were really as light as a feather, so that I could keep you moving in front of me with a word or a wave of the back of my hand, we could make a good pair. I can dance, you know." He was up again on his one leg, and, putting a hand lightly on one shoulder after another of those who stood between him and the floor,

144

he launched out on it. A waltz was being played. After a moment of slender balance, he began, turning on the first beat with a swing of his shoulders, and for the second and third with arms outstretched like a tightrope walker re-establishing his poise. His long hands were held at right angles to his wrists in oriental butterfly actions, and his one foot zigzagged, rocking from toe to heel, carried round by the momentum of his body. The performance had a weird elegance, emphasized by a frown of concentration and an occasional flash of teeth.

The dancers checked their clumsy, safe left-right to watch, the visitors with obvious alarm, but there was applause and laughter from his friends. His dance put authority in its place. The sister had moved off and was standing with a doctor, watching him. He finished in perfect, almost reckless balance, and stood holding his pose, suggesting with his too few limbs the multiple arms and legs of Siva as no normal man could; then, with a sudden grimacing "Hoop-la!" addressed to the visitors, he sidled and leapt back to sit by Zephy. She was stunned with admiration and ashamed to be so earth-bound.

"You see," he said, "what I need is a one-legged partner, someone who would have the same rhythms as myself. Your two poor little feet would be one hazard too many."

Two legs now seemed to Zephy almost as shameful as four. "How did you lose it?" she asked tenderly.

"In the war. I never realised, when they said they were going to take it off, at last, after God knows how long of messing about in hospital, that the loss of it would make my body into the magic three-in-one, the shape of the True Cross. There's a challenge for a man! Bearing always in my body. I had implored them for months to take it off, I had chosen to be without it before I knew what it meant. It's often like that when you choose, the reason is clear afterwards. Not to the doctors. They only see a cripple. Of course on a walk I take the old tin leg, just as other people take a bicycle. It's easier and quicker. But the hospital staff doesn't admit the existence of spirit. They don't admit you can choose. Spirit is mad, according to them. The very last thing they value. Value! They hate it."

"Now then, Shaft!" said the sister repassing them. "Don't start browbeating Zephy with one of your long talks. She wants to dance."

"All right, Sister." He leant backwards in his chair and insinuated an arm among the group behind him to tap the shoulder of someone sunk in the chesterfield out of sight. "Here a minute—I want you."

A figure heaved itself reluctantly up and came round to them.

Zephy stared in unbelief at a puffy, weary young man whose eyes were dead with despair, across whose puzzled brow creases ran like ropes. The puffiness she already knew was a result of the insulin treatment. It was one of the depressing aspects of the place that there were so many dreary balloons among the patients.

"What do you want, Shaft?"

"I want you to dance with one of the Holy Innocents who has—of course—been shut up and should be made welcome."

"I'm awfully sorry. I had my insulin this morning and I feel half-dead. I really couldn't. Please forgive me. It was my last, thank goodness. So perhaps we can dance next time."

The voice was final proof. Zephy's eyes lit up so that Dr. Fisher would hardly have recognised her.

"G. de Fol!" The name floated out on her released breath. "You here! How lovely—for me, I mean. What a surprise!"

Geoff stared back at her, unrecognising, astonished at this affection.

"Don't you remember me? In the milk float from Silverstone Tower? Don't you remember having breakfast at the Red Rose and watching the tide come in? Last summer?"

Geoff put his hand over his brow and answered, frowning with effort. "I remember, I think. You had some funny name. Aphrodite—Artemis—Primavera—what was it?"

When she told him, a faint smile rewarded her.

"That's right. So we meet again." He sat down beside them, but that was the end of his conversation. Shaft, however, talked volumes, all of which Zephy took for wisdom though her thoughts were occupied with Geoff's face. Those rope furrows became for her the focal point of a tender pity. They expressed so well the twist of a tourniquet. She interpreted them with an understanding that made him more lovable, present and thus marred, than as a joyful memory. Biddy sat patiently by, making such assenting and evasive noises as were necessary to accompany Shaft's wealth of ideas.

Afterwards these three, Geoff, Zephy, and Shaft (whose real name was Shaftsbury), were constantly together, and Biddy smiled to further it. Zephy had found in Geoff a link with her essential self, something that made her loves and memories available to her again, and through the medium of devouring pity established them in the contemporary scene. She felt half-cured already. It is true that Geoff's friendship was of the most indifferent kind. They were united in their adherence to Shaft, whom they hero-worshipped, Geoff for his war record and Zephy as a prophet. His constant affirmation that you could choose—it was up to you—seemed to her the true and difficult word. From Shaft's uncensored and ranging flow of talk she learnt much about himself from the inside. Conversely, later on, he gave her outlines of Geoff's troubles from the outside, but the inside she had to imagine for herself.

Sometimes she ran, panting like a little dog, after the buoyant stride of Shaft wearing his "tin" leg, but if Geoff came too, he was soon tired and they lay in the fields under the June sun.

On one such day Zephy had been watching a tower of white cumulus being jacked up higher and higher by the compacting of its unruly base, which seemed to draw in loose grey tatters from the surrounding sky to swell its own excitement. Between Zephy and the toppling heights swallows flew high, and less air-borne birds purred over her with their old-fashioned feather engines. It was only when a wood pigeon's note surprised her like a loved tune without name or context that she realised that she was being happy. The cooing, with all that it stood for, was not merely an awakened memory. It was actual. She turned to Geoff, but he was lying on his back with his eyes closed, his mouth grim. Shaft began singing "Like as the love-lorn turtle," larded ad lib with embellishments exactly rendered in a proficient counter-tenor. Zephy had never heard, or heard of, such a voice before, and did not know whether to laugh or admire. When Shaft talked he mimed, took on the face and voice of different characters as he thought of them, laughed at what he might be supposed to have meant, laughed with astonishment at what he did mean, so that his homilies, instead of being aimed at anyone, were as distractible and ricochetting as a prep-school boy coming out of class—with this difference; his was not the chatter of release but of high tension.

On learning that Zephy had been in a convent, he said he had thought himself of going into a monastery.

"But they are so obsessed with killing the present for the sake of the future—afraid of living even a moment in the world they have been given to live in. They think the spirit of man is wholly and altogether bad, must never be allowed a moment's choice lest he choose wrong, must be kept like a fat woman in corsets lest she bulge in the wrong place. Brother, I'm getting *such* an odd bulge! They dun themselves with prayers and psalms and bells. One only wonders they don't beat gongs. They must not look, *they might see something.* They must not think. Oh Lord, Thou knowest I have a filthy mind. Every movement

147

is by rule. Brother, a *little* less upright. It's not humble. Striding about like a shepherd on the mountains. Anybody would think you were going to see a girl. They do not see that by killing the present perhaps they are injuring eternity. What is eternity but eternal *now?* Suppose their eternity is just an eternity of mortification and stultification—what a yawn! Sinners at least are always finding out that God is everywhere. And if man is made in the image of God, by doing such violence to himself doesn't he risk defacing the likeness? They are afraid, and that in itself is un-Godlike. It would be better to sin and love than to be afraid and fossilise. For every one monk saint there are generations of monk hypocrites. If you see a lot together they give you the creeps. It is easier for God to look at you suddenly out of the eyes of a murderer than out of one of those tortoises."

"The sisters weren't like that."

"Why did you go away then?"

"I don't know. I suppose because Reverend Mother didn't really want me to stay. She thought I was born wicked. She thought it would be like letting the Devil in."

"Isn't that just what I was saying? She was afraid—afraid of a little goblet full of good wine. Afraid like teetotallers. Absolute security is what they want, no risks taken of the Spirit blowing where it listeth, for thou hearest the sound thereof and canst not tell whence it cometh or whither it goeth. I don't like the wind. You never know where it's been. Well, I mean, do you? Fear all the time, not love. Cast-iron defences, and damnation, like the hydrogen bomb, ready to hand in case anyone works loose. But at least the orders have chosen. They have chosen Eternity without Nowness, whatever that may be supposed to be. But a clergyman is in such a position he can't choose anything. My father's one, so I know."

"I don't understand what you mean about choosing. Not altogether."

"Well, look. What else can it mean that the Kingdom of Heaven is within you except that you can have it if you choose it? Do you prefer the world where millions of men are threatening each other—seriously, mind you!—with hydrogen bombs? Every reasonable thinking person knows, as they say in absolute unison, that having a bigger one than the other party is security. Every reasonable thinking person also knows, though they don't say it, that you have to be ready to drop yours first, or it's too late.

148

"Big bomb, little bomb, bouncing B,
They're all at a conference and can't see me.

"Do you feel comfortable? I prefer the Gloria. You can't destroy God, not even if you had a bomb big enough to wipe out the earth and the solar system, and so on, unravelling the whole universe to the farthest star and leaving nothing but 'gaseous vapour.' It would only be re-establishing the First Principle, Alpha and Omega; Allah, Allah, Allah. Who's mad, they or I? And do you know who put me in here? My father. Because if he didn't, his congregation would fall off. Dreadful affair. His son is a Communist agent. Grows his hair long. The Tories would stay away and the Socialists would stay away. They would be embarrassed. *They all want their bomb.* My father wants his bomb too. There's even a text for it: 'It is more blessed to give than to receive. Yes.' "

"Well," said Geoff, speaking for once, "if we received it, that would be that."

"What would it be? It wouldn't alter the Gloria. *Gloria in excelsis,* that's my Excalibur. They can have their bomb. It just goes off with a big bang. They say the world started from an explosion. If a race of dangerous homicides is extinguished by its own act, God can make a new world. I suspect He often does it."

"That's all very well, but supposing a race of reasonable beings is extinguished by a race of lunatics? What about all the children who would be burnt or terror-struck before they had time to choose anything?"

Shaft's exalted expression was clouded by a spasm. His pupils dilated till he looked at them from out of a pit.

"That is the measure of the sin. That is exactly what I am talking about. There comes a time when a man has to act as if he and all his nation were one and the same thing and to decide on behalf of them all that there is something they may suffer but will not on any account do. Something they will die without having done, and be glad of it. I've been through a war. I took my father's and mother's values on trust. But now I've seen and chosen for myself. I'll no more of it. It has made me mad. 'We find a grave deterioration of the mental faculties, leading to some aberrations in the reasoning processes, failure to form proper concepts of cause and effect, and the presence of suicidal tendencies.' WHO'S MAD," he suddenly shouted at them, "they or I?"

149

Shaft was refusing to have any treatment. He was a so-called voluntary patient—out of indifference, so he said, to where he found himself; and also because he saw clearly enough that, holding the views he did, he must eventually be imprisoned either voluntarily or involuntarily.

"After a war, you're mad," he said. "Before a war, you're a traitor. During a war, you are just shot."

❖

There was in the grounds an enclosure of high wire behind which the patients who could not be trusted took their noisy exercise, or more often sat dull and immobile on the benches. This was an aspect of Hell which the other patients kept as far as possible out of sight and mind. Any of them might have time enough to spend there, for all they knew. Shaft knew the segregated by name, and would always stop by the wire and speak to the hopeless old animals slumped there. He seemed to have some power of direct illumination, so that, as he moved along, the dead faces lit up for him and burned for a moment with a human expression.

He had an influence over Zephy stronger in proportion to her almost total receptivity. She was conscious of suffering a painful vacuum where the convent had been torn out. Its love was not for her. Its great promise had dwindled to set rules and personal antipathies. Shaft offered her wild, unearthly love for everything and everyone, with bubbling personal joy—which she did not discount because she found it in an asylum, but for that reason considered it remarkable beyond all comparison. Following after him, she met also the free patients like themselves, many of whom were young. Shaft was popular among them for his nonsense and good nature. If they were capable of laughter, it was in his presence that it broke out. Zephy felt wonderfully free with him. He did not, like Reverend Mother, turn everything she said into something she ought to be ashamed of, or, like Dr. Fisher, so distort its meaning that it became in effect a lie. The words that she spoke to him were her own, and he liked them that way. Love towards him seemed to her something that everyone must feel, in no way peculiar to herself. It did not embarrass her to express it. With Geoff, on the contrary, she was acutely shy, afraid of speaking. She blotted herself out but did not deceive herself. The mere fact that he was linked with Silverstone and innocence, that she had known him *before,* gave him a unique position. She felt he was connected with her: he concerned her in a special way. He was marked out by fate and piety for her to cherish.

Geoff remained silent and indifferent. He accepted her for Shaft's sake, but never sought her company, nor did she seek his, though Shaft was there to bring them together. She longed to know what had happened to change him so much. She was patient and gentle, putting on no airs, least of all offended ones. She hoped silent affection would help to tide him over. Biddy was her confidante. Talking to her was as easy as throwing stones in a well. All went in, was received without criticism, was quite safe, never to be brought up against you. Biddy's kindness closed over all, unchanged.

❖

There was a second dance, in which Shaft took no part. He had been allowed a weekend at home. This time Geoff asked Zephy to dance with him, and she stood up big-eyed, lifting her arms and offering her slim torso as though she could hardly believe he would really take hold of her. Courteously and distantly he steered her through the monotony of the appointed steps. The buttons of his coat clicked against the buttons of her blouse. He was so much taller than she that without contortion it was impossible for them to speak. This is a Noble Pleasure, she thought whimsically, but her idea of dancing had been that it was something mutual and spontaneous, essentially care-free, a taking flight like two birds. And yet this was Geoff's hand holding hers, Geoff's buttons on her buttons.

"Thank you," he said, leading her back to her chair before she had finished clapping. And that was all.

However, before the full anticlimax had time to be appreciated, a bearded man, whom she had occasionally seen in the hospital Studio, gravely presented himself. He was hardly taller than Zephy, of unguessable age, and very neat. His beard hung straight from his underlip with no jut from the chin beneath it. It was carefully brushed, like his hair. His nose was long and melancholy. It turned neither up nor down, but reminded Zephy of a wedge of cheese.

Biddy gave her a push, and she was standing up again. Instantly she was gripped like someone being strapped in at a fun fair. The little man rolled his blue eyes to the ceiling and they were off. They raced, they spun, they reversed, they flew, they checked, they syncopated. They ran smoothly, they separated and met together again with a snap like machinery engaging. The hand, small and ringed, that held hers, was moved now up, now down, now pressed with hers into the small of her back. The little man drew fierce breaths and when the music stopped he had timed his performance to end in a dramatic, gripping posture. Only then, like a yachtsman letting go of the tiller, did his eyes come down.

"I want you to take me *very* seriously," he said, and escorting her back to Biddy he bowed ceremoniously and withdrew to the far side of the room, where he sat and looked at her.

"He used to be a professional dancing partner," said Biddy. "I thought you'd have fun."

"I found I could do everything he wanted me to. But with a beard on your ear that wants to be taken seriously it's not worth it."

After this Zephy was recognised as a possible partner. Before long a young man with very thick spectacles stood before her, perspiration breaking out on his forehead and neck. The business of asking her to dance was so much more than he could manage that she dispensed with it out of pity and embarrassment. He had two immense white handkerchiefs, the manipulation of which took all his presence of mind. He held one between his hand and hers, the other he clapped on her shoulder blade to protect her blouse from his anxious clutch. Since she also had a screwed-up wisp in her palm, either hers or his was continually dropping to the floor, and he, with crimson apologies to her and the other couples, then bent to pick it up, dropping his own as he did so. When they were both upright and facing each other on the move, Zephy thought they might each have had eight legs, because it seemed impossible for either to find a place where the other's foot was not. And not only feet. Their kneecaps jarred almost as often, no matter how frenziedly he held her to his chest. The help-ful contact of hips as practised by the bearded bantam was the thing he was determined to avoid as worse than death. They leant together like tent poles, with their legs operating so far behind them it was devastating that they still trod on each other. After long-drawn misery for both of them, the ordeal came to an end. Her partner looked in a desperate way and could not even think how to leave her.

"Have you your handkerchief?" he asked, dropping his own.

"Thank you," she said to his bending back, and fled. His glasses fell off, and were trodden underfoot by a disbanding couple.

"This business of dancing is more of a mixed pleasure than I had supposed," she commented to Biddy.

❧

Dr. Fisher congratulated herself when Zephy's soliloquies began to be haunted by clothes—clothes worn at dances, seen in magazines, on visitors to the hospital, in films shown in the recreation hall—all that she had hitherto been denied. Zephy was frightened by the delicious passion of vanity that was erupting in her. Dr. Fisher took no interest in clothes. She was so far above anything of the kind that to Zephy these confessions were the most pathological she had yet had to make. She did not understand why brassières and off-the-shoulder glamour were suddenly so obsessing. Dr. Fisher, however, knew from text-books and statistics that this was normal at Zephy's age—rising seventeen. It was much better than slaughterhouses and nunneries.

❧

Shaft returned from his weekend in a disturbed state. His eyes were fixed and his always rapid movements were exaggerated to twitches. Coming out from his interview with Dr. Richards, he met Zephy, who had been with Dr. Fisher.

"How was the weekend?"

"Dreadful. Scene after scene. What's so awful is that they stage them beforehand. A family conclave. They all know in advance what to say and what to leave unsaid, what position to put you in; and they give your mother all the dirty work because she'll do it best. And she does it. She does it." He put his arm through Zephy's as they walked. "You're the only person who doesn't think I'm mad. Or should it be 'Blessed are the Mad for they shall see visions'? Well, here we are together. Are you mad, my lamb? Where's Geoff? I need the company of my peers."

Smiles and tender looks were so naturally directed to and received by Shaft that sometimes they escaped Zephy's vigilant censorship towards Geoff and lit on him. Often he was suddenly and unaccountably rude.

"Why is he sometimes so horrid to me?"

"It's your fault, spring lamb. You are deliberately trying to trouble him. He's got a thing about women."

Zephy blushed from the valves of her heart, gasping that one who had done prodigies of self-effacement should be so accused.

"Why has Geoff got a thing about women? Do you know, Shaft? He is so changed."

"He met a woman who was pretty notorious, but as beautiful as a race horse. He thought she was the love of his life, and he hers. He had a fearful row with his people about her because they tried to force him to drop her, threatening to cut off funds and all the usual. So he went with her on a skiing holiday, and before they came home she thought he might be good enough for a weekend. But she was wrong about that: by the Sunday night she had found somebody better—a ski instructor. In the meantime, a photo of her and Geoff had got into the Sunday papers. He came back to London, but he wouldn't go to his people and he couldn't pull himself together and here he is. He has failed his final exam and has no money to take it again. Away goes his career—he can blow kisses after it. He hates all women, and most other things as well, naturally enough. Hate spreads, like love. Of course he's got it all wrong, but if I try to talk to him he boils up and gets rabid. The only thing that matters is how much you love—you, yourself. The scope or intensity of the other person's love is quite outside you. It doesn't really concern you. It's like a sunrise or a sunset—you can't do anything about it. But she just couldn't understand that. You understand, don't you?"

"Who are you talking about? Geoff's girl?"

"You see," he went on, speaking a semitone higher and breathing in gasps, "the same sort of thing happened to me, only the other way round. There was a girl. . . . I loved her so much it was like a fire. You know how a fire carries with it anything that can be caught, runs unseen along the ground, snatches at trees and bushes even at a distance and makes everything it shines on fiery too. It was like that. I loved lots of women, all women, because I loved her far more, beyond measure. But she couldn't understand it. We separated after the sort of hellish scene that only those people can make who love each other beyond bearing. I've never seen her again, and if I can't love her I can't love anyone else."

By the time Shaft reached this point in his story, both he and Zephy were trembling like quiver-grass.

"Is it always like that?" she asked. But he went on with his soliloquy, thumping his chest with his fists.

"Never believe people who talk as if love were a sin. Love is the one thing it is impossible to repent of. You can't do it. You may be sorry so much wrong and suffering came from it, but never sorry it happened. Love is the besetting virtue of sinners."

Zephy burst into tears and ran in search of Biddy, to whom she poured out a troubled account of the terrifying world disclosed to her, freer and far more dangerous than Dr. Fisher's scientific farmyard obscenities. "I'm frightened," she said. "I don't want it like that."

"Don't take everything Shaft says for gospel. He's got the gift of the gab and he'll talk as long as anyone will listen. He's a dear creature, but it all sounds nonsense to me. As for Geoff, don't take any notice of him. He's not himself. Anyway, men are cross creatures. What's wrong with him is that he's made a fool of himself. He'll get over it."

Meanwhile Dr. Richards patiently explained to Geoff over and over again that he was not trying to prove that Geoff's love and mortification were illusions, but only that if he had learnt to control his jealousy of his mother he would not now have had a breakdown—he would have been in some sort of training for dealing with it. He had leeway in adaptation to make up; otherwise every time his ego was wounded it would be worse. Geoff glowered, biting his nails.

"All right, all right! I know I made a fool of myself. But it's not only that. You talk as if it were all simply natural—that it happens to everybody. That it's *meant* to be like that."

" 'Meant to be' is a very questionable form of expression. It *is* like that."

"Well, I don't want a life where you mayn't even resent treachery and vice. It's not worth having."

" 'Treachery' and 'vice' are big words simply meant to take a charge of hatred, to be filled up with explosive. Cassidy was a nymphomaniac. She could no more help it than you can help hiccoughs. You couldn't have known she was like that, and you may never in your lifetime meet another."

"I don't care if I do. I've damned the whole bloody lot to Hell."

"The trouble is they do pop up so," said Dr. Richards, smilingly showing him out.

❧

Shaft had been long-haired and thin when Zephy first saw him, and after a month his hair was still uncut, the parting had vanished in an uncombed tangle, and he was much thinner. It was a hot June. The dining room smelled of plastic table tops on which the sun blazed through glass, and also pervasively of better-forgotten meals. Shaft would not eat the travesty of food provided for them.

"Food and drink are honourable," he said. "They were chosen as symbols for the Godhead. By eating muck you make nonsense of the Sacrament. This is the exception that by going in defileth a man." He pushed about on his plate a few tepid half-boiled potatoes and a piece of liver of identical density but grey and rubberoid. "No. A man can choose. I do not choose to put this revolting substance *in my mouth*. After all, we are human, not starving dogs."

The others, however, got it down somehow. They had no feeling whatsoever of choice.

"It's no good, Shaft," said Geoff. "They'd be prepared to give everyone in the hospital forcible feeding, electric shocks, and the whole bag of tricks, but they'd never even consider giving us food we'd *want* to eat."

"I wish I had the cooking of your meals, Shaft," said Biddy. "I'd soon see you putting on weight. I wish you'd eat something. You're a real skeleton."

"Well, I'm alive, aren't I? Look round at some of the others. Are they alive? You wouldn't know. You can't call that liver *vivificantem*."

Zephy smiled at him for the use of her favourite word.

Another time he stood in the crush round the serving table and asked the sister what they were offering today. "Any Panis Angelicus?"

"There's rissoles and spring cabbage," said the sister, indicating two immense pewter dishes, one containing brown tennis balls and the other a battered green mattress. "And bread-and-butter pudding."

Shaft shrugged his shoulders with a characteristic sweet smile. The flesh on his face was so slight and creased that one remembered, seeing him smile, that the teeth belonged to the skull.

"Come along now," the sister said breezily. "There's nothing wrong with it. You're too fussy. Dr. Richards said I was to see that you ate a proper meal."

"That was nice of him. But it was unrealistic. He should perhaps be among us? He's losing contact with life. They tell me not to think so much about what would be better, but to see clearly what *is*." He pointed with a delicate skeleton finger at the rissoles.

"You're very naughty," she said with professional roguery. "You'll get into trouble. And so shall I if you don't eat."

"Do you eat that, Sister?"

"Yes, of course. There's nothing wrong with it."

"It lacks dignity," said Shaft, and seizing a bread roll he went away, tearing it ravenously with his splendid teeth and shaking his long hair.

❂

The young women who were reaching a convalescent stage in the hospital were generally dressed in the style of glamour-for-all. The majority had sun dresses in which they lay browning on the grass. Geoff, who had finished his insulin and was now beginning to lose the puffy fat, played tennis with some of these copper nymphs. Zephy could now think of the smooth and confident face he used to have with wild joy at the thought of seeing it soon restored. He still had those ropelike creases over his brow, but less so when he was playing tennis, which he did, to Zephy's eyes, brilliantly. To him it was Purgatory in slow motion, a ghastly performance.

Zephy envied these girls almost beyond bearing. She was still wearing the skimpy oddments in which she had left Silverstone almost eleven months before. Her sickness benefit was accumulating, however, and she intended to buy new clothes as soon as she could. Her excitement and delight when Bess sent her some money to buy herself a summer dress nearly choked her. She and Biddy spent hours discussing what it might be like.

"Look, Shaft," she said, showing him her postal order, "I've got some money. Isn't it wonderful? For clothes."

Shaft had ideas about money. "In the Kingdom of Heaven there is obviously no such thing. Currency is nothing but a way of measuring selfishness—so much that I've got that's not for other people, all totted up in units of ill will. And people think the more you have the better it is! There is as a rule lots of everything for everybody, except good will. However, your mother had the right idea. Shall I take it? I'm going to the post office. I'll get it cashed."

Zephy had to stay in for her treatment, so she handed it over and positively skipped into the consulting room.

Biddy was waiting for her when she came out. "I can go!" she said, quite aghast at the breadth of her good fortune. "They are going to let me out next week." Zephy and she hugged each other.

"Where will you go? Will you go home again?"

"Of course I shall. The children are there."

"What about your husband? What will you do about him?"

"I shall just have to get along like I did before. You don't catch me complaining again! I'm sorry to leave you here, but you'll soon be out too. I'll come and meet you when you come out. I'm all in a whirl now. I feel so queer at the thought. I wonder what sort of a mess my house is in. And the children will be wearing clothes I've never seen. The Welfare Officer saw them yesterday and she says everything's all right. But she wouldn't see how many sheets were torn or cups broken. It comes on you all of a sudden, when you know you can go—as if I hadn't been thinking about it day and night since I came here! There now, I'm forgetting to tell you. Shaft wants you and Geoff to meet him at the North Lodge. I don't know what it's about, but he looks as pleased as I ought to be."

"Are they letting him out?"

"You bet they aren't! Not if they know their job. He couldn't manage outside for a week."

"I think he's the most wonderful man I ever met."

"Why, bless him! He's clever enough and as sweet as can be, but cuckoo if anyone ever was."

"I think he's better than everybody else. It's only that he looks queer, with his long hair."

"People don't look queer for nothing."

"Lots of the others have long hair."

"Yes, but that's showy, for vanity or to look artistic. None of the others look like cave men."

"Would you say St. John the Baptist was cuckoo?"

"Don't ask me. I never set eyes on him. You'd better go and find Geoff. Shaft said he would be in the Studio."

"Oh, at his hateful caricatures! Come on then, let's tell him about you."

"I've never been in the Studio."

Free artistic expression was a part of occupational therapy, and also a useful aid to diagnosis. Zephy spent a good part of her time there, as did Shaft. He usually talked and joked incessantly while painting, and had produced during his year's stay a series of variations on the same theme—the Annunciation—which he referred to as his "Unconceiving Virgins." In the course of experiment his angels developed steadily through splendour and strangeness to *terribilita*. The "Virgin" in the earlier pictures was merely hiding her head in refusal. "Love," he had expounded while painting a discarded tandem in the foreground of a picture, "is neither singular trying to be plural—the bicycle made for two—nor plural trying to be singular—the famous 'either neither.' But it is triune—the creator, the lover, and the new life, Holy and Blessed Trinity, altogether one. That's why I say there aren't to be any unconceiving virgins."

In later pictures the Virgin's place was taken by people of either sex, often recognisably the staff, and in the latest, the most startling, the sacred madness of his Gabriel was confronted by a spangled tight-rope lady hand in hand with a jeering clown, white face split from ear to ear, wearing a silk hat and bishop's apron and gaiters. He had chosen a new name for Zephy while engaged on this, and now addressed her as "Conception."

Zephy was concentrated and serious and painted childishly. When she and Biddy now went into the Studio there was an unfinished picture on her easel. It was going to be somebody gathering flowers. Geoff and half a dozen others were standing in front of it laughing.

"Zephy, my love," said a fat girl in a very tight scarlet jumper, "we were just saying we shall lose you soon if you don't make your pictures more peculiar. Whatever can poor Dr. Fisher find to say about that? I've just been touching it up a little. One or two of the flowers are putting out their tongues at her. Just a little fancy of my own. Wait a minute, I must do the ones she's holding so tightly round the neck. Here you are—you carry on."

She handed the brush to a blond, double-jointed young man, who, after deep thought and several bursts of giggling, altered the fingers of the figure's outstretched free hand into five pens, all with different nibs.

Geoff, without stopping to think, wrote across the waistline MY NAVEL IS MY INKPOT. Everybody laughed except Biddy, and the fat girl said: "I'm sure you've got something there. Next, please."

A huge woman took the brush and pushed them all aside. "We've no use for these pastel shades. You can't have wishy-washy complexes. What they want is some red, lots of it. Slosh it on. They like that. There's no face. Who was it going to be?"

It was going to have been St. Francis, but Zephy hardly liked to say so now.

"I can make it into Dr. Fisher. Hair *screwed* up."

"Let's have a machine to screw it tighter," said the fat girl. "Who can do a Screwing Machine?" The giggling young man thought he could.

"It's a top-heavy affair. Worse than any garden-party hat."

"I'll put hatpins. Don't nudge. Ow, it's gone right through her head."

"Have a go, Biddy."

"I can't, no really, I couldn't." But under pressure she added a balloony pig such as children draw blindfold.

"I think that's all quite interesting," said the fat girl. "The figure isn't as clearly defined as some I've seen. The feet are awfully big. You might think it was a man."

"That's subtle," said the huge woman.

Biddy was still shocked by Geoff's verbal addition. "You shouldn't have put that, Geoff."

"I dare you to take it to Dr. Fisher."

He never smiles, thought Zephy. "All right, Geoff, I will, so there."

"You should take art seriously," said a voice from the far corner, where Zephy's bearded dancing partner was at work on a mobile. "I always take Dr. Richards very serious work."

Geoff and Zephy went off to find Shaft, taking Biddy with them. He was waiting some way outside the lodge gate, sitting in the shade on a milestone, his coat pockets hanging heavily and a packed rucksack on the ground beside him. His brown cadaverous face looked wolfish with pleasure.

"Come on," he said. "Under the big walnut tree beside the field." He shouldered his rucksack and strode off.

"What's it all about, anyway?" said Geoff, annoyed to see Zephy running after Shaft like a little schoolboy after a big one.

"Spiritual food," he answered, forging ahead. "Offerings and oblations. Joys and laughter. Good will to men and dogs, and so perish all plastic cruets."

"He's a caution," said Biddy. "What is he playing at?"

While Zephy was walking along the narrow footpath between the corn and the hedge, she looked over the bright sienna surface of the shouldering grain and desired passionately to be herself wheat-coloured evenly all over. Her blouse clutched her round the chest and tweaked at her armpits, so much was it now too small, but in imagination she felt the sun on her bare back and shoulders. She could even feel the passing coolness of leaf shadows playing across her skin and the light fanning of branches which had been pushed aside falling into place behind her. She could perhaps find a gold-and-green-striped wheat-coloured dress. Cotton chintz perhaps, that would ripple round her. Long, that no one might mistake her for a schoolgirl. A sun dress, with a little bolero. She would be golden-bread-crust brown underneath all over except for her front; that would be crumb-coloured. She would be free from the ugly russet triangle over her collarbones, and the silly body that she saw in the bath naked except for red-brown ballroom gloves and football stockings. She would not be unequal to other girls, might even be pretty. Or Geoff might think so. You don't have to be pretty to everyone.

When they reached the walnut tree and had got their breath, Zephy said: "Biddy's going home."

Shaft gave Biddy his dazzling though near-skeleton smile. "An occasion to celebrate. Just what we needed. We'll celebrate the joy of Biddy's children. Sit down and wait a minute for me. I won't be long." He unhooked the gate and disappeared into a leaning thatched hut in the next field.

Zephy stood where she was and looked at the wheat for itself, ashamed to have used it for such little silly, particular dreams.

It was a level field, so wide that between her eyes and the far margin there were wispy streaks of dancing blue mirage. At first sight the corn appeared to stand as still as dead water in the windless heat, but after a moment she saw that there was wind, about as much as she would expect her own breathing to make, or the passage of a bird, and the ears acknowledged it with the slightest inclination, not in waves, but one by one. If she turned her face to the sun, she saw the field dark-topped and dense-stemmed, but if she turned and looked in the other direction it was bright like old polished brass and the primrose-green stems were striated each with the shadows of its neighbours. In among the stalks were field flowers grown unnaturally tall and held upright by the gentle pressure of the field, as water weeds in water. In the enclosed and silent reaches harvest mice must here and there have built their nests aloft between harnessed stalks. A sparse population, venturing many yards from home along jungle paths, they would be climbing to the swaying top in search of the ripest ears. Silent, she had thought. As she listened it was not silent. Far from it. Bees passed along between the stems like cars on a main road, touching nothing till they alighted on a flower and weighed it down. Only a bumble, careless fellow, bumped his shoulder on a stalk as he went. And what was that sound, a ticking, flipping, cracking that now seemed to fill the whole wheat world like the tick of a clock suddenly noticed in a still house? Was it the pedestrian population of grasshoppers, beetles, shrews, or the dry-skinned adders? Could there be so many mice nibbling, here, there, and there? Or was it the ears bursting in the sun and showing the pale grain within the sheath? If one trained one's ears for only a little one might even hear the undulating flight of white butterflies travelling over the spiky surface purposefully as they sometimes cross a river or a bay. This awe-inspiring field, she suddenly thought, is not a natural thing like the sea. It is made by mean people like Grandfather, who never even see what they have done, and have done so much more than they ever meant. They only meant to make money for beer.

Biddy meanwhile was thinking with anxiety of her imminent release. Geoff's thoughts were harder to guess. He was thrashing the ground with a head of ribwort in frustrated savagery. None of them noticed Shaft's return.

"To a baby harvest mouse," said Zephy, speaking to the air, "the wheat field must seem an eternal thing. I once watched one eating the ears. It knew just how good they were—all milky."

"I've been watching you watching the wheat. I always eat a handful as I go through the field." Shaft spoke from the bole of the walnut tree, where he leant with arms spread out along the branches, one-legged, the spare trouser folded over his belt.

"Shaft! You've taken your leg off. Are you going to do a corn dance?" He looked to Zephy's eyes like an inspired magic-man.

"No, not now." He talked because he must, but rapidly, as if he couldn't spare time to say it. "I might do that at full moon when they have sown the seed. I would coax and tickle it up with my hands, swaying like wheat myself, like Adonais. My real fertility rite was in France when I nearly bled to death in a furrow, most unwillingly. Or I could do my well-known scarecrow dance. Very spectral and effective, peculiarly terrifying to parsons. They can't endure long hair. I wonder why, as Chopin said. I must ask Dr. Richards if he has any ideas. It ought to remind them of patriarchs and prophets, but they seem to skip that one. Women, perhaps. Whoa man! Come off it. Drop it. Put it down. We'll skip that one too. Mothers' Unions. That's better. Nothing irregular there. Mothers' Helps. *Soup!* Could it be soup? Or perhaps parsons, having more repressions, have their associations in contrary motion. What does it *not* remind you of? No, I am sure no one was ever asked, 'What does the dome of St. Paul's not remind you of?' "

"Oh shut up!"

"Yes. I talk too much. It's to keep back the saliva. I took my leg off because a tin leg and a real leg are like the Army and the Church supporting each other because you have to be practical! We are not asked to take the WORD literally. You had better not or you're in for it. You must take the symbols literally and the WORD symbolically. I thought this was no occasion for make-believe and easy ways out. My leg is a leg of integrity. This is to be the Real Thing, a Ritual Feast honoured and *meant*."

Geoff was in a bad mood. This high priest pose of Shaft's is boring, he thought. Also propping himself up there like a crucifix is too much of a good thing. He looks ridiculous with his beatific wolf's grin and his one leg. No, not that. A man with only one leg can't ever look ridiculous again, whatever else he looks. Also he is not posing as being the shape of the cross. He really is it. Can't be anything else. What a size the man is. Makes me think I'm dreaming. He got up to hand him the rucksack that he was reaching for.

"Now then. Here are, first, two bottles of Nuits-Saint-Georges 1949. Much better than a blood infusion. I had one once, and now every time I see an apoplectic man with far too much, or skinny spinster with none left at all, I wonder if it's the donor." He hauled out two collapsible horn tumblers. "Biddy and Zephy will have to share. One for Geoff, and I'll drink out of the bottle. Here is a loaf of stone-ground whole-meal bread, containing, Conception, whole ears tasting just as they do off the stalk. Here is some *pâté de foie gras*. Veal-and-ham pie, skewbald inside with eggs. Strawberries. I only got three punnets, but Biddy can have mine with love and kisses. Sugar. Real Emmentaler. Knives. I pinched them out of the pantry when it was my washing-up session. Spoons ditto."

"Strawberries! I've never had fresh ones."

"I've never had wine," said Biddy. "I hope it tastes nicer than beer."

"It is as wonderful as anything that has ever been said about it. A libation!" Shaft poured a cupful on the ground. His expression was of high joy.

There were things that Biddy believed absolutely. For instance, that lunch was at one o'clock and you ate it.

"I can't possibly eat all that before lunch."

"You certainly couldn't eat it afterwards," Zephy laughed. "But what a lot!"

"I am as empty as a creek at low tide. As pants the hart. You'll see, there won't be anything left."

Shaft and Zephy, both with bulging cheeks, laughed into each other's eyes. Undoubtedly it tasted good! She drank the wine wonderingly. Who would have thought just grape juice would taste so soft, so deep, so many-sided?

Geoff, getting up to refill their cups with wine, unconsciously threw the grenade into their jollity.

"However did you get all this?"

Shaft was eating bread and *pâté de foie gras* like a happy dog. He answered with the free side of his mouth. "With Zephy's postal order."

Zephy was left with a mouthful, unable to swallow, paralysed and dumb.

"But it was Zephy's money!" Biddy was slowly crimsoning with indignation.

"Conception and I don't have money."

"You mean you haven't now," said Geoff.

Shaft was looking at Zephy with seraphic love, not in the least put out by these protests. "She's one of the Holy Innocents. Her currency is love. She'd be absolutely spoilt if she had money."

"She wouldn't be spoilt if she had a decent dress to her back instead of near-rags."

Zephy choked at Biddy's words and had tears in her eyes.

"Near-rags!" said Shaft with the same loving tone. "What a way to describe the aura of Conception. She's dressed like the flowers of the field—woodbine, campion, clover, camomile, hop." He was on the veal-and-ham pie now, and took a mouthful between each flower name.

Zephy picked a piece of camomile and turned over its raggy little flower sadly.

"She's dressed for Galilee. Do you want her with uplift and an expression that's always being undressed?"

Geoff's fidgety hands froze into stillness and he didn't speak again, suddenly far away.

Zephy looked up, gallant and laughing. "I'd much rather be dressed like a rock pool. I have grand ideas, really. Like a shrimp. Don't take any notice of what they say, Shaft. I'm enjoying this feast. Come on, everybody. Strawberries!"

"I shall take these back," said Biddy, still red and deeply offended. "You can at least have them for your supper. I couldn't eat them. But I'll have a drink, please. It's so hot."

Geoff held out his cup for a fourth round. "This cheese brings out the flavour perfectly."

He doesn't care at all about me, Zephy thought sadly. He doesn't mind if I'm robbed. I know I ought not to think like that, and I don't really. But I think he might. He doesn't think at all like Shaft.

The young dog that sooner or later finds all picnickers had joined them and was being fed by Zephy with leftovers. It was a large white mongrel, but it had a friendly wet nose and a faceful of laughter. Zephy hid her sad thoughts in its twisting neck. Biddy appeared to be asleep. Shaft sat propped against the tree with his hands folded over his belt. His expression had lost its elation. His long hair hung round a face that was mediaeval and scholarly. "I am a man full of good things." The bottle was beside him. Geoff had resumed his rhythmic thrashing and was becoming, under the influence of the wine, pugnaciously talkative.

"You're a cool chap. I suppose it comes from being a Commando. You certainly have the courage of your convictions—if you call free for all a conviction."

"It's two-way," Shaft answered gently. "And Commandos were murdered as well as murdering, poor blighters. That's the only way they could forgive themselves. Only I wasn't finished off, so I was left to work it out for myself. You must possess nothing, not even your own life. And you must resent nothing that anyone does to you."

"Ah, that's Dr. Richards' stuff. Everything's all right, it doesn't matter what people do. There's no good, no bad, all just ordinary. I don't see how anybody can love anything without good and bad, without a sense of honour."

"The honour is in the loving."

"Fat lot of good that does you. The honour of being made a fool of. The honour of having your heart pulled out alive. Any God who made this kind of a world and found it good is by any standards BAD."

"Oh, take the lid off! Good and bad are ant-heap words, crawling, blind, finicky, tidy, scheduled, town councillor's words, quite irrelevant to love. One loves Life passionately without question or doubt. Damn it, one is in love."

"It will be just another letdown."

"The trouble with you, Geoff, is that you are enjoying hatred. You're tasting it like brandy, getting all the fire and flavour out of it. But the God you are hating is just a shop-front lay figure, a national passion inflater, an apotheosized vulgarity. Every man has to create his own God out of himself, and he recognises it when he worships it, and when he worships it he becomes it. And that's your real Trinity. How do I create, how do I recognise? Because I am. I say to Dr. Richards, I am God; and that is what he has been waiting for. He writes it down in his book and is very pleased. That is textbook madness. From the moment you've said it they know where they are. 'You are not the first person who has thought that,' he says, kind and helpful to the poor mad bloke. No, I am not the first who has said it either. And I don't draw the same conclusion from that that he does. The First Person! V.I.P. The very First Person, the Great I AM. Everybody is the First Person Singular in their own universe. Nothing can happen to them that they don't do to themselves. If I am not afraid, there is no danger. If I don't resent, there is no injury. That's the only possible meaning of the Redemption. At the Crucifixion no sin was done. No one can injure God. He turns it into something different. That's why I won't repent in Holy Week, the festival of stillborn sin, of rapturous holiness. I don't believe in the Man of Sorrows. It doesn't make sense, Burning furnace of charity, Holy, Mighty. They gave Him evil and it was not. Instead there was the Abyss of Virtue. Taking away the Sin of the World is literal. And everybody could do the same. Of course this is heresy. The Church is determined to have every man's sin tattooed onto him. They would like it chalked up somewhere that it's not to be counted against him, but not taken away. Oh no. Sin is a vested interest. And do you know what I've discovered?" Shaft was getting worked up, suddenly acute and excited. He fixed Zephy, the only one who was still listening to him, with eyes like a dog's that has sniffed at a rabbit hole and knows the rabbit is inside.

"You can change the past. People are always talking as if the past was fixed. But it isn't. Suppose, for instance, that you are acting in a play. You do the first and second acts, but when you get to the third the producer says, 'No, not that way. Very good up till now, but I want this just the opposite.' Then you see that though the stance and voice and expression you used in the first part are just the same, that part you were playing is totally different. You see what I mean? You can alter the *real* past. You can choose."

There was a silence, partly embarrassment, partly heat and inertia; then Geoff burst out at Zephy. "For God's sake stop mauling Willi. It sets me on edge all over."

Zephy offered the dog a stick to worry instead of her forearm and wiped its puppy saliva off her skin.

"Willi. I knew a dog called Willi too. A white poodle," she said.

"Bloody Hell! Can't a man speak without having his words snatched up and pinpointed? I might as well be in the consulting room. Bloody women!" His last words came back to them as he strode away.

"Bad day today," said Shaft. "I suppose he's getting better. The wound's itching."

Zephy sat in the immense bleakness of revelation. She was not conscious of being wounded by Geoff's bad temper, only that if he had loved Lady Penhellion, what chance had she, insignificant camomile? The lost dress no longer mattered. She was out of the running.

❖

Shaft walked openly into the dining room to return the knives and spoons. The sister on duty was so relieved she permitted herself a burst of rudeness. The loss had been noticed and a message, "Three Knives Missing," had been circulated to all the staff, advertising to the farthest department that she had not seen to the counting of them at the proper time.

"I am sorry, Sister Poppet," said Shaft with a smile that took away all impertinence strangely playing over his unkempt wild man's face, "but here they are again, and no innocents have been massacred or unworthy personal throats cut. I shall not be needing any haddock today, thank you very much. The decision is irrevocable."

Zephy also found another meal impossible.

"Are you feeling unwell?"

"I've been out in the sun too much, Sister. I just couldn't."

Biddy, out of fear of having her release revoked, managed the impossible, pudding and all. Geoff had not appeared again. Shaft reported later that he was lying down with a splitting head. Shouldn't have had any alcohol.

It was a bad evening for Biddy too. The late post brought her news that her husband, his mother, and the children had vacated the house that was her home, and had gone, leaving no address. They did not want her to return to them. Zephy and Shaft did their best to comfort her where no comfort was possible, and when she had wept her heart out she accepted the blow with a dignity that would have proved to anybody that she was absolutely sound.

"I shall go to my sister while I'm looking for a job. I'll try to find something where you can join me when you come out, if you want to. It will be somewhere for you."

❖

Dr. Fisher considered the painting that Zephy handed to her.

"This is quite different from anything you have done before. It has more confidence, more abandon. What have you to say about it yourself? What is it about?"

Zephy's nerve failed. "It was a joke," she said miserably.

"Jokes are not without importance. In fact, they usually spring direct from the unconscious. There is a great deal here that is most interesting."

"It's not real. It is not at all what I meant to do. It—"

Dr. Fisher smiled. "You don't have to explain it away. Nothing happens without a reason. Patients are always saying things are accidental or could just as easily have been something quite different. It is not true. The machinery is very intricate but what comes out is simply what had to. Now this is obviously a mother figure."

"It was going to have been St. Francis."

"Very likely, but you have really lost interest in St. Francis. He is just a hangover from the convent. His monk's habit is easily used for a maternity gown. She picks flowers—and here is an interesting double meaning, a treble meaning. The flowers are yourself; she injures them by her touch, and they resent her, putting out their tongues. That means also clearly that they have themselves become beastly. You feel contaminated. You told me yourself that flowers—representing yourself in your childhood—meant nothing to you any more. This picture is all in the past except for one important feature."

While this was running its course, Zephy was thinking that the hair-screwing machine was hardly exaggerated. It seemed as though the hotter the day the more Dr. Fisher was determined to get her hair up and off. She wore a tweed skirt always, but in summer paid tribute to her unconfining principles by wearing a silk shirt under which she noticeably omitted her brassière. She had thin sad legs and sandals. She was, in fact, a fright, and yet her face was fine and to Zephy's eyes tragic, within a recurring decimal point of being lovable. But the point was there. Perhaps she was beautiful in spite of everything if one got the knack of seeing it.

"It is obvious that the mother figure is here combined with myself. You need not wriggle with embarrassment. You are making a satisfactory transference with a clear desire to do injury. I see you have put the hatpin right through my head. This hand too—the pens that

168

write down all you say and do. And this most illuminating remark! The navel, as you know, is where the child is separated from its mother. Your unconscious is quite witty. Have you anything to say about this sea—of blood perhaps?"

Zephy had nothing to say.

"It is in the background of the mother figure. The pig suggests slaughtering, but you have shied away from that. It is only a symbolical pig. You have set out here with complete lucidity, and even some enjoyment, your whole case! The disguise is so thin that one must suppose you are practically in control of your thoughts. Are you satisfied yourself with this explanation?"

"I don't mind about Mums as much as I did." Zephy was thinking of Shaft's difficult doctrine, according to which God was even in that horror-striking bedroom where Bess and Sam had slept like contented children. She gave a prodigious sigh. "I wish I could have stayed in the convent. I don't understand about sin."

"Of course you don't, if by sin you mean sex. You've had no first-hand experience. Secondhand experience is always shocking. When you stand on your own feet and live a normal life you will find that sin, in the mystic sense, is just a bogey. But of course all things, as St. Paul wisely said, are not expedient. Some are just silly and harmful."

"Shaft says there is sin. He says you know when you do it. He was in the war, and I think he killed people. Perhaps children, I don't know. But he says you know when you do it."

Dr. Fisher drummed on her desk, but her face was elated with contemptuous, if sympathetic, certainty.

"You must remember that Major Shaftsbury is himself seriously disordered. He is not my patient, but he causes a lot of trouble."

Zephy had never yet, however relaxed and freely associative, given away her feelings for Geoff to Dr. Fisher. That she was suffering from new currents of experience, and shaking now before the future as much as previously before the past, was evident to an experienced eye. But Dr. Fisher attributed it all to Shaft, whose name and views were constantly on Zephy's lips.

"You are not the first girl whose cure he has greatly retarded, and to some he has done serious harm. He is an aggressive. He must have someone to dominate, who will give up her personality to him, if not physically, then mentally."

"If I had a hatpin now I would stick it into you," said Zephy in a rage. Where had her self-control gone? But after all they had tried to undo it. "Shaft is wonderful. He's not mad at all. He's a saint. And people do get here by mistake. Look at Biddy."

Dr. Fisher went a little red, and replied, viciously shoving in a hairpin: "Biddy is much better for being in here. Because a person is cured, you can't say they were never ill."

❖

When Dr. Fisher came into Dr. Richards' consulting room, he did not find it necessary or possible to meet her with the charm that never failed his patients. If she had been one of them, he would not have felt any impatience towards the cut-and-dried fixture of her tenets. If she had been a patient, he would know exactly what was wrong with her. As it was, they were colleagues because she had been chosen by the board, but he did not think her a very useful one. Also she annoyed him beyond bearing, so that he could hardly force his glance towards her. He received her sulkily. It would be hard, seeing this childish rudeness, to remember that it was the patients who saw the real man. Though he was Dr. Fisher's superior, she spoke as though she were his. He was always conscious both of his ignorance and of his failures. He tended to think of the hospital as a wasp trap where all were in deadly trouble together. She thought she was doing the real work under constant obstruction and ineptitude from the rest of the staff.

"Have you a moment to spare, Dr. Richards? I want to talk to you about one of my patients."

"What is it?"

"Persephone Stalker. I should like to move her on to the Convalescent Branch. She's not really ready, but she has come under the influence of one of your patients, Major Shaftsbury, and he is doing her more harm than I can counteract. I've spent all these months getting the convent out of her system and now she is soaking up his nonsense like a sponge. Will you interview her and sign her as ready for the branch? She isn't, but it would be better for her than staying here."

"She is due for a routine interview in any case, I see. I'll report to you when I have seen her. Is that all?"

"I'm very anxious to do the best for her."

"Oddly enough, so am I."

"I think it would be a good thing."

"I'll let you know what I think when I have seen her."

❖

170

Zephy was always pleased to go and see Dr. Richards. Since he had handed her over to Dr. Fisher she had seen him only once a fortnight, and it was never anything but easy conversation. He always made her feel confident and well, so it was with unguarded pleasure that she answered his questions and joked with him about the nervous boy he had sent to dance with her. It came like a bullet fired across his desk when he told her she was to be moved to the Convalescent Branch. To leave Shaft and Geoff! She would never see Geoff again. She held on to the seat of her chair and her words were meaningless to her. Dr. Richards was answering, was looking at her with his melancholy dog's eyes, but she never heard what he said.

She went outside and walked aimlessly about the garden, trying to keep consciousness of the outside world, if it was only the feel of the asphalt under her feet. She could not concentrate even enough to tell what kind of a day it was, and when drops of rain fell on her bent neck she only thought, It's weeping. Never till that minute had she really taken in that there must be an end to her time at Symington Hospital with Geoff. No one had told her how long she might or might not be there. Many people were there for years. She had ceased to think of it. It was true she was better, but now that she was to go, the old pain in her chest was there again. She was faced not only with the loss of Geoff and Shaft, but also with a life outside, an unknown hostile life containing all the terrors under which she had broken down, in new forms, perhaps, that would touch her even nearer, and she would be bitterly lonely. It was true Biddy had said she could go to her, but that seemed as little comfort as being told she could be buried in the same coffin. She tried to imagine the different ways of earning her living that were open to her—farm girl, shopgirl, factory girl, nursemaid, waitress, bus conductress; all but the first would set her among jostling throngs of indifferent and exploiting strangers. She knew the Welfare Officer would want to send her to a farm. They always did; even patients who had never done farm work before were sent. It was supposed to be vegetative, without anxiety. But she had now, she found, an absolute horror of farm work. Dr. Fisher had seen to that. It was overlaid with six months of revolting talk. In nothing opening before her could she see a spark of joy.

She was sitting thinking of the convent and Sister Clare, of the quiet rustle of habits, the gentle voices that said so little, so happily, the midnight murmuring in the Chapel, the sound of the Angelus blown seaward by the south wind, the cries of gulls over the roofs in

171

winter. She did not notice the arrival of Biddy, panting a little, until she had sat down beside her.

"I've been looking everywhere for you. It was your day to get the dining room ready. I suppose you forgot. I did it for you, so it's all right."

Zephy put her arm through Biddy's but said nothing.

"I've been looking for you," Biddy began again. "I've got some news for you that you won't like, I'm afraid. I wanted to warn you."

"I know. They told me."

"Don't take it too hard. Perhaps he'll write, and that will be something to look forward to."

"Write! Of course he won't write. He can't even bother to speak to me."

"That's because you're always there. It will be different when he's lonely."

"It's me that's going to be lonely."

"He will be too. He won't know anyone there."

"I don't know what you mean," said Zephy, suddenly out of her depth.

"I thought you knew. Geoff's going to the Convalescent Branch."

Zephy hugged Biddy, in paroxysms of laughter. "Biddy, you old dear! *I'm* going there too."

❖

Now that the time had come to say good-bye to Shaft, Zephy, however truly sorry she was to leave him, could not help a certain feeling of guilt. When she had told him she was to be transferred to the Convalescent Branch he took it with a jerk, almost as if it were treachery.

"I can't understand your choosing to go. It's the last thing I ever thought of in connection with you. Geoff, yes. But not you, Conception."

"I didn't choose. They are sending me."

"They! They are like priests in cassocks made of newspaper. You shouldn't have let it happen. You can't have made your point of view clear. You aren't made for *out there*. They won't let you be yourself, my unique and heavenly lamb. They'll set on you and never rest till you are altered."

Zephy was made to feel that she was forsaking the Kingdom of Heaven yet again, and at any approximation to her last interview with Reverend Mother her knees trembled and her hands sweated.

"No, no, Shaft, no please," she implored. She even had to bear a lash of personal angry lightning from the starved-lion eyes that till now had always burnt with a passionate but suprapersonal brilliance. It was a miserable week. They were constantly together, as before, but he was different, wounded, sometimes coaxing—"Conception, you could have a high place in the Kingdom"; sometimes jeering—"Conception will be using rouge and lipstick in a fortnight." He let her feel the full weight of his hold on her. Even Geoff said, "Let her alone, Shaft. We all want to get out of here as soon as we can. So do you." Zephy would have felt less like a forsaker if Shaft had not been so ghostly thin, so nearly disembodied, burnt up in his own fires and glory. Also if this setting out with Geoff had not seemed such a sweet and promising adventure.

Biddy left a day or two before her, much distressed to see her so tormented. Her own unhappiness was something shut up inside herself, never to be opened again. She had shaken off the welfare workers who had beset her—one had been looking after the children's interest and the other Biddy's supposed own. They were sent out from two different organisations and had never met or collaborated. Between them they had seen her whole life fall to pieces, but were just as busy now offering her substitutes. She turned her back on them and set out to do what she could alone. She promised to send Zephy word immediately she was settled. When she was gone, Zephy felt alone on the high sea. Where would it take her?

Finally the time came for her and Geoff to go. It was a drenching day. The penitential Victorian pile of the main building was half-hidden under the driving opacities of white rain, a wing showing here, a portico or turret there, tatters of cloud flying for flags, looking as much like Balmoral as it was ever likely to. At the porter's lodge the ambulance that was to take Geoff, Zephy, and half a dozen others to their destination stood glazed under swilling rain, spouting a jet at each corner of the roof. The sisters concerned had waved good luck from the door; the other passengers were snug inside. Geoff and Zephy in mackintoshes lingered to say good-bye to Shaft. Geoff's shoulders huddled his mackintosh round his ears, but even so he shuddered at the water that ran down the groove in the back of his neck, contracting his upper lip. Zephy's hair was plastered round her face, where the rain streamed over the curves of her eyelids and cheeks and ran into her smiling mouth.

Shaft had come out in a shirt without coat or hat. He gave

no slightest sign of having noticed that it was raining. His attitude was the easy one of a man under a blue sky. His head was not bent against the pellet drops, his brow was clear, his eyes wide open. He did not defend his neck or hands, or step as if conscious of puddles. It was impossible to imagine that the rain touched him. He alone seemed immune.

"Good-bye, Shaft," said Geoff, extending a hand out of his shelter-ing contraction. "I wish you were coming with us." It rang false in his own ears, much as he was attached to Shaft and grateful for his friendship. "Don't let them get you down. We'll write."

"Don't worry about me. The doors haven't closed on me for ever yet. You never can tell. Maybe I'll persuade all the staff that they are really madmen and I'm your only philosopher. All things are pos-sible."

"You'll never persuade Dr. Fisher," said Zephy, laughing.

"You don't know how she might react to a few electric shocks. They say it jerks out the most obdurate *idée fixe*. It would be interest-ing to try. Imagine all the staff without their convictions! What a Bedlam. What a bleating of sheep. Good-bye, Conception, lamb of God. Never let them teach you to whittle love down till it's reason-able. Don't be an unconceiving Mary."

As the car started, they saw him moving off, gaunt and solitary, stride hop-stride, stride hop-stride, the mettlesome gait of the one-legged. Zephy, peering through the window, wondered unhappily where he was going. His face was remote, unconcerned with the whip-lashes of hair that the wind tangled and untangled round it. She watched him making his way through the rain until its hissing col-umns and the fans of muddy spray thrown up by the wheels of the ambulance came between, and she lost him.

❖

The atmosphere of the Convalescent Branch was quite different from that of the hospital proper. In the first place, it was the stepping-stone back to that much discussed Reality. It was on the map, at least, whereas the hospital was in Limbo. In the Convalescent Branch the patients were like repairs done by a helpful amateur who hands the gadget back saying, "Well, try it out, dear. It may work." If they held good, the real test would follow, and to all of them it was a formidable hurdle to take.

In these circumstances, with their thoughts fixed on the future with every variation of feeling from panic to painful hope, with the

174

knowledge that once in the outside world they would be regarded with suspicion and hostility for having been "inside," the patients were much more reserved towards each other. Fear of the contempt of that world of people who had not broken down was reflected on the other inmates of this marginal camp. The struggle was closing in. One must not squander one's forces before the time. Even Zephy, whose natural characteristic was friendliness to all, felt a disinclination to expose herself to new acquaintances, and Geoff was locked up like a safe that has once been burgled. He dreaded new people. Zephy had learned his moods, never gave him any sense of criticism, was gay without chattering, and, though boringly shabby, was, one had to admit, a constant pleasure to look at. And if they looked like a pair, other people would leave them alone.

To Zephy's surprise, on the very first evening at the branch, Geoff put his arm through hers and said: "Come on, let's get away from this ping-pong. I can't stand it. I can't stand the sound of it. I don't think I shall ever hear it again without risk of a relapse. Let's go and explore."

PART IV

The Old Hall

It was already November, but winter had not begun. There would be, with luck, another two or three days before the trees would expose their branches. The leaves, though turned to buttercup and rose, were still dense, so that the sunlight, before it could enter the old Hall, had to filter through their blaze, and took on itself the colour of white wine. Inside, this liveliness shone through the ancient window arches and flowered on the opposite wall. Stone was the keynote of the room. Stone outlined the doors and windows, and the fireplace was like a shallow cave in a cliff face. Between the bare stonework was plaster, patched here and there from century to century with varying tints as though the walls were covered with very faded maps. When the sunlight, ruffled with leaf play, had turned a wall to peach, the colour was reflected back onto the opposite side, and from there, by virtue of the wide splay of the recesses, relayed to left and right until the room trembled with light like a full wine glass, and one forgot that the walls were of fortress strength.

A man in his early thirties, wearing an overall, was resting on the steps of the dais and giving the room his full attention. He had a bony face and his hair was cut round like a Crusader's, so that he fitted well into the twelfth-century room. His widely spaced and steady eyes had the characteristic, outward-inward stare of those who translate the idea received into the form created. His hands were strong, with quick concise movements, but at the moment they were still and all the action was in his eyes. If, he was sadly admonishing himself, a sculptor who had been offered his first commission and lent this room as a studio could not produce anything, he was a fraud. Here he was in fact, and had been for a month, and there was nothing to show for it. The drawings he had brought down with him as "possibles" and the plaster models he had made from them since were no good here at all. Very probably it was the place that showed them up. It imposed such a standard. It was certainly not enough that a thing should be clever, or tuned in to the thoughts and tastes of the moment. He had outgrown the fashion snobbery of the young, and his ability to meet that demand already revolted him. It had seemed inevitable among his contemporaries, postwar strugglers whose work was restricted by economy to experiments in new and cheap processes, unlikely, and indeed not intended, to be placed in any setting more exacting than a modern flat, among lightweight furniture durable enough to sit on while waiting for the hydrogen bomb to go off. He was no longer interested in breaking prejudice. On the contrary, he had for some time been blindly feeling his way towards the ultimate prejudices that are the inescapable attitude of man.

This ageless room should have given him a new liberty. Here simplicity and integrity were taken for granted. The walls themselves were a lesson on the qualities of stone. Verrocchio had been able to make stone blossom and play while still retaining its own qualities. What were they made of, those people? A design had to be very good indeed if it was not to turn out as stone merely diminished. It was lucky for people of his temperament that the formidable material was supplied in blocks machine-cut, because that gave one courage to begin, if only from the itch to chisel away the unnatural sharpness and restore its life.

The room around him, in which the short-afternoon sun was already fading, was suggestive of a sea-sculptured cavity, with its rounded upper surfaces and the overhang of the middle wall surprisingly corbelled out halfway up. The stairs fitted into a crack like steps cut for rock climbers. When he had first seen it he had felt there would be no difficulty here, only pure inspiration, but it had resulted in despair. Perhaps he was suffering from the lack of company, the feeling of having left the world. He turned over his drawings again, considered them deeply, and sighed, "It won't do. I'm not good enough." Then, as so often before, he went down the outside stairs to wander round the garden, to see whether, if he chose a site, it would not be suggested to him what to put there.

Among the big trees that constricted any proper view of the Hall, he reflected that the fall of the leaves would have the effect of parting a stage curtain. What play would then begin? He felt lonely, keyed up and in suspense, as if something must soon happen. If he put his creation, whatever it ultimately turned out to be, near or under the play of the trees, where it could be seen from the main windows, it would perhaps need, or be given, a slightly melancholy feeling. Or gravely beatific. But that would have to be in itself remote. To the unresponsive, just a piece of stone there among the ivy. If something were set up at the end of the long lawn it could be gay, or sinister, or both, according to whether the sun was on it or behind it. Or perhaps it could stand among those profuse and careless rose tangles. Not a Cupid, but as abstract as you please. However, complete abstraction was not his line. She would have to commission that elsewhere. He turned the corner of the building and walked along, his head sunk, forgetting to look about him. It was ridiculous and humiliating that after a month of somebody's generosity he was back at this less than preliminary stage. He would have to write and give an account of himself, to explain that he had rejected what she had already passed with approval, because he couldn't pass it himself. And he had nothing else to offer.

A longing for stimulus reminded him that Biddy was out and he would have to get his own tea. He had gone round the outside of the Hall and now came in at the opposite end, and went along the uneven brick-floored passage to the kitchen and put on the kettle. He leant against the wall, waiting for the water to boil, deep in thought. When he raised his head, his unenquiring eyes were met with a view of the garden and river through the open door where he came in. The sun was in the act of setting, and a brief light of the utmost strangeness lay over the trees and walls, transfiguring them as a room is transfigured when, at teatime, it being still daylight, someone pokes the fire into a blaze. Then, while he watched, it was evening. The golden cherry trees were eclipsed in a dusk that rose up from the ground as rapidly as the sun sank beneath it—and it was time to pull the curtains.

The room downstairs where Constantine now sat was, as befits an undercroft, even more rugged than the Hall above it. Instead of arches it had heavy beams, and instead of splayed window recesses it had uncompromising right angles. It was architecturally as positive as the one above was imaginative, positively comfortable, also, with quilted curtains and big armchairs, and a log fire under a Tudor chimney. This was the winter living room, domestic, established and asking for the companionship of intimates. Well, he had books, his own and those belonging to the house.

After tea he lay sprawled in the easy chair, his back on the seat and his knees jutting out into the room like a landing stage. The fire burned without urgency, making little sounds like a disordered clock that ticks, stops, and then ticks again. In all the house there was no other sound. Ancient as it was, it stood in a silence of its own that was astonishing. Even in a wind the noises were all outside. They beat upon the doors and windows, but inside there were none of the expected creaks and groans. Rain travelling down the steeple-like central chimney could splutter softly on the fire, and a real north gale, when it blew, whistled in the letter box. But this was a breathless evening, anticipating frost and a full moon. There was not a sound. He considered the letter that was on his conscience.

Dear Thorny,

I have to confess to you that I have as yet done nothing at all except reject everything I have done so far. This is the effect your house has on me. I mean its walls and windows and roof, its doors and internal communications, its substance and its concavities, its silence and its outlook, combine to make it at one and the same time so spiritual and so actual that it is hard to imagine what could add to it. But you can never have meant me to suppose that you were asking me to try anything so ambitious. When I feel most discouraged I have wondered whether that wasn't really your idea—to jerk me out of my infancy. I can assure you the process is painful. Meanwhile, of course, I am enjoying your hospitality, well looked after by Biddy, ravished by the whole place, thoroughly upset and on edge.

What was that little noise? A mouse, or a foot on the gravel under the windows?

Your inadequate cousin,
Constantine

Letters like that, he thought, are written lying down. If one was sitting up, pen in hand, nothing so ingenuous, or perhaps some people would say, so affected, would get onto the paper. . . . A mask to hang on that whacking great square pillar opposite. . . . Constantine reached for the sketchbook that was never far from him, and crossing one leg over the other began drawing faces. A woman who was like a lioness. He knew her. She was very beautiful, but unlovable. Her face was a mask, all right, but without secrets. It had no interplay between itself and what it hid. He began on another subject. This might go. He had often admired the relation between brow, nose, and cheek, and yet as he now drew it, without the fine tension of the whole skull, the face was tragic, broken, and weak, the balance lost. No good for a mask.

There *was* a slight noise somewhere. Someone knocking? How typical of this place to have four outside doors and no bell. He got up and went to the side door. It opened on bright moonlight, the glitter of gravel, and the dark solid of yew tree and shadow. Anybody there? No answer. He closed the door, retraced his steps through the living room, and went along the corridor to the front. Here was a sky full of moonlight and the open garden bleached with the condensation of nightfall, stretching to the river, but nobody in sight. There remained Biddy's quarters. To make sure, he crossed her snug little sitting room to the back door and opened it.

Outside, lit from above by the moon, stood a small bareheaded figure that one might in that light have mistaken for a garden statue, with an originality of proportion and poise that made her loose coat hang in straight Gothic folds. She was standing back from the door as if ready to withdraw at half a word. He let a pause hang between them as he looked, simply because no words came.

"Is Biddy in?" she ventured, coming a little forward. The light from the house now found her face, and lay softly over its moulding, detaching it from the long column of neck that made the whole figure so singular.

"No," he answered, still looking. "I'm afraid she's not here."

"Have I come to the wrong place? I'm sorry. I thought she lived here."

"She does live here. But she's out tonight." He noticed that the visitor was trembling. "Have you been knocking a long time? I thought I heard something quite half an hour ago."

"I tried the other side of the house first. When do you think she will be back?" Already she was retreating, had passed out of the warm house light into the stony moonshine. He shot out and caught her by the arm.

"Come in. You mustn't go. She'll be back soon. Come in. You can wait in the warm. She didn't tell me she was expecting anyone. Did she know you were coming? Come in."

She allowed herself to be drawn in, and he let go of her arm guiltily as soon as he realised that she was not going to vanish.

"This way, it's warmer in here." He led her towards his own sitting room. The uprush of relief and excitement that he felt on seeing her, his determination to keep her at all costs *in sight*, made him feel slightly dishonourable, or at any rate less than well mannered. Fortunately she showed no sign of suspicion, hardly even of having noticed him personally.

She did, however, give a gasp and look round unbelievingly at the living room over which the firelight leapt as he poked the fire into a welcome. When he straightened his back she was still gazing.

"It's jolly, isn't it?" he prompted.

"It's queer. It reminds me of a place I used to know. But that's a ruin."

"Ah, that's what's so wonderful about this place. It isn't a ruin."

"When I walked up to it in the moonlight it looked just an ordinary house. Or perhaps I wasn't looking. It makes me feel dizzy." She put her hands up to her temples. Queer little fingers, he noticed. Like a bundle of thin bamboo canes. He made her sit down in a big chair, which she did without relaxing.

"You can't see the old part from the front where you came in. Are you really feeling dizzy? Would you like some coffee?"

"Oh! I would!" she said, looking up and smiling, and then added without embarrassment, "Do you think I could have some bread and butter?"

"I'm sorry! How rude of me. You didn't have any tea?" He was looking at her differently now, humanly.

"No."

"Nor lunch?"

"Now I come to think of it, I didn't."

"Heavens! Have you had anything today at all?"

The question seemed to alarm her, to put her on her guard. She distanced into reserve. Her face was a mask over a world of secrets.

"I haven't had my supper yet," he volunteered. "We'll have some together. Biddy won't be back till half past ten probably, so you've got a lot of time to fill up till she gets here. Do you live near?"

"No. If she gets back so late I am wondering how I can get—on."

"Anybody waiting up for you?"

"No."

"Then you can share Biddy's room. She's not had a visitor since I've been here. I won't be responsible for letting you go."

"Do you think I really could? Oh!" She changed entirely, dropping a layer of gallant pretence, and her head sank back onto the cushioned chair, so that the candlelight fell on other curves and planes, lids rounded over the eyes as over large grapes, a delicate high-bridged nose, and from under the firm but uninsistent chin a long flowing line down the throat to the collarbone. Michaelangelo did necks as long as that in the "Madonna and Child" and "Youth Triumphing Over Age"—thrilling deliberate distortions. Constantine had felt slightly ashamed of his willing reaction to them. But this throat was as untheatrical as the flight of a lark.

When she opened her eyes he was abashed.

"Sit where you are. I'll bring something to eat as quickly as I can get it. Just stay there. Have a snooze, if you like."

He was tempted to lock the door after him as he went out, still half expecting she would take fright and bolt. Not till she has had something to eat, though, he reassured himself. She won't move till then.

He returned with a tray, trying hard to be more casual, but feeling that in spite of himself he was showing excitement. Even his hands spreading the cloth betrayed him.

"I can do that," she said, getting up.

"Would you like me to take your coat now? Are you warm?" Again he was ashamed of himself. He wanted to see what was under it. She wore a jumper and an oddly long skirt, of original well-chosen colours, both rather loose over a slim-waisted, disturbing body that moved without consciousness of itself. He pushed his fingers through his hair and looked anywhere but at her.

They sat down to supper.

"We had better introduce ourselves. My name is Constantine. What is yours?"

"Persephone."

"Delightful." His voice surprised him by squeaking.

"Do you and Biddy live alone here?"

"I don't live here. I'm a guest, like you."

"How can you ask me to stay then? Are you sure it's all right?"

"Of course it is. There's nobody else here. This place belongs to my cousin, Mrs. Thorn. My name is Thorn too. She's in Spain recovering from an operation, and she has lent me the house for six months. In return I am supposed to do her a piece of sculpture for the garden. I'm a sculptor. Oddly enough, although I've known her ever since I was a child, I've never been here before. And the place has taken me down so many pegs that I dislike everything I've ever done." Heavens! She's eating like a lost dog. I don't believe she's heard a word. "In fact, I was thinking of throwing it all up until I saw—well anyway, what do *you* do? Hi!"

"What did you say? I do beg your pardon. I'm afraid—I had just forgotten to listen! What do I do? Well, just at the moment, as it happens, I'm looking for a job."

Constantine tossed up an apple and caught it with emphasis.

"Excuse my table manners. So you thought Biddy might help. She might know of something near here. She seems to make friends easily. She's at the Women's Institute tonight. Is she an old friend of yours?"

"Yes. She's my oldest friend. That's why I came to her first."

Constantine determined to have a word with Biddy privately at the first opportunity. Meanwhile he studied his visitor. It was not difficult. She was so remote, oblivious of his eyes. It was impossible to guess what she was, or how old she was. To start with, there was clearly something to be hidden. She seemed to have come a long distance, apparently on the spur of the moment, since Biddy had not been warned. Had she been turned out of her job, or her home? If so, for what? Was he to imagine her in habit and bowler, prominent at the meet, daughter of the Master? You might think so from her straight back. But then she wouldn't be wearing worn-out sandals. Or selling hats and undies at Southend? The sandals ruled that out equally. Or had she merely run away from school? No. Whatever else her clothes were, they were not the British schoolgirl's. Could she be sixteen even? And if so young, how did she get that ageless expression? And where did she learn those fresh but always exquisite movements? A ballet dancer? He had lived near a school of ballet in London and remembered the pupils at the lunch hour pelting out in their black tights to cross the road, leaping like dogs after a bouncing ball, tingling young animals in the round, all alive-O. No, she was certainly not one of these. And if Biddy was her oldest friend, that was limiting. There was no mystery at all about Biddy. You could sum up her class and all her possibilities at sight. But certainly friendship was one of them.

While all this was going through his mind, Persephone's attack on the food had slowed, and after a very small helping stopped. She excused herself, saying that she was afraid she couldn't eat any more, but she looked at him over the rim of a big cup of coffee and smiled. Constantine stretched his legs under the table and stiffened himself into unconcern.

"I feel much better now," she said.

"How far have you come today?"

"From London. I hitchhiked."

From London to this Saxon backwater to look for a job! It was so unlikely that he found himself unable to ask any more questions. If he could only persuade Biddy to keep her long enough for him to be able to do at least a drawing.

As they sat facing each other on either side of the fire, he was plagued with the urge to ask permission now, before Biddy came in. There was time enough, and she had to sit and wait anyway. Half a dozen times while he talked about the Hall, about his absent cousin Mrs. Thorn, about Biddy, he was on the point of asking if he might draw her, but he could not bring himself to risk it.

As his eyes came back to her again and again, he realised that she was trying to hide a great weariness, that her thoughts were elsewhere and his talk was wasted breath. In his excitement and pressing need to escape from an artistic impasse, fidgety with inspiration as he now was, he admitted reluctantly that he must let slip what might, for all he knew, be his only chance.

"Look," he said at last, putting down the pipe he had just started, "I can see you are tired. I don't know how much space there is in Biddy's room. It's not my house and I've never been in that part of it. But I do know where the sheets are kept. Suppose you write a note to Biddy, and then I'll give you some sheets and things and show you the spare room. You can go to bed, and Biddy will come and see you when she comes in. I'll watch out for her and be sure she gets the note. I don't suppose you want to sit here for hours listening to me."

"I would really rather like to go to bed. Hitchhiking is awfully tiring. And I wouldn't be wasting your time."

"Don't think it's that! Visitors are a great luxury here. I haven't spoken to anybody except Biddy for a week. So you must promise me not to go off in the morning without seeing me. Promise!"

"Of course I wouldn't. You've been far too kind."

She took the notepaper that he found for her, and sat seriously considering its blankness. Her wavy hair pinned up high at the back made her head look like a young fir cone. A real shape. There was no artifice in it. Given the very personal quality of her hair, crisp and fine like a distaff of carded wool, and the shape of her head, it had to be like that. He stood behind her and pulled out his pocketbook, making a quick surreptitious sketch as she wrote.

She turned round, moving easily from the waist and shoulders, just as he was slipping his book back inside his jacket.

"There. I've just told her that I'm longing to see her and that you've been very kind and let me stay."

"All right. Come along and see for yourself that the note is prominently displayed. She's bound to come through the kitchen. Put it on the table, in the middle of this red tray. She can't miss that."

Afterwards he took her upstairs, handing to her out of the airing cupboard the necessary linen, smothering in himself the inescapable thoughts that go with such simple actions. It would also be simple, and indeed polite, to offer to help her to make the bed, but he did not. He showed her the room and switched on the light.

"I'm afraid I can't offer you anything else. You'll be able to borrow from Biddy when she comes. There's lots of hot water."

Persephone stopped in the open doorway. She turned to him blushing.

"I've got an embarrassing confession to make now. You'll think I'm awful. I've got some luggage. I left it just beside the drive gate to avoid carrying it so far in case Biddy wasn't here. It must look as though I had meant to stay." She laughed, really amused. He laughed too. All that careful planning and inducing and fearing and treading on hot bricks when she had been meaning to stay all the time! His spirits soared.

"All right. I'll get it. You can make the bed while I'm gone."

Beside the drive gate, hidden under the hedge, Constantine found a small shabby suitcase and a bass bag. He carried them back with emotion, as if they contained the secrets of his own life, weighing the suitcase—it was half empty—and looking at the bass bag with affectionate amusement. She would have that!

Her room door was open and she was waiting for him on the stairs.

"Thank you very much."

"Are these two bags all? I hope nothing has been stolen."

"Oh, nobody steals from me."

"Well, good night. Sleep well. I'll wait up for Biddy, so you needn't try to keep awake listening for her."

"Good night. Thank you very much."

He turned on his heel and was going downstairs before her door had closed.

❖

Constantine was too excited to sleep early. He was on fire to work. Also as he lay in bed a continuous murmur of soft voices came from the spare room where Biddy and her visitor seemed to talk all night. He dozed off in the last dark before the dawn, and woke with the arrival of the milk cart, leaping out of bed into a day where every minute was an opportunity.

The night had brought a sharp frost, out of step with the mild autumn weather. Last night the garden had looked milky. This morning it was stiff with the glitter of crystallisation and held the morning sun like a glass bowl.

He was standing in front of the fire newly lit when Biddy came in with the coffee. She was solemn with difficult decisions taken.

"Good morning, Biddy. You and your visitor had plenty to say to each other last night. Did you go to bed at all?"

"Oh, Mr. Constantine! I hope we didn't keep you awake."

"No. I was awake anyway or I shouldn't have heard you. Is it a long time since you saw each other?"

"Yes. Nearly two years. Oh, I am glad she came here. It was very good of you to let her stay."

"What else could I have done? No reason to hurry her away. She's the first visitor you have had."

"Mr. Constantine, I've been wondering—it seems a very impertinent thing to ask while Mrs. Thorn is away—but do you think she could possibly stay with me a few days? You see, she has nowhere to go. She hoped there might be somewhere quite near where she could either work and live in or go into lodgings. But you know what it's like here. There's nothing except odd jobs cleaning. Nothing for her."

"What sort of work does she want?"

"I don't know what to suggest. I don't really. But if she might stay here a little—share my room, of course; I don't mean for her to be in your spare room—and if I paid her keep out of my wages until she's settled? She could help me. She'd be very useful. Mr. Constantine, she's all I've got. And that's true for her too."

Constantine turned to his bacon and eggs to hide the amusement that was twitching his face. He was having everything made easy, just as he wanted it. There was no need to give himself away. He filled his mouth.

"That's all right, Biddy," he said unconcernedly. "I can't see how Mrs. Thorn could possibly mind. I shall be writing to her anyway, and I'll explain. As for your friend's—Persephone's—keep, it needn't come out of your wages. I could employ her for a fortnight if she doesn't mind sitting for a portrait drawing. I was stuck for a model anyway. I want her head." He went on eating. "It seems to me it might suit us all very well."

Biddy withdrew as obviously radiant as Constantine appeared indifferent. She could hardly wait to close the door before running to tell her success.

Constantine sat at breakfast in the blissful silence that spilled over round him. What brought that metaphor into his mind? There was indeed an unusual sound, like the basin of a fountain spilling over, a soft continuous noise that had none of the urgency of pattering. He sat immobilised to listen, and then rose and opened the door to the garden and listened again. It was space filling. His ears were inadequate. The morning sun lit up as if with its own fire the summit of the pyramidal beech tree which still carried its full output of leaves. Yesterday they had lain almost as smooth as feathers on a pheasant's back. Now they were curled and crinkled with the night's frost and overlaid with silver. As the warmth of the sun snapped the frail topmost threads of ice it released the leaves, which then slithered down from their place in the sky, flicking over the watersheds of the lower branches till they pooled on the rimy earth. This was the sound that had reached his unconscious before he heard it. This was happiness spilling over. Now as he listened the other trees joined in, elm and cherry and acacia, pizzicato, pianissimo, in the breathless morning.

After his breakfast, Constantine, whistling and active, went up to the room where he worked, and began to tidy it up. He collected his scattered drawings and put them into a portfolio. He paused in front of the clay model he had made the day before, and hurled it back into the lump. He took a couple of small models cut in plaster, knocked their heads together, and dropped them into the waste bucket. He took up the dust sheets with which the floor was covered and shook them out from the top of the garden stairs. He swept the floor and dusted the dais and the chair and took the dust sheet off the couch. A cleanliness unnatural to a sculptor was imposed on him by the use of a borrowed room. What little furniture remained in it was tucked up in heavy sheets till it might have passed for works waiting to be unveiled. Only one example of his month's work was left exposed, an eighteen-inch figure in clay, smoothly spiral, based on the idea of a young boy twisting his body and head to follow the course of something in the sky. He turned this round once or twice, ran his thumb up its spine and round the neck, sighed, and set it on the stand at its best angle. It would never look better than it did here. The room was kind to things put in it, and yet took away their importance. It took away, that is to say, his importance. The thousand-year-old Indian stone heads over the fireplace were in a relationship with it of perfect give and take. It was a question of being good enough. This, however, no longer weighed on him. There was something he had to do, by inner compulsion, and the force of its necessity removed all doubt.

His model was not to sit for him until the afternoon. There were still four hours to get rid of somehow, two hundred and forty minutes uncomfortably inflated with energy and impatience. Nor did he find it possible in this leaf-floating weather to stride out over the country-side. The whole rhythm was rallentando; one was forced to drift, to sit on gates and smoke, to watch the kitten boxing the falling leaves with pulled punches, or the cock in the sun, scratching in a litter as gorgeous as itself, or the stolid bullocks, untickled by the drift of leaves past their shoulders and ears, looking up at him with elm leaves stuck to their wet noses. By the riverside the launches were battened down under tarpaulins, and the leaves lay on them like flowers scattered on a coffin. The unmoving water was solid enough to carry a carpet of pale serrated ovals. Elm boles showed hugely bulbous with the cracked grain of the bark eddying round humps, callouses, and warts. Over their crevasses and *séracs* small birds travelled, apparently enjoying the terrain as well as searching for insects.

Constantine headed for the gravel bank on a bend of the river a mile distant, where he could idle time away. He would sit on the shoal of pebbles picking out those that took his fancy, and watching the swans who sailed there, airing their arched wings, which were ruffled inside like snow caverns. It was a good place to sit on a wind-less day.

At length, between watching, idling, whistling, and walking, thinking all the time of the pleasurable work before him, the morning had gone, and had not dragged, but had been exhilarating and enjoy-able. For the first time he regretted that his meals were served him in gentlemanly solitude. He had never specially desired Biddy's presence or thought of altering his cousin's arrangements. Biddy's visitor was another matter altogether, and Biddy was to have the pleasure for a fortnight while he ate alone.

❖

Persephone presented herself promptly at two o'clock. She was de-mure but unembarrassed.

"Am I too early?" she asked.

"No, not at all. I am anxious to begin. There isn't very much daylight now, you know. Are you rested? It's tiring to sit if you aren't used to it."

"It couldn't be tiring, sitting here, with so much to look at. I've been round the garden with Biddy. And I sat by the river this morning, it was so warm. Isn't it a divine place? But I expect you were working."

"I was wasting my time—even more than I knew. Well, let us go up to the room where I work. Did Biddy show you that?"

"No."

"Good. Then the pleasure will be mine. Will you come? I'll lead the way."

The studio was even more full of sun than on the day before, because of the melting of the leaves from the curtaining trees. As Persephone stood there, the light enclosed her, playing over the goblet cheeks and pedestal throat both directly and by reflection, so that her face in the round was as gliding as it was solid.

Constantine drew a deep breath. It was better than he had been able to remember.

"Let me see now; where shall we put your chair?" he deliberated with assumed casualness.

But Persephone had forgotten him. She was gazing about her with eyes that seemed to occupy the width of her face from temple to temple. When she spoke it was to ask surprisingly, "Are all the walls standing—I mean the originals?"

"One has got a lean out of the vertical. You can see where it has been made up, in the corner there. But it has been like that hundreds of years already. Mrs. Thorn told me that when bombs were dropped round about during the war the walls wriggled like accordions. And yet the leaning wall never worsened. I shouldn't worry."

"I feel so much at home. And yet I never imagined it looking, and feeling, so happy."

"Are you thinking of your ruins?"

"Yes, of my ruins." Her eyes were suddenly wet and bright. Constantine hastily pulled forward the chair.

"Let's try how it does here. Sit here, will you please?"

She sat erect with her hands folded in her lap, as if at the photographer's, guyed it, and then smiled at him. His heart seemed to kick him in the ribs. It was an archaic smile, reminding him of the very

192

earliest Apollos—those short-legged, live-wire apparitions with huge eyes, whose upper lips curl so firmly at the corners. He had supposed that smile to be a sculptural convention, but now he saw it before him. It was a smile of pure gaiety. It did not exclude tenderness, but tenderness was irrelevant to it. That was why, on the Apollos, it was so alarming. Who knows what amuses the gods? And the upper lip remained smooth, undistorted, with just that curled tip. None of the widening that lifts the cheeks like the parting of a stage curtain where you see creases along the line of the pull; still less of the grand Hollywood O-for-Open.

"You can sit however it is most comfortable for you. All I am going to do today is a sketch of your head. Chose some particular thing to look at—a branch, for instance, outside the window—and then, if you lose the pose, you've only to look for that and you'll be right again."

He moved round her, looking from each side at the pose she had chosen, till he found the viewpoint that suited him best. She sat motionless, only blushing slightly as he stared. He moved his easel and his stool, pinned the paper to the board, then took it off and chose another piece of a different colour; sat and looked, doing nothing; got up to fetch his charcoal; fidgeted about and finally moved the whole paraphernalia to a different position. He told himself that he would do one or two straight portraits from different angles just to familiarise himself with the subject and see how it went.

By the time he had blocked in the shape of the head, his sitter had lost the first freshness of the pose. The Apollo gaiety had vanished. He found he was drawing a Gothic head, a creature as mysteriously sad as the other had been brilliant. Where had she come from, what was she thinking, how could she be two persons so opposed? And how disconcerting it was for a man sitting down to draw the one to find himself confronted with the other. He drew, rubbed off, and drew again with double concentration. Then, sighing, he looked at his watch.

"You can move now. I've made a mess of this."

Persephone stretched her limbs and jumped up. "I could never have believed it would seem so long. May I walk about? Did you do this boy?"

"That rubber neck!"

"May I pick it up? Isn't it nice to handle! Oh, you can get down into the garden from here."

She went out onto the platform at the head of the steps. Constantine joined her and, leaning over the rail, shoulder to shoulder, they watched the spraying waterfall of leaves. One after another slipped past her shell of a face. Constantine remembered how only yesterday he had stood down there among the trees, looking at the empty platform, sensing that something was due to happen. The drama had begun.

"Catch the leaves," he said. "A month's happiness for every leaf you catch. Steady on! Don't fall over."

"Can we go down?"

"Yes. Come on!"

He played with her as with a child. On the lawn they chased the elusive leaves. "There you are! That's an easy one. Higher! You nearly had it. Ha, I've caught one! Allow me to present you with a month's happiness. Do you think it counts if I give you one?"

"Of course it doesn't. In this sort of magic the rules are very strict. Look, if you don't snatch, if you just hold your hand out"—she held her hand at right angles to her wrist, Egyptian fashion—"one will surely land on it. Of course, now there doesn't seem to be a leaf coming my way at all. Who would have thought the air could be so empty?"

Constantine watched her movements. It seemed to him that no one before had ever moved quite like that—spontaneously, without the slightest trace of wildness.

"There!" she laughed. "What did I say? This leaf left the tree and flew left and right, high and low, looking for me, till it landed on my palm. A whole month. That will do to be going on with. Shall I sit again now?"

The drawing took form. Constantine pursued it, paring down, shaping up, simplifying, evoking; but the more like the model it grew the more acutely he became aware of what was absent from it. He became merciless towards her, sitting there, and at the same time passionately aware of her, with a projection of himself onto the elusive uniqueness of her face, as if his being depended on it. He had had this feeling often enough before, and it usually vanished as soon as he had made what he wanted out of it. Never before had the target seemed so out of range, as though he were not exploring an external form, but feeling for the limits of himself.

The afternoon was waning. As the sun ceased to shine transversely on the splayed recesses of the south windows, where it lingered long on its way to the west, there was a brief interval of premature dusk, during which Constantine began to admit defeat for this day. Persephone was becoming as vague to his sight as a boulder on the shore at twilight. He looked up to say that they would stop work, when the setting sun, having fallen clear of the intervening branches, reached the west windows. The room glowed rosy and resplendent, but Persephone's head eclipsed the sun and she herself vanished into a corona of vermilion fire.

"Thank you. I can't see you any more now. You sit beautifully. Did it seem very long? I'm afraid I am a brute when I get going."

"No," she replied out of her aureole, "not when I settled down. There's plenty to think about."

"What do you think about?"

"My whole life."

"What's the grand total in years?"

"Nearly eighteen."

"You must have been at a very interesting school!"

"School! There wasn't much to think about there. But I can read and write."

"Holidays, then. Surf riding, skiing, hunting, dancing."

"You have very grand ideas. I haven't done any of those things, except perhaps dancing."

"Why do you say perhaps?"

"It hardly counted."

What, Constantine wondered, had counted? She volunteered so little and he could not continue to ask direct questions. He felt himself to be only in the perimeter of her consciousness. He was not one of the things she had to reckon with, not even as much as the sun-crimsoned stone that she was stroking with her bamboo fingers.

"You must be longing for tea."

"Yes, I am. Have you finished with me now?"

"I've finished drawing for today, but I haven't finished with you, not by a long chalk. Will you sit for me in the morning as well from tomorrow? There will be less and less light in the afternoon."

She baulked.

"Will twelve o'clock do? I—like to help Biddy first."

❖

It was Biddy who brought in his meal, contrary to his faint hope.

"How did the sitting go? I hope you will show me the drawing when it is done. I'd like to see it. She used to draw too."

195

"She was at an art school! How stupid of me. I never thought of the obvious thing."

"Well, no. She wasn't at an art school." Biddy was retreating. "She says you want her in the morning as well. Don't work her too hard, Mr. Constantine. She's not very strong, and I want her to take the mornings easy."

"She suggested twelve o'clock. It's not physically tiring. She is sitting down all the time."

"I don't know what to do for the best. I'm really worried. You will write to Mrs. Thorn today, please? What if she doesn't like it?" Biddy had always seemed calm before. It was surprising to see her wringing her hands. Was she in a panic lest she should lose her job?

"Don't worry, Biddy. I'll write. Mrs. Thorn won't mind. Why should she?"

"I don't know. Ladies are sometimes very particular. I'm only the housekeeper and I haven't been with her very long. And most of the time she was in hospital. I don't want to leave Zephy now I have got her. In fact I won't. And it would be awkward to give Mrs. Thorn notice while she's away and can't see to things. It does seem for the best if the child can stay."

"Of course it is. I don't know what you are fussing about."

❖

In the evening he tackled the letter to Mrs. Thorn. It certainly presented new difficulties, but the old ones had vanished. He could confess his failure and idleness now that it was over. She had done enough creative work herself to know that these languishing periods happened. In any case he and his cousin were on very good terms and he enjoyed writing to her. The first part of the letter was written at speed. The second part required several drafts.

You once said to me that the old Hall was a magnet that brought to itself what it needed, as well as what once belonged to it. Well, it has done it again. Last night when Biddy was out the figure that we both want presented itself under a full moon at the back door to call on Biddy. Such a model can occur only once or twice in a lifetime. It is not just that she will do for what one has in mind. She brings teeming ideas. As luck or the old house would have it, she has, for unexplained reasons, nowhere to go. Biddy, who is like a hen with one chicken, asked if she might keep her here till she found a job and offered to pay for her keep. I leapt in with both feet and said she could share Biddy's room for a fortnight and sit for

me. This is taking a liberty with your house for which I apologise,
but I feel sure that if you saw her you would say the same. She says
she is seventeen but looks much less. A Mélisande. That is to say,
there is quite obviously a mystery about her, even if she were not so
cagey. But she is not weepy-waily like Mélisande, who after all was
a fish-boned creature. She's Mediterranean, one of Apollo's by-blows
ex nymph. Anyway I am from today furiously at work and quite
certain something will come of it. Please if you agree to the ar-
rangement write and tell Biddy it is all right, since, of course, she
is popeyed with anxiety at doing it without proper authorisation.
Of all things, the girl's name is Persephone. I hope you are enjoy-
ing the Mediterranean. . . .

Having got this off his mind Constantine sprawled in the big chair
by the fire that was yet hardly necessary except to play on the walls.
He was both satisfied and anxious—satisfied because things were
going the way he wanted, and anxious because he wanted everything
at once, to be sure of having had it, lest it should yet escape him. It
was impossible to take one's time when for all one knew everything
might go wrong. She might go as unexpectedly as she had come. He
felt so greedy it was like a fever. However, there was tomorrow and
she had apparently agreed to a fortnight, though that was uncon-
firmed. Tomorrow must not be like today, oscillating between two
faces. He must try to keep his mind on the job. Where had he really
seen what he thought of as the Apollo smile before? Was it the Apollo
of Nemi? The head found at the pool of Cyane? He got out a heap of
books—Etruscan art, archaic Greek sculpture, Graeco-Indian. He
went through them face by face, and found with surprise that he had
never seen that particular curve before. His memory was working in
reverse and presenting him with the image of something seen that
was as yet only in his intention. This was immensely encouraging.

Meanwhile except for the books he was turning over there was
nothing for him to do. Sounds of washing up and intimate voices
came distantly from the kitchen. He might ask if his shirt was
mended. In the month that he had lived here he had never intruded
on Biddy in the evening. Now he was tormented with reasonable
things to see her about. There was the electric iron. She had asked
him to have a look at it, days ago. It must surely be urgent? He sprang
from his recumbent position with alacrity, feeling a fool as he did so.
He knocked at the kitchen door. Biddy said, "Come in." She was
alone there.

He repaired the iron, taking his time over it, while she sat knitting. He talked to her while he worked, but neither of them mentioned Persephone, though her absence could be felt. Finally it became ridiculous not to mention her.

"I've written to Mrs. Thorn, so you can set your mind at rest. I'm sure it will be all right."

"Thank you, Mr. Constantine. It's very good of you. I've sent the child to bed, but I'm sure I shan't sleep myself for worry. How long will it be till we can hear from Mrs. Thorn?"

"A week at the very earliest. The child, as you call her, is nearly eighteen."

"I know. But she's such a little scrap."

"Is she ill? You don't put an eighteen-year-old to bed at nine-thirty."

Biddy became uncomfortable. "Oh, no. She's not ill. Don't think that. There's nothing the matter with her, like that. It's just that I enjoy having someone to fuss over, I suppose."

Constantine put down the iron, which had been in order for some minutes. He felt an exasperation directed against all women and Biddy in particular. What they said never added up to make sense. Biddy was being as evasive as water. He said good night abruptly.

Through the window of the passage that ran between the kitchen and the Hall, a square of moonlight competed with the cosiness of electric light. Constantine took his coat off the hook and strode out with a sense of relief that seemed to assume that moonlight was exclusively masculine. At least it was anticosy, anticoddle, direct and even cruel. In its cold light he could look again at the pollard willows and pollard elms and the slopes out of which they leaned. It was bright, but had not the black-and-white exactness that moonlight sometimes has. It was hazy; it simplified forms but also rarefied them. How could one catch the quality of rarefication in sculpture? The memory of Persephone as he had first seen her outside the back door—only yesterday—haunted him as he walked, while he looked at the landscape with eyes that felt twice their normal size because of the dilation of his pupils in the deceptive light. He walked far, taking a footpath through a tangled, beautifully looming wood, a bird sanctuary where the rolls of bramble and masses of ivy, the skeins of hop and clematis draped over the hawthorns and hanging down over the brushwood, were never hacked and tidied up. Even the old posts set upright in the path to deter cyclists looked in this light individual and significant. There was a dead tree trunk lying beside the way, long since stripped of its bark and polished like alabaster, over which he lingered, feeling its breadth under his hands, its wooden muscle and the depth of pockets of shadow. The thick end was rough from the passage of the saw, the other huge with limbs, one crossed over the other. Even with his hands back in his pockets the shape was more felt than seen, and so was the space in which it lay, as though his body were surrounded by a sensitive aura that was pretactile.

As he walked, the light not only brightened as the moon rose higher, but also his eyes grew accustomed to it. There were no animals in the fields. The cows had been taken in. Horses, alas, have become rare. One could walk miles without seeing their rich and massive shapes. Owls were about, unseen, and beside a backwater swans were asleep on the bank, compact as cowrie shells, their heads buried in the crack along their backs. Moonlight was feminine, after all. Loneliness struck into him as he turned homeward, walking fast to warm up before he went to bed.

When he reached the Hall, the moon was high over it. In its brilliance, as he crossed the lawns, leaves, glittering as they tacked, came to meet him, gliding parallel with the earth. Odd that as the planet whirled its way through space the wind of its motion did not penetrate the atmosphere enough to deflect a leaf from its course. One happy month. As she said, it would do to go on with.

❖

Constantine was frustrated in his ambitious scheme for a daily studio lunch for himself and Persephone, which would not interfere so much with work. Biddy would not hear of it. "She must have a proper midday meal," she insisted, and when he insisted too, Biddy added: "She doesn't touch her breakfast. A good midday meal does you more good than anything else."

"Oh, if it's a matter of principle!" He shrugged in annoyance.

Biddy looked irritatingly hurt.

"What does she do all the morning anyway? It's a frightful waste of daylight."

"She helps me," said Biddy primly. "At this moment, if you want to know, she's mending your shirt."

This was a mollifying thought.

❖

Constantine had decided that he must make an effort to entertain Persephone during her sitting in order to prevent her expression from changing to its opposite as had happened yesterday. He never talked while working, and the necessity to do so made him nervous. However, when Persephone came smiling into the studio, to catch and embody *that* seemed the overriding necessity.

He talked copiously. It did not matter if the smile faded so long as it was still, so to speak, in the face. As he worked he lost direct connection with what he was saying. He had simply left orders with that part of his mechanism to carry on. Now and again the sound of his own voice came through to him like that of the dentist's when one comes round after an extraction. But it was succeeding. Though perhaps she wasn't listening. Perhaps his monologue was simply the background noise against which to swim off in her own thoughts, and she was sitting there thinking of what had "counted." The idea upset the agreed balance between surface and concentration. While he was trying to restore order in himself, the sitter's face suddenly broke up into outright, helpless laughter. Her shoulders shook and she buried her face.

Constantine's first thought was that she was laughing at him for his predicament, for being jealous of her thoughts.

"Have you any idea what you are saying, at all?" she asked at last.

"Not much," he admitted wryly.

"You have just said, 'One must always COUNT one, two, three, before speaking, to make sure one does not say what one means.' "

"That's what comes of a split personality. I was drawing, I was drunk with work. I wasn't bothering about what 'he' said."

"Well, I won't have to bother much about what 'he' says either, after that confession."

"You won't meet 'him' often on his own. 'We' are very truthful. This drawing is better than yesterday's muddle. But exaggerated. That's because the whole man wasn't on the job. I'd better bring the wireless up here and give you paid comedians."

"What a threat! Just leave me alone. I like listening to the room."

"Will you come for a walk with me before work tomorrow? You can't sit still all day."

"I'm going to the village shopping with Biddy tomorrow. Another time, perhaps."

❧

In the later session he worked without attempt at distraction, beginning a second drawing, aimed at her second personality. In the silence that enveloped them, tinged with the melancholy of starlings outside the window which ruminated on the nature of sunless afternoons, Persephone withdrew into herself, and her exterior was left unconscious of his eyes, for him to work on and analyse. It is a face like good prose, he thought, so clear-cut as to be a revelation—a revelation of just how mysterious it is. As he considered it, he lounged on his stool, one foot on the ground and his hands on his knees, quite forgetting to draw. He had thought at first to do as many drawings as were necessary to get her out of his system, so that he could detach himself and approach his work freely. Already he knew that was impossible within any foreseeable time. The re-creation of her head, as he saw it, in the medium of wood, stone, or bronze was the only work that interested him now. Mrs. Thorn, however, had not commissioned a portrait. If in sculpture one does a figure, the head is only a part of the whole, no more important than the limbs. Any finesse of likeness or expression would be out of scale. In fact the head is very often either minimised or left off. The limbs win. They are very real, the face a mere indication or a concavity. For him, Persephone's face was the dominating factor. Perfect as her body quite obviously was, without her face it was uninterpreted, so lessened in meaning as to be dreaded. This was a problem to give him hard thought. Meanwhile all he could do was to pursue absolute clarity and simplicity without sacrifice of essentials. One advantage he had as a sculptor, though hardly as a man. He had to deduce the essentials from the form only, confronted by an exterior of bloomy skin as free from lines as a child's, yet able to vary between pagan mysteries and a Pietà; concerning whose history, future, or present circumstance he hadn't a clue, and whose indifference to himself was devastatingly easy.

In this way, day by day, work went on. On a surface level Constantine and Persephone exchanged easy banter, but she volunteered nothing about herself, and the more he tried to formulate an indirect way of asking leading questions, the less he could bring himself to ask them. Biddy was still harassed, asking every morning whether Mrs. Thorn's letter had come yet. It came after ten days, containing pages of descriptions of galleries, of Spanish particularities, of incidents and meetings. Constantine had to wade through all this, and only in the postscript did he find what he wanted.

I am glad you have found a good model. Certainly keep her as long as you want her, if she will stay. I am glad Biddy has company. My impression was that she was a very lonely person. I enclose a note for her to put her mind at rest.

Constantine burst triumphantly into the kitchen waving his two letters. He gave one to Biddy and the relevant part of the other to Persephone.

To his consternation Persephone broke into tears and he had to watch her being consoled by Biddy.

"It's nothing," she said to him over the girl's bent head. "It's only the relief."

Persephone pulled herself together almost immediately and smiled over the top of her handkerchief as she blew her nose. From then on, the atmosphere existing among the three of them was suddenly warmer. Biddy was all smiles; the catering seemed to have become for her an absorbing pleasure. Persephone shed her outer defence, and her attitude to Constantine changed, even as she put her handkerchief back into her pocket, into one of grateful friendship. He himself was dizzy with pleasure.

As they pottered about the studio together—for she had offered this time to help him clean it up—even her conversation was unconsciously more candid and her expression, for the moment, utterly gay. Ledges and sills in the studio were now cluttered with maquettes that Constantine did in the evening to catch remembered actions. Drawings of Persephone from all angles lay about, for the fortress-like walls would not take drawing pins.

"I wish I knew which of them was like me. They are all so different. Those two are just like boys."

"They're meant to be. Young Apollo before he knew his power."

"I don't feel like a boy. I could run and climb and swim as well as they could anyway. And I never want to kill things. Boys are always killing things. It seems to be their greatest pleasure. Just like dogs."

"I don't kill things for pleasure."

"I suspect that's why I feel so safe with you."

"Don't talk as if you were my tame rabbit and I just happened not to be wringing your neck. Look at the drawings. Is *that* like a tame rabbit? If it is, I'll tear it up." He thrust a drawing under her nose threateningly.

"No. It's really rather frightening."

"Good. It's meant to be." He shuffled the drawings together in sudden shyness and stowed them in a portfolio. As he did so, it flashed upon him that all this time spent on analysing her into two possible and distinct forms was completely futile. She was, somewhere within her, both those characters, which she showed alternately. Both, and all the time. If he could only think of an *idea* requiring both, the form would come of itself. It seemed to him that he had made no progress at all. A welter of feelings and not an idea. Well, shake up the dice—and keep the potential stirring!

"Do you think you could stand for a change? It's much harder, of course. Could you do twenty minutes?"

"I ought to be able to. At the convent we always stood for the offices. Sometimes it was forty minutes. It's not nearly as tiring as kneeling."

"But that was not absolutely still. People tend to rock like pendulums after a minute or two if they aren't used to it. But you could lean on the end of the stairs." He went on speaking, but her words "in the convent" had slid into place like a keystone. He had stood aside from the faith of his ancestors, yet he did not query the reverence that her words sanctioned in him. He did not even ask why she was no longer in the convent. The whole atmosphere of withdrawal and purity was hers. He understood now the tenderness of her movements and the Madonna-like brooding that he had so carefully drawn. For the alarming gaiety of the other face it was harder to account, but it was certainly a plus to her otherworldliness, not a minus.

"If you could only stay like that for a bit!"

She was leaning on the newel post and looking backwards up the stairs.

"I know it's a bit of a strain, but do try. Tell me when you've had enough."

He began to draw furiously, forgetting her, forgetting everything but happiness in the bite of his crayon on the paper. This was it. This would do. She had grown plumper since she came, was not nearly so shrimplike. It was wonderful, just wonderful. He rubbed something off with his little finger, corrected it, and rubbed it off again, broke his charcoal, drew the line in to his own satisfaction, and looked up to hear her give a little sound and sit down precipitately on the steps with her head between her knees.

"Oh God! But it was worth it. You've given me the very thing I wanted. Come on, I'm awfully sorry. I'll put you on the couch for a rest. Put your arm round my neck."

He carried her across, keeping his cheek away from her hair; but he still felt it against his neck, soft, crisp, and electric. He laid her down.

"Want a drink of water?"

She lay for a moment with her eyes closed, her face like faded pearl. He permitted himself to try if her skin was cold; and for this he brushed the abundant fringe back from her face and for the first time saw her whole brow. He was surprised to feel the tightness of his eyes and throat. He laid the back of his fingers against her temple. God! he thought. I'm in a bad way.

"How silly of me," she said, coming to. "I'm so sorry. It happened quite suddenly. I'm all right now."

"I'm sorry too. I did warn you Standing models often faint, but I didn't think it had been long enough. In fact, I didn't think it had been any time at all. Don't move. Let's have your pulse. Your wrist is all pulse! There's nothing else in it."

"Don't you know," she said, smiling, "that beginners, when they take somebody's pulse, only feel their own?"

"I must say," he admitted, reddening, "that I thought if it was yours there must be something wrong. All the same, what a funny little arm to have!" He held it up. "Just about room for an artery and a vein. Well, yes. I *can* feel something like a harvest mouse breathing."

"It takes two of them to weigh a ha'penny." She volunteered this with closed eyes.

"You are full of interesting information. Stay where you are and I'll get you some tea."

Studio teas had been organised for a long time now, so that Constantine was able to make her a brew without informing Biddy, who would certainly have rushed up and taken charge.

The rest of the morning was spent in quiet conversation while Persephone lay on the settee and Constantine sat on the arm above her feet. He looked down on her, aware that even their positions were masculine and feminine. She talked now in the most natural way, and apparently with great pleasure, about the convent.

"Until I came here it was the most beautiful place I had ever been in. I think it will bear comparison with anything I shall ever know. You see, it was the sort of surprise one never recovers from. Like some nasty ones. But there are good ones too, sometimes."

"Indeed, I know. Surprises that alter the world."

How often Persephone's thoughts went back to the convent, Constantine soon learned. Now that the ice was thawed, any long pause in conversation was likely to be broken by a dreamy voice saying, "At St. Hilarion's . . ." He came to know a great deal about it, but when he ventured to ask why she had left he got only the vaguest of answers. Sometimes these seemed to point to the Mother Superior, whom he came to dislike as much as anyone he had ever heard of—though Persephone had apparently withdrawn any censure she had ever felt.

"I haven't noticed that you go to Mass here. Do you?"

"No," she answered sadly. "You see, when the whole impetus of a way of thought has been smashed, you can't go back to it. You have to start again from the beginning." She seemed to be feeling her way among immensely puzzling thoughts which, when she found that he was not laughing at her, she tried to put into words. "Sometimes the most darling people do quite dreadful things, but that doesn't make them dreadful people. People are stupidly cruel with their labels."

Constantine also learned that her birdlike fragility had been put to farm work; that his treasure had been the handmaid of pigs.

"Pigs!" She laughed at him. "There's nothing more endearingly funny in the world."

She was too naturally easy with him, he thought. Cool and light. Every questing instinct reported that if anything troubled her it was not his presence. She was on top and did not even notice it.

The interrupted pose had been very profitable to Constantine. He ate his lunch alone in the living room that was by now so much his own. Every stone's surface had become a recipient of his thoughts, as if a print pulled off them would show his heart. The folds of the quilted curtains hid his desires. The wooden ropes carved on the rails of the chairs took the twist of the self-control cramping his hands. The room, as it was the symbol of his solitude and privacy, was also the shape of his imprisoned will. He often paced the floor, and the wall as he reached it was not what pulled him up. He had already reached his own nervous impasse. There was only one thing staring him in the face: the future of his love. The mere thought of it, either way, came to him no more explicitly than as an alteration in his pulse or breathing. From now on the heights and depths of feeling were astronomically distanced.

On this particular occasion he was relieved to be with himself in his concentrated aura. Upstairs the morning had been too distracting. He was conscience-stricken for having overworked her, exhilarated at the sudden bound forward of their intimacy. He felt rich and rushing with ideas like a river unfrozen. Throughout the meal he passively received his own kaleidoscope of images, each coming up continually in a different association. By the time he reached the cheese course he had discovered that his sculptural problems were solved for him. He would do a life-sized Daphne at the moment of turning into a tree. This would allow him to portray the body as tree trunk and give free play to the character of the piece of wood, while the head could take the interest he wished it to have, would take it of necessity however much he simplified. The pose she had accidentally taken had given him the idea. It would not be a desperate arm-flung Daphne. She would sink into her tree as into Nirvana. She would smile at Apollo's helplessness. All her conflicting qualities would come in together as one idea.

His plan of work was to first model a portrait head in clay, to establish it in the round. He would do also a head in alabaster, for which she would not have to sit. Then he could go back to wood with what he had learnt, and begin the real work.

From now on he lived on two planes, his brain and will stimulated with new concepts of work, while he as an individual inhabiting his body was discovering every day new tortures. It began with that soft touch of her hair under his chin and the weight of her body as he laid her down. He could not get it out of his mind. It was in his thoughts like an eddy drawing to itself similar ideas. The idea of kissing the finer loose curls on the white nape of her neck particularly haunted him. The desire to kiss grew overwhelming and became exhausting, like a haemorrhage, followed in its turn by the desire to kneel, the fear of weeping. He began to hate the night. He took long walks before going to bed and still was up early, searching the countryside with brooding eyes as he waited for his real day to begin.

The weather was wild and changeable, like April in a minor key. As in spring, two weathers fought for the blue sky, slate-grey tatters against billowing white mainsails of cloud. Here and there the sun picked out a patch in the wide landscape, like a detail enlarged from the familiar masterpiece. The wild-rose hips blazed in tangled hedges over the bleached and flattened windlestraw. The trees were bare, the shapes of the earth in the nude reappearing, the final, the absolute, the essential form which a thing has by the necessity of its nature. This, however, was not a sculptor's country, unlike some that bewilder and excite with mass and hollow, forcing themselves on the imagination. Here, outside the garden where the multiple shapes in the yew-tree boles caught and held him in frequent speculation, above the rugged and savage elms and the writhing pollard willows there was the semicircle of the sky, across which regal or invading clouds for ever passed, stealing attention from the flat land. The long slow lines of the river meadows suggested little to inspire him, but they were ready to take on the interpretation of ideas already too absorbingly present. The river itself was a creature with limbs, languid and wide-flung.

He sighed an immense sigh, drawing in his breath again in an effort to control its regularity. He must have her bare shoulders. He could not model her body even if it were offered him. He loved her far too much. Only if they were established lovers and quite sure of it, might he perhaps be able to leave love aside with a smile and absent himself temporarily in a sculptor's concentration. At the mere thought he was in turmoil. He quickened his pace and cursed the banging of his heart and the loss of himself.

In the important matter of his work, however, the period of feeling his way was now over, and Constantine's energies were concentrated and impetuous. Neither he nor Persephone was aware of the vulnerability and unusualness of their long days and weeks together. Persephone was in sanctuary. She had no desire to be anywhere else. Shelter and time to think were her most pressing needs. Constantine represented for her, as he was painfully aware, no more than impersonal kindness, for which she was grateful. He also, in the studio at least, was now in sanctuary, since he was passionately at work and saw nothing in the immediate future to stop him.

The portrait in clay was done and left behind, signifying for him, apart from the pleasure he had had in doing it, only so many short-comings to be improved on. The alabaster head and shoulders was well under way. He had found, with Biddy's help, a cashmere shawl in one of the cupboards, and had persuaded Persephone to wrap it tightly round her under her arms instead of wearing her jumper. Drawings and maquettes had been made, experimenting with the position of hands and arms, which must be kept close to the upper part of the figure. A drawing had been sent to Mrs. Thorn. There had been days of snow, drifting dreamlike and silent, when the yew boughs encircling the walls had held their white reflectors to the window and lit up Persephone's face like an opal. I must do a study of her hands, he thought, before I commit myself to the big work.

Thoughts of Daphne circulated in him with his blood. Though the actual piece of wood in which he would carve it would impose its own qualities and to some extent suggest the form, the idea that he wished to interpret was growing and taking in more and more of his life. The fact that the opposites in her would have to come to terms was as exciting as any zero hour, and counterposed that other zero hour with which he must ultimately be confronted. The love he felt for his Daphne's inviolability might be explained as helping him to love his own helplessness. Inviolable she was, tender, smiling, and distant.

He told her that in spite of so many preparatory drawings he still needed her to be looked at, and to pose when called upon. She could read, sew, or play the gramophone, but she must be there. This was true ideally, and in fact also, because if she was not there his thoughts strayed after her and concentration was almost impossible.

Only once in five weeks had he broken out of his bubble of tensed imagination, when they made an excursion together to choose and order the tree trunk that was to become Daphne. It had been a day of intoxication for Constantine, as of a dream that is found to fit perfectly into the outside world. He returned more deeply enchanted and enchained, and the delivery of that piece of yew, calculated to contain Persephone whole, was looked forward to as the beginning of life without end.

In the evenings, if there was a special concert on the air, he would ask Persephone and Biddy to listen with him. Biddy always refused for one sensible reason or another, but Persephone came and sat with her sewing. Her presence against the background of domestic security going back as far as the Anglo-Saxons in their forest clearance, in the room which had become the shape of his heart, disturbed him to the depths and yet was bliss. As he watched her spreading her little feminine bits and pieces of cambric and lace on her knee, cocking her head sideways to look at them, patting them and fitting them together, he was assaulted with desire no sooner brought under control than suffered again. Only the fear of her imagined displeasure, of the cold frown never yet seen, of the wreck of their partnership, was strong enough to keep him in check. He leant his hands and brow against the beam of the fireplace, and the fire was reflected in the black pit of pupils which had usurped his eyes.

After such an evening he would lie awake half the night waiting for the moment when the sight of her should make the agonising strain worth while. No term was set to these days and nights. The Hall, islanded in time and space, visited only by passing wind and weather and the faithful sun and moon, embodied for Constantine and Persephone their feeling of security and gave it back to them as apparent fact. They were as surprised as if the impossible had happened when Biddy interrupted the play of Constantine's chisel by announcing: "Visitors to see you, Mr. Constantine."

Two persons came in, dressed in duffle coats, their sex indistinguishable at first sight. The man was the shorter of the two, or at least gave that impression. He was muscular, with a thick torso, and his head was animal, with heavy hair. He was handsome by the regularity of his features, but taken separately eyes, nose, mouth, and chin failed to escape meanness. In the same way his abundant vitality was felt not to go beyond lust. It was with a sense of disaster that Constantine forced himself to make a show of civility.

"Hello, Caspar! However did you get here?"

"Thought you'd be surprised. This is my friend Soph. I'm taking some things of mine up for a show in Nottingham and I remembered you were somewhere round here. So I got your address from your lodgings."

Constantine shook hands with Soph. She was slim, high-shouldered, and awkward, with a peculiar charm in her slow, angular movements, reminding him of a heron. Her face, however, was cat-like, Sphinxlike, intense, and shameless. Her conversation, carried on mostly in ejaculations, was translated and expanded by her laugh, which conveyed intelligent sympathy and malice in equal proportions. It was gruff, and her high shoulders came higher at each outburst.

"Well!" she said. "This is nice!" Her laugh suggested, "And I see all there is to see in this setup."

Persephone had left her pose and stood waiting. The visitors were treating her as a studio model who socially is not there.

"This is a friend of mine, Persephone Stalker," Constantine unwillingly introduced her.

"Sorry if we are interrupting," said Caspar, showing small even teeth in what he thought was a smile. "We couldn't go past without looking up old Constant." Constantine frowned at the attempt to represent them to Persephone as old friends. He had always disliked Caspar. "Besides, I was curious to see how the great commission was going."

"As a matter of fact, he hoped we might scrounge some lunch from you," said Soph, the smoke from her cigarette closing one eye.

"We've brought some beer along with us," Caspar apologised. "Thought you'd welcome some gossip from the metropolis during your banishment. But of course now we're here I see you're in clover. Are you doing a portrait? I thought it was going to be a figure group —Lollobrigida and the Dentist."

"Give me time. I haven't got that far yet. All my plans are laid."

"You shouldn't be short of time here. There isn't anything else to do. No pubs, no cinemas, no night life. I must say my inspiration would dry out pretty soon in those circumstances. I like to keep in touch with things. Nowadays the fashion in art changes so quickly. You've got to keep your finger on the public pulse—see what's in the shops. It all hangs together. You always struck me as working for a public that simply doesn't exist. This place belongs to a relation of yours, doesn't it? That's a lucky leg up for you. We don't all have relations. Well, I should have thought you would embark on a huge marble group—the Cosmic Forces at loggerheads or what-have-you. Something guaranteed to take a lifetime to do. Not a little head in alabaster. Sting the old lady for something. She's wide open."

"Huh!" Soph's laugh came like a hyphen between this and Constantine's retort.

"Spare me your lewd advice. The world is your sewer. You and your cosmic forces! Your abstracts are simply concrete obscenities so blatant that the mugs think you couldn't possibly mean it, and they buy them and put them on their mantelpieces to prove that they aren't dirtier-minded than you."

"Huh!" again.

Caspar never resented insults, of which he received many. He placed them in the category of pet names.

"This is a practice detail," Constantine went on. "As I say, give me time. I was just settling into this nicely and don't want to lose a day's work. I should be very glad to have you for lunch, but it's early yet. Could you amuse yourselves for an hour? Have a look round the place."

"We did that before we came in. Lend me a board and I'll have a go too, seeing that you've got such a nice model. Soph doesn't need any entertainment."

"Don't mind me," said Soph, picking up the maquettes one after the other and dropping cigarette ash on them.

Constantine turned in despair to Persephone. "Would you mind if Caspar joined in?"

"Why the hell should she mind? What's the difference between sitting for you and sitting for me?" Soph's gruff laugh was the only comment on this. "Do you mind sitting for me, Miss Venus, pocket version?"

"I don't mind your joining in."

"One in the eye for you, Caspar."

Persephone resumed her pose. Caspar was fitted up with a drawing board and crayon.

"What about you, Soph? Do you want a board or some clay?"

"Me? Huh, my interest is engineering. I'm out of this. I'll just watch it going on."

Constantine, with nerves on edge, went back to his chiselling, no longer with assurance, but with apprehension and a divided mind. Soph prowled around trailing cigarette smoke, examining every object in the room with close sardonic attention. She was interested in the equipment, prodding the clay, testing the edges of the tools on the corners of a block of plaster of Paris, comparing Constantine's drawing with the measurements he had marked on it for the block of wood. She also apparently was getting rich amusement out of the human scene in its placing and cross-tensions.

"Why aren't there any mobiles? That's the only kind of art I like. You could have them dangling all along that tie beam. Lively and nice, twiddling in the sun."

Persephone, with practice, could now pose for longer at a time, but today Constantine was only too anxious to break off.

"That's enough for me," he said as soon as he decently could. "What about you, Caspar?"

"Sure."

Persephone came down from the dais and went behind Caspar to see what he had done. Constantine, who always knew at any given second what she was doing and how she was looking, saw her blush deeply. Soph had been waiting with expectation of amusement for this moment, having herself visited Caspar's corner earlier.

"I'll go now," said Persephone to Constantine.

"Yes, all right. Tell Biddy to lay for three, please. I'll let you off this afternoon. Buzz off somewhere with Biddy."

"Good-bye, Soph."

"Oh, good-bye! Aren't you having lunch with us?"

"No. I have mine with Biddy in the kitchen."

Soph smiled with catlike benevolence.

Meanwhile Constantine had been to see Caspar's drawing. Caspar was putting in the finishing touches. He had managed an adequate caricature of Persephone as a huge-eyed kitten, tiny nose ridge and an upper lip curling round the two cushions that hold the whiskers; but his time had been spent in translating her clothed body into the nude he would hope to find there, drawn with his own inimitable coarseness.

"What an ill-mannered lout you are." Constantine was so angry that his words came out with dulcet quietness.

Caspar went on improving the details. "We're always told never to be dominated by the model. The model is there to be used. Funny state of affairs if you were answerable to the model for your work."

"She is not a model. I told you she was a friend of mine."

"He means she is the skivvy," interrupted Soph. "She's just told me so."

He addressed Caspar. "I didn't think even you could be so gross."

"If you think a nude gross, you should change your profession."

"It's not nudeness that's gross. It's confronting a young girl with your very common imagination of what she would be like undressed. She is straight out of a convent and more sensitive than most. I don't know how to apologise to her."

"Don't talk like a bloody parson. She won't mind. They like it. She'll probably offer to show me what she is really like. You're making a jealous idiot of yourself."

Constantine was choking with the desire to kick Caspar down the garden stairs. But there was Soph, who, however ambiguous, was a likeable person in her way, and his guest. His first instinct was always to keep his temper in hand. His sense of fairness told him that all Caspar had done was to carry over admissible studio behaviour into a private house—and not even an obvious private house. From Caspar's point of view not a private house at all, but merely a house without its owner, a house for anything, "wide open." For all this, his anger was still white hot, his eyes murderous.

"You men!" Soph was grinning from ear to ear like the Cheshire cat. She was being excellently amused. "Caspar like an unthinking animal and you all tangled up in your complexes! Huh! You are jealous of each other for looking at her, and yet for all your looking neither of you can see that the dear child's pregnant."

Constantine laughed. His rage was dissipated in the rising flood of their preposterousness. Can people be so stupid?

"Whatever next! You must be crackers. You don't know what you see when you see it."

"What I'm just telling you is that I do know pregnancy when I see it. I've seen it often enough. I've heaps of sisters-in-law. You can always tell. There's a look in their faces."

"Congratulations," said Caspar to Constantine.

"Hold your tongue."

"Shut up, Caspar. He's touchy about it. Don't get us both turned out before lunch. How about it? It will sweeten our tempers."

"Come this way. I never heard such impossible nonsense."

"Why impossible? Huh! Very ordinary. I say, this is fine!"

Constantine detested the necessity of showing them into the living room. He did not want them there, contaminating its associations and moving among his dreams. He need not have worried about Caspar, who was not sensitive to atmosphere and merely said what every gaping sight-seer says, though giving it a ruder twist: "If walls could speak!" Soph was a more subtle, more inquisitive introduction. She was horribly intelligent.

In the first moment Constantine had laughed spontaneously at her outrageous supposition. Almost immediately afterwards it became a necessity to find it funny, and he found himself in the state of buoyancy that accompanies a sense of imminent danger. This enabled him to get through lunch, though resenting every minute of it, with a cool civility that was a stylised minimum and that managed to omit Caspar from its circuit. It was Soph who brought it to an end.

"Come on, Caspar. We're gate-crashers here and we've blotted our copybooks. We'd better get on and leave the Ivory Tower. Thank you for lunch, Constantine, and for letting us see the place. I hope the work goes on well. Come on, Caspar—cut it short."

When he had seen Soph's wonderfully doctored old brake turn out of the drive, Constantine flung off into the fields almost at a run. Persephone's company was the only thing that could have brought him any relief. He had never wanted her so badly. But he had dismissed her for the afternoon. She had stood before him with the touching childish dignity that he found had absolute authority over him. "I'll go now," she had said. And he had replied: "Yes . . . buzz off." He needed her to comfort himself by the sight of her, unchanged by a mere blast of beer and fug from the underworld. He was not yet fully aware what the poison was that worked in him more and more as he walked.

As long as one stayed in the grounds and neighbourhood of the Hall, the old, wild, measureless countryside was implied. It lived in the memory of the place, was inseparable from it. And there was always the incalculable river with its outlying territories of islands and marshes. But for that, the country would soon have been planned so that traffic was always within hearing. Happily, the river was still willful and liable to go one better than the Catchment Board. When all the natural world is tamed and safe, the mountains ribbed with hairpin bends, the wild animals extinct, the jungle a park, drought and rain controlled, the sun harnessed, how will a man be able to endure the force of his own passions, for which there will be neither counterbalance nor prototype? Perhaps that is the real reason for the hydrogen bomb—to supply the missing element that will remind us that we are but dust.

Constantine found his own passions at the moment enough to blow him up unaided. He felt like a goaded bull not knowing which way to charge. It was infuriating to be so pricked by that clot Caspar. He was angry with himself—that is to say, absolutely angry. Miles of deep solitude would be needed to cool him down. People who live in a place like the old Hall, when they leave it do so seeking the very heart of the stillness out of which it seems to be distilled; while town dwellers leave their walls, vibrating with wireless from above, below, and at either side and their windows rattled by traffic, to find a higher-powered point of activity.

Constantine chose the lode, a long bank tapering in the distance, raised above empty fields and giving just enough height to overlook the winding line of rushes that marked the course of the river. The banks of the causeway sprouted blackthorn and furze, pulled by cattle and checked by slashing, but always more determined than either. Over the wide land, which here had as much character as it lacked feature, something of past centuries remained, caught like wool in the brambles. When at last the lode changed into a positively domestic farm track and slanted off towards buildings, Constantine took to the low fields. Behind him when he turned he saw the sun, rayless, crimson, and deformed, lying on the couch of purple vapour that swallowed up the distance. Somewhere there, in the haze between him and the sun, the Hall was standing, coloured on the west side and throwing a long shadow on the east. Empty now. A huge fossil on a green lea.

It was now dark, and a byroad to nowhere in particular was as good as anything else. He had walked in a circle of eight miles before a poster advertising the joys of an old coaching inn, now a roadhouse, confronted him as he came out of a lane onto the highroad. The front was floodlit and its car park full. As he pushed through the door, the hothouse warmth and the smoky, overbreathed air struck him as comfort and relief. The smell of beer was delicious as roast beef. He joined the crowd waiting to be served at the bar and looked with his trained observation at the faces round him, reflecting that what makes bars so dear to men, over and above the satisfaction of a simple need, is a parodied version of the instinct that sends Italians crowding to High Mass. In Italy one sees not the pious conventional masks usual in English churches, but faces marked with naked sensuality, treachery, brutality, and the knowledge of these. They come together simply as mankind. As mankind, they have been let off. A man also comes to a pub to enter the anonymity of the crowd, to be allowed to be just another human. And there is a ritual to it, an assumed brotherhood, a particular tone of voice, a solemn step timed to the non-spilling of beer.

He appraised the grouping round the bar, where attitudes are unstudied and often take on a likeable bravado. The high stools induce interesting poses, loose and dramatic.

With his third drink he found himself wishing that Soph would walk in so that they could get drunk together. Soph would be good company, blast her. Besides, he wanted to talk to her. You never know what women think. She was crackers. But they had made him understand that he was ridiculous to them in his ivory tower. After his fourth drink he argued that a place like this, made to fit the lowest common denominator in man without any strictures, was just as limited as an ivory tower. If the one leaves too much out, so does the other. Any barman knows that. Whatever he caters for, he knows it for what it is. He is not escaping to either extreme. He is on the job. If anyone knows who's rotten, it's a barman in a roadhouse. What a figure he was too, with his stylised movements, continuous as a ballet, his rapid eye and his closed-in thoughts. And of course his bottles, his lovely bottles. The rest could be models for a bas-relief of the Seven Deadly Meannesses. Sponging, showing off, selling it, lying, smearing, secondhandness, round-the-corner-ness. Pure Caspar. And all wrapped in such wide bonhomie. Except for that scowling young Apollyon that he could see dimly in the angle mirror, sitting in a corner that he could not locate from where he sat. Damn it all, it was himself! He must be tight.

He hunched himself out through the swing door into the night of bright stars and rising wind, and set off for home. Before he had gone halfway the wind reached gale force, with sudden and prodigious squalls that could be heard travelling across country before their shock was delivered. As he staggered in the blast he acknowledged it with half-tipsy cheers. It was better to be exhausted from without than from within. Walking into the wind was nearly as tiring as pushing a dead car. Walking sideways to it was an acrobatic performance. It was entirely to Constantine's liking.

Worn out and practically without a thought in his head, he arrived home about eleven o'clock. Round the Hall the yews lashed their snaky branches, while the more rigid trees made sounds like music through a comb. He was in time to see two shadows against the kitchen curtains before the lights were turned out and Biddy and Persephone went to bed.

In the living room the fire was white with wood ash but capable of flickering into life. There was a cold supper laid out, and lying beside his plate a little note:

> Thank you for the afternoon off. We went to the pictures in Cambridge.
>
> P.

She must have been in the bus that passed him on the windy road home. Even that changed his nerve-deadening tramp into a long walk under a star.

❂

The gale blew all night, and in the morning there was a wide high sky looking as if the wind had polished it. Distant white clouds travelled rapidly over it, furling and unfurling as they went. Constantine woke late, with a feeling that some accident had happened, or that something very serious was threatening, without at first being able to recall yesterday's events or connect them with his mood, other than as a great anger that had burnt itself out. He lengthened his breakfast with a book, deliberately losing himself until Caspar's intrusion should seem too far past to think about again. While he was sprawling in the big chair in front of the fire, sitting with one leg draped over the side of the chair and an arm curved along the back, Persephone came in, sparkling with excitement, and leaning over his arm in gentle unexpected familiarity announced: "The wood has come. Three men and a lorry."

216

"Do you mean Daphne?" He swung his legs up and brought them down again to seesaw him out of the chair in one movement.

Persephone was wearing an immense fisher-knit jersey in which she was lost.

"You funny little koala!"

"Do you like it? Biddy made it for me."

"Well, we can't see much of you, but you won't be cold!"

"It's *very* fashionable just now."

Whatever was changed, it was not Persephone. He feasted and refreshed himself on her face, and he drank her voice. She was supremely all that he believed. She was the very form of his belief. She was perfect in sincerity, detached from everything that was not-she.

They spent a morning of unshadowed happiness manoeuvring the tree trunk across the lawn into the garden loggia, where it was to be worked. This was a glass-fronted affair put up as a compensation for the sun lost to the Hall through its thick walls and encircling trees. The windows of the loggia reflected the neighbouring shrubs and the sky and trees as bright ghosts, and their shadows played over the brick wall against which Daphne was to stand, as also over herself. When the wood was finally upended on the stand and the men had gone, their lorry wheels scattering the gravel as they vanished, Constantine stood Persephone against the block and laid his hands on her two elbows to perfect the pose. He was within a split thought, as near to the action as it is possible to be, without doing it, of kissing her peachy cheek; but he was himself the Apollo of the story. He had a superstitious feeling that to alter her personal inviolability would be to imperil the work. And yet that much, he felt—with today's peculiar boldness and assumption of her as in one way at least his own— she would have allowed, as a kind of dedication to the future Daphne. It was so near a thing that he was more elated than if he had taken the kiss.

❈

There followed a period of prodigious energy. From early morning Constantine was at work on the alabaster head. Nevertheless, in spite of his assertions to the contrary, and the diversion of a passionate part of his attention to that magnetic tree trunk, there was a persistent Cassandra in his subconscious who looked at Persephone with unprotected eyes and sometimes spoke with Soph's voice. Who could tell, now, when that enormous fisher-knit obliterated her figure? And when he asked her to pose for her arms, she appeared in a roll of blanket instead of the clinging cashmere draperies. She said she was too cold, which may well have been true, for it was now well on into December. Constantine blamed Caspar's grossness for the appearance of the fisher-knit and the blanket. But he could no longer reassure himself by looking at her slender waist and reiterating "Nonsense."

Then there was a little characteristic pose she slipped into again and again when she did not know he was looking at her—a darling position with an expression of rapt tenderness. He had seen it with awe and fear many times, attributing it only to love for something or someone not known to him. Now he heard Soph's voice saying: "You can always tell. There's a look in their faces." The sweat broke out on his brow and the chisel slipped in his palm. Jealousy was too much to bear.

One evening as he sat opposite her by the sweet-smelling fire where green willow blazed over a bed of incandescent ash, he decided that since he had loved that expression so long he had better take the plunge and draw it for future use, make it his own in the only way he could.

Biddy had gone to the Women's Institute, but Persephone had not wished to accompany her. It was to be a demonstration of drawing poultry—a subject with which she was all too familiar on the farm. She said she had no inclination for a social evening with entrails. There was, as it happened, no music he could turn on for her, but if one could cut out one's response to the exhilarating fireworks in the hearth, there was the occasional tinkle of wax falling from the candles into the glass sconces, and behind that a silence that made one's ears sing. The light, flame-coloured from the many separate sources, flickered, caressed, and evoked, but never made a bald assertion such as electric light puts before one, take it or leave it. The familiar massive angles of the walls, the curtain folds, the knobs, the shadows beneath the table, the bulk of armchairs, the pile of logs ready for burning were all explored from different angles, winked on, rounded, cross-shot with light manifold and interacting, touched as with fingers, the effect being not merely to show where a thing was but to divine its nature. Among it all sat Persephone, a mirage and a torment, his Credo and the query of queries.

He drew, and while drawing had no other problem but the snaring of her face within his power. She was quiet, thinking her unguessable thoughts, sewing and enjoying the warmth on her shins. Though her feet were uncoquettish in wool socks and sandals, she habitually sat with them pressed together, and now extended them, still demurely paired, to the blazing hearth as she held up her piece of material for her own admiration. It thus came between her face and Constantine and forced itself on his attention. Till now he had never wondered what she sewed. Who knows what women's bits of things are like before they are sewn together? For the first time he considered the small irregular trapezium of stuff on which the fire laid its own colour. How small would it have to be if it were not for herself? She was so small anyway. Perhaps she wore those ridiculous but charming trifles that his sister called "briefies." He could not ask her what she was making, though he knew she would not lie. As she lowered her handiwork she met his eyes fixed on her, with what expression he did not know, but she smiled suddenly.

"It's a sleeve," she said. "You'd never think it, would you? It ruckles up like this." She pinched it up into a short puff. "I'm looking ahead, to the spring."

Sleeves, of course, can be any length, he thought. His heart must have stopped, for it then beat so furiously that afterwards he found that her information was lost. It had been pounded out of his memory, and, try as he would, he could only remember her holding up her fire-lit scrap of white and looking at him with her laughing eyes; but what she had said was, for better or worse, a blank.

Not till the next day did the complication occur to him that perhaps she had told him something she wanted him to know. Perhaps she was now content that he knew what in fact he did not know. His mind could give him in her voice equally convincingly what he most feared and most desired.

Outside in the loggia before breakfast, chiselling with a concentration like a surgeon performing a life-or-death operation, he had tears on his cheeks that he knew nothing about. He wiped them off when he stopped work, and blew his nose. It's bitter out here, he thought. Even with the oilstove I can hardly have Persephone out here till the spring. The spring—what was it he knew about the spring? Mrs. Thorn would be back in June, but that didn't necessarily end everything. She would surely let them carry on if Daphne was going well, until it was finished.

❈

It was in vain that Biddy, anxious and sympathetic, tempted him with food and urged him with counsel. He grew thinner day by day, his eyes brilliant and steady under a settled frown. To Biddy's questioning disappointment as she cleared away neglected meals he answered that he was working. It was always like that. As to his sleep—of course he wasn't sleeping. How could he until he knew he hadn't spoiled it?

To Persephone he was alternately absent-minded and of a tight-lipped gentleness. She was as excited over the progress of Daphne as any child watching any workman. She wanted to hang around, handing tools and standing to admire. Constantine laid the mallet on the bun point of her fir-cone head as she bent to stroke the smooth base of the wood where the bark had been stripped off, leaving the muscles of the tree showing.

"Be off," he said to her laughing upturned face. "It's too cold for you out here, and I don't need you at this stage. I not only don't need you, I mustn't have you. If you are so keen, go and try your hand in the studio. Go on. Go and model something. I can't think why you haven't done it before. I'll be there before long."

When he came in, hours later, it was lunchtime and she had gone. He ate something and then went upstairs, where he was to work on the alabaster head. Here he found her morning's work. She had selected an alabaster pebble that was already halfway to her intention, and had filed and coaxed it into a swaddled babe that would lie in her palm. He was looking at it as if it were a pistol that had just shot him when she came in and ran eagerly forward. "I was making a Crib for Christmas. We always had a Crib in the convent. Don't you think it's nice? I like the feel of it. Of course it was there before I began. I would hollow out a cradle but I'm afraid it might look like a pestle and mortar." She looked downcast at his silence, so he smiled and said: "You've got the idea. Do some more."

It was true. She had shown sensibility and tact with her stone.

"Tomorrow I'll do the donkey. Look, this stone will do it. It's got turned-over haunches, lying down. The ears will be very hard. If I make it braying, they can be flattened back?"

"Donkey yourself," he said gently, sighing.

❖

Shoals of letters for Mrs. Thorn formed under the letter box every morning now. Constantine weeded out those that obviously need not be forwarded. He divided them first into three groups—Christmas cards, catalogues, and the rest. Only the last category needed to be looked at twice. Some decisions were easy. "This Means Money for

You" went straight into the fire. Oxford Famine Relief, Distressed Gentlewomen, Cancer Research? He would send a small sum to each and let her know; then if she wished to send a larger donation she could, and he would have done nobody out of it. PRIVATE. That meant the bank. Thank heaven it was not for him, anyway. Messrs. Mortlock, Cain and Mortlock, Valuers and Antique Dealers. Sealed, typed, but with the indefinable look of a private letter. Better send it on. Bills. Keep them back till after Christmas. Half a dozen envelopes for himself. Card from Soph. Some local postmarks for Biddy. Nothing ever for Persephone. She must have made friends in her life. She could not but be loved. The conclusion was that nobody at all knew her address.

By Christmas week the alabaster head was finished. It glimmered hauntingly with a mocking smile, the secrets of its rounded eyes hidden under lowered lids. In the loggia, Daphne was a rough outline of herself. The head was positive but as yet not fully detached. Brow and temples and chin were fixed, and hints showed here and there above the rough, like rocks on the surface of an ebb tide. Already it showed a promise of poetry, but it would be a different poem from her alabaster sister's. The eyes would be open and the key minor. The neck was still a thick block and the arms lay in projecting courses. The real excitement was just beginning. Constantine grudged the cessation of work for the days of Christmas, but it would be churlish not to join in such festivities as Biddy and Persephone were anticipating. He thought he might take them both on an excursion to the circus that he had seen advertised at the bus stop. He spent hours wondering what he could give to Persephone that would be unique and all-significant, short of stealing from the Mycaenean case in the British Museum. What can a man give instead of, as a symbol for, his unacceptable self? She would not at present even accept her pay from him, which from the beginning it had embarrassed him to give, because it was so little and he dared not offer more. Then she had taken it as if he were giving her the earth, with childlike eagerness. Now she said she was not posing properly any more, she was not necessary, and she would not be paid. This terrified him, for it took away his only hold over her. He said it was a retaining fee because he would need her again, but she only shook her head. Anyway, she added, she was helping Biddy to make Christmas cakes and mincemeat and was learning all sorts of useful things.

Constantine was planning a Christmas party for the three of them, which he himself would prepare, and Biddy would for once be an idle guest. He bought a bottle of wine and cut evergreens for decorations and dreamt of an extravagant outlay on flowers. Even in this he was disappointed, because while he was feeling for the perfect opportunity to suggest it, Biddy and Persephone presented their invitation for him to join them, and so robbed him of the comfort of including Persephone in his own milieu.

The kitchen part of the Hall, though very ancient, was tagged on outside the main walls in a cottagey jumble. Biddy had made coloured paper chains, as for children, and had draped them from the central point of the middle beam like a velarium. Nowhere could he stand upright without paper loops in front of his eyes or worrying the back of his neck. Persephone and Biddy were as comfortable as rabbits in a burrow, but he felt like Gulliver. Biddy's few Christmas cards were prominently displayed. All her friends seemed to have chosen the same motif for her. There were babies squeezing cats, babies sticking out of the top of stockings, babies clapping their hands, babies in the nude, praying. Constantine was unreasonably angered by them. Biddy and Persephone laughed and chatted round him in an intimate co-operation that made him feel like a booby, like a baby at a children's party, only there to be fed. However, Persephone was wearing around her neck the amethyst-coloured chiffon scarf that was a present from him.

When at last they were all set in front of their steaming plates of roast pork and crackling, he opened the bottle and poured the wine into the tumblers provided.

Persephone watched, gay and goggle-eyed, but presently her laughter faded into thought. She lifted her glass towards Biddy. "It makes me think of poor darling Shaft. A happy Christmas to him."

Constantine froze. So now his troubles had a name. Poor darling Shaft. His throat was too tight to swallow.

Biddy saw his immobility. "A great friend of ours," she explained. "Major Shaftsbury."

He had provided the wine in order to toast poor darling Shaft, who equalled Major Shaftsbury, who equalled the worst that could happen.

"Here's to the happy man," he said, icy and casual, hating himself for being as crude as Caspar.

Persephone, holding her tumbler in both hands like a child and sipping appreciatively, looked at him and said: "Not a happy man at all, except in his own way. He's in a mental hospital."

"I'm sorry. I drink to his recovery." He made a great effort to push consideration of the shattering information into the background until the necessity of being a convivial guest should be over. Persephone seemed unaware of having said anything. Her whole attention was on his face to see if he was enjoying the food she had helped to cook. She would interrupt a sentence to study him as a mouthful of crackling and applesauce went in. She could not be disappointed.

❖

In the loggia he looked for oblivion. He worked with a harsh effort to separate himself from all that had hitherto made his conception as much emotional as intellectual. What was different? Nothing but a name for what he had known nameless. As he chiselled rhythmically to establish the key line of the back of the neck, he discovered a dismal couplet in the self-imposed emptiness of his mind.

> My love is in a looney bin,
> Some come out, but some stay in.

He couldn't have been in very long. How do you know that, he challenged himself, unless you are accepting Soph's verdict? He may have been in a long time. He may be due out at any moment. Or not for years. Perhaps never. He may come out quite different, so that she does not want him. If only he, Constantine, knew something, anything, rather than this torturing guesswork. He put down his tools. Impossible to work if your mind is not on the job. It had been like this for days. He went to the kitchen to put before Biddy his plan for taking them to the circus.

Under the paper velarium Biddy was ironing, pulling and patting the garments with her friendly, sud-creased hands. When she saw him bending his head to come in, she quickly put a cloth over what she was doing. But it was too late. He had seen a neatly folded pile of infant vests, fresh knit, with ribbons tied in bows. Now they were underneath her lying cloth. Constantine leant with both hands on the table.

"I'm going away this afternoon, to spend New Year with my sister. I'll let you know my plans—later."

❖

Like a horse that shies and bolts, Constantine left without even an intention. It simply happened to him that he walked in driving rain and stood with his suitcase at the bus stop. In the same indifferent way, at his sister's New Year's party he tagged on to a friend who was going with a group of climbers to Snowdonia. The car in which they were travelling up skidded on an icy corner and overturned. Constantine suffered mild concussion and compound fractures of the knee and shin. He was left behind in the hospital.

Days followed with no conscious thought beyond pain, and after them days of futureless tedium and nights of artificial sleep. He seemed to have been thrown onto a scrap heap of unwanted time. Meanwhile the mind was exerting its mysterious capacity to rearrange itself, to let the grounds settle, to shift the point of balance, to accept the unacceptable, to jettison untenable hopes. Now and again, when indifference left the field of thought empty, a clear picture slid into his mind of the immutable factors, such as his love for Persephone or her need of help, and then he slept. When the pain had gone he alternated between apathy and impatience. Either he was going to write to Mrs. Thorn and throw up the job, or else he couldn't possibly put off going back till tomorrow. It was nearly six weeks before the doctor would let him go, and by then he was frantic with anxiety, having heard nothing from Biddy or Persephone since his departure. There was no one but himself to blame for this, because he never wrote until he was preparing to go back.

❖

When he returned to the old Hall it was one of those mid-February days that are as warm as spring. A thrush was singing musingly on the top of a tall ash, launching its controlled notes into the space above the garden, above the Hall, singing for the unbelieving birds, for the lean trees, for the bronze ivy underfoot. Constantine heard its song from beyond the drive gate and it grew clearer as he walked. An overture, he thought, setting the mood for Act Two. For he must now, however panic-stricken and uncertain of his words, take the stage again and take part in the action. Even if he did nothing, that was a rôle too, and would weigh, even decisively, in the final God-knows-what.

He saw that Persephone was in the garden, beyond the house, standing beside a clump of pussy willow and having a conversation with a robin. She raised her elbows luxuriously, as if to stir and feel the spring air round her. Her long coat showed an appreciable obtuse angle in the folds that used to hang free from the shoulders and bust,

224

and her carriage had the characteristic backward leaning of the spine to redress the balance. When she heard Constantine she hurried to meet him, showing no embarrassment, as if she had always assumed that he knew, and smiling as she searched his face.

"You are thin," she said tenderly. "Biddy must stuff you. Are you really all right now? It has been queer without you."

Constantine looked, with eyes starved after a month of miserable thought, at a new Persephone. He saw as the skin feels the sun, as the heart feels the blood passing through it, and the love that had tormented him for so long became like a prophetic dream of something still to come, happening to him now for the first time, accompanied with a spasm of pain and helplessness, as if he had skidded again on the icy road.

❧

During his illness Constantine had been obsessed by his Daphne. Between dreams of fever he worked on it in imagination while his hands were imprisoned under the bedclothes. Mentally it was slippery work. What had to be done was continually changing, as was also what he had done already. It never came right. Sometimes he made a false stroke, and a vital part cracked and flaked off. More often he was totally unable to remember what he had intended it to be. It was a nightmare of frustration, from which he tried to free himself by repeating that when he was dealing with actual wood and chisel it would be definite and straightforward, and his confidence would return. Later, when he was convalescing, he had felt only a blank disinclination for work, which he attributed to his condition.

Now, when he went into the loggia and pulled the sheeting off the figure, receiving, as he looked at it, the full revival of all that had gone to produce it, he realised that he had suffered an immense bereavement. Daphne was dead. He would never work on it again. He looked with passionate sorrow at the head, which was farther advanced than he had known. He appraised the rarefied posture, the transition into tree. He kicked caressingly at the unqualified tree base, divided into columnar limbs, untouched as yet, and too heavy for the whole. Then he sheeted her up, no longer to preserve her from the frosts and mists, but to hide her from sight.

In the evening, unable to settle in the room that contained so much of the self he no longer possessed, he took the bull that harried him by the horns and wrote to Mrs. Thorn.

Dear Thorny,

This is a letter that has to be written, and I am only glad that it is you and no one else to whom I have to write it. I have been away for six weeks, having hurt my leg in a car skid, and am just back, confronted by difficulties that stagger me seen from the beginning. I don't somehow think they will look much different seen from the end. Your little visitor, Persephone, is with child. Please believe me that I am not the cause of it. If I were, I should be the proudest man living. I think it is someone now in an asylum. I have had doubts before, but it wouldn't have been fair to tell you until I was certain, or to leave you in ignorance now that I know. I implore you to continue to give her your protection—now more than ever. I can't tell you how touching I find that position of the spine just over the vertical, like someone carrying a basket of apples or washing. There are words I find I just can't put down.

Then there was Daphne. You know it was the focal point of every idea in my head. I can't go on with it. It means nothing now. This would be trouble enough if there was nothing else. I don't know if you can imagine what it is like to have a creative act killed in full swing. I just don't know what to do with myself. I shall have to begin again from the beginning. I feel like someone looking where something was, after a bomb has fallen.

Pushing the pen was a penance like that of Sisyphus. Constantine gave up. He was writing an appeal for sympathy for himself. He was possibly exposing Persephone to being turned out. How could he tell what Mrs. Thorn would do? Some people mind violently when it concerns their own houses; other people not at all. One would expect her to be one of those latter, only that she loved her house so much more than people normally do, as if it had a *mystique*. Perhaps he was a prig himself to think he ought to tell. In any case, he realised now, he couldn't do it behind Persephone's back. He would have to speak to her. And wasn't that more impossible still? He lay slumped in leaden weariness.

Biddy knocked and came in with a tray of hot egg flip and brandy.

"You had better have this before you go to bed, Mr. Constantine. You don't look too good yet. I've lit the fire in your bedroom."

"Come and sit down, Biddy. I want to talk to you. You can't keep your secret any longer. It's plain for all to see. I'm horribly worried and perplexed. We ought really to tell Mrs. Thorn. It's her house; we can't use it as our own. I suppose the baby will be due just about when she comes home?"

Biddy looked at him with surprise and without any embarrassment.

"Why, didn't Mrs. Thorn write anything about it to you? We told her right at the beginning. It wouldn't have been right not to. She wrote a very kind letter indeed, and said she was glad to give Zephy a roof, and she was to come back here after the baby was born, and she would see what she could do for her when she got back herself."

For this honesty on their part Constantine was as grateful as for his own salvation. Of course they had told. He should have expected simple candour from Persephone. He should have known. For a moment it seemed as if nothing was now wrong. Then he came back.

"Who is the father? Is it this Major Shaftsbury?"

"What, Shaft! Lord bless you, no. He had nothing to do with it. But they were all there together. I was too. That's where we met."

"Where do mean, 'there'?"

"In the mental hospital."

Constantine doubled the brandy in his egg flip and drank it off.

"Then where is the father now, and is he going to marry her?"

"He doesn't know anything about it, and I can't persuade her to write to him. She just ran away. But I'd rather she told you herself. You talk to her, Mr. Constantine. She won't tell you any lies."

"How can I talk to her!"

"You can. She won't make it difficult."

With the brandy and the stimulus of shock, Constantine was able to finish his letter.

> *P.S. So you have known all along. I could kiss your hands and your feet for your goodness to her. But why did you never write me a word? You must have known how it is with me.*

❖

"What do you want me to do?" Persephone asked next morning, when Biddy sent her up to Constantine in the studio. "You see I cleaned it all ready for you."

Constantine was standing in front of the alabaster head. He ran the back of his fingers up the line from collarbone to temple, then turned to look at Persephone. A sculptor's hands are a sense organ. They demand contact. But he was condemned to sight only. He wished he were blind and allowed a blind man's privilege to take the living face in his hands, to escape out of the prison of imagination and know the reality by direct sense. He thrust his hands deep into his pockets. He moved around, passed her and returned, with that handless, would-be detachment that deceives no one. It only makes the labouring breast into the hands' deputy, the part most sentient and vulnerable and demanding. Persephone watched him with hyacinth eyes that filled her face from temple to temple. Were there ever eyes that said so much and left so much unsaid? He felt like shouting, "Sphinx!"

"Why?" he said, stopping in front of her and then moving on so that he finished the question with his back to her. "Why did you tell everyone else and not me? Don't I count?"

"I thought you knew. I didn't try to hide anything. But it isn't the sort of thing one talks about."

"Well, talk now, for God's sake. Tell me all about it. I've got to know, please."

"I knew you had a right to know."

Constantine whipped round, facing her with avid hope, but she continued, stuttering a little, as if frightened. "It didn't seem fair to let you start on something big with me for a model. I was worried in case you didn't get far enough before my shape got too funny. And now you have been away six weeks, and I don't suppose I'll do. Can you go on with Daphne all right?"

"I'm not going to. She's on the scrap heap."

"Oh!" Her cry expressed new surprised grief. "Is that," she asked, looking at him ambiguously, "because of my shape?"

"No. I could finish it. I got far enough—as you say. It's just one of those works that don't get finished." He groaned. "There are always lots of those."

She came to him and held out her hands.

"I'm terribly sorry. She was going to be splendid. What will you do now?"

Her hands went down as his were not drawn out of his pockets. She rested them on the new slope of her stomach.

"I don't know what I'll do yet. But don't wander from the subject, please. Who is the father, and why doesn't he know about it? Biddy told me that much."

"I don't have to tell anyone his name. I knew him when I was a child, and we met again in the hospital. He was very important to me."

Constantine heard the past tense. But that is easier for a reserved person to use than the present.

"You loved him?"

"Yes. But he didn't love me. He only needed me. That's not the same thing. When we both left the hospital I went with him to help him. You see, he wasn't at all the same afterwards as he was before his breakdown. They didn't really cure him. Somebody had to help."

"And you? Didn't you need help?"

"Well, of course, at first we were only fit for each other. When you have been in one of those places only the people from inside seem to know anything about life at all. But I hadn't had such a shaking up as he had. And besides, Shaft cured me. It was Shaft and not the doctors who taught me a way to live. And he's mad, you know—really mad. I know it's a black mark against you if you are sure you personally aren't mad. But I couldn't leave Geoff like he was. I wanted to help. Shaft told me never to whittle love down till it's reasonable. He used to call me 'Conception.' You see he and Reverend Mother were both right from their own point of view."

She slowed up and stopped. Constantine saw her struggling with a distress that surged up and threatened to overwhelm her. He was beside her in a moment, and this time it was he who took both her hands and spoke most tenderly.

"For heaven's sake don't cry. You'll break my heart. Don't tell me any more if you don't want to. It's only that I could perhaps help you. I want to—I shall always want to."

He kissed the bamboo fingers, which were wet with tears.

"I wasn't much good at helping, after all. He used to get very cross with me. I used to think it was his illness, but as he got better that got worse. When he began to stand on his own feet he cared for nothing but making a career. He was hard and cynical. You mustn't blame him. He had been too idealistic before, and in hospital they turned him inside out. Perhaps someday he'll suddenly be himself again."

"What is he doing now?"

"He's in a furniture shop. A very grand one. You see, he never got his degree, so it was difficult for him. But his family had a wonderful old house and he knew quite a lot about furniture. I think his uncle helped him to get the job. He never let me go there because I hadn't got any proper clothes and he didn't want me to be seen. We were very poor. I used to go out as a char, secretly. He would have been furious. But he never knew. It was great fun buying a good piece of steak with secret money. He got on awfully well. He was always good-looking, and twice as handsome wicked as he was before. You know how it is. With other women, at any rate. When I say wicked, I mean damaged. I'm talking to you as if you understood. Anyway, if you really want to help somebody, the least helpful thing you can possibly do, just when he is getting on, is to present him with a baby. So when I was certain I slipped away."

"God almighty, you might have killed him. At the moment my sympathies are with him. What a thing to do to a man!"

She looked up at him with a face that shook, like water disturbed from underneath.

"I did make myself wretched at first by imagining him trying to find me, and terribly hurt. But I knew it wasn't true. I still have one dreadful nightmare—that he'll think I am like somebody else he knew, and that it might send him back into hospital. And then I think, perhaps, really, if he thought *that*, it would be the easiest way for him, because he's been given the antidote to it once. He's laid down rails, so to speak, to take him across, and it would fit into his new cynicism. But I think I couldn't bear it."

"But it's his child! A man should be given at least the option of fathering his own child."

"Dear Constantine! Don't identify yourself with him. He's not a bit like you. When I am feeling extra weak-willed I try to imagine his face while I am telling him—and that cures me."

"And you still love him."

"I am him, with this inside me."

"All right, you blessed, candid creature. What are you going to do about it?"

"I can stay here till it's born, Mrs. Thorn says, and perhaps afterwards. She is very good. Biddy and I thought perhaps Biddy could look after the baby here, while I go out to work, if Mrs. Thorn will allow it."

"Thank heaven there is Biddy."

"The most wonderful thing about Biddy is that you can accept anything from her. There are not many people you can say that of."

"I want very much to be one of them."

"Why, think what a help you have been," she said hurriedly. "If you hadn't needed a model, what should I have done? I'm terribly sorry that I'm no use to you any more. I did feel I had a sort of share in Daphne. I was very proud of her."

If the unique relationship between model and artist had a value for her, it had incomparably more for him. His consciousness opened to receive the forgotten room in which they sat—time-softened in surface, cavernous in shape, impregnated with memories, winged with impulse. It was the wind in the trees outside that moved the light and suggested the lifting of wings. And in the moment of recognising and reappraising the room he realised how exactly she was the right person to live in it. She had the same quality of enduring softness. Like it, she had chosen a great simplicity. What a fool he had been to fret and grieve like an adolescent over a broken dream. He saw her now, her rounded body, and hair feather-easy like a bird that has just preened itself, with that neck that gave her head a carriage and freedom such as swans have, and some savages, and perhaps Cleopatra. What odd comparisons to group around her! The carriage of her head was peculiar to herself. It had no pride. It had remoteness and yet suggested a wider field of sensitiveness, a greater willingness to acknowledge. A control tower. A delicate warm column of flesh and bone carrying the most beautiful face he could imagine. Round her the legend-evoking walls rose and arched—pagan temple, Héloïse's cell, Iseult's tower, cave of Ariadne, or the great shell of Aphrodite—taking their character from the fact that she was in them however you saw her. And then suddenly pressed home like reality when one comes out from an anaesthetic, the greater marvel that here was this unique room NOW, with Persephone herself sitting there, inspiring in him a love as great as any legendary one, since to him none of these could have exceeded the greatest he could imagine. All this surged over him in a moment while she waited for him to answer. But the words he spoke were, to his ears, hideously banal.

"What nonsense to say you are no use to me any more! Quite the opposite. New ideas are pouring in. You just wait till I get going. But I suppose you will change every day and I shall have to be quick. Stone this time. Wood takes too long. How long have we got?"

"Four months."

" 'I had a little pear tree.' " He was suddenly, tenderly happy.

" 'Nut tree,' " she corrected. "If I have a boy I shall call him Conker." Her cold fingers had not been withdrawn, and he chafed them between his hands. He would make that which she carried in her body into his own—defiantly, arrogantly his.

"I'm not Caspar," he said. "You'll have to wear a sari or something, that I can see you in. I like you in your coat if only it hadn't sleeves."

"When it gets warmer I won't have to be so muffled up. Will you really and truly want me? Will there be something you will mind about as much as you minded about Daphne?"

"Far more, when I get going."

"I'll be able to stand much better now. I'm awfully well—quite different."

"Come then. Let's get started. Take this wastepaper basket and hold it as if you were receiving apples off a tree. That's right. Push yourself well out, bless you."

Zephy pushed herself well out, and was as gay and as mischievous as he had ever seen her.

Mrs. Thorn's answer came so quickly as to surprise him.

Dear Constantine,

I have a great deal of sympathy for you after reading your letter. Yes, of course I knew. They have behaved with perfect sense and manners to me. I like everything I hear about Persephone. I admit I had guessed how it was with you, but God forbid I should butt clumsily in. I am sure it came better from her. Don't grieve too much for Daphne. I thought she promised to be really fine, but you will probably come back to her sometime. She may improve with keeping. Try some drawings for a Demeter. I really would prefer stone, because I had always imagined something standing out-of-doors, under cloud shadow and all the rest of it.

Thank you for sending on all the Christmas mail. You sensibly forwarded a letter from Messrs. Mortlock, Cain and Mortlock. They are a firm that I have dealt with for a long time. Old Mr. Mortlock is quite a historian, and he has standing instructions to let me know if anything comes into his hands that has a real historical connection with the Hall—engravings, silver, etc. There are lots of things in the house that he ferreted out, such as the green Staffordshire dinner service with the Lovel initials in the centre. This time he is offering a portrait of an eighteenth-century Lovel. Probably one of the last of them to live there. They sold out in 1780. Have a look at it when he sends it, and report to me if it seems to you worth keeping. The last of the line shot himself soon after the death of his father, about 20 years ago. Lady Lovel had the reputation of an inflexible family tyrant. I never met her.

I am beginning to dream of drifting willow fluff and swans in

*flight, and steamy mornings, after all this rock. You must stay on a
bit when I get back. I shall enjoy your company. I know you are
making the house uninhabitable by using my dearest room as a
studio. I shall just turf you out into a shed.*

❧

The year had turned. If the days were sunless and sometimes spat
their rain, there was a taste in the roving wind, a gloss on the sky-
ward twigs. The birds rootling among the ivy and snowdrops had
abandoned their monotonous winter clucks and chirps and seemed to
exchange with each other an excitement that was not yet song, except
the thrush who daily carried his music farther into the heights of
prophecy.

"What weather for smelling things," said Persephone, wrinkling up
her nose, which could just, if given the benefit of the doubt, be called
aquiline, or, more precisely, wrenlike. "I can smell not only the violets
and witch hazel and all that, but the gravel and the hedge and the
river! I ought to have been a dog. Every time I go round the garden I
find something new. Smell this. What can it be, with its heavy leath-
ery leaves?" She held up twin white flowers.

It was the season of beginnings, of stirrings, of buds and lambs, of
grinning, nudging cavalcades of dogs along the lanes, of boys whistling, of young girls looking with wild desire at spring fashions, of the
babe in the body. Constantine worked with the intensity and the
supernormal availability of images that comes when the normal instincts are cruelly starved. He blinkered himself to all but work, and
found himself, with the Demeter on which he was now working,
much freer than he had been before to escape the possession of himself by the model, and almost savagely, in this sphere alone, to assert
his mastery. Persephone had said that she was part of the man whose
child she bore. It was for Constantine to create her again, his, and the
swelling body that he would give her would be, in its line, in its
meaning, in its essential conception, only his. He worked grimly, his
chisel-sharp eyes looking up from frowning brows, and if she met his
glance there was no recognition in it.

She stood for him willingly, her arms wrapped closely in the cashmere shawl and folded over her belly; and week by week the folds
hanging from her waist grew farther from the ground in front. When
she was tired she just sat down and laughed at him. Always he protested that it was an impossible moment to stop. Sometimes he even
swore at her, but she was not at all put out.

233

"If I waited for you to say 'rest,' I'd be there as long as the room. You must do the best you can in the circumstances."

Constantine had now temporary security of a sort. His stay and Persephone's under Mrs. Thorn's roof was indefinitely prolonged. He knew the worst, and it looked as if his rival was finally out of the picture. He himself had a continuing real relationship with Persephone, though not the one he must eventually have if he were not to crack like overheated glass.

The preliminary work was done, the stone obtained and set up on its stand in the garden under a contrived shed. Here he worked alone, starting early in the morning in order to gain time for new work which he kept on hand to make Persephone sit for him. When he was with her he watched her movements, noted and fixed them in drawings. If she pushed in a slipping hairpin, if she stretched out her legs and looked at her sadly worn sandal toes, if she carried a tray, if she laughed, streamlined in the wild March winds, it was all inspiration for him. To all these movements her pregnancy added its astonishing sculptural dignity.

When the weather grew warmer and his tarpaulin shelter was found to have been pitched among daffodils and the small flora of grass and thicket, Persephone came out to sit with her sewing in the loggia, where Daphne, swathed in her shroud, had been pushed away. With its glazed front the loggia was too narrow for working in stone, where the flying clippings might have broken a pane. From its open entrance Persephone could see Constantine at work, though he was inaccessible to conversation, owing to his mood more than his distance. Here she sat, perhaps darning his socks, and marvelling as she looked around her, like someone who had died and is surprised to find herself convalescing from it in the Elysian fields.

On one such day Biddy, coming from the house to call them in to lunch, saw Constantine throw down his tools and take up a conversational attitude at Persephone's feet on the steps of the loggia. His hair was powdered with stone dust, as were also his overalls and the out-at-elbows sweater that he wore for work. His long legs sprawled out into the garden. "Anybody would take him for as nice a working chap as you could want," she commented to herself, and thereupon laid a tray for two and carried it out to them.

"This sun would do anybody good," she remarked as she put the heavy tray down. "Mr. Constantine, don't you let her carry that tray. I'll come back for it." She returned to the house and ate her solitary lunch on the sunny back doorstep out of sight, very well pleased with herself. "The more she tells him now, about her dad and her mum and everything, the better for both of them."

❖

In this way some weeks passed. The cherry trees had opened over the garden like so many ruched parasols. In every direction there was trilling and sparkling, flowers bowing and straightening again (bowing before the wind, bowing to each other, bowing under the bee's weight, flipping of stalks upright, scattering of pollen, dancing of sun and shadow); there was play of breezes chasing in and out of the bushes, incalculable as children; purr of wings, slither of twigs rubbing together like grasshoppers' thighs, grunt of frogs swimming in the moat with an affectionate arm round a lady love's waist, rise of marsh gas, bamboo leaves whipping like pennons, alchemy of every kind, sun drawn in and scent given out—a to-do all over the garden, in which the Hall was the only quiet thing, like a mother who is placid because her family is so big.

Constantine was aware of all this as he worked doggedly. The earth would have to turn in its orbit and leave him out of account. Persephone was entirely of it and with it. She sunned herself and her burden as happily as the bumblebee trundled his bulk or the birds brooded their eggs.

Biddy was out for a day's shopping, leaving them together, happier than they knew.

Towards midday their thoughts were interrupted by a shrill whistle coming from the Hall in the near distance. The window cleaner, familiar, as everywhere, and having taken note of the absence, or whereabouts and occupation, of the inhabitants, as is second nature to him, withdrew two fingers from his mouth and made urgent signals of "Wanted."

"Damn," said Constantine, looking round without putting down his chisel. "Oh, I think I know what it is. It won't take long. It's only something of Thorny's. I had a postcard this morning. Stay put. I'll be back in a minute." He tossed his chisel into Persephone's lap. "Pray over it that I'm not kept too long, this morning of all mornings."

As he came into the living room by the garden door, stopping to beat off some of his dust at the threshold, two visitors rose. The young man, dressed with unself-conscious style, smiled attractively, and the lady's eyebrows went up, though she was careful to hold them there so that it became the surprise of pleasure, a "gracious" mannerism.

235

Constantine looked like a miller's mate and was indifferently aware of it. She offered a card: *Messrs. Mortlock, Cain and Mortlock.*

"I am afraid we are interrupting you. I hope our visit is not inconvenient. I am Miss Mortlock, and this is my father's assistant." She added his name in the usual disinterested mumble of syllables cut short. Snob, was Constantine's mental note.

"Sorry I'm too dirty to shake hands. Forgive me."

Miss Mortlock was not good-looking, but she was smart to the nth degree and groomed as for a competitive show. She was well set up and conformed ruthlessly to the line of the moment. She wore a black cloth suit with impressive pearl earrings and necklace, and showed long nylon legs the shape of Indian clubs, jacked up on those very high heels that tip a woman forward in a perpetual *élan*. Her features were sudden and irregular, but by wearing an exaggerated hat she contrived to make her face look as though it too was that way on purpose. She had assurance and drive. Nerve, was Constantine's second reflection. And if she did not get what she wanted he would be much surprised.

Her companion was considerably younger and remarkably good-looking. He had by nature the breeding she assiduously cultivated. He was aloof, and there was a wry, tight set to his lips that was forgotten when he smiled. Constantine turned to him with more warmth than he might have done but for Miss Mortlock's patronage.

"I understand my cousin Mrs. Thorn has dealt with Mr. Mortlock for a long time. Is this your first visit here?"

"Yes, it is. A wonderful old place, and what a situation! I'm immensely taken with it. Full of atmosphere."

"My father says atmosphere is the only thing he can't sell. It would fetch fabulous prices, but it won't keep. There's hardly a ghost of it about the oldest thing in the shop. I believe one of the things Father hopes for from you, Folly, is that you might persuade Americans they were buying it. You have it yourself."

She used what Constantine supposed was a nickname as if she meant to imply that her brothers had been to the same public school and the name had been borrowed from them. But there were undertones of both possessiveness and wheedling.

"Bunkum," the young man answered, unsmiling. "I hope your father will have better reasons for keeping me."

Miss Mortlock looked at him quickly with an intake of breath and then turned with redoubled assurance, as if a tap had been opened farther, to Constantine.

"We took the liberty of examining the room while we were waiting for you. As her agents, I hope that was pardonable? It helps us in selecting for her. Mrs. Thorn isn't really what I would call a collector. But I daresay the extreme age of the place imposes a certain rudimentariness. And of course it's not big enough to take much. I'm sure she is right and shows the restraint of good taste. All the same, I had not expected it to be quite so simple. Surprisingly she seems almost to prefer the moderns, at least in art."

Folly, who seemed to feel himself in a position to dispense with deference, took her up.

"The moderns, however sophisticated they really are, are more like the Stone Age, the Bronze Age, the Africans or Mexicans, or for that matter the early Middle Ages to which, after all, this house belongs, than anything that is likely to pass through our hands. The thing that worries me, as a layman, is why so much of it—I'm thinking of sculpture now—has to be eroded or skeletal. Minimal. Metalwork that looks as if the surface had rusted away in a bog and only the framework is left, or stone rolled and hollowed by the sea. When I was a boy I used to clamber about in a Cornish cove where every stone is spherical and you can hear them churning under the water. I used to think, you can't know which of these was once a god's or a bull's head from some toppled temple on the cliffs. But you don't get the same thrill from something that has not yet *been* developed. Is the mood of the time obsessed with the Long Death, or are they going back into the Great Womb with the interested patronage of the psychologists? It seems that I personally prefer the Long Death. But not pseudo." He smiled at Constantine, addressing all this to him.

"I had no idea you were so poetical, Folly."

"Had you not?"

"I have a feeling that you may be putting your foot in it. Something tells me that Mr. Thorn is an artist."

"I came to the same conclusion. I hoped to lure him into explaining his point of view. What do you do, sir, if I may ask?"

"I am a sculptor."

"There, Folly!"

"I agree with you up to a point," Constantine contrived. " 'Minimal' is an adjective that frightens me very much, in its bad sense. But if one could eventually reach the minimum that expresses what one means—and it may be a lot—then it is really the maximum, since anything that could be eliminated without loss diminishes the thing by being there. And though I think many of the famous relics have been improved by the rough and tumble—I love them with all protuberances broken off down to the simple bulk, pitted till they hardly look as if they had been worked on—yet I confess that I do find myself compelled to a certain *plus* that I hate to think of being rolled smooth in the sea bed. I hope the ghosts Miss Mortlock was talking of will always hang on to it, and that if it must become undistinguishable stone, it will come into the hands of someone with your susceptibility."

"It does sound *thrilling*, Mr. Thorn. If you have something on hand, might we see your point of view for ourselves?"

"I have something on hand, Miss Mortlock, but I am afraid it is not on view. I hope that doesn't seem too discourteous. It is good of you to be so interested."

"May we know what it is?"

Constantine looked at her, and felt the greatest reluctance.

"Not that either, I am afraid."

"How disappointing. It's still wrapped in the mists of futurity. Well, I hope it will be a great success. Folly, did you bring the parcel out of the car?"

"It's in my suitcase. I'll get it."

"I hope Mrs. Thorn will like what we have brought. I daresay your tastes are similar to hers? However, if you don't like it, that doesn't matter at all. We are on our way to the sale of Bramble Haggard, Lord Overman's place. I daresay you saw it in the papers. He had quite a wonderful collection of Bohemian glass, among other things. My father asked me, since we were passing on the Great North Road, to deliver the picture by hand. It's always safer with glass, however carefully it is packed."

Folly now brought forward a parcel about eighteen inches by twelve and handed it to Constantine.

"May I cut the string for you?"

Several sheets of best-quality, loud-rattling brown paper came off, intractable, refusing to lie anywhere, followed by eellike strips of corrugated wrapping. Folly gathered them up and folded them, as Constantine took off the tissue paper beneath, till he held in his hands a concave gilt frame of which the glass was covered by a final piece of card cut to fit. That lifted, he looked at the charming portrait of a young woman in an elaborate evening head-wrap or bonnet, shaped high like a mitre, made of ruched lace and ribbon and tied under her delicious chin. Beneath this demure elegance she wore a dress cut so low that her little breasts were almost naked. The paint was applied to the underside of the glass, and this gave it a brightness and life as unlike varnish as spring water is unlike chlorinated tap water. The pictured face laughed, its eyes shone, its skin was transparent. Constantine laughed too, dumbfounded. It unquestionably was, it could only be, a portrait of Persephone at her most mocking. It was not that it resembled her, or reminded one of her, or suggested that such a bonnet for fancy dress would become her. Somebody with a genius for likeness had done it. Electrified and hilarious he exclaimed: "It can't be true! It's not possible. Do you say this is supposed to be eighteenth century?"

"It is, quite certainly."

"It must be a fake."

"Father is not easily taken in," said Miss Mortlock, brushing imaginary dust off her skirt. "It's genuine, all right."

"May I look?" said Folly. "I haven't seen it yet. What makes you doubtful?"

Constantine had just read the spidery calligraphy at the bottom.

> The Hon. Persephone Harcourt-Lovel
> daughter of Lord George Harcourt-Lovel
> fecit.
>
> pinx.

He drew an expanding breath, and looked round to explain. Folly, at his shoulder, was looking at Miss Mortlock with the expression of someone on whom a vicious practical joke has been played. His overbright eyes were fixed on her with savagery.

Does he think she is trying to pull something off? Well, but it's not a fake, after all, Constantine thought. If Thorny isn't pleased with this I'll be very much surprised. The old house is at its tricks again.

"I'll show *you* something now, and you'll see why at first I thought there was something queer." He went out through the door into the garden and signalled enthusiastically to Persephone, repeating the window cleaner's actions. He watched her approach across the sunlit lawn. How lightly she still walked, like a pregnant doe, big-eyed. Birds and their shadows took off as she came past, and the shadow patterns of leaves in the breeze joined the flower pattern on her faded smock and slithered across her round advancing body.

Constantine caught hold of her hand and drew her in, unconsciously proprietary in his excitement. "I've got a surprise for you," he said. He was longing for the moment when he would say to her, "Look, you belong to the house. You've been here before."

On the threshold she stopped, wavered, white as honesty pods, and dropped her arms to her sides. Constantine had the feeling of having become suddenly invisible to three people. There was a long pause, and then Miss Mortlock moved nearer to Folly, as if to remind him that she existed.

From the doorway Persephone's hesitant voice scarcely crossed the room.

"How did you . . . did you know I was here?"

"Isn't it self-evident that I didn't? I am learning it now."

"You see . . ."

Miss Mortlock now spoke. It sounded like a shout after the strangled voices of the other two. "If this is a friend of yours, please introduce her to me."

"You are mistaken. You must ask Mr. Thorn." He turned to close the lid of the suitcase in which he had brought the picture. Constantine, who was paralysed as well as invisible, saw on the lid the name "G. de Fol." He turned back to Persephone, whose eyes were expanded and brimming in her diminished, blue-veined face. So might a desolate but unvanquished ghost materialise in such a house as this. She stepped back into the garden and vanished out of sight.

"You are absolutely wrong in what you suggest." Constantine spoke like a stranger to himself, without indignation, without animosity against de Fol, or any passion except pity for Persephone. He had at the moment no feeling that referred to himself.

"You must excuse me. Will you please let yourselves out. Leave the picture. Mrs. Thorn will certainly want it." He went after Persephone.

When he had looked for her in the garden and house in vain, he crossed the kitchen and penetrated into Biddy's quarters as far as the bedroom door. It was closed, and from beyond it came sounds of physical and mental anguish that it was intolerable to hear. He knocked on the door and called through.

240

"Zephy, Zephy, my darling, are you ill? Can't I do anything? Ought I to send for the doctor? Oh my God, let me come in."

After a moment her voice came back, weak but with a trace of jest.

"I'm being sick. Not at home." Constantine withdrew a few yards and sat down on an ottoman chest, pushing his hands through his hair in distraction. If he went for a neighbour, he would leave her alone with no one to call to if she wanted anything. Supposing she was really ill, supposing it was the baby coming, what was he to do? He heard Miss Mortlock's car go down the drive, and realised that he had forgotten their existence. Another groan, and he got to his feet and went to telephone to the doctor.

"Can you come at once to the old Hall?"

"Is it urgent? I'm busy. No time at all today. What is the matter?"

"It's a girl who's going to have a baby."

"Is she one of my patients?"

"I don't know. Persephone Stalker. She has been taken ill. I'm alone here, no women about. I don't know what to do."

"Is it her husband speaking?"

"No."

"Where is he?"

"She hasn't got one."

"Oh, I see. Symptoms?"

"She is being sick all the time, that's all I know."

"Can't rush round to every pregnant woman who's sick. How far gone is the pregnancy?"

"About seven months, I should think. She's had a shock."

"Sorry, but I can't possibly come myself now. I'll get in touch with the nurse and send her. She'll report to me. Best I can do."

Constantine, sweating, went back to his post outside the bedroom door. He listened for sounds of life with ears like those of a threatened animal. He imagined himself after her death, looking up and seeing in the doorway the face he had seen there an hour ago. Seeing it always. He wondered, straying to a quieter level, what the history of Persephone Harcourt-Lovel had been. He heard the springs of the bed creak, and a deep sigh. And then, unexpected, Biddy's well-known unhurrying steps.

"Something's the matter," she said, as he came to meet her. Her broad, gentle face showed nothing but concern to help. "What's happened, Mr. Constantine?"

241

She darted into the bedroom, and through the open door he saw Zephy, with her face buried in the pillow, move a blind hand to welcome her.

"Gracious, you are cold! Mr. Constantine, can I trouble you to fill two hot bottles and bring them? And put the kettle on again for a cup of tea."

Constantine went, humiliated to a cypher. He had wasted himself in frantic anxiety and had not been able to think of such an obvious sickbed thing as a hot bottle. It was such a warm day. And yet now he found that he was shivering himself.

Biddy came presently to collect the hot bottle. The kettle was boiling but he had not noticed it.

"She'll be all right," said Biddy. "Don't you worry. The nurse is here now. But what a thing to happen! If I'd been here, it wouldn't have happened. And yet I couldn't have sent him away without knowing what he'd do when he saw her. She loves him, little as he's worth it."

Constantine was infinitely weary. "It wasn't really fair to him. He thought the child was mine."

"Don't you make excuses for him. That's what he wanted to think."

"I got the impression he was as good as engaged to his boss's daughter."

"Then he wasn't likely to be claiming any illegitimates, was he? Here, give me those bottles. And make yourself a pot of tea. You look nearly as bad as she does. Don't worry, it's not the baby. She'll be all right, she's only upset. It's her nerves."

❖

The next day Zephy was up again. She was blue under the eyes, and it seemed to Constantine that her shape had altered, was less buoyant. Otherwise she appeared gay and unchanged.

"Don't stand waiting for me as if you were to escort your grandmother to her wheeled chair. I'm all right again. What a wonderful day."

It was a dove-coloured morning, blue-grey and feather-still. They rossed the grass together where the narcissus stood in motionless groups. The cherry blossom leant outward on threadlike stalks all down the boughs, and the open tree was dense with scent that no breeze disturbed. Short-necked crimson primroses were buttoned into the ground like the leather flowers sewn into mattresses. The flight of a bee could be heard in the whole of its transit across the lawn. It was as if spring had decided not to haste away so soon, but to show itself for once as eternal as it is so often called, to sleep away eternity in a chosen moment. Zephy even today was a sharer in all this. She loved to catch things, like this spring morning, in the act of being. Little as Constantine imagined it, she felt exhausted but released. The worst she could imagine had happened, but she had suffered it all before-hand. The ordeal was over, and here was still the wonderful world—more wonderful because nothing so dreadful could ever happen again. It's like Shaft's leg, she thought. He was glad when it was off. Constantine was blind to everything but the fright he had had the day before, hearing her moans. The day hung round him like a brood-ing menace, as if all the pounding insistence of his vitality would never be free. He had been awake all night, and today was zero hour.

How was he to force himself upon her at this moment, the very day after he had seen the face she lifted to the other? If she were to glimpse the terrible size of his love, she would be frightened clean away. He supposed that her present state was one of absolute reserve, a modesty in which even a husband would be a third person in a magic circle of two-in-one. If she would let him fill that third-party position, he would at least keep her with him, and a little hope.

"I've got an idea," he ventured desperately, taking her arm, "that I think would be wonderful."

"What is it?"

"I am afraid to ask, because I don't know what you will say."

She laughed. "Have a shot! I'm not so dangerous. But don't ask me to pose standing."

"If I could marry you—if you would marry me—I would be proud to look after you. We could be as happy together as we are now. And I would be very fond of your baby." His breath gave out.

She stopped and turned to look at him with amazement.

"And me too, I should hope! You preposterous darling. I wouldn't dream of it." Her emphasis was final. "Do you think that if I wouldn't do that to Geoff, who is its father, I would do it to you? Just because you are that kind of person? You must not think on those lines. I'm all right. I've got Biddy. I'm not anyone to be sorry for. Do you know what Shaft used to say to me? No offence can be given unless it is accepted. Well, I have accepted no offence and none has been done to me. Thank you for being so good, and please never mention it again."

Constantine had the sensation of falling into the abyss. And yet the bottom of it was where he lived, where he had lived for a long time, holding at bay the powers that assaulted him.

"Will you be all right in the loggia?" he said shortly. "I shan't work today. There's no air. I think I'll take a boat up the river. I'll tell Biddy you are alone." He turned his fiercely contained face and went, and did not see how Zephy wept. Her head was still in her arms when she heard the too-impatient creak of his oars going upstream. The bee, its bag now full, passed in a straight line, like a minute circular saw, down the length of the deserted garden.

❈

For two weeks Zephy was about, lying with her feet up, pinched-looking across the bridge of her nose, with the blue showing through the skin round her eyes. If she walked only a few steps she was liable to double up and press her hands to her body. However, she read the books Constantine provided for her, and laughed as she read, and gave the impression of revelling in the garden from pure idleness.

"Look what I've had!" She waved an envelope at Constantine.

"From Thorny?"

"Yes. Read it. It's nice."

Dear Persephone,

I hear from Constantine what a remarkable piece of evidence has come to suggest that you belong to the old Hall. If your father really was Richard Lovel, I cannot claim that I knew him, but I knew of him, and it would give you a double claim on our welcome. I am looking forward to meeting what the old house has sent me. It is an affectionate old place and can't bear the past to be forgotten. Meanwhile you must let Biddy and Constantine look after you and I hope all goes well.

"I think I'll screw up my courage and write to ask Mums about Dad. I don't like to be receiving such nice welcomes when perhaps it isn't true. Poor Mums thinks I'm still with Geoff. I didn't write and tell her because she would have wanted me home. I don't want my baby's earliest impression to be Sam. When it is born and I am fixed up somewhere I'll go and see her. So long as I have enough money to come away again. I think about Mums a lot just lately. And I long for mountains. Sometimes here there's a bank of cloud on the horizon that makes a sky line like the fells. You can't think how I want it to be real then."

Constantine was inexperienced and could not know that the last

244

phase of pregnancy is usually more vigorous than the first. He thought that things were following the usual course. His agitation was probably greater than that of a natural father. He had not willed this frightening state of affairs. He worked like a demon.

The doctor and nurse came and went, often unknown to him, and finally one day Biddy, coming out to him in the garden, broke the news.

"They are sending the ambulance for Zephy this morning. She's to go into hospital at once. I want to go in with her, Mr. Constantine, so will you please get your own lunch? I'll leave it ready."

"Is she in pain? Is it the baby? It's still six weeks too early."

"I don't know what it is. They don't say, they never will tell you. But it's not going right. She's not in pain except in spasms, but they are not the right sort."

Constantine said good-bye to Zephy as she was carried out on a stretcher, wrapped in hospital blankets. Her face was peaky and big-eyed like a fledgling's, and had something of the same anxious expression. They hoisted her into the ambulance and the doors were shut between her and him.

❖

Zephy was adamant that he was not to visit her in the hospital. Biddy brought back this ruling.

"She says—you know how she talks—it's not as though you could just edge into the crowd round her bed. You'd be the only one, and she says she's not going to have the nurses and patients thinking you are the father. She says she may or may not be a Lovel, but she is not going to let herself be foisted onto the Thorns under false pretences. She says it isn't manners to Mrs. Thorn. She says maybe *you* wouldn't mind, being an artist and all that . . ."

"Biddy! She didn't *really* say that!"

"Well, no. She didn't say that bit. I did, but it was all in the same conversation. She says it's because of Mrs. Thorn being so kind. And I think she's right."

❖

The emptiness of the house and garden had a positive quality like a cutting edge. Constantine found that his greatest trouble was a curious physical one. His longing for Zephy was so much greater than any power he had of apprehending it that it translated itself for him into an effort, moment by moment, to draw his breath. It was a continuous struggle in which he consciously laboured to fetch each lungful, despite the pressure round his chest of those grappling hoops of iron recommended by Polonius.

He heaved splitting breaths without relief. He had trouble too with the particular brightness, sharpness, and significance of what he saw around him, the attributes of early May which seemed not less than sacred. Sometimes it rarefied itself to pure illusion, a painting on his retina, beyond which, externally and internally, was vacuum and darkness. At other times it was a terrible and glorious reality from which he was absent, a man who could not be where she was not. Movement in space was tiresome. Since it made no difference where he was, space had taken on itself an inertia through which he had to force his way. Time would not progress. What! Is the church clock still showing the same minute that it was when I climbed over that last mountain, when I breathed that last breath? Every day he posted something to Zephy. Twice he went to the hospital just to stand outside. Once he disregarded her order and went in. They told him she was too ill to see anybody.

❧

Zephy lost her baby and very nearly slipped away after it. To Constantine's pleading to be allowed to see her Biddy opposed herself, her usual furthering attitude to him reversed now that Zephy was in danger. "It's no time to be crossing and vexing her," she said sharply. However, when Zephy was out of danger, Biddy brought back from the hospital a note which Constantine thereafter wore over his heart, for its few friendly jesting words affected him like an unexpected kiss.

As time went on, Biddy, who went between them, became, to his sensitivity, irritatingly complacent and mysterious.

"I told her," she said, "that you're like a dog with fleas that can't settle anywhere."

"Don't only tell me your side of every conversation. Tell me what she said to you."

"Why, if she thought I would do that she'd never tell me anything. But she was very pleased with that sweetbriar you sent her, pinching it and sniffing it."

"Is she very much upset about the baby?"

"Poor child! Judging by how much I was looking forward to it myself! All those lovely little clothes."

At last, on a day, the clocks began to move again for Constantine. The emerald pasture land blazing with buttercups was no longer a simulacrum, the voluptuous shuddery breath of cows nosing into the long grasses spoke for him, the sedge warbler poured out continuous excitement, the sun poured content. Zephy was due home.

When at last, apprehensive of strange alteration, he saw her again, she was still her precious self, half waif, half apparition. But she wore a new summer dress in which she was bewitching as an uncertain, experimental beauty, not knowing if it had come off. Under his fierce assessing eyes she blushed crimson.

"Poor Constantine! I let you down every time. When you want Daphne it's Demeter, and when you want Demeter it's Daphne again."

"Demeter is finished long ago. What do you suppose I have been doing all this time? It's a wonder I haven't turned Thorny's treasured house into a jungle of stone foliage and peeping faces, in my fidgets, like a schoolboy carving up his desk. Demeter's fine, thank you."

Persephone was hesitant and nervous. He supposed that was because she was still weak. Also he was unable to imagine how much a woman might sorrow for a child she had never had. Imagination of a grief one can never know oneself is apt to run to extremes. She looked, for the first time, as if he had power to hurt her. Biddy had witnessed their constrained meeting with anxious disappointment, and hurried away to the kitchen.

Their conversation was interrupted with silences like pitfalls.

"I must see the garden," she said suddenly, as if it were more important than he was. "You can't think, after that glossy ward, how I long for dandelion fluff and bird droppings!"

They went out together, and her starved eyes were confronted with the immense copper beech just coming into leaf. The lawn under her feet had as many discarded silken leaf bracts as blades of grass, and the tree itself was a presence. Its shape had materialised in miniature glazed and pleated leaves that shone amber and coral where the sun lit their surface. They offered, along every outswinging bough, immediate joy too new for any shadow. They intercepted, played with, and transmitted the light into a dome that was radiant and subdued, through which the trunk ascended colour-flecked like a mullion but carrying the arteries of spring.

Zephy walking in a world drawn out thin with suspense, sighed with momentary longing, to be Daphne to this tree, to be dissolved in sun-gold, to rise in sap, to spread at ease in serene rhythms under the May sky.

Constantine beside her shuffled his feet in the confetti of leaf bracts, blown cherry blossom, and elm sixpences.

"This should satisfy your craving for litter."

"Do you know where the nests are? Oh, it's good to be here!" And yet she looked apprehensive. If she found herself near him she put distance between them. Her laugh was unsure.

Beauty or not, he was glad she still wore her wonky old sandals. He had an affection for them; they held her in the past. Without them he would have been terrified that, like a newly hatched butterfly, she would float off. They arrived at the loggia.

When a girl wears no make-up but lets her complexion be seen in depth, when its petal surface reflects frankly the grass beneath her, on chin and lower lids, the sky above on brow and cheekbones; when her face is bonfire-lit leaning down to put her nose inside a tulip, and loose wisps of hair cross shadows on her temple with the silky bent grasses; when not only her bewildering eyes look out on the spring but also her face slides into it, takes part in every muted sun fleck, is mixed in the blush of the cherry tree and turns mermaid under the yews, assuming unconsciously the panic beauty as her own, a man may be excused for looking at her and seeing nothing else.

"Why, you've begun again on Daphne! I'm glad. I hated her being all shrouded up in a corner. I felt it was me in disgrace." She stopped, startled at what she had said, and shot him an anguished glance.

"I began on it yesterday. I was fidgety and I thought I'd see if it would go. The neck was asking to be done." He was considering, while he spoke, that look and how it should be interpreted. "Do you want a rest? Are you strong enough to walk about like this?"

"Of course I am. I want to see Demeter."

"Are you sure you really do—not just to pacify me? I thought she might perhaps make you sad."

"I want terribly to see it."

The sheets of corrugated iron out of which Constantine had made a work shed had been taken away. Demeter stood under a tarpaulin in the open garden with cowslips round her feet. He pulled the sheet off, and Persephone looked, saying nothing. In her face he saw her reaction to the memory of all that had gone between them, out of which this had come, and just as once he had been bereaved of Daphne, so now she seemed, attributing Demeter to an attitude of his already in the past, to be bereaved in her turn. She was trembling and she mopped the palms of her hands. At last she turned to him stuttering.

"I like it," she said, most miserably. Suddenly it dawned on him what had happened. A rush of joy and power swept him into recklessness. He took her and held her where she could feel his heart racing in a continuous thrust like a flywheel.